Remember
Next Week

For John and Lillian
thanks for your friendship
and support over the years,

Major Roscbrough.

Remember Next Week

Major Roxbrough

Print information available on the last page.

Rev. date: 10/12/2017

To order additional copies of this book, contact:
Xlibris
800-056-3182
www.Xlibrispublishing.co.uk
Orders@Xlibrispublishing.co.uk
767637

Once again dedicated to Clare:
because she insisted I had to!

A special thank you to my editor, Paula,
I could not have done it without you.

Also by Major Roxbrough and published by Xlibris:-
Glimpserama.

Contents

PROJECTOR …

Into a sober pleasure, when thy mind
Shall be a mansion for all lovely forms,
Thy memory be as a dwelling-place
For all sweet sounds and harmonies; Oh! then,
If solitude, or fear, or pain, or grief,
Should be thy portion, with what healing thoughts
Of tender joy wilt thou remember me,

Wordsworth.

ONE

GLEVE ORCHVESTIGE HAD been sent back to his own body. The wasted, starved body that had no more than seconds to live. He was strapped into the second chair and even if not bound, would have lacked the strength to rise. Had he managed that, he would never have gotten out of the laboratory, hidden as it was in a concealed fortress built into Lomonosov crater. At the very same instant that the Brain machine failed to keep the two brothers in the body of one another; they switched back to their own fleshly shells............

Darcie came too rather gradually, he had been strapped into one position, near starved to death and in the darkness. He did not truly know what had happened to him. The last thing he recalled clearly, he was seating himself under one of the cowls and allowing his elder brother to lower one onto his head.

He lay thinking. The machine had not been a diagnostic tool after all. In some super scientific way, known only to his brother, his mind and Gleve's had been swapped, they had occupied each other's body. Why had not Gleve explained this too him? Why had he kept the true details of the unit to himself. Darcie would still have allowed the experiment, it would have been curiously fun to walk about in his brother's body.

He lay beside Cylvia and gave the matter some thought. Darcie was not usually a deep thinker, but on this occasion he discovered he was seriously introspective. He concluded there was only one possible answer to Gleve's treachery; he had intended the exchange to be permanent! It was the only explanation that made sense. It answered all the other questions in one fell swoop. The restraints, the hiding of the laboratory, it's fortification, his brother's need for secrecy.

Then he realised what it meant to he, Darcie. It was a death sentence!

Time had passed while he had been in the cave. He was dimly aware of that. He had gotten gradually weaker and no matter how he had called out in the first few days it had been hopeless; no one came. The conclusion was inescapable, he would have died. With his death, Gleve could have carried on acting the role of his younger, more attractive brother. Then there was Cylvia. Cylvia Dortbrooke, the shapely and beautiful red head that Gleve lusted after. It had amused Darcie, he had never felt threatened by it. Gleve would not have had her in a thousand centuries. Whilst Darcie was in the cave though?.....He wondered.

Still, no matter, it was not as though she had cheated on him. In fact he rather hoped his brother had finally enjoyed her, before returning to the dried husk that was his own; close to death - soon to be, corpse.

Darcie rose from the bed, discovering that his own body felt as it had always done, good, Gleve had not damaged it in any way. He had slept and dozed for an untold period though and now the bedside chrono read zero thirty hours he was wide awake. Leaving Cylvia sleeping, he padded to the kitchen and made himself a cup of lichenmint tea. What should he do about his older brother?

If he did nothing he knew he would die. If he was not dead already. If he went to the constabulary and raised the alarm, would they believe his somewhat naive story? He might even find himself under suspicion himself, for his elder brother's murder! After the horror of his experience that would be cruel irony indeed.

The project must remain secret for some time then. Not for ever though. Darcie was not the mental genius Gleve had been, but he was a salesman and he knew a marketing opportunity when he saw one. Was it a marketing opportunity though? Who would want to spend time in someone else's body? When he thought about it, he could think of many.

The disabled for one. They would pay for a few days in a healthy whole body. The owner of the body would be compensated financially for spending a few days in a spastic condition. With Darcie taking his commission for the rendered service of course. Yes the tomb that now housed his brother could not remain hidden for ever.

How to go about finding it and opening it though? How to work the machine once it was in his possession? Darcie realised it was barely possible that he could perform the latter himself. No, he would need a totally trusted confederate, or an employee who worked for him. There was a couple of problems there, he was not exactly solvent, nor did he have a high paying job. To get into the fortress would either take explosives that would risk damaging the machine, or a genius who could fathom out the code. He had seen his brother press a series of keys quickly and had not bothered to even attempt to commit the sequence to memory. So he needed someone very accomplished at that sort of thing. An expert code breaker, or a criminal.

For both he needed money.

Or, cunning.

Darcie considered his various options and realised the one thing he had on the plus side of the balance sheet was guile. Indeed he had that one particular asset in spades. He could *hire* what he needed with promise of a share of the prospective profits. Who though, would believe his fantastic claims and take it on trust?

Once again the most likely alternative to him would seem to be the criminal fraternity!

TWO

WHEN SPIDER HOURGLASS was caught for the first time, he knew he was in big trouble. He would never survive in prison.

He was short, light and had never experienced violence nor buggery ever before. He offered his solicitor all he possessed to get him some sort of alternative. To bribe someone, anyone, so that he could avoid incarceration. All to no avail. He had cracked the security lock on the safe and though he had left no DNA, when the constables had raided his pad, some of the jewels were still in his possession.

Spider never professed his innocence, he knew he was guilty, the constabulary knew he was guilty and the judge knew he was guilty. He just knew that prison would destroy him. So, to use his own vernacular, he greased a few palms in the hope of being declared too feeble minded to go the a correctional facility. An asylum would have suited him much better. The judge, as it turned out, took the bribe and then, without a second thought, sent Spider to gaol. Not just any prison either, but the Correctional Facility at Argentia Planum. The prison in question housed the worst criminals on all Mars. It was also by far the coldest, being just north of the south pole. It was widely held that there was no glass in the cell's barred windows and during the night the southern wind blew through the metal obstructions with teeth cold enough to tear at the flesh of the dead.

Dead was what Spider thought he would be within a week of being transported to Argentia Planum. So as he was escorted out of the court cells and hustled into a reinforced flitter wagon, his state of mind could not have been any worse. Inside the wagon were facing rows of iron benches. The prisoners were cuffed to the metalwork for the duration of the journey. Each bench held four prisoners. Spider was cuffed in place and found himself forward most of the right hand side of the flittruck. One slight stroke of good fortune, at least he would only have one other prisoner seated beside him.

He waited while the vehicle filled up and stole a glance at the convict who had been cuffed at his shoulder and his heart sank. The man was half again his size and weight and the long ragged scar down the side of his face did nothing to inspire confidence in the safe cracker. Added to that visual indication of the nature of he at his elbow, was a harsh buzz cut and two days growth of beard, who went unshaven when depilation was so cheap and so permanent?

The flittruck suddenly commenced the journey with a lurch and the giant (or so it seemed to Spider) was thrown against him with the acceleration. He emitted a sort of basso animal grunt, which Spider could not fathom. Either it was threat of violence if the incident repeated, or something beyond Spider's criminal imagination. For a good thirty minutes the journey was conducted in total silence and then one man at the flittruck's rear asked,

"So guys are we going to introduce ourselves to one another and relate our reason for being in this predicament"?

The man to his left suddenly elbowed the speaker in the face and the sound of his nose breaking could be heard by all.

Someone else dared to mutter "Muller ain't feeling sociable today".

Spider struggled to hold onto the contents of his bowel, Muller was in the same flittruck. Muller who had killed, how many was it, with a machete? The little safe cracker slumped even further down on the bench, convinced his life was soon to get absolutely terrible and then get worse from there! Even though the homicidal maniac had been violent to the first of the criminals to speak however, it set the others to muttering. Someone wanted to know if anyone had a cigarette. Eagerly Spider fished into a pocket and produced a pack of Dreadnoughts; real tobacco with no medical filtration of any sort. In order to be popular, he offered them around, for anyone who wanted one. The packet never came back and everyone was smoking then, except him.

"That was a mistake", the heavily scarred individual to his left told him under his breath. "You never give anything like snouts away so eagerly, now you have none left for yourself".

"Thanks for the advice", Spider was glad of the chance to express gratitude, "I'll be certain to remember it for the future, I'm Spider by the way, Spider Hourglass".

"Bil Klip", the heavy set giant returned, what you in for Spider"?

"Robbery", Spider replied and resisted the temptation to make a joke about Klip's name.

"I'm doing a third stretch for a bit of G.B.H. but it was a bum rap, no matter, I've seen the best and the worst of the slammer".

On an impulse Spider offered the heavy his hand. Klip's smile was not a pretty thing to behold, but he took it and nearly crushed the life out of the safe-cracker's fingers as they shook.

"I've a proposition for you, Bil", he dared to offer then, knowing this to be a rare moment of opportunity. "Keep me alive while I do my eighteen months and I'll give you some of my stash when I get out".

"Stash? How much we - talking about"?

"Five hundred"? In reality Spider had three thousand hidden away in various safe places. He knew his first offer would not be good enough, but it turned out that Bil Klip, despite his amusing name was not greedy, he looked at the safe-cracker with his steel grey eyes and asked him,

"If it's seven fifty, I'll look out for Spider".

They shook for the second time in as many minutes and then Spider asked, "How do you know I'll pay, Bil. Do you accept my word, after all we've only just met"?

Klip returned darkly, "No one wants marking and being given good hiding for that sort of figure Spider, so, you have the lucre"?

"One thing I do keep beyond all others is my word Bil, I have the whazumahs".

"Honour among thieves eh Spider, you really green aren't you? We have deal and I don't renege on my word neither".

Spider resisted the urge to correct his new friend's grammar and they lapsed into silence until the flittruck sighed to a halt. They had reached the most infamous prison in the solar system.

The back of the vehicle hissed open and they were double cuffed before being undone from the bench and then armed guards took them into a secured waiting room. Spider was about to ask what happened then, when the iron door clanged open and a guard said,

"Hourglass"?

"That's me", replied Spider.

"Is it"? The guard smiled, but it seemed without mirth, "Well would you like to come to reception Mister Hourglass, so we can book you into one of our luxury suites"?

The others laughed and Spider hurried forward as well as he was able, with ankles cuffed together. As he shuffled down a corridor of unpainted breeze-block, which terminated into an area, at the end of which was a hatchway, one of the other guards was waiting for him, stationed in the hatchway.

"Hourglass", the guard at Spider's shoulder informed his comrade, "Green as grass, may need keeping an eye on".

The other nodded, "We'll put him on blue level one. Now; Hourglass, I'm going to ask you some questions and then we'll list your items and strip search you, before you go to the wing. You address me as sir, or boss, okay"?

"Yes sir, boss", Spider replied and was asked an interminable amount of personal questions, that the guards surely already knew the answers to. Finally the next question was,

"You're going to blue one, Hourglass. Would you like a sea view"?

"Oh, yes please", Spider returned in naive honesty.

"And will you be wanting to make use of the swimming pool"?

"Yes please".

"Can we also book you down for a twice weekly massage from our female Scandian masseuse"?

Finally Spider understood, while the two guards suddenly burst into laughter, the one at his shoulder suddenly said, "Okay green-grass let's get you behind the screen and get you searched and then we'll list your belongings, after you've changed into our wonderful well fitting pyjamas".

His ankle cuffs were removed and he began to undress. The second guard had come from out of the hatch and the two of them were going to search him together. Spider took off his watch and the guard he handed it to, whistled,

"This real, not a copy"?

"Yes sir, it's genuine", Spider assured.

"Makes you laugh doesn't it", the guard observed to his colleague, "We're on sixteen thou a year and this con here has a genuine Samsung Anolog in palladium, what do you reckon this is worth, Ramone"?

The second guard nodded toward Spider, "Ask green-grass he'll know. Hey, how much's this worth"?

"Two and a half g's", Spider returned, "And before you ask, I bought it, it's not hot".

"Bought it with someone else's money", Ramone laughed, "Okay get the rest of your bling off so we can enter it into the pad".

In a moment of inspiration, Spider said, "Get me in the same cell as prisoner Klip and the watch is yours"?

The two guards looked at one another and Ramone spoke first, "Don't do it Vlad".

Vlad pondered aloud, "I'm just going to look at Klip's screen, see what can be done. Ramone, when we come in for shift they don't search our wrists do they? Green-grass isn't going to complain it's gone missing; are you green-grass"?

"What's gone missing Sir"? Spider replied perfectly.

"Hey", Ramone conceded, "It's your job Vlad, not mine. Okay Mister Bling, get the clothes off and lets get you in the prison stripes".

Spider had just gotten dressed again, when Vlad came back, "I can't do it kid", he reported sadly, "There's no way I can put Klip on blue one and in black and white stripes, he's a three time loser and it's always G.B.H.".

"So where does he go, Sir" the safe-cracker asked.

"He'll end up on black three, with his record". Vlad actually sounded apologetic and made to bag the Samsung.

"If you can't put him on blue, can you put me on black"?

"Are you serious"? Ramone asked, "Do you know the sort of villain ends up on black, they'd eat you for breakfast green-grass, after they'd raped you that was"?

"I'd prefer to go to black and if possible in the same double cell as Klip, for the watch Sir, is it a deal"?

Vlad grinned and turned to Ramone, "I've just realised what's going on here, it's love Ramone and who am I to stand in the way of sweet romance? Okay sweetheart, I'm not heartless enough to keep you two love-birds apart, you can go on black with your husband. Get out of them stripes, I'll go get the green hoops while I try on my new watch".

While he was gone Ramone advised, "It's none of my business newbie, but just stick close to your boyfriend while you're in here, there's some pretty mean animals get on the black".

"You mean like Muller"? Spider offered.

Ramone looked gravely, "Muller won't even get on a wing kid, no he'll be going straight to segregation".

THREE

"I'M GOING TO try and get myself a better job, Cylvia", Darcie told his girlfriend at breakfast.

"Is this another one of your attempts to change, Darcie"? she wanted to know.

"Oh, yes it is, have you any connections, could you put a word in the right ear, I'll not let you down".

She looked thoughtfully, "If you'd said this to me two months ago I wouldn't have believed you, but right now, Darcie, I do think you're making positive moves in the right direction, regarding your life, so I'll see what I can do".

"Thank you babe", he kissed her lightly on the cheek and she gazed into his face for a while before, suddenly moving to the door.

"See you tonight, you know Darcie, I sometimes wonder who I'm coming home to, you're like a chameleon".

Then she was gone, leaving him alone with his thoughts. He could not hope to get his hands on the Brain Machine with only soda pop money behind him, but could he improve himself enough to get a responsible better paid post?

FOUR

AS THE DOOR slammed shut behind Klip and he saw who was lying on the top bunk, his face almost split into an amused grin. It was a face that could have split all too easily as well.

"How in Hades you manage to get yourself on this wing, Spider and even in same cell as me"?

"It cost me Bil, it cost me dearly, but if I'm going to survive my stay in this pokie, I figure I'm going to have to stick close by your side".

Klip threw his bedroll onto the lower bunk, "Did they give tobacco and papers"?

Spider threw them to his bodyguard, "For you Bil, I've given up the habit, so you'll be getting double ration from now on".

"Only if I stay healthy, I saw one or two of the guys as screw was escorting me here, people Spider not want to know. Did you get ping card as well"?

"I was hoping to use it to read, to pass some time with it, you know"?

"Okay, keep then", Klip agreed and began to make his bed. "When it comes to association do not wander off on your own".

"You don't have to tell me twice, not anything. What about chow"?

"We get our scran and eat in here. During exercise hour you walk just ahead of me, no variation. They'll begin to say you my bitch, do you care"?

"No, if it keeps me alive they can say what in Hades they want. It's going to be a long nine months isn't it".

"You think you going to get parole"?

"I'm going to keep my nose clean, so yes. I'm not figuring on doing more than fifty percent. When you get out, the money will be waiting for you".

"Let's not get ahead of ourselves, first we have keep you out of harms way to get that parole". Klip observed, in his economical mode of speech.

FIVE

DARCIE HAD BEEN a sales rep for 'ReaditwithUs' for three months, before he began to feel he was getting into his stride. The difficulty was that there were so many titles to remember, so many author's names. Selling door to door was not like going to company address's either. Sometimes it was incredibly difficult not to punch someone in the face. Sometimes a semi naked woman would answer the door and try to seduce him and that was hard in a much different way. Why didn't their men keep them satisfied, what was the problem?

Darcie stuck to his plan though, he saved and he stayed faithful to Cylvia. Though it made him miserable at times, he became more resolute and determined as a result. The goal was a machine that could potentially make him rich beyond his wildest imaginings. The fringe benefit was that Cylvia seeing his resolve, without knowing the reason for it, began to love him in quite a different way. She began to love *and admire* him. As a result, their love making took on a new and delicate tenderness that both found deeply satisfying.

Darcie resolved to wait until he had saved a thousand or so, before determining who he would need for his team. He wanted a breaker of codes and a computer genius, but neither of them must be too honest. He needed an edge, to keep him in charge and that edge - together with the promise of riches to come, was the need for secrecy and the threat of a return to incarceration. In short, Darcie was going to look for two cons who fit his requirement.

SIX

"WHAT IN HADES is this"? Spider groaned looking down at his metal segmented plate. It contained three sections and then two more over to one side.

Klip informed him, "That's dinner and duff".

"Duff"?

"Pudding".

"So these five globs of gloop are supposed to be edible"? Spider asked in desperation.

"The brown stuff lichbeef, the green lichpeas, the white lichspud. Then the shizula on the other side lichsponge and the yellow, lichcust".

"There's nothing to chew, we'll lose all our teeth".

"That's what canteen is for".

"Didn't this come from the canteen"?

"No", Klip was more patient than one would have expected from a violent man convicted of grievous bodily harm. "Food comes from kitchen, canteen - prison shop".

Spider shook his head and tried some of the brown goo, it tasted like yeast, "So when do we go to 'canteen' then"? he asked in desperation.

"I'm not sure it would be good idea for you to *go* canteen", came the disappointing answer. Klip felt obliged to explain, "There are usually disputes there, things get heated, most shankings are at canteen".

"Shankings? They sound ominously like stabbings", Spider mumbled unhappily.

"They are stabbings", the more experienced convict assured, "With a shank, a home-made knife".

"I can see my stay in this boutique is going to be fun filled from the get go", the safe-cracker observed sardonically.

"You can either throw yourself into population during association, or you can stay un-raped and alive, my advice is what you are paying for and I'm telling you to keep your head down".

"Okay, okay, I get it and Klip, thank you".

Later during association Klip was met by another who had been in prison with him before.

"Hey man", Fingers Sponsogil began, "Word has it you've got yourself a bitch, I didn't think you were into that sort of thing"?

"I'm keeping him safe is all", the heavy replied, the question had not annoyed him, such rumours were rife in prison. "So what you in for this time, Fingers? You been hacking computers again"?

Fingers nodded,

"The detection programmes are getting harder to avoid now-a-days though, Bil. The Constabulary were on to me in days, I'm doing eighteen".

"So you'll be out in nine, just like Spider".

"Spider"?

Klip confided in his friend, "The guy I'm sharing a cell with, first time in the slammer and he's a safe-cracker. He must have stash all over the place, you get out together if you keep your noses clean, you could do worse than getting to know him".

"So what are you waiting for then", Fingers grinned, "Introduce me to the newbie"?

Klip did and the duo became a trio, because Spider and Fingers hit it off from the first moment they met. For a few weeks all went without incident, but prison, though grindingly dull, was never free of incident. It happened when Klip and Spider were taking a shower. They always chose to conduct such activity when most of the other prisoners had finished, just before *bang up* in fact. They had almost finished when three figures entered in unison. Klip was instantly alert, he recognised the body language of their purposeful tread and saw it was full of menace.

"Hey Klip", the foremost of them began and that was as far as he got. For Klip's towel shot out like a whip and snatched the shiv from his grasp. The bodyguard to the safe-cracker dived down into the water and snatched it up, before anyone else could react, he had buried it to it's hilt in the front most of the trio, into his chest.

Spider watched in fascinated horror as blood gushed from the man's fatal wound and mixed with the soapy suds that were sliding down the shower's drain. By the time he slid to the floor, the would be attacker was already a wet and messy corpse. The two who had been following him hesitated, but Klip did not. With a bound he was at them and his spade-like fist connected with another's jaw. Spider heard the cracking of bone and instinctively knew it was not the snapping of finger bones. The last of them turned on his heels and ran.

"Come on", Klip grabbed Spider's arm, "We're 'outa' here before screws find the bodies".

Hurrying to do as instructed, the dazed Spider asked urgently, "We'll be split up, you'll go to 'seg' and then get a bigger sentence when it all comes out".

Klip pushed Spider into their cell before answering, "The two who lived won't say a word, if they did every con in the joint would be after them, no one grass' in prison Spider it just isn't done".

An investigation was conducted over the fatal stabbing, but no one did offer any verbal evidence, especially the prisoner who had his jaw wired up for several weeks. He was sent to segregation but still offered nothing and the authorities reluctantly left the case cold - but unsolved.

Time passed, Spider endured freezing nights when the wind blew straight off the pole and through their bars. He asked for more blankets and the guards just laughed. During these miserable times another prisoner hung himself in his cell, while another slashed his wrists with a broken light bulb and bled out. A grim depression descended upon the black three wing. It was decidedly the worst period and just when it was needed most, the Mars' World Cup began. The rules were slightly different to Terran football, due to the differing gravity and the fact that all football pitches on Mars were made of pseudo-turf, but the contest was as keenly fought and just as importantly, as keenly followed.

Spider said nothing to Klip during the early rounds, but when it got to the semi-finals he dropped his bombshell.

"I want to watch tonight's match on the tri-vid; in the association screen room", he told his cell mate and protector.

"Why, we have perfectly good two dimensional television in here"? Klip wanted to know indicating the plasma with a wave of his brawny arm.

"Are you kidding me, Bil"? The safe-cracker objected. "You can hardly see the ball on that poxy fifty nine centimetre screen". The association room had a one hundred and seventy eight centimetre three dimensional presentation and surround sound in addition.

"It's China against Poland tonight", Fingers, who was now an almost permanent guest in cell twenty three over the last month added.

"So what"? The violent offender wanted more information.

"I've been telling you, the bookies have China as favourites and Poland as second favourites, this is really the final tonight", Spider informed the sport ignoramus in frustration.

"So the game's worth getting stabbed over"? Klip was not convinced.

"I've got ninety grammes of tobacco riding on China", Fingers added, "And I got odds of three to one before the contest started from Nostrils Finandra".

Ninety grammes, at three to one, why'd you not say so in the beginning"! Klip exploded then, "If you'd said it was *important*"!

Of course once Klip had given in on one game, he was on dodgy ground when Spider wanted to watch the second semi final. Fingers was less supportive, he was still sulking over the fact that China had lost one-three and he had lost three months tobacco allowance to Finandra.

"So what's the bet this time"? Klip wanted to know.

"There's no bet, but it's the semi final, Bil".

"But you said the other match was like the final and the actual final would not live up to it and this is only the semi-final".

"Well, yeah, I know I did, but this is England against Romania and the Romanian's are the competition's dark horses".

"Really"? Klip grinned his hideously scarred grin, "Well don't you go putting any snout on it Fingers, because you don't know much about much if you ask me".

The trio survived another game, in which Romania knocked out England on penalties after one each, after extra time. Klip put his foot down on the third place play off. England surprised all the experts by beating China two-one, to claim third place.

Klip then knew there was no way he could talk the duo out of going to the final. Poland against Romania were the teams from the two largest populations on Callisto and Venus. On Mars alone, did the Chinese outnumber the two. Klip had gone to the exercise yard on his own the afternoon before the final. He was just doing his fourth circuit of the yard when he became aware of a presence at his shoulder. It was Nostrils Finandra,

"A word to the wise", the prisoner bookie began without preamble. "If the three stooges are going to tonight's game, someone might get hurt"!

The three stooges was the name the trio had been given by the wing and mind it, they did not.

Klip suddenly gripped Nostrils in a vice-like hold that was bound to be causing some discomfort, "Lay a mitt on Spider; you or any of your girl's and I'll......"

"Spider"?! Nostril's gasped, trying to pull himself free, "Spider's not to be touched, we all got the message after that incident in the showers. No Klip, it's not Spider that anyone wants to hurt, it's Fingers"!

"Fingers? Why, he's a regular stand up guy".

"Not since the semi's he isn't", Nostril's informed and then it dawned on Klip,

"He never had that ninety grammes did he? He couldn't pay you when who was it got knocked out"?

"China", Nostrils practically spat, "It was China and I gave him three to one. So I can't help it if some of the boys who were waiting on payouts from me feel a bit sore can I"?

"You've held back, because he wouldn't cough up"?

"I had to lay part of a bet like that off, Bil, what could I do, but tell them how the whole thing went down"?

"Put jam on it Nostrils you've more snout in this joint than the canteen".

"Hey, I've got a rep too you know? A guy has to have a rep or he doesn't last long in a place like this. Anyway I have to tell you some of those he owes now are the Romanians. Now that might not be so bad if they win tonight, but if the Romanian team loses, they might get to thinking about the smokes they're missing out on because Fingers welshed on his bet".

"Not your girls at all then"!

Nostrils shook his head, "I'm just putting you a word to the wise, Bil. Call it my good deed for the day".

"Alright Nostrils, thanks".

Ten minutes later Klip crashed into cell twenty three, where Fingers and Spider were playing cards, "If you're playing for money Spider, don't expect the welsh-er to cough".

"Oh"! Fingers tried to explain, "I can pay Nostrils eventually, but he'll have to wait for my allowance".

"You didn't tell him that when you placed the bet and as he'd laid some of the wager off, some Romanians who are waiting for tobacco are thinking of taking it out on your hide. So you're not attending the game with us two".

Finger's shoulders slumped, "I'd better go and explain to Nostrils; again".

"Wait a minute", Spider cut in, halting the hacker, "Take him this". He rummaged about in the foot locker under the bottom bunk and produced a small plastic package.

Fingers took the package and examined it, "Snufz", he gasped, "Cut this to make 1 in 2 and there should be some to spare. How can I ever thank you Spider"?

The safe-cracker grinned, Bil can't have eyes in the back of his head, you can watch me as a second bodyguard. Do we have a deal"?

"We have a deal", the hacker agreed and went in search of Nostrils.

"I think Romania will beat the Poles, but you never know"? Spider told the heavy.

He was wrong, Poland won three two and the Romanians smashed up several cells.

SEVEN

"**V**ISITATION SPIDER", THE guard told the safe-cracker.

"What"?!

"You've a visitor, are you coming or do we send them away"?

Spider was intrigued, he had not the slightest clue as to who would be waiting to visit him. He followed the guard and went into the visiting corridor, walking down the partitions, wondering if he would recognise someone. He got to the end and had passed no acquaintances when a voice said,

"Mister Hourglass, it's me who's come to see you, do you want to talk, I have some supplies to hand in for you"?

Spider took the seat opposite the plexi-glass screen and asked, "That's kind of you stranger, but I don't recall our knowing one another"?

"We don't yet, I'm what you might call a prospective business associate".

"What supplies"? Asked the convict.

"Soap, toilet paper, writing paper, stamps, shampoo, toothpaste, toothbrush, pen, chocolate, snufz and tobacco. All have been inspected by the visits officers and will be delivered to your cell".

"Well thank you Mister ah......."

"Orchvestige; call me Darcie".

He was clean cut, well dressed and strikingly handsome and Spider was impressed by appearance.

"What business are we going to engage in then, Darcie, my new associate"?

"It's a rather delicate matter", Darcie began.

"Yes, I thought it might be. As you are conducting it in a correctional facility, Darcie".

"I have something valuable locked inside a vault. I suppose you could almost call the vault a fortress, actually. The trouble is the contents are delicate and could be damaged if the door was blown off, so I need someone who can get into it with out resorting to such drastic measures, even a torch of some kind, or a laser, might do damage to the contents, the only way to get into that vault is with someone expert at cracking security codes".

Spider grinned, "And the contents aren't exactly legal is that it"?

"Amongst them is my brother's dead body. He died because he could not get out of the vault, there was no foul play, but I would not be able to answer certain questions and be believed by the Constabulary".

"Being as you were the last one to lock the vault before *forgetting* the code perhaps"? Spider offered helpfully.

Darcie shook his head, "No, he was the last to lock the fortress! There was no key pad inside the vault, so he had no way of getting out".

"You do realise that your story makes little sense"?

"I do, yet it's the truth. Do you begin to see my dilemma"?

"That the truth cannot possibly be the truth. Yeah Darcie, I can see how that might be a knotty one", Spider quipped. "So this is how it would be; I open the vault no questions asked, after you have given me my fee"?

"Not quite, I cannot afford your services *until* the vault is open and then I can pay you handsomely, for the contents are worth a fortune"!

"So you want to hire me, on the promise of payment *after* I have done the job"? Spider laughed. "That's not how I er... *work* Darcie".

"I understand your reluctance and I also point out that, unless you are confident in your abilities, you would not take the job anyway, but I would like you to name your figure if I did have the cash"?

"Let's just get one thing straight Darcie there isn't a safe made that I can't open, for your job, I only need two hundred".

"Do it for my promissory note and I will give you four hundred once I've made money from the contents", Darcie offered.

Spider mused for a second and then returned, "I have two associates who look out for me, if you understand what I mean by that Darcie, my new partner", he began, "They come along with me, just to make certain we don't have any sort of *misunderstanding*, if you follow my drift. Once I have opened the vault and you have realised the sale of the commodity, whatever it happens to be, you pay me four hundred and my associates fifty each. Oh, Darcie, the item is worth that much isn't it"?

"It's worth more than that, so I agree to your terms. Enjoy the items I brought you sir. Once you are at liberty, free from this facility please ping me at *orchvestigesales@mckimberley&droozfandin*. I will then give you some details of where the vault is situated and meet you at an agreed time", and with that Darcie rose to his feet.

"Darcie", Spider told him by way of farewell, "We'll meet again, good health my new business partner".

EIGHT

THE SUN WAS low on the horizon and did little to warm the cool wind that was called the vanquil, as it gusted across the plain, sending endless clouds of pink and red dust swirling into the air. Due to the smallness of Sol's diameter, the illumination was meagre and the cupola was an angry ruby. Underneath this heavenly splendour, for it was splendid in an alien way, two figures waited at the base of a now dormant volcano. They were dressed in thermal breeks and long frock coats of emerald, both had their hoods up. From a distance, therefore, it was not possible to discern that one was male the other female. A car slowly weaved it's way across the rusty plain, in their direction. It was an actual ancient Fiat 1400s, the steam driven vehicle that perambulated by means of the traction of rubber tyres on the very road it rested upon.

One of the figures turned to the other, but said nothing, it was very rare to see cars on Mars, but not totally unheard of. The Fiat must be at least thirty years old, more than likely more ancient still. It was evidently on it's way toward the couple and they were not surprised at that, for they were waiting for a rendezvous. Finally the car reached the duo's side and pulled up. From out of it's quite cramped interior, a very disparate trio climbed, with evident difficulty.

The foremost of them hailed the cowled couple, "Hey, Darcie, we made it. In that too"!

Darcie Orchvestige threw back his hood and approached Spider Hourglass and the two shook hands. It was the first physical contact they had ever enjoyed.

"It feels great to be under the sun again", Spider remarked with obvious relish, "You don't know how depressing it can be to see only grey painted breeze-blocks for nine months".

"Nine months, I've waited that long for this meeting and I saw you when you had done five", Darcie complained. "Don't tell me you were saving up for that pile of junk".

"Hey man, we *were* saving up for that", one of the other of the trio chuckled, "And it got us here didn't it"?

"Darcie, this is Fingers Sponsogil, one of my minders", Spider made the introduction. "The silent partner, as it were, is Bil Klip".

"Obvious aliases, if I ever heard one", Darcie grinned. Spider shook his head however.

"Mister Klip was given the name by his father. Fingers is a nick-name though, you are right there. He earned it by being a master of the keyboard, the P.C. keyboard".

"A hacker"! Darcie sounded delighted. "If Spider gets the fortress open, I may be able to pay you for further services, Mister Sponsogil".

"So there's a computer in there"? Fingers asked.

"Not exactly, but it is controlled by one, as are most inventions of the last few hundred years".

"An invention then", Spider concluded, "I see now why you needed me, force may have damaged it".

"Just exactly where *is* the fortress"? Fingers wanted to know. He was gazing about the landscape and could see no clue as to it's whereabouts.

"That's part of the clever camouflage", Darcie replied, "Come on, we'll show you"?

"One moment"! Klip suddenly froze them all by speaking for the first time, "Who is your *friend*, Mister Orchvestige"?

By way of tacit answer, the final member of the strange group lowered her hood and Fingers gasped loudest.

"Whoa, a beautiful friend then and a singularly attractive redhead"!

Cylvia Dortbrooke's auburn hair cascaded over the hood and shoulders of her parka, in ringlets of spun copper and bronze. Her face was heart shaped and the bridge of her nose dotted with freckles, she had a small mouth and large eyes that she was currently wearing emerald green. The three former convicts tried to tell if her body was as fabulous, but the parka withheld the possibility of delightful contours.

"I'm Cylvia", she told them simply and Spider returned.

"To men such as we, you are Helen of Troy my dear, I presume you are Darcie's romantic attachment"?

"She is", Darcie answered perhaps a trifle too hastily. There was a sudden undeniable tension in the air.

"Where is Troy"? Cylvia asked then.

Spider and Fingers laughed, "In Turkey, don't trouble yourself with it my dear".

Spider turned to Darcie, "Hadn't you best show us this concealed vault then, my dear partner"?

"Of course, come this way"?

Five sets of boots kicked up the red rust, in clouds to rival those stirred by the vanquil. They rounded a slight flair in the surface of the volcano and then Darcie told the safe-cracker,

"You'll have to squeeze through this gap, it's actually a very narrow entrance that leads to the code-sealed door, only one of us can squeeze in at a time".

"Then I go check it out before Spider", Klip said and Cylvia could not take her eyes from his ragged scar.

It was a very tight fit, but Klip went in and squeezed out again, in seconds, "It's a door as he says, the sort they have in large banks and on the left hand side, opposite the massive hinges, is a keypad covered in letters and numbers".

"Letters as well as numbers", Spider almost groaned, "That means it could be a Proncsel-Minotaur, or if we are in real trouble a Proncsel-Kaleidescope. Here let me go and see it for myself"?

The safe cracker went into the narrow passage and was gone much longer than Klip. When he returned Darcie asked,

"Well, which was it"?

"Neither. What by the sacred phases of the moon, is inside that thing, Darcie"?

"Why"? Darcie asked "Can't you do it"?

"It may take a while, but the safe that I can't get into hasn't been constructed yet", came the assured reply.

Fingers suddenly guessed, "There's a Daytrine-Obsidian in there, isn't that right"?

While Spider nodded, Cylvia asked,

"Is that bad, it's still just a safe; isn't it"?

"The Obsidian, my dear, is claimed to be totally crack-proof and to date the only way anyone has ever gotten into it was with E5 plastique".

"Well can't you get one of them then"? The red-head asked naively. Darcie told her,

"E5, is powerful explosive Cylv, it would tear the door off and the resultant rush of air and debris might damage the machine and the computer. Or even bring the whole of the volcano's side crashing down on us"!

"Do you know what I think"? Spider suddenly began. "I think we should all go back to Lomonosov, over a drink you tell us, Darcie, exactly what's inside the fortress, vault or safe, what ever you want to call it"?

"If I do", Darcie began, "Can you crack an; - er something Obsidian, or not"?

"A Daytrine-Obsidian. As I told you, the safe hasn't been built that I can't get inside. First though I want to know how your brother locked himself inside it, when there's only a pad on the outside. If, indeed, that's the situation"?

"You go to Lomonosov in your car and we'll take my flitter, we'll meet you at the Gold Earring Eatery, alright"?

Fingers took one of Cylvia's slim hands, "Would you like to ride with us my dear, you can sit on my lap if you wish"?

Before Darcie could object to the hacker's clumsy advancement, or Spider could scold Fingers, the girl surprised them all by smiling and replying,

"I've never been in a car before, sure, I'll go with you".

No one was more astonished than Fingers, while Darcie knew exactly why Cylvia was behaving as she was. It was punishment for his own behaviour with his secretary.

"Oh! Right then. We'll see you at the eatery, Darcie"? Fingers offered uncertainly.

Grimly, Darcie nodded and strode off toward the flitter which was out of sight.

Without a seconds hesitation, Cylvia climbed into the somewhat cramped rear of the Fiat 1400s. Eagerly Fingers joined her and the front seats were then pushed back into seated position. With Spider at the wheel, the aged car slowly moved off and began a wide arc, ready to travel to Lomonosov.

"I sense all is not well between you and Darcie, my dear"? Fingers began.

"He's building my trust once again", Cylvia smiled sweetly, "But I will never forget that he tupped his secretary".

"He cheated on *you* is he right in the head"? Fingers wanted to know.

"Oh I'm not certain, while I've known him he's changed abruptly, twice. Sometimes I wonder if he's gotten personality issues, you know, bi-polar"?

"Has he told you what's in the cavern"?

"Some, his brother Gleve managed to get himself trapped in it, it seems".

"Do you think he locked him in and then forgot the code to get him out"?

"Well, I can't accept that Gleve locked himself in, how could he"?

Fingers fell momentarily silent. He glanced at Klip who nodded.

"You don't plan to harm him do you"? Cylvia wanted to know. "He'll pay you, I can tell you that, despite his faults, he always honours his deals".

"If he does, then all will be well", Spider assured over his shoulder. "Unless there is something beyond our imaginings inside that curious fortress".

Cylvia fell silent too and there was an unspoken tension in the air before they reached the eatery. Fingers rushed to help the girl out the car and they entered in unison. Of course Darcie had preceded them by some considerable margin.

"I've ordered us all the beef cobbler and hot tea, on me". He told them, this proved very acceptable. Cylvia took her seat beside him and the trio seated themselves opposite. The cobbler arrived, accompanied with lichenbeets and lichen-spud, but the beef was excellent and no one spoke for quite some time. Finally as the were enjoying their tea Darcie said,

"I guess it's time to tell you what is in the fortress".

When he had finished the trio from prison were silent for some seconds before Klip spoke,

"That has to be the most fanciful piece of entertainment I've heard in a long time".

"It explains why Darcie seemed so strange for a month or so", Cylvia told them, "I can't expect you to believe that, but I find that I do and opening the vault will tell us for certain".

"A Daytrine-Obsidian would be used to conceal something that was potentially worth thousands of silver shillin", Spider mused.

"Yes, indeed", Fingers agreed, "I believe the story and I would love to have a crack at such a sophisticated computer".

"Without damaging it in any way"? Cylvia reminded.

"Of course", Fingers agreed with a smile just for her. "To access the programme, there will certainly be a series of code words and for that, you will need me. Or it could take you aeons to get the Brain machine to work".

"So what's the best stratagem"? Cylvia wanted to know.

"There's no sense in all five of us going back out to the fortress", the safe-cracker told the two of them, "I can go with one of you, while the rest of us stay in the warm here in Lomonosov"?

"Then Cylvia will go with you for the first trip", Darcie decided and eyed Fingers as he did so. The girl smiled at her boyfriend's discomfort.

'Good', she thought, *'It's just what you deserve you cheating vole'!*

NINE

"THERE'S NO SHAME in admitting defeat, Spider", Darcie told the safe-cracker, blowing heat into his cold fingers. The wind was gusting directly into the crevice containing the fortress key-pad.

"The safe isn't built, that I can't crack", came the muffled response. For Spider had his muffler over his nose and mouth and goggles over his eyes, the latter to protect them from the dust. He looked like a figure made of rust. He was caked in it and as he had moved little, the dust clung to him and built up a rind, making of him, some bizarre inedible fruit.

"We should get back, it's getting close to sundown".

Spider took one earpiece of the stethoscope from his ear for a second and promised,

"Half an hour more, do you realise how close I am".

"After twelve whole days I would hope close", Darcie observed with a certain amount of sarcasm in his basso utterance.

"I have fourteen of the sixteen inputs".

"How can you know that".

"I can hear the tumblers sneck into place, I just need two and fifteen and we're in".

"If you're so sure, then why don't we get back while it's light and all five of us can return in the morning"?

"Alright", Spider agreed suddenly, "I'm starved anyway".

Darcie groaned, "And my thumb is already volumed to red".

"Get the chick, to pay out of Finger's share"?

"That's not funny and if he so much as touches her, he'll have to change his name to Broken Fingers".

"Come on then, let's go before we lose the light. I wouldn't fancy our chances of navigating in the dark"?

The duo left the crevice and got back to town, but once they had eaten they decided everyone should return in the dark, for the opening of the fortress was so unbearably close, not willing to wait for the others to stir the same duo began walking toward the flitter when a voice suddenly cried out,

"Make like statues! M.B.I.I".

Spider instantly stood stock still, while Darcie turned in astonishment,

Take out your weapons and drop them on the ground and then walk away from them. Do it now, I've a blaster trained on you".

"What's going on"? Darcie asked naively, while his partner suddenly produced a needle gun from his coat and dropped it on the ground. He then obediently began to back away from where it had fallen.

"Don't be stupid", ordered the man in the grey jacket and trousers decorated with orange flashes, uniform of the M.B.I.I. (Mars Bureau of International Investigations). Do like I said"

"I don't have a weapon", Darcie told him candidly, "Who the Lamb of God are you and what do you want with us"

"Agent Spagliatelli", the officer said, "Now go to your friend, we've been keeping tabs on the activity around the volcano, just what's going on out there"?

"What's it to you"? Darcie dared, "It's private property and belongs to me".

"It may be your real estate Orchvestige; yes I know who you are. It may be your property, but I think it might have your brother inside".

"It has".

"Then you're guilty of kidnap and the misappropriation of military grade components. That's larceny, Orchvestige".

"We've not been able to get inside, Spagliatelli", Spider told the agent honestly. The place is locked with a Daytrine-Obsidian sixteen code pad and we cannot crack it".

"Not even you, Hourglass", the agent replied with satisfaction, "No one can crack one of those little beauties".

"So what now"? Spider wanted to know, "Are we under arrest"?

"No", said a deep voice just behind Spagliatelli, "No one's under arrest just yet. Drop the weapon *rosser*, or this blaster aimed at your neck might accidentally go off"!

"What are you doing, Klip"? Spider gasped, "You can't take the M.B.I.I. Hostage"!

"It seems I just have", Klip argued with satisfaction.

"What are we going to do with him, we'll get years for this"? The safe-cracker wailed.

"Put your own cuffs on Spagliatelli and give me your pad or telephone, which ever you have on you". Klip instructed the former constable with relish.

"If I don't check in, they'll come looking for me", the agent told them, as he did as instructed, while Klip continued to hold the blaster to his neck. Only when he was trussed up, did the huge body-guard relax and lower the weapon.

"You think I fell off a Yule-log, but you're wrong", Klip said to the agent. "No one's coming to look for you, this is a private project of your own, otherwise there'd be two of you, M.B.I.I always work in pairs".

He was gratified to see the shoulders of the agent slump as he spoke, he then knew that what he had suspected, was in fact, true.

"What did you have to come here for"? Darcie asked desperately. Looking at the short stout agent with the greying hair, "We aren't doing anything wrong".

"If that's so, why do you need military grade film capacitors and utensor diodes"? Spagliatelli wanted to know. "Who stole them from Aeolis Space-force Base? You or your brother? Where is Gleve too, is he inside"?

"Shut up and get in the flitter", Klip cut in. "Spider you drive the Fiat, I'll drive the agent's Volkswagen".

"To where"? The safe-cracker wanted to know.

"The fortress of course, where else, all six of us are going back out".

"In the dark"?!

"Yeah", Klip told them, "It's going to be quite a party, but you can work by flash-light Spider. We've got to get whatever's in the fortress out and be away from there before anyone wonders where this rosser is".

The lights of the Fiat were not able to penetrate very far, so Klip lead the procession, with Spagliatelli, still cuffed, as his passenger. Behind them in the Fiat was Spider and Fingers, while Darcie and Cylvia brought up the rear in his flitter.

"This affair is getting out of hand now Klip has kidnapped the M.B.I.I. Agent", Cylvia told her partner.

"What were we supposed to do"? Darcie asked in frustration, "I didn't know Gleve had stolen some of the machine's bits".

"A machine you'll now not own, once your convict friends get into the fortress", Cylvia pointed out.

"Once I sell the patent to it, we'll be able to buy thousands of cap-things", Darcie told her.

"And the charges for kidnap"?

"Will be levelled at Klip, not us".

"Darcie. We are accessories unless we go to the authorities right now", Cylvia warned. "Come on, pull the flitter around and we'll use our pads to inform the constabulary"?

"No"! He firmly contradicted her, "We've gotten too close to give up now".

"Some things are more important than money", Cylvia told him, "Like staying out of prison".

"Look babe, I forced you to stick with us right? If anything goes badly, that's what I'll tell the rossers"

"Rossers", she echoed, "You're starting to sound like a convict now".

"Cylvia", Darcie returned very quietly, but through gritted teeth, "Shut up"!

The rest of the journey was conducted in atmospheric silence. They climbed out the flitter and into the cold night of Mars. It was fearfully dark, the moons providing next to no illumination. The wind had grown frigid too and they threw their hoods up. Ahead of them they could see flash lights dancing as they lit the way to the front of the concealed entrance.

When Cylvia reached a trio of shrouded figures, Finger's voice assured her Spider was already at work,

"How long"? Darcie asked obtusely

"As long as a pleasant morning jog", the hacker promised, even though he could not have the slightest idea.

"Are you warm enough officer", Cylvia asked Spagliatelli.

"Quite ma'am", the agent returned, "My uniform is thermal and the volcano is breaking the wind at the moment. It's agent by the way not officer".

"Is it necessary for you to throw yourself at every man we meet"? Darcie demanded in agitation then.

"I don't throw myself at every man", she returned acidly, "I don't throw myself at you"!

"It's not too late to make this right", the M.B.I.I. Man tried then, "I can forget Klip's misguided loyalty to you, Orchvestige, if you undo my cuffs and surrender to me now"?

"Forget it", Klip growled, "And he ain't in charge any more anyway, *I am*"!

"Now just a minute Mister......."? Darcie began, but Cylvia said quietly,

"Darcie. Shut up"!

Suddenly they heard a whoop of triumph and a figure joined them, "I've got another, just one more to go", it was Spider's voice. In the rusty light of the flash-beams features were difficult to discern.

"You came out here to give us a progress report"? Klip grizzled, "We're out here freezing our behind's off and you still ain't opened the door! Get back in there and get the job done already".

"Well okay", Spider sounded genuinely hurt, "I just thought you'd want to know. It's not a ball in there either you know? It's cramped and cold too".

Klip made a growling noise and Spider blurted,

"Alright, alright. I'm going. You're here to protect me Bil, just remember that. Get out that foul mood, for solstice sake"

"Go Spider, the dialogue isn't amusing nor helpful, we need to focus right now", Cylvia urged. Strangely at that moment the dynamic shifted to her and the safe-cracker replied,

"Okay, sorry, I'm on it".

It was noted by Spagliatelli, "It's just hit me now, you're in charge".

"No", Darcie was quick to correct, "She knew nothing about this until I told her I was taking a trip and asked her to come, she's innocent, agent. Innocent of any crime you can think of, or accuse any of us of".

"We should have brought a portable stove", Fingers thought aloud, "So we could have at least make some hot drinks, maybe next time"?

"Let's hope there isn't going to be a next time", Cylvia noted, "Spider is very close".

"And once he's in", the agent wanted to know, "What then, what are we going to find, Miss Dortbrooke"?

"Your precious parts, used to create a diagnostic tool that will save lives", she told him calmly, suddenly believing every word Darcie had told her. "Plus the dead body of Gleve Orchvestige, who gave his life for the project".

"There was an accident"? The constable in Spagliatelli instantly came to the surface.

"That's right", Cylvia replied as though she were telling the truth and her voice was totally convincing, "Gleve lost his life creating the machine that took it, no one is guilty of murder, agent Spagliatelli".

They waited another hour in almost silence, the wind chilling them to the marrow. They even huddled in a tight knot to try and conserve body heat, but it was a battle that they all knew Mars would ultimately win. Then suddenly Spider cried out,

"Holy Ostre, I've only gone and done it"!

They heard a quiet click, felt the rush of air drawn into the crevice the safe-cracker was working in, saw a flicker of light as systems began to quietly whine into activation and L.E.D.'s begin to turn on. There was a whoosh and the fortress door was opening, leading into an almost sterile environment.

"Go girl", Klip instructed and Cylvia was second into the crevice, just behind Spider. She hurried to see. Hurried to check, despite her former evident conviction, that the fantastic yarn Darcie had told them all was the truth. The dessicated body of Gleve Orchvestige was strapped into a quite plain tubular steel framed chair. It had shrunken with the dessication that the trapped dry atmosphere inside the fortress had acted on the body and become it's tomb. The head had sunken down onto the chest and the bald pate had lost it's constant gleam. The tubes that lead into the body were thus incongruously large and useless. Thankfully thanks to the absence of water vapour, there was no putrefaction and therefore no odour, the water that had existed in the body in life had evaporated in death. The group seemed to assemble around the dead man, momentarily silent as though in a respect that some of them did not feel. It was the agent who broke the observance,

"This proves nothing in itself people. I see the attempts at medication, but what story does it tell"?

Darcie told the group at once, "He had strapped this body into this chair, so that I could not get out of here. From this other chair, in my body, he left the cavern and locked me inside. Something went wrong though, for some reason the exchange was not permanent and before I could reason out what had happened to me and even attempt to get in here, he died of starvation".

"Not a pleasant way to go", Cylvia observed with a shudder.

"Don't feel sorry for him", Fingers pointed out, "He raped you"!

"This is all very tragic in the tradition of the ancient bard", Spagliatelli observed, "But obvious crime has been committed here and by my capture, is still being perpetrated".

"Never mind that for the moment", Klip observed coldly, "Does this thing work even for a short time, Darcie. Don't forget you have bills to pay".

He touched the back of the corpse's wrist and it promptly begin to cave into powder. Within seconds it was spilling onto the cavern floor and the hand fell off and was dust.

Cylvia held back the gag reflex and asked,

"It's your turn now Fingers, can you get this thing to work and provide us with a demonstration"?

The hacker grinned, clicked his fingers and took his place in the vacant chair, he replied, "Does this all turn out to be a wild Dodoprot chase, or will Fingers Sponsogil save the day"?

The plasma monitor danced into life and displays of numbers and letters began to descend down it with increasing rapidity. Without realising they were doing it, the group tightened into a knot around his shoulders, entranced by the possibility of using the Brain Machine. Even Spagliatelli was intrigued and not just from an agent's perspective. Could any two of those present be able to change bodies for a certain period?

"What we have here is an electronic encephalographic computerised recorder. Radiography demonstrating the intra-cranial fluid-containing spaces after the withdrawal of cerebra-spinal fluid and introduction of air or other gas; it includes pneumo-encephalography and ventriculography. Not only that, but the computer then makes a detailed recoding of the encephalograph and is able to reproduce it into a second brain, replacing it's original settings......".

He stopped suddenly,

"What is it", Cylvia was first to find her voice, "What have you seen"?

"This machine.........",

"What about it; what"? Cylvia was persistent.

"It's just that, with the slightest of modification, the projection of the recorded image needs no hardware receiver! In theory, with a better power supply and a couple of components, namely a Saladrium leaf capacitor and a couple of Vhransistors - the brain pattern can be projected an almost infinite distance"!

"Alright, I'll tell you what"? Spagliatelli began then, "Take the cuffs off and give me an undeniable demonstration and I'll hand this over to a pal of mine in the M.I.I.I.I.".

"The M.I.I.I.I. What in tar-nation is that"? Cylvia wanted to know.

"The Mars Institute of Intelligence for Internal and International Investigation", it was Spider who answered her. "They're a more science based outfit than the one Spagliatelli here's in".

"That's right", Spagliatelli agreed. "But I want to go in the machine first".

"You want to swap bodies with someone", Cylvia deduced, "With whom"?

"I'll do it", Darcie volunteered, "After all, my pattern should still be in the computer".

"And then no more larceny", the agent warned them.

"There won't be any need", Fingers grinned, "I've got the components I spoke of in my trick bag in the boot of the Fiat".

"If we choose to make the swapper a projector", Cylvia added. "I get to be the first to experiment with it's possibilities"?

"Why"? Darcie wanted to know. "If you're thinking of going into ..... ".

"I'm not"! Cylvia cut him short, she turned to Fingers, "You said infinite distance right"? The hacker nodded causing her to announce,

"I'd go into hyper-space, to see if I could help one of the astronauts who are trapped in it".

"A worthy, if dangerous cause", the agent nodded, "But could this so called projector pull her back if things went wrong, could you monitor it at this end and finally Sponsogil, if you're so damned clever how come you didn't build one of these machines yourself"?

"Always the rosser eh"? Fingers grinned, "Yes I would be able to monitor events on this display here and retrieve her brain patterns if there's no one out there. As to why I didn't build an *Encaphlotron*; firstly I didn't conceive one, that takes brilliance, secondly I'm a programmer not an electrical engineer, that takes quite a different skill set".

"Yet you're sure you can adapt it to another use"? Darcie pointed out.

"Yes, but again building on someone else's ground work is comparatively easy".

"All of this is very interesting", the agent remarked, "But all we've seen so far is computer language and a lot of talk from you Fingers. While I'm still in cuffs, now; is anyone confident enough in the machine's abilities to un-cuff me"?

"Klip. Please take the restraints off our friend in the Bureau"?

"Why don't we keep them on while Fingers does the demonstration"? Klip wanted to know.

Before Darcie could argue with him, the agent told them,

"I can live with that".

"Alright then gentlemen, take your seats please"? Fingers chirped.

TEN

EDUARDO SPAGLIATELLI FELT his brain begin to itch. It was as if cold fingers were tracing over what he thought was his skull. Tiny sparks of light danced before his closed eyes and then he grew frighteningly dizzy and unaware of his surroundings. He felt like he was rushing in every conceivable direction at the same instant. Yet none of the exertion caused his breath to become laboured. Suddenly he was enveloped in a neutral grey and he went deaf and lost all feeling of touch, he could no longer realise that he was in his body. He tried to open his eyes, but he had none. He tried to speak, but he had no throat. He did his best to remain calm, realising then that the sensation of the out-of-body experience was not in any great way frightening. Then the whole process seemed to begin afresh, but in reverse. The instant he could open his eyes he did and it was obvious at once that he was viewing the cavern from the chair over to the left, he could tell that quite easily by the shift in perspective.

Fingers voice said, "It's done, you can get up guys, you should feel no ill effects of any sort and should tell me if you do".

Spagliatelli stood, he threw off the parka, it was making him too hot. Then he gazed down at his arms and hands. They were covered in coarse black hairs! They were the arms of Orchvestige. He flexed the fingers, turned the hands over a few more times, noted the absence of the wedding ring. Noted the absence of the cuffs. He went over to his own body, it was still seated. Laughing he told Klip,

"You'd better un-cuff our boss".

Klip drew his snout nosed blaster and aimed it at him, "Take that needle gun from it's holster and you're fried, rosser".

"I have no intention of doing so", Spagliatelli heard himself say in Orchvestige' voice, "And you'd be killing your boss if you shot this body".

"Klip"! The girl retorted sharply, "Put it away and help Darcie out of those cuffs will you.

She turned to Spagliatelli, "Well, agent, is the demonstration enough of a success for you? Are you now willing to be seated and put back where your thoughts and aspirations belong"?

"I hope he is", Spagliatelli heard his own voice say, "I don't relish being out of my own carcass for long this time".

Spagliatelli seated himself once again, "Once we're back where we belong and trigger happy over there gives me my radio back, I'll put a call in to Archie Normanton, he's the constable I was telling you about, the one in the M.I.I.I.I".

ELEVEN

TWO DAYS LATER Spagliatelli had returned to his headquarters and been replaced by the tragically thin Normanton. He of the M.I.I.I.I. Klip and Spider were also gone, having been paid from Cylvia's bank account, she had taken over the bills, bailing out her boyfriend, intent upon being the first woman to use the Encaphlotron, as the Brain Machine was now known.

"Don't worry", the girl had told Darcie, "If you want to sell it as a simple swapper, Fingers can always change it back for you".

She had questioned the hacker extensively as to how the projection would work. Her mind would be projected into hyper-space, there her thoughts should be able to journey in search of human brain patterns and lock onto one. Then she would share the mind of the target until both agreed that one of them should leave the body. Fingers would then recall the appropriate brain waves that would inhabit Cylvia's body.

The prospect for human travel in the galaxy would thus become fantastical. No longer would there be the need for ships, distance would not be a problem. Once Darcie registered the patents he would be the richest man in the solar system overnight. His personal wealth would be greater than the entire holdings of 'If You Want It, We Stock It', Venus Water, and English Tourism, added together. He could then sell forty nine percent to the highest bidder and simply watch the money just roll in, whilst still controlling the board as the chief share holder. Darcie had already named the corporation *Orchevestments* and Cylvia was not sure she liked the glint of avarice in his beautiful blue eyes. She knew she would soon be cast aside, to make him the most eligible bachelor in the solar system. Nothing short of a duchess would be good enough for Darcie Orchvestige, owner of the company that created the Encaphlotron, the future for mankind itself.

So when Fingers finally climbed back to a standing position and announced to her and the two men,

"Done. The new components are in place, the second hood is now redundant. What you have now Cylvia is an Encaphlotron-ic Projector".

"What Cylvia has"?! Darcie exploded.

"She is paying the bills isn't she"? Fingers was deliberately annoying the man.

"It's alright Darcie", Cylvia soothed, "We know Gleve originally built the machine. Fingers is just teasing you. Well, you two; you too also Archie, it's time for me to try the mysteries of hyper-space, see if I can help some of the vessels that have never sent word back to Earth, word of their arrival at Proxima".

"Are you certain you want to make your first projection so powerful"? Fingers wanted to know.

"It can do it"?

"Of course, I've written a plotter into the programme, but...."

"Then that's where I want to go", she decided firmly.

"Get in the chair then", the programmer and erstwhile hacker instructed.

Darcie suddenly went over to her and kissed her on the cheek, "Good luck and safe return".

"Of course", she answered. Her voice lacked total conviction however.

The cowl was lowered, Fingers activated the programme and then leaned back.

"That's it"! Normanton asked after an interval.

"The programme is automatic, she's out there", Fingers told them.

"So what happens now".

"You take me to the patent office in Eos and damned fast", Darcie ordered briskly

"I meant what happens to the girl's id", the constable persisted.

"I'll monitor her progress on the screen and be able to tell when she finds anyone, if she can. If not, I'll bring her back, you might as well take Mister eager trousers here to Eos".

"Alright then, Orchvestige, let's go and remember, the agency gets one half of one percent of all shares".

Darcie grinned, "You won't let me forget Archie, come on, time's a wasting".

Fingers watched the two men leave and was then alone in the fortress. Not even the corpse was there to keep him company, it had been removed for study by Normanton's science team. He could suddenly hear the cold wind gusting across the souther plain outside. It was accompanied by the steady whir of the computer's fan. He wondered how long he would have the place to himself. How long Cylvia's mind would be drifting through hyper-space in search of another human thought process, be it alive, damaged or dormant. What happened to the crews of those disappeared vessels, their fate was beyond his imagination?

He settled down for a wait. In the two days since the machine had been reactivated, the fortress had enjoyed the installation of some creature comforts. It now boasted a stocked freezer, hypoven, three sets of bunk beds with Mars Season sleeping bags. Around the rear of the volcano was a chemical porta-closet. There were two laptop computers which could provide contact with the rest of the net on the planet and any form of entertainment he might want. Cylvia had spent shillin like they did not matter to her, which, they probably did not.

For a while though, Fingers watched the screen and wondered what his female friend was experiencing. A strange instinct suddenly caused him to glance at the girl's dormant body and he jumped violently. Cylvia had opened her eyes!

He looked back to the screen and saw the information the computer was providing, a new set of brain waves had been brought back to Mars by automation. Just who was the woman who now possessed the beautiful frame of Cylvia Dortbrooke?

"Do you know what has happened to you"? Fingers asked.

"I agreed to this, I'm First Officer King of the space vessel H.M.S. Искатель-Seeker".

Fingers had heard of neither, "I'm Sponsogil", he began, "Please allow me time to look up the details of what you've just told me".

The beautiful red-head waited patiently, although her eyes were everywhere.

"The H.M.S. Искатель-Seeker was privately and jointly funded by Lloyds of London and the Royal Bank of Moscow, it was crewed by four Astronauts - English and four Cosmonauts - Russian", Fingers read aloud, "That was five years ago Officer King"!

"Five years, yes, Miss Dortbrooke told me that, I have to confess I was shocked at the wasted time".

"So what happened when you found Cylvia in your mind, as you are the first to realise the experience it would help me to know. Oh and can I get you anything dear lady? Food, drink, do you need any facilities"?

"I wouldn't say no to a hot chocolate", King smiled, "And can I firstly ask you what you do Mister Sponsogil"?

As he arose to get the drink for her, thinking it lucky he actually had some hot chocolate, Fingers told her,

"I'm the programme designer and operator, Miss King. Should I call you officer, or what mode of address is appropriate"?

"Josephine".

"Josephine King! Good job no one shortens your first name".

She groaned, "Don't travel that road mister Sponsogil, believe me I've heard them all, do you have a first name"?

"Everyone calls me Fingers, due to my occupation, I prefer it to my given".

"Okay, Fingers, I was actually in some sort of induced trance when Cylvia entered my brain and then my mind. Her intrusion brought me out of it".

"What had caused the trance, hyper-space"?

"Yes. At least I think so, it's all new territory isn't it"?

"You can say that again, here's your drink".

Thanking him she continued, "Of course my first reaction was,

'Get out, I will not go insane'! Until Cylvia convinced me she was a separate person and how she happened to have reached me I then asked her about your machine. She explained that the missing vessels were her very reason for transmitting her mind through space and asked if we could swap minds for a while. After an indefinite period of unconsciousness I was happy to agree to anything, but waited until she had roused the rest of the crew. Captain Garin reset the controls and the ship was just entering normal space when I *left*".

"Normally a great period of excitement for a girl surely"?

"Absolutely, but this exploration is too and Cylvia has a very dynamic personality, I actually feared for my sanity if I refused her, so here I am. Are you alone here"?

"For the moment, the owner and science agent are on their way to Mars patent office, they'll be back in a couple of days".

"I thought I felt light, I've never been on Mars, do you think you would take me outside please"?

"Sure. You're not a prisoner anyway, Josephine. You might want to put a parka over your uniform though, it's in the deep south here and the weather is brisk".

As she tugged on a coat he asked her, "You say Cylvia had a very dynamic personality, strange she never exhibited it much while she was with us. It hardly sounds like the same woman"?

"Perhaps her experience in this projector device changed her then, I don't know, all I can tell you is that I did not wish to share a body with her for very long".

"Don't you fear for what might happen to it, while it's loaned out, so to speak"?

"I do, but then she must face the same fear and the swap is by no means permanent, so I just jumped into yet another adventure. Now let me outside, I've never been on any world other than Earth".

Fingers lead her beyond the crevice that hid the fortress entrance and the redhead gazed open mouth at the raw splendour of the open landscape.

"It really is red", she almost whispered. "That is the iron oxide we're told about, the planet of rust, I'm a woman of rust".

"Especially with Cylvia's colouring", Fingers agreed, "You might be able to see the ends of your long hair Josephine, but you also have freckles deep green eyes and are quite stunning".

"It must be hard for you then, this substitution, when you're clearly in love with her".

"I...., no, she's with someone else actually, one of the duo I spoke of earlier, the owner of the site and machine. He will soon be a very very rich man".

"Oh and is Cylvia one who goes for wealth over feelings"?

"What feelings, did she say...think something to you, while the two of you shared your body"?

"No", Josephine admitted openly, "But it's strange Fingers, vestiges of memory and feelings linger in this body, remnants of what Cylvia left behind in the dregs of her brain I suppose. She definitely felt a warmth for you and a growing dissatisfaction with whom ever she's with at the moment".

"Why are you telling me this"?

"In case I say something endearing to you, it might not be from me, but her. I'm sorry this is very confusing".

"I guess feelings always are", Fingers noted, somewhat obviously. "There again it's very new territory for you. New world, new acquaintances, new body"!

"And what a world! Were you here when everything was under bubbles, before the special plants managed to make it a bit more Earth-like"?

Fingers nodded, "I was a youth, but yes it took a while for all the bubbles and tubes to come down, there's still a museum, that's preserved some, if you ever want to see them".

"Where"?

"Up in Hellespontus Montes. Who knows you may have time for a visit"? He jerked his head suddenly to one side at three musical notes played in quick succession. "I have to go inside, the computer is signalling that Cylvia wants to communicate".

The duo squeezed through the slim corridor into the cavern and saw on the screen that a message had appeared;

Fingers, we are in trouble, I've managed to rouse the
crew from the torpor of hyper-space, the captain has even

got the ship into normal space, but we don't know where we are, the on board computer was expecting the constellations when viewed toward Proxima and cannot decipher what is being fed into it. Surely the Encaphlotron is capable of far more if it can read a human brain, please respond to this plea for assistance?

Finger began typing,
Josephine told the hacker, "That's English, not Standard it......"
Fingers was already replying, in English.

Stand by.

"Could the Искатель-Seeker be way off course"? Josephine asked, switching to standard.

"Unknown", Fingers was not willing to commit himself, "We still don't know the nature of hyper-space, never mind it's behaviour. That's why this machine is such a terrific break through. Mankind can reach the stars with his intellect, whilst still in the solar system".

"Can you help them, before they run out of supplies"?

"I'm guessing you had supplies enough for a couple of years, so there's a good chance the Encaphlotron can make something of stellar charts, once someone aboard sends them to us".

He typed the appropriate request and the two of them waited for a response.

TWELVE

"IT'S NO USE", Garin, the captain told them in desperation, "We're lost".

"May I try and make sense of the computed astral charts, captain"? First officer King requested.

Pavel Garin spun around in his command seat, "If I cannot fathom our position with the aid of the computer, what can anyone do, King"?

The English first officer said quietly, "I am not the enemy here, captain. Ignorance and fear are those, will you let me try or not"? The conviction in her voice was some new quality the others had not noticed in officer King before. She had woken them up after all, even if Garin had gotten them out of hyper-space.

He rose slowly from his chair, "Very well, *first officer*, have a go, make sense of the constellations".

King seated herself and began to type into the console, she typed in English rather than standard, so the four Russians could not understand what she was doing. At her shoulder astronaut Henti Varety read what her officer was doing and was astonished, but she contained her surprise and said nothing.

Added to her surprise was the fact that also in English a reply appeared on the console, which King promptly deleted.

She turned to the other six members of the crew, "I've input some data, it will take a short while for the calculations to run, we might as well get something to eat".

As the rest of them drifted to the galley, Varety took King to one side, "What's going on Jo"? She demanded. "Who is *Fingers* and how can you be in touch with anyone from England"?

"I can explain later, but not now, the others will notice we've held back and make the wrong assumptions about us. Keep it between us for now Henti, alright"?

Varety nodded, "I just hope you know what you're doing that's all".

The crew ate together. In addition to the captain there were three other cosmonauts; Alina Krivova, Tatyana Avilova, and Viktor Blok. The male astronauts were; J.P.Tornell and Drax Malunderain.

Cylvia excused herself as soon as it was politely acceptable and went for'ard once again, a message was already waiting for her on the computer screen;

> The ship obviously has no stern sensors, the answer to your dilemma is really obvious. The ship has drifted off the plain of the ecliptic and the northern pole of Nyjord is actually beneath the stern of the ship. Though we know space to have no up nor down, you are above the entire system of Proxima, looking up from it and that's why the constellations are not recognisable.

Cylvia deleted the message after typing a thank you and made the necessary course change. Nyjord was just swimming into view when she heard someone join her in the command section, it was the captain.

"Another inexplicable act on your part first officer", he noted without a great deal of pleasure, "How did you perform this latest miracle".

"It wasn't a great mystery captain", Cylvia began, "We had simply drifted from the ecliptic, pointing nose upward. The vessel is now yours to land".

Garin grunted his thanks and then opened the ship wide intercom, ordering the crew to take their landing hammocks and strap themselves in. It was hardly necessary, his entry into the planet's atmosphere was smooth and extremely well executed and he then began to land Iskatel-Seeker, as it was called in Standard.

The instant the craft thumped down onto firm terrain, he accessed the map that had been sent from Explorer One and correlated it to their position. As various members of the octet were beginning to free themselves of their restraints he informed them,

"We are on one of the large northern island land masses that Explorer One named Hyderabad. I will call this landing site Samara. We know we can breathe outside, that we'll be fine as long as we eat only from our rations, so get into the outdoor wear provided and we leave the ship in ten minutes".

Cylvia could barely contain her excitement, she was going to set foot on a world, that lay beyond the solar system.

Ten minutes later the airlock hissed open and the landing steps were lowered. The first officer was second to poke her head outside the ship. A myriad of incredible visuals smote her in an instant. The multi coloured grasses, the slightly pink sky. On the horizon were the blue fronds with their silvery leaves and huge white and orange flowers. The planet had a fragrant smell of vegetation and unpolluted air. The crew stunned to a daze, slowly descended the steps and stood in silence for several moments, just surveying the vista that lay before them. Then they heard the crashing of breakers on rocks, waves that no storm on Earth could possibly reproduce and knew that Samara lay on a coastline. When they sniffed and smelled what was in their nostrils, there was the tang of saline.

Avilova urged Garin, "I must administer the shots that we have, we're inhaling water vapour and will get microbes into our system nasally".

The formula of the injections was that transmitted from Explorer One, the vaccine against the phleege.

"Agreed doctor", the captain consented at once, "Do it before we do anything else".

Cylvia rolled up her sleeve and waited for Avilova to press the hyper-spray to her arm, the sub-dermal mist was totally painless.

"Alright", she cried then, "First things first, let's get a camp under way before nightfall. We know the days are short, so let's use minimum delays and maximum application".

Garin nodded to her and went back into the ship to send a hyper-space message back to Moscow and London, Iskatel-Seeker was on the planet Nyjord.

THIRTEEN

"ALLOW ME TO introduce first officer Josephine King to you", Fingers began with mock formality, "Formerly of the trans-stellar ship Iskatel-Seeker. As you can see she currently occupies the body of our own dear Cylvia Dortbrooke. Josephine this is agent Archibald Normanton of M.I.I.I.I. And this dashing specimen of manhood is none other than Cylvia's boyfriend and owner of the Encaphlotron, Darcie Orchvestige".

"Director of Orchevestments, now the patent is registered", Darcie told her with pride.

Jo looked at Darcie with strangely combined fragments of memory and new interest,

"Nice to meet both of you and to be here", she simply told them courteously.

"What's been happening to the ship"? Normanton desired to know.

"It has now safely landed on Nyjord and the crew are making preparations for a camp on the island mass formerly named Hyderabad", Fingers told them.

"Now I know the code, there's no need for us to constantly endure this cavern", Darcie pointed out. "We can go back to warmer climes and wait for interest in the projector to begin building. I will market it myself, as I have experience in sales".

"In collaboration with M.I.I.I.I. of course", Normanton was quick to add.

"I can't actually leave here", Fingers contradicted, "The crew might message for further assistance".

"Neither can I", King added, "I don't belong here, surely Dortbrooke will wish to return to her own body, sooner or later".

"Can't you come and celebrate with me and return afterwards"? Darcie wanted to know, awarding her with one of his winning smiles.

"I can't message the Iskatel-Seeker without perhaps giving Cylvia's position away", Fingers added.

Darcie's face fell, "You mean to tell me, I've just become potentially the richest man on Mars and we can't celebrate the fact"?

"I got the impression Cylvia wished to stay in my body for long enough to truly experience the wonder of Nyjord", King then admitted weakening, "I can come with the two of you, for a couple of days I reckon".

"I'll stay with Fingers", Normanton offered then. "Sooner or later the M.I.I.I.I. are going to be all over this place".

"Well just remember that I now own the patents", Darcie reminded somewhat superfluously. "So madam it's you and I, your carriage awaits".

He offered the girl who looked exactly like his girlfriend his arm. She took it and as they left Fingers scowled and returned to the keyboard.

On Nyjord however, the crew, having hastily erecting two large perma-huts, were sleeping. All save Cylvia that was, who was taking first watch.

Though the star filled canopy was quite dark, the crescent of Brahma the moon-planet, cast a cool blued-green glow over the landscape. She had a needle rifle nestling in her lap and twice rose to her feet at the sound of rustling over to her left. Seeing nothing she was grudgingly forced to deduce it was the wind, but she remained vigilant. After two hours J.P. Tornell came to take over.

"Anything"? He whispered so as not to disturb the others.

"All sorts of sounds", she returned at the same volume, "But I think it's the breeze". She huddled down into her fleece, Hyderabad was around fourteen degrees in the darkness. Tornell put his arm around her shoulders and she shied away,

"What's the matter, have I done something to upset you"?

"Er... no, sorry...J.P. I guess I'm a bit jumpy".

King had told her nothing of the familiarity between the two of them, Cylvia did not even know how far the relationship extended,

"I'm exhausted, I stand relieved, see you at dawn okay"?

"Okay", he echoed, but his tone sounded hurt.

The minute she got into her sleeping bag, she was asleep.

A pink tinged mist was rising from the red grass when the crew roused themselves. It would take some time to get used to the shorter day, but they fully intended to adapt. Proxima shone down from a flesh coloured sky putting Brahma into shade, the globe of the moon-world became a deep mineral aquamarine, but it was possible if one looked closely enough to see thick cloud and weather systems on the half sized sphere of the orbiting world.

The crew busily prepared and ate a breakfast, they had just finished clearing it up ready to begin the days experiments when Malunderain made the first sighting,

"Captain"! He barked to Garin, "Natives just beside that clump of blue fronds at around eleven thirty".

Garin looked in the indicated direction, as explained by an imaginary clock face, sure enough brown skinned natives were watching the camp.

"Presume them hostile", Garin snapped, "To the armoury quickly".

No sooner had they scurried up the steps and into the ship than Malunderain, who had kept vigil at the airlock shouted, "There's more, many more and they're armed with spears and clubs".

Garin turned to his closest crew member, who happened to be Blok, "Get a mortar, the needle rifles may not be enough if they're arrogant and hostile enough to attack in force".

"Do you think these are the Barabora, Darren reported"? Krivova wondered.

"Well they don't look like Khela do they"? Varety reasoned.

The natives were now a quite sizeable raiding party, no sooner had the crew gotten out of the ship once more, than one of them gave a yell of command and with whoops and cries, they began a charge. A spear landed at Garin's feet and he opened fire, the rest of the crew followed suit without hesitation.

Cylvia had not fired a needle gun before, but fortunately it was simply a matter of pointing and depressing the trigger. Barabora, or whoever the natives were, began to fall as the needles did their work. They were the instantly fatal variety and the brown bodies began to pile up, but still they came on, climbing over their fallen comrades to get at the invaders from off world.

"Blok"! Garin screamed, as he hastened to reload his rifle with a fresh clip of needles, "Let them have it. Put one right in their very midst".

A dull sucking pop proclaimed the mortar had launched from it's tube and then a thunderous explosion. The report preceded chunks of grass soil and mangled seared flesh, interspersed with a spray of blood, hurling up into the air and falling like pernicious rain. The natives suddenly froze in abject horror and disbelief, unable to conceive of such destruction with such devastating results. They suddenly turned tail and scattered in all directions, a confused and panic stricken retreat.

"Keep shooting", Garin ordered, obviously he wanted the defeat to be total and one which would convince the natives to stay away, for a very long time to come.

Despite her personal convictions, Cylvia managed to down at least two brown bodies, as they ran, terrified of the power of the newcomers to their world.

Finally Garin decided, "Alright, cease fire, hopefully that will be a powerful message to any others of Hyderabad who think to harm our mission".

"I'll make some tea", Tornell said. The answer to any eventuality, when English, was to conclude it with that beverage.

The others began to slowly walk toward the fallen, needing to know the strength of the attack they had so successfully repulsed. They reported in turn to Cylvia who totted up their individual counts, she went to Pavel Garin,

"We believe there were in excess of five hundred in that raid, captain".

"Then despite the message we gave them, we'll need to stay alert to the danger", he decided, "Thank you number one".

Cylvia went for her tea, Tornell sought her out,

"Are you alright", he asked squatting beside her on the crimson grass.

"Fine", Cylvia responded, still unable to understand the depth of their friendship, "What a pity we had to do that. Nyjord could be a paradise".

"You might feel differently if we manage to contact the Khela".

"Of course, it's just a setback, I'm delighted to be here".

"And what about us"?

"Can we agree to put it in stasis for a while, we have other matters to focus our concentration on. Just a hold, if you follow"?

"That's up to you, but you know Krivova is interested in me".

"Don't threaten me J.P. You know that doesn't sit well".

Tornell looked shocked, evidently King had never spoken to him like that in the past. No matter, Cylvia had ceased being bothered with the posturing of men.

She rose and went to sit with Varety, she began,

"I've something to tell you. However, it's so fantastical, I will understand if you don't believe me".

Josephine and Darcie were in Merce Insula, they were stopping at the Wielki Hotel, which was run by the Polish proprietor who owned it. The Wielki had every convenience and was opulent by Martian standards and Darcie's thumb was in danger of going red.

"You can thumb Dortbrooke's print can't you"? He asked her over dinner that evening, they were drinking champagne at his insistence and even so the question shocked her.

"It's not my money to throw away, Darcie", she told him honestly.

"Do you not think so? He countered, "Do you really think she's coming back"?

"I think it's time we returned to the fortress", she told him, the mood utterly spoiled by his suggestion of larceny. "Or, Darcie you need to seriously consider the offers made to you today".

"I'm broke and they know it, otherwise they'd be offering me more", he observed not for the first time.

At his insistence, she had sat in on the meetings, so replied,

Then sign with one of them. Orang-U-Can offered you the best deal, get back to Speakman and agree to let him have forty nine percent of Orchevestments for the three thousand gold shillin he offered".

"Three thousand"! Darcie groaned, "It's a pittance".

"It's not three thousand shillin, it's not even three thousand silver shillin, it's in the gold coins, it will make you rich and you will never need to worry about money ever again in your life. Not only that you will still control fifty one percent of the stock".

"Alright"! Darcie suddenly agreed somewhat capriciously, "I'll take the deal under one condition".

"You're making *me* conditions"?!

He nodded, "The condition is that you take the position of deputy director, stay in that body Josephine and help me run Orchevestments"?

She was lost for words, when she did regain the ability to speak she pointed out, "You've known me for a week, what makes you think I'd make a good business woman? Also Darcie, what other positions are you expecting me to assume"?

"I *know* you'd be the perfect foil for me, help me run the company, keep a rein on my capricious nature. As to the other matter, well only time would tell with that, but I don't expect you to do anything you didn't want to do".

"You forget the most vital matter", she reminded him then, "I'm just the lodger here, this body, that you find so incredibly attractive, yes I know you do so don't try to deny it, isn't mine"!

"You don't know that for certain do you"? He asked. "I'll tell you what; come back to Lomonosov in the morning, if Cylvia wants to stay on Nyjord, then take the post I'm offering and together we can run the firm. No pressure on the romantic front, I promise".

"I'm a trained astronaut, not a business woman"!

"This will be an adventure to rival anything you could have expected, a different type of adventure. Wait to see what Cylvia thinks, please"?

Josephine smiled, "I suppose it does have the advantage of being longer term, before Cylvia, we were sort of doomed…."!

Cylvia was sitting on a the cliff top, west of Samara. She kept a careful eye on the swirling Pteranondon high in the sky, but they showed no sign of descending and anyway she had a needle rifle lying beside her. At the base of the rocky promontory she could hear the massive breakers crashing against the rocks. The bright star of Proxima lit the seascape brilliantly and it was good to see a turquoise horizon for a change. She realised how at peace she was, how much she was enjoying the simple and unsullied beauty of the alien world. She wondered when a message would come from Fingers, *the* message in fact and she examined her feelings toward it, what would King want to do? What would she Cylvia want to do?

The breakers continued their ceaseless pounding and a fine saline breeze wet her face as she turned it toward the sun. She had skin that tanned rather than burned, for the first time in her life and that was something she found very enticing. Indeed one of many things she found enticing. Suddenly a call turned her attention inland and over the red, yellow and green grass a figure was approaching her, it was Varety. She waited calmly for the fellow astronaut to be close enough to hear her, knowing what the other would say,

"We've all sent a personal message back to the solar system now except you, Jo. It's your turn for time on the hyper-space transmitter, are you coming back to the ship before darkness catches you out"?

"Of course", Cylvia replied, "Just give me a couple of minutes more on my own will you, Henti. I want to collect my thoughts before I use the radio".

"Sure", the other girl returned and then was gone as swiftly as she had arrived.

Cylvia gazed back out to sea and listened to the breakers.

---------------- fin ----------------

TIME'S FOOL

"Love is not love which alters it when alteration finds, or bends with the remover to remove: O no! It is an ever fixed mark that looks on tempests and is never shaken; it is the star to every wandering bark whose worth's unknown, although his height be taken. Love's not Time's fool, though rosy lips and cheeks within his bending sickle's compass come: Love alters not with his brief hours and weeks, but bears it out, even to the edge of doom."

Shakespeare,

ONE

IT WAS ENTIRELY possible that the Falstaff flit-taxi was the finest on the planet! With it's acid-resistant cobalt blue livery and anti-glare windows, underneath was the smoothly purring three hundred brake horsepower engine. It was also not beyond the realms of possibility, that Pujol was the most attractive taxi driver on all Venus too. Mia Pujol only reached one forty seven centimetres when standing at her full height. She was a slight forty seven kilos, but in that package came a slim, yet shapely chassis. Mia Pujol was of Spanish decent, she had a gloriously olive complexion, a shock of ebon tresses and the most beautiful brown eyes, that any man could lose himself in, given the chance.

An acidic laden wind was gusting across the plain of Waking Ruins, buffeting the Falstaff, as the sun was partially screened by the floating satellites in orbit above the second planet in the solar system. Pujol took the taxi from the outskirts and into the heart of the city down Shakespeare Avenue. Not that any trees were lining the acid pitted road yet, but named in Venus' progress toward total Terra-formation.

A figure on the pedestrian walkway suddenly caught Pujol's eye. Strange she had not noticed him until the taxi had almost passed? His up-raised arm was enough to cause her to slow and let the rear passenger door sigh upward. A hot acrid blast entered the taxi causing the atmospheric control to sigh into action, bringing the internal temperature to something comfortably appropriate for a human passenger. The slender form of the man practically hurled himself inside and the door closed behind him.

Pujol always used the central mirror above her windscreen to view her passengers, preferring those on the wing's as rear driving aids. The man was out of breath, sweating, his hair all about his face, stuck to it with perspiration. His clothing was quite bizarre, it looked to be made of some sort of mixture of cloth and fine metal, judging by its lambency. It was light and darker blues hooped with an open neck that was held partially closed by laces that were threaded through copper eyelets riveted into the garment.

Pujol looked directly into his deep green eyes,

"Where can I take you mister", she wanted to know, her rich contralto betraying her Spanish origin.

"Oh, er, just drive for a few minutes will you, while I find out where I'm going con su permiso"?

He had been courteous enough to use a little Spanish and Pujol was comforted by that, her occupation could present hazards to her safety at times, but to date, she had always dealt with them.

As she pulled smoothly away, noting the beginning of the rush hour, she spotted the Rhodium pendant that hung at his throat, momentarily concealed by the laces of his strange garment. It did not so much shine, as would have been usual for the semi-precious white metal, as glow! As though there was some curious power supply within the tiny device. For it was only twenty millimetres at the base and maybe twenty five wide and could not have been more than two deep; curious?!.

He seemed to make a decision then and asked her,

"Do you know the town of Perseus, it lies just north westerly of the Mount Dragonis area, por favor querida señora"?

Pujol had to think, she believed there was a new development up in the north by that name,

"That's the new build no"?

"Correcto, will you drive that far"?

"I would have to take the meter off and agree on a price before the journey commenced", Pujol told him reasonably, "It would be half up front señor, is that agreeable"?

He nodded, "I will give you dos de plata shillin. One now, do we have agreement"?

It was a generous offer indeed; two silver shillin.

"Deal", she agreed and he leaned forward and reached over her shoulder to place one of the promised coins in her hand. Their hands touched for the merest of instances and a curious feeling of power ran up her arm and through her body.

"Was that static"? She asked, "You're not radioactive"?

He shook his head, "Merely chrono-tic energy and totally harmless let me asegurarle,(assure you) there is no threat to your health nor well being. Now; I have a solicitud"?

"What might that be"?

"May I get in the front, por favor, I do not like this being in the back of the transporte"?

By way of answer, Pujol pulled up gradually to let him move from the rear to the front passenger seat.

That was when the freak accident happened!

The acid wind must have been corroding the tube and coupler type scaffolding for some time. Eating into the steel and at that very instant the load on the joints must have been too great. As the **ride** climbed out of the back of the Falstaff, there was the scream of metal pushed beyond endurance and the structure instantly lost integrity, as two joints sheared in the same instant.

The pendant at his neck suddenly grew quite bright and then the entire scaffold crashed onto the flit-taxi. It's tremendous weight caved in the roof and Pujol felt one tube strike her cranium with sufficient force to be fatal!

TWO

THERE WAS A period that had no duration. Time did not flow within it. All was blackness, all was limbo. It was an inestimable period of non being. Pujol floated within it, yet she knew nothing, she did not even possess self awareness, she was not even *olvido,* she was oblivion!

An acidic laden wind was gusting across the plain of Waking Ruins, buffeting the Falstaff, as the sun was partially screened by the floating satellites in orbit above the second planet in the solar system. Pujol took the taxi from the outskirts and into the heart of the city, down Shakespeare Avenue.

She had a curious feeling that she had taken the very same route before and of course she had driven it many times. The sense of deja vu was not of a repeat however, so much as a total re-run down to the finest detail. Shaking her head slightly to clear the fuddle. A figure on the pedestrian walkway suddenly caught her eye. Strange? She had not spotted him until the taxi had almost passed him by. His arm was raised enough to cause her to slow and let the rear passenger door sigh upward. A hot acrid blast of acid-wind entered the taxi causing the atmosphere control to sigh into action, bringing the internal temperature to something comfortably appropriate for a human passenger. The slender form of the man practically hurled himself inside and the door closed behind him.

Pujot scrutinised him in the mirror she used for such a purpose. Why did his bizarre mode of dress look strangely familiar when he wore clothes in the style and texture that was unique to anyone of Venus?

"Where can I take you mister", she wanted to know, but her enquiry was uncertain. For some reason she could not explain, his presence in her vehicle, filled her with faint dread.

"Oh, er, just drive for a few minutes will you, while I find out where I'm going con su permiso"?

He had been courteous enough to use a little Spanish and Pujol was comforted by that, her occupation could present hazards to her safety at times, but to date, she had always dealt with them.

Or had she?

Pujol pulled smoothly away, noticing the beginning of the rush hour. Her scrutiny of the mysterious passenger directed her attention to a Rhodium pendant that hung at his throat. It had been previously concealed by the laces of his strange garment; a mixture of metal and cloth. The unsettlingly familiar object did not so much shine, as would have been usual for the semi-precious white metal, as glow! There was evidentially some curious power supply within the tiny device. Yet it was only twenty millimetres at the base and maybe twenty five wide and could not have been more than two deep; curious?

He asked, "Do you know the town of Persius, it lies just north westerly of the Mount Dragonis area, por favor querida señora"?

She switched totally to Spanish, "Sí he oído hablar de él antes (yes I have heard of it before)"!

Where had she heard of it before? She tried to bring the memory of it to the front of her mind, but nothing would come, it was most frustrating.

He asked her how much she would want to take him all the way north westerly, right over Venus' equator and then up to the marginally cooler north. The entire journey would be done in daylight, bright; searingly bright - sunshine. For they were in the middle of Venus' two hundred and forty three day - days! The sun would burn brightly on the harsh world for nearly six thousand hours, then the night would come and it would last just as long.

The price they agreed was generous and Pujol set off taking the Somersby Street that would lead onto the Ishtar Commons Road. Though it would not get dark, the clock would indicate when it was time for a break and after two hours she pulled into a service station at Acid Plains. She climbed out of the Falstaff, glad of the chance to stretch her legs and bend the crick out of her back. She half turned to speak to her fare and he loomed over her, but then a lot of men did.

"If we are going to spend the journey together am I to learn your name"? She asked him.

"Of course", he readily agreed, "My name is Onyx; Rhai Onyx", he held out his hand and as they shook she told him her own.

"I must rest, for a while", she informed him then, "And I'm hungry too, are you joining me, there's little else to do in Acid Plains"?

"I could eat", he agreed and opened his arm in a gesture that indicated she lead the way. They took a seat near the huge plexi-glass window, so that the alien plain of Venus was the vista at their side. A young woman came to serve them, she gave them a semi- interested glance, she too noticed the strange appearance of Onyx' clothes.

"What can I get for you"? She wished to know. The two of them had been looking at the listing beneath the glass topped table.

Pujol ordered a hot meal - pork, carrots and potatoes, all nurtured under domes on the harsh world itself. For desert she had Arroz con leche and finished with liquen-café Onyx went for beef which was considerably more expensive, his choice of vegetables was the same while he had Tarteletas y flan and finished with cafélatté.

"What takes you to Perseus then señor"? Pujol asked just to break the silence that threatened to engulf them.

"Call me Rhai, por favor and I go to escape my destino".

The answer was enigmatic, but she persisted, "And what might that be"?

"Why muerte of course, is it not the destino of us all eventually"?

"I suppose that's one philosophy, but a grim one. I do not give it much thought and have no desire to rush toward it".

"Who would"? There was a grim sadness about him as he asked her that and she found her heart going out to this stranger who had such a moribund outlook on existence. Thankfully the food arrived then and for a while they ate in silence, while they were waiting for the second course, he asked her,

"What is your story señora? For it is surely a strange occupation for a young woman to pursue and especially one as attractive as yourself. Is there no man in your life, who can take care of you and free you from the need to work"?

She smiled at the compliment and told him then, "I choose to be unattached at present, I don't feel the need to cease work at my age and have no family for the time being".

"Ah an amor de corazón roto (broken hearted love affair), in your recent past ¿No es así"?

"None of your business", she laughed, yet it was the case, and at times the nerve endings were still raw.

They finished their meal, went to the señoras and caballeros rest rooms and then got back in the flit-taxi. That was when it happened!

The heavy goods articulated flit-truck's skirt blew away and the massive and heavy vehicle went into a totally uncontrolled slide. Only the flitter stopped it from ploughing into the café. The impact was fatal to Pujol, the strange pendant at Onyx' throat glowed brightly once again.

THREE

Shards.
This time there was the semblance of memory.
Residue.
Something had happened to the flit-taxi.
Splinters.
Something had happened to her.

T HERE WAS A period that lasted for an inestimable duration. Time was not calculable within it. All was harsh browns, all was silent floating through a soup of weightlessness. It was an episode period of non perceived being. Pujol floated, yet she knew she had been there before, knew this was some twist of fate that cruelly let her possess self awareness, she *esperando repetir*, she was waiting for the loop to start again!

An acidic laden wind was gusting across the plain of Waking Ruins, buffeting the Falstaff, once more the sun was partially screened by the floating satellites in orbit above Venus, the solar system's second planet. Pujol drove her taxi away from the familiar outskirts and into the centre of the city that she knew so well. She chose Shakespeare Avenue, not that any trees were lining the acid pitted road, but because something in the back of her mind told her that was the way to go.

A man on the pedestrian walkway suddenly appeared is if from nowhere catching her eye. He could not have been there, before, she instinctively knew that. She almost ignored him, until the taxi had almost passed him by. His insistent upraised arm was eventually enough to cause her to slow and let the rear passenger door sigh upward. Yet she knew that it was going to prove to be an error of judgement; but how did she know that?

A hot acrid gust blasted into the taxi causing the air conditioning to purr into action, bringing the internal temperature to something comfortably bearable for her and the passenger. The slender form of the man hurled himself inside and the door closed to again.

She always used the central mirror above her windscreen to view her passengers, preferring those on the wings as rear driving aids. The man was out of breath, sweating, his hair all about his face, stuck to it, with perspiration. His clothing was quite bizarre, it looked to be made of some sort of mixture of cloth and fine metal, judging by its lambency. It was light and darker blues hooped, with an open neck that was held partially closed by laces that were threaded through copper eyelets riveted into the garment.

Pujol looked directly into his deep green eyes,

"Where can I take you this time Onyx", she wanted to know, her rich contralto betraying her Spanish origin.

"Oh! Ah, fragments of half remembered pieces still remain then. Just drive for a few minutes will you, while I find our where I'm going con su permiso"?

He had been courteous enough to use a little Spanish but Pujol was no longer comforted by the gesture. Her occupation was presenting her with a hazard to her very existence, something she could not deal with.

As she pulled smoothly away, noting the beginning of the rush hour, she spotted the Rhodium pendant that hung at his throat, momentarily concealed by the laces of his strange garment. It did not so much shine, as would have been usual for the semi-precious white metal, as glow! As though there was some curious power supply within the tiny device. For it was only twenty millimetres at the base and maybe twenty five wide and could not have been more than two deep; curious?

She made a decision then and asked him,

"The town of Perseus right? It lies just north westerly of the Mount Dragonis. We will agree a price......it will be, oh; it's gone! Tell me about the pendant instead, Onyx"?

"Dos chelines de plata and the pendant is the cause of my misery, señorita. Alas it seems to be involving you also".

Pujol pulled to a halt, she half turned in her seat and demanded, "I don't want it to involve me, Onyx, why don't you get out of the taxi now"?

His head suddenly hung in shame and he acquiesced, his hand going to the release mechanism of the rear door. Something within her caused her to ask,

"Can't you tell me what's going on, maybe then I'd have a better chance of helping you"?

He looked up and his beautiful green eyes were misted with tears, "Let me start by asking you a question", he begged and when she nodded, went on, "You have now fragments of memory sí"?

"Some, they are not consecutive but I know if I let you stay in this vehicle something catastrophic will happen".

"Si, always it is so, this is my curse, this I must flee from, until my physiological clock runs down. You though, you Mia, you do not remember all the times it has been. What has developed between us, that we have been *enamorado* and then the pendant he save me by going back".

"You're not making sense", she complained, cutting the motor and putting the parking lights on. "I don't love you Onyx, I don't love any man. Now start at the beginning and tell me the whole story, or get out of the taxi and I don't want to see you again".

"You want the story from the beginning"? He smiled sadly, "Very well, mi amor, I will tell you the story from the beginning".

FOUR

I WAS BORN in the year six thousand five hundred and fifty five, the sixty sixth century in the region of Doñinos de Salamanca, which is in the country of Spanuguese. My family were a proud and traditional one and encouraged we children to learn Spanish despite it being spoken less and less over the years. So when I was ten, I was sent to the Universidad Salamanca, where I underwent an intensive hypno-course. I was one of eight and loved my sisters and single brother dearly. My childhood was a happy one and we wanted for nothing.

My father was a Chronotist and once I became of age at fourteen I left my hypnocourses and decided to follow him into his field of study, which was the machinations and physiognomy of the fourth dimension. You see, we of the sixty sixth regarded time as an almost biological entity. Something which could exert it's *will* onto the ley-lines of continuity.

Of course I was keen to learn and also keen to receive my first *'Colgante-de-tiempo'*. Before you ask the Colgante-de-tiempo is the miniaturised machine which you have many times admired, at my throat. It allows a body or even two, if they are in close proximity, to traverse the barriers between the ley-lines, in essence to travel through time!

I pursued my studies in temporal mechanics and finally the day came that I had eagerly anticipated; the day of my first chrono-voyage.

Having had the upbringing that I'd experienced, the choice was easy for me. I went into the past and watched the Crucificción del niño Jesús! I found it as upsetting as one can imagine any crucifixion would be. I even felt great sympathy for the two bandits that were to die either side of him. Over the next year I made several similar journeys; always after having hypno-taught lessons in the appropriate language of the time and place. For the crucifixion I had learned both Aramaic and Latin. The latter was most useful when I was in the boat containing Gaius Julius at the occasion of his landing in ancient Britain, in fifty five B.C. I never heard the words Julius was supposed to utter, but I did witness that the troops were reluctant, and according to Caesar's account were led by the *aquilifer* (standard bearer) of the 10th legion who jumped in first as an example, shouting:

"Leap, fellow soldiers, unless you wish to betray your eagle to the enemy. I, for my part, will perform my duty to the republic and to my general.". The British were eventually driven back with catapultae and slings fired from the warships into the exposed flank of their formation and the Romans managed to land and drive them off.

I returned to the Salamanca and my reports were favourably received. Then I was down-when once more, armed with the knowledge and currency of ancient Germany to see the hysteria that Adolph Hitler could instil in the Reichsparteitag . The rallies took place near the time of the Autumn equinox, in the year nineteen thirty three under the title of The German people's National Party days, (*Reichsparteitage des deutschen Volkes*), which was intended to symbolize the solidarity between the German people and the Nazi Party. I personally added a total of one more, to further emphasize by the yearly growing number of participants, which finally reached over half a million from all sections of the party, the army and the state. I have to confess I found Hitler a magnetic and dynamic personality, despite not desiring so to do.

Finally I went to the FrancoÉcosse Tunnel disaster of twenty eight fifty seven, when the massive under sea route from Dunkirk to Dunbar collapsed and was flooded by the North Sea. I witnessed the trial of Andrew McKenzie, the engineer who the French blamed for the disaster and who after his execution was posthumously cleared, when it turned out that the tunnel had been sabotaged by none other than Michele Desroches, the underground leader of Celte Gratuit France.

About this time I began to feel tempted Mia. Tempted to do two things that were forbidden by the, 'Temps en Voyageant Conservatoire'. The first was that one should not travel to times after the year four thousand, for fear of making an accidental change that could effect the future, no matter how slight. The second was that one should *never* travel into the future, *especially* the future that was conceivably in ones own life expectancy!

The rule I most desired to break was to see what the solar system and other systems would turn out like in a few years from my birth. I desired to see if Spanuguese would rise to become an Atlantic power. There was opportunities for many countries to fill the void since the devolution of the American states, which had each declared their independent sovereignties hundreds of years in the past. If any could take control of Atlantia, it should be Spanuguese, the birth place of *temps en voyageant* (travelling through the fourth dimension).

The problem I had, if I was going to flaunt regulations, was doing so and in such a way that I would be avoiding detection. The unit that each of us was given, in the shape of an amulet was only the focusing device of the Contemporariness main frame. The main frame was a huge computerplex using the now famous thirty third technology devised by Gleve Orchvestige and further developed by Fingers Sponsogil. The addition of saladrium leaf capacitors and vhransistors had been a master stroke of Sponsogil's. Add to this the forty seventh century development of techdridium power packs and the chronocrystal and the focusing device had the ability to allow the user a field, through which, he or she could slip the leylines of the fourth dimension. The only trouble was, also, incorporated into it's micro-circuits, was the lock and tracer section of it's functionality.

An unlocked amulet could travel into the future and an amulet without a tracer would not register on the main frame. If I had an unlocked amulet with no tracer functioning the enceph-projector and chronocaster of the Colgante-de-tiempo would allow me to go where I wanted and no one else would know.

To achieve that however I needed to *walk the wavy* [comit a crime, break the law] and the only way I could do that was with the help of *dimrouters* [criminals, specifically criminal hackers]. I had heard of the most famous of these, Donna Trum, but I had no idea where to find her and thankfully neither did the *combmen* [officers paid to protect the law and the honest citizens of the country]. I was stuck, unless....I thought I might know a fellow *Tiempoviajero* [time traveller], one who sometimes walked the wavy. I went by space-flitter to her apartment, which was on Venus. The woman I sought was called Conta Aracage. It took me three presses of her intercom, before she answered,

"What"?! She demanded sounding furious, "Whoever you are, don't you know it's the women's singles final"?

"It's Onyx, Aracage. May I please come in"?

"Onyx.........oh, the keen one from Temps en Voyageant Conservatoire. Alright; but don't issue a peep until the game's over, understood"?

"No problem, I wanted to watch it myself, just forgot it was on".

The door unlocked and I positioned myself outside the holographic field of the match. It was Wimbledon and Algern versus Friss. The Scandian was winning, one set up and Friss from Hungary looked to be only managing the honour of being the runner up. However the Hungarian had a massive serve of two hundred and twenty seven kilometres per hour. This had become possible since the development of graphidium rackets and balls and of course the playing surface was no longer grass but cosmo-turf.

So I was forced to sit through the game and watch Friss win the next set and then go on to beat the Scandian in a third set tie breaker. One of the best finals of recent times in fact. Aracage had not even offered me a drink while she was glued to the holograph. She looked up,

"What a game, Onyx, what a match eh? Want a drink, or a smoke"

"Please, Conta", I began in forced friendly tones, "Could I have a blanco vino and an uno-en-horno (1in4, the safe mix of med-bacco and snufz)"?

"I don't have any wine, have a calientefuerte, I can put soda in it for you if it's too much for your delicate palate"?

I forced a chuckle, "No a calientefuerte is fine por favor".

I waited while my colleague but not friend, got me the drink and the smoke and once we had thumbed the latter to life I asked her casually,

"Do you still wonder what it's like to travel into the future, Conta"?

She peered at me through the smoke of her own uno-en-horno and returned with a question of her own,

"Do you"?

"I do, but the lock and tracer is the problem isn't it, now if I could have those circuits disabled, then I'd be sorely tempted indeed to walk the wavy".

"You"! She laughed, "Señor Top-of-the-class, Señor Papá Chico, walk the wavy"?!

I leaned forward earnestly, "Yes I would Conta, but I need the services of a dimrouter, namely someone who can disable the parts of my amulet whilst maintaining it's function, I need the help of Donna Trum".

"Why are you telling me"? She asked suddenly guarded in her manner.

"Because in you, I recognise a fellow spirit, admittedly a female spirit, but similar in many other ways".

"You and I are nothing alike Onyx, now finish your drink and leave, I have things to do and people to meet. It's been lovely we must do it again some time, at your palatial apartment".

"You'd always be welcome to visit", I told her lamely and was shortly there after almost thrown out of the place.

My lack of success was depressing, but also I suspected, if I had judged the situation correctly, it would not be the end of the matter. I drove through a lovely day on Venus. Since the development of the grav-field generator and the relocation of Venus to the same orbit as Earth, but on the opposite side of the sun, the weather was like that which the English Empire enjoyed, with the exception of the fact that the day on our home world was still two hundred and forty three days in duration, the night just as long and very cold as a result.

I had been in my luxury apartment on the second point fifth planet, only six hours when my pad pinged and the message indicated voice only communication. This brought a sardonic smile to my face, voice only, how antiquated, how *misterioso!*

"Hello", I began in standard.

"Onyx".

It was not even a question really but I returned, "This is he".

"You require the service of Donna Trum"?

"I do, but how'd you know", no sense in letting the caller know I knew Aracage, she might have contacted the dimrouters by some subfusc machination.

"Never mind how it's known, do you wish a meeting"?

"Indeed".

"It will be seven dinero-fichas".

"Seven just to meet her"?!

"Seven; just for the meeting. Do you have it"?

"I'll pay five and fifty dinero-porciento", I offered, not because I couldn't afford it, but because the figure was outrageous.

"There is no room for bartering, seven gets you the meeting, less does not, do I cut the connection"?

"Very well", I agreed, I'll bring seven".

"You will have seven with you and wait where you are. Involve the combmen or try any sort of trick and there will be an immediate *contracto* issued upon you for your death".

The connection was cut and for the first time I realised just how deeply I had gotten involved with the dimrouters.

I spent a couple of sleepless nights in my apartment. I'd taken rest days from the Temps en Voyageant Conservatoire fortunately and was not missed nor needed. Then without so much as a warning by net, there was a knock on my door and when I went to view who was without, was surprised to see a beautiful, tall woman waiting for permission to enter. My thumb activated the entry pad at once and the door hissed open. The woman moved with a grace that few possess; you are another with such quality Mia.

"When will I be taken to see......er, to see whom I seek"? I asked the beauty.

"If you mean Donna Trum, I am she", was her reply and she possessed a lilting tone to her voice that was both melodic and entrancing, just like yours Mia.

"You're Trum"! I gasped, "I didn't expect.....".

"To do the unexpected is what keeps me one step ahead of the combmen", she told me, "Now, you have the money", and she held out a long fingered slim hand.

I self consciously placed it into hers, she was putting it into a ditty bag as she further informed,

"To unlock the amulet will be a further twenty, I don't expect you to carry such a sum about your person so you will wire it to an account, the number of which, I will give you, if you agree the fee"?

It was around fifty percent of my entire savings, dinero-fichas were the highest rate of money in our time and then beneath them there was dinero-porciento (one hundredth) and dinero-milésimo (one thousandth). Most everyday items were in the latter.

"I agree, where do we go to get it done, or will you meet me somewhere once you have the money"?

She took the ditty bag from her shoulder and told me, "If you have a power supply it can be done in five or so minutes. You don't need reminding about the consequence of non payment do you"?

"I do not", I removed the amulet from around my neck and placed it before her on the table, then offered, "Can I get you anything"?

"A double Pacharán liqueur, if you have some"?

I nodded and then went for the drink silently, allowing her to go about her somewhat nefarious work.

No sooner were I passing her the drink however than she told me, "Done, you now owe me twenty dinero-fichas, you have twenty hours to settle the debt. Failure to do so will result in an immediate contracto being issued upon your head. Contacting the combmen would give you a similar result. Know this, if my name is ever mentioned by you again, you will be the *para caminar muerto* - the walking dead, do you understand"?

"I understand señorita, you will get the fee and I will never mention you after that".

She then gave me a beautiful smile, so incongruous on the visage of evil,

"Enjoy your trips into the forbidden areas then señor and ¡buenos días"!

She left without touching the drink. I looked down at the amulet, certain it had not been opened, all that had been done was that she had fried the lock and tracer without damaging any other parts, a very selective laser of some sort perhaps? I neither knew nor cared. What I did know was now I could journey anywhere and with impunity. I could also make the money I had lost and then some, for I would soon know the future!

I see you wonder what went so badly wrong. Listen Mia and I will tell you. I was nervous before my first foray into the future, I was going to explore where few others, if any, had been before. For the first time since becoming a Tempus Voyageant, I felt the need to take Dylatrin; the anti chronospasm medication. Traversing the ley-lines of the forth dimension had never caused me even the slightest queasiness in the past; my past. This was a new area of exploration for me though and I did not want to spoil it by being anything less than one hundred percent fit.

I was also too frightened to stay on Venus and promptly flew my private space-flitter back to Spanuguese. I mentally set the date, something the projector would detect, but then delete and then I activated my now unlocked amulet.

For an initial voyage I elected to go to seven thousand five hundred and seventy five, one thousand years into the future. That could not cause me any problems surely, I reasoned.

How wrong I was.

How naive.

I found myself in the same place of course, the automatic corrections in the chronocrystal ensured that, the only thing that was different was the duration. *Spanuguese was a radioactive waste!*

I had no protection from radiation and immediately fled back to my own time in history, for indeed it now was history, when considered from my viewpoint. As I drove my flitter to the clinic at Doñinos de Salamanca my mind buzzed with unanswered questions:-

Had there been some sort of atomic war on Earth?

Or was the radioactive panorama I had witnessed the result of terrorism?

Who had the war been between, if there was one?

Was it just Spanuguese that was so devastated, or had the war been inter-planetary?

A good job therefore that I had chosen a millennium to travel. The only trouble was radio active wasteland would last ten thousand years, so who knew when it had started, it might be conceivably in my own life time.

Whilst I was being checked for radio activity [I told them it had been an industrial accident and paid them to keep the matter confidential] and given the all clear, I realised I had to know if nuclear war or a nuclear attack on Doñinos de Salamanca was going to be in my lifetime, because if it was I was going to escape into the past.

I had learned my lesson the hard way and well at the very first. Going into the future was not a sensible thing to do. Now though, I had to do it again and less years forward.

What was my life expectancy? With medical science of the sixty sixth century I expected to reach one hundred and twenty at the most and then, no matter how repaired and rejuvenated the body, the mind failed and no one had found out how to do brain replacement and remain the same person.

I therefore reasoned that if I went one hundred and fifty years into the future and found no evidence of nuclear destruction, my existence would be assured. Even so I bought a radioactive protection suit and saw even more of my savings depleted. Taking the Dylatrin again, I activated my untraceable amulet. Spanuguese was fine! What a relief.

It also threw up more questions though. Questions I did not want to consider nor face. After my lifetime why should I care about events that I could not alter nor witness?

As I've mentioned I was running short of funds. I did not want to ask my father for a loan, but if I didn't get money soon, I'd have to let my apartment on Venus go. Then I made the next decision that would take me down the same path toward disaster. I decided to do something that was thought totally hazardous. I decided to trip forward to a date within my own lifetime!

Firstly I was sensible enough to return to Venus. The last thing I wanted to do was run into myself. Chronotist's had postulated that if one did, it would lead to either madness or the instant death or winking out of existence of one version of the same person, or the other. As I knew I lived in Doñinos de Salamanca, the chances of meeting myself on Venus seemed incredibly slight, to zero.

I set the amulet for just a week!

The instant I arrived, I hastily checked the net on my own pad and recorded the numbers of the Venus lottery, then I fled back to my own time. I then rushed to buy a ticket and smiled in relief when I had completed the on-line sale. All I had to do then was wait one week in the apartment and share the win with whom ever had won it in one weeks time.

It happened exactly as I had hoped and known it would, the week before. My share was four thousand vensustes, one hundred times greater than centisustes and one thousand times greater than kilosustes. In short I was a rich man.

Now you might think that it should have satisfied me and I would give up on the future and continue my safe traversing into the rich past. With my good fortune, or rather nefarious planning however, there returned a naive recklessness and a renewed need to flirt with time yet to be!

I desired to see how many years of life I would have on either Earth, Venus or any other world that mankind currently occupied. I could do it all from one world of course, for the solar wide net was available to me on any pad. Now that I was rich and had my own bank account number and passwords, all I needed to do was journey a given period future-ward and check my balance, this would also tell me that I was still alive without the risk of meeting myself.

I went forward in time one hundred and twenty years!

There was no bank account in my name!

I was not greatly alarmed at this notion, extreme old age is not comfortable for the majority of people, illness and malady frequently accompanies the final years. Better to live slightly less time and be vital to the end. So I cut my next jump to one hundred years. There was so much I could have learned if I had stayed a while in the future, but for me then the only piece of data that burned into me being with insatiable curiosity was my own bank account. I went on the solar wide net once more.

There was no bank account in my name!

This was disconcerting, but not tragic, one hundred years was a considerable distance into my future and I was only young. I could make that century a time when I really swung. Now you may think that at this point that cutting the duration further was asking for trouble, but I realised then that I *needed* to know the length of my vitality. I reset the amulet in my head and journeyed forward eighty years.

Again no account for Rhai Onyx. I typed in my name into the general search engine, I would not read the detail of the description of me, simply that I was alive and had closed the account for some reason. Up came my name.

Like an imbecile I read the date's beneath that showed my lifespan!!

Rhia Onyx
6,555/03/15 to 6,575/11/23.

Twenty at the time of my death and I was twenty years old!

I looked at the months, it was November and I was in November back in my home time, it said the twenty third, I had left on the twenty second!

I only had a day left to live!

It would help me nought to go and live in the future, for in less than twenty four hours I would simply wink out of existence. I could go and live in the past, but then that would create a paradox and time had a way of avoiding paradox. I only had one course of action available to me, go forward twenty hours or so and try and save myself from what ever had killed me, tomorrow.

If it looked like I was about to die whilst in the twenty third, I could instantly flip back a day and begin the last day of my life again. I could do that endlessly until I was successful, or until I became too old to continue journeying and living the same twenty hours over and over and over.

FIVE

ONYX SIGHED, "THAT'S what I've been doing for the past six months of my life mi amor. I have already cheated time of six months, I'm still alive, but the moment of my death remains twenty four hours in time's future".

"That's not all the story though is it", Pujol asked, "You said a few moments ago that *'Mia, you do not remember all the times it has been. What has developed between us, that we have been enamorado,* you have met me many times and some of those times I was ....ah, different to today"?

"We've met many times", he agreed, "And I'm in love with you. You, on the other hand are not always in the same mood, sometimes, as it is with women, you find me enchanting, sometimes pathetic, sometimes vile".

"You always tell me, if you have chance, don't you"? She demanded and was angry with him, "You tell me to get sympathy and sometimes to lay with you, until something happens and you have to flip back. Do I always end badly, or is it sometimes just you"?

"If we are together, we go together", he admitted, "But if I'm alone.......".

Pujol threw open the door to the flit-taxi, "Get out you selfish cerdo, I don't want to die because of you".

He did not hesitate but climbed out of the vehicle. He walked around to her side and she let the window slide down.

"I'm so sorry Mia, can you find it within yourself to forgive me", he pleaded.

"Could you forgive someone who has gotten you killed over and over again"? She demanded hotly.

"But if I go back, back to the ever decreasing window in my own physiological time, so that I don't meet myself setting off once more, you live again. So do you really die"?

"I don't want to try and think about the implications, Onyx. If you had knowingly let it happen even once, it would be a crime. I suggest you walk, try to find your destiny and perhaps to accept it".

"Death"?

"You don't seem to mind it for me"!

As she spoke she became suddenly aware that another vehicle was coming down the street and slowing as it reached them. One of the polarised windows slid down as it drew parallel to the taxi and Pujol heard the muted phut of a weapon discharge. Onyx fell forward as the vehicle sped away. Pujol had to push the door very hard to get out and see the time traveller's condition. He had been dead before he hit the floor. A wave of dizziness suddenly gripped her mind.

"No"! She gasped, "I wasn't with him this time, I was inside the flitter, this is so unfair". Then her conciousness began to tumble down into the inky pit of conscientiousness, or repeated death!

SIX

Fragments.
The semblance of half remembered incidents.
Scraps of mental information.
Something had happened to her near the flit-taxi.
All was edges without any central filling.
What had happened to her?

THERE WAS A period that lasted for a duration that none could hope to calculate. Time was not a factor within it. All was deep browns, all was silent floating through a sea of weightlessness. It was an episodic period of non perceived being. Pujot drifted, yet she knew she had been here before, knew this was some twist of fate that cruelly let her possess self awareness, she esperando repetir, she was waiting for the loop to start again even though it was something dreadful

An acidic laden wind was gusting across the plain of Waking Ruins, wafting constantly against her Falstaff. The sun was partially screened by the floating satellites in orbit above Venus, the solar system's second planet. Pujol drove her taxi away from the familiar outskirts and into the centre of the city that she knew like the back of her hand. She chose Keats Avenue, not that any trees were lining the acid pitted road, but because something in the back of her mind told her that she had not been that route in a long, long time.

The fact that it was a departure from the usual was what decided her choice. She remembered a man, a man who's destiny had been interrupting her life. She parked the flit-taxi on Keats Avenue in order to think. Closing her eyes she dredged half-forgotten memories from her back brain. He had a short name, the man who was perhaps twenty to twenty five, his former being the same length as the latter. What was it? Did it begin with an 'R'? What did he want with her? Rhai! Rhai Onyx. What *did* he want with *her?* Why did she not desire to rendezvous with *him* again?

Pujol opened her eyes and turned on the net-cast, she desired to distract herself despite the myriad shards of memory tumbling around in her mind. The tennis was on, the men's final. Despite the fact that Slonin was only six months from having a plantroniumprismatic atomic pump implanted in his chest to replace his diseased heart, he was beating Londeran by two sets to one. Normally such news would have had Pujol on the edge of her seat, another victory for Slonin and he would have won Wimbledon for the fifth time in succession. She could not concentrate though, she cut the connection and remained staring out of the windscreen. Then; on the urban horizon she saw a figure purposefully approaching.

The man or woman looked impossibly tall, or maybe it was a trick of the light changing her perspective. The longer she watched however and the closer the man, for it was a man, the closer he got, the more she could see he was approximately two point one three metres in height. His limbs were in proportion with the exception of his head, which was bigger than on any other man she had ever seen.

The veritable giant was heading directly for her flitter. Determined not to give a ride to anyone else mysterious she climbed out of her taxi and stood waiting for him to get close enough to speak to her. When he stopped he asked,

"Pujol"? She was not surprised. She nodded. He continued professionally,

"I am from 'Temps en Voyageant Conservatoire', I am a combman. These terms mean something to you I imagine"?

"They do, bits of my memory are coming to me, I want this experience to end, have you come to help, or to hinder"?

"I've come firstly to apologise on behalf of 'Temps en Voyageant Conservatoire', the directors have instructed me to do so on their behalf. I know of Onyx' crimes, I now know of the confusion and upsetment he has introduced to your life. I have come to end that confusion".

"Are you from the sixty sixth century"?

"I'm from the seventy first in point of fact. I would tell you my name but I don't think you want any more fragments to interfere with the rest of your natural progress through the fourth dimension".

"You said firstly to apologise"?

"I did. I have important news for you. Onyx will not disturb your life any more. It took until my point in time for his crimes to be detected by our central systems, but finally they did. Ironically I found out about him in our historical records. He was living the last few hours over and over at your expense, do you remember this"?

Pujol nodded, "But you say it's over now"?

The combman nodded his elongated head. "The memories can be scrubbed from your mind. If you so desire, the process is quite safe"?

"I'll leave my brain as it is if it's alright with you"?

"Of course if that is your choice".

She got the impression he was about to turn to leave, staying him, she asked,

"So what happened to Onyx, did he finally meet his death, like all men eventually must"?

The combman nodded that huge head of his once more, causing her to reflect upon what strong neck muscles he must possess.

"His crimes carry the ultimate punishment in my time", he shocked her then, "He was fleeing from his execution"!

"What was the manner of it, did he......".

The combman gave a grim smile, "Did he suffer? No, I shot him with a needle gun, a fleeting second of pain and then it was done. He did more suffering by avoiding it for so long. You helped him with that Pujol. I hope that knowledge helps you in some small way"?

"I cannot make sense of it", she confessed. "He was executed by someone from the seventy first for fleeing the sixty sixth and committing crimes in the thirty third. He committed the crime in the first place because he died in history, by the hand of someone from his future"

"Once one takes a 'Colgante-de-tiempo', the normal rules of cause and effect are subject to change, Pujol. Onyx knew that as well as anyone, he thought he was beyond those rules and the laws of time exacted their balance".

"So, así es como resulta, such is the way of things. Is that all you have to tell me, Official"?

"One last thing, use your pad please to access your bank account"?

Pujol reached into the taxi and removed her device and quickly opened the appropriate net-account. Her balance was two hundred and twenty five vensustes greater than what she was expecting.

"Compensation", the combman told her.

"Thank you".

"What will you do with it in this time"?

It was more money than she had ever had in her life before,

"I think I'll let the taxi go and return to education", she decided. "I will pay for a medical degree course, I've always fancied I might like to be a dentist".

The combman nodded, "A worthy profession Pujol, good luck with that". He turned and began to walk away. She watched him until he had disappeared onto the dusty Venuser horizon.

---------------- fin --------------

NATURE'S LAW

This girl, for whom your heart is sick,
Is three times worth them all;
"For those and theirs, by Nature's law,
Have faded long ago;

Tennyson

ONE

T HE PROBLEM STARTED during the physical act of making love.

Reen began to gasp as though she were fighting for breath and Senifer thought the noises were one of pleasure until she looked up. Reen was going a slight shade of blue.

"I can't get my breath and the pain in my chest........oh, call the med-cent get an ambula-flitter"?

Senifer remained as calm as she could, after all this was not the first problem Reen had exhibited. Her failing heart had been replaced only five months previously with a plantroniumprismatic atomic pump. The pump was guaranteed for fifty years though, so that could not be the cause of her lover's distress now.

Leaving Reen gasping on the bed she hastened to ping for the ambula-flitter. It came admirably quickly, yet still was not swift enough. By the time it reached their apartment and the med-squad had rushed inside, Reen Glynfandell had stopped breathing altogether.

The med-squad tried everything to revive her, all futilely, she was pronounced D.O.A. At Zephyria General Infirmary.

Senifer sat in the waiting room when the surgeon came to see her, she had not wept, not drunk, hardly moved, she could not believe that the past few hours had truly happened.

"Miss Treadby", he began. All she could manage was a nod, "We did everything conceivably possible but in all honesty it was already too late by the time Miss Glynfandell arrived here, I'm very sorry for your loss".

"What did she die of Doctor"? Senifer wished to know and still the tears would not come.

"The P.A.P. Stopped, a very unusual situation, the first one I've seen".

"Stopped"?

He nodded, afraid to say more.

"But when we bought it Cydoniamech Industries told us it would run for years and years, it was guaranteed for fifty"!

The surgeon nodded, his expression grave, "I don't doubt your word, Miss. I suppose you have their helpline"?

Senifer Treadby's jaw set firmly, "I do Doctor. I will be giving them a ping".

"Good luck, Miss Treadby, is there anything I can get you? Do you need a ride home"?

Senifer nodded, "And the email of a good interment company if you can recommend anyone, doctor"

The taxi-flitter was at the front entrance as Senifer walked through the gleaming antiseptic tinged corridors of Zephyria General Infirmary. She knew that the next few days would not be easy, she tried to make a mental list of who she needed to ping. Her mind did not work though, she was still in a state of shock and the only person she could think to turn to was her brother Clement.

Clement Treadby was her big brother and life long confidante. He was the first she had spoken to before 'coming out' and he was the one who had not judged her because of her sexual orientation.

She walked out into a cool Martian night and saw the wonder of the night heaven's before climbing gratefully into the waiting vehicle.

"Where to, Miss"? the driver was cheerful, unaware of her loss.

"Twenty three Kingsite Flats please, do you know it"?

"Just across town, I'll have you there in ten minutes", he promised and the flitter roared forward with admirable velocity.

Senifer pinged her brother, thankfully he had still not retired for the night. His chisel cut features swam into focus on the ninety millimetre tall screen,

"Hi, Sis, everything alright"?

Senifer knew only one way to tell him and that was the direct one, "Reen's dead and I need you, Bro"!

Clement's face went from grave concern to disbelief, "What happened? Some sort of accident"?

"No, the P.A.P. Failed".

"What"? He was momentarily incredulous, "But it can't, Sis, there were too many safeguards, Cydoniamech Industries' record is......"

"That's the top and bottom of it, Bro, it stopped pumping", she cut him short and the tears suddenly came and the gush became a torrent, "I need you here, can you come"?

"Give me six hours and I'll be there", he decided then, "I've a couple of things to do before I can set off, but then I'll be in the Morphy-Richards and with you by the early hours".

"Will Gholina be with you"?

"She's really backed up at work right now, but she'll attend the service, don't worry about anything, Sis. Just try and get some rest until I'm there; okay"?

Senifer cut the connection and slumped back in her seat.

"I couldn't help but overhear, Miss", the taxi driver told her, "Sorry to hear you lost someone dear to you, no fare for the ride, it's the least I can do".

"That's kind of you", she replied, before he was pulling up outside her apartment. It was with a certain amount of dread that she entered the apartment that actually belonged to Reen; the very place she had laughingly referred to as their little love nest. The door swung open at her hastily keyed code and she walked slowly inside. She could smell their body heat, the soft after bathing cream the two of them had shared. The walls dripped memories. The first thing she would have to do was sell the place and move away from the ghosts. The ghost of Reen and the ghost of herself. Sell it if she could that was. She knew she could though, knew that before her surgery Reen had shown her the will in which she, Senifer inherited everything. She realised then that she was a wealthy woman. Yet she would easily give it all up and more just to have her partner back.

Two things had to be taken away and placed out of sight at once. One was the holographic cube of the two of them together on the synthetic beach of Ascraeus Lacus lake. The first real body of water that had been created on Mars. They were together in bathing suits, how beautiful Reen looked, pressed together like the lovers they were smiling into the lens of Clement's pad. What a lovely time that had been. Even Gholina had seemed happy, even though she was in the company of 'weird sister and her butch lover'.

The second thing was the Roxbrough painting, entitled 'La Ascraeus Lacus în Seara Umedă' (the wet evening street of Ascraeus Lacus) that they had bought from the Romanian art dealer who owned a gallery there. It had been Reen's favourite for so many reasons. The Scalla and two Fiorento's could stay up, they had been Senifer's choice.

She thought about the coming interment and decided that a cremation would be better, for no doubt Cydoniamech Industries would want to remove the failed P.A.P. in an effort to avoid a costly suite, which Senifer was intent upon starting against them. Why bury a body with an empty chest cavity and anyway Reen had not believed in the hereafter.

"When you're gone, you're gone", she had joked with Senifer more than once, "So we might as well make the most of this one brilliant journey".

It had not been a brilliant journey for Reen though had it, Senifer mused and went to the drinks cabinet? No sense in going to bed. Going to a bed with sheets still rumpled from their last love making. She would not sleep, she knew she could not sleep until Clement arrived and began to organise everything, just like he always had. She poured herself a double Romanian Tuica. The first of many she intended to sink while her brother was slowly on his way. She would get so drunk that she did not care that she was alone.

Then she realised Aunt Gwinifrit would expect to be invited to the funeral and she sank the drink in one swallow and began to cough violently. Gwinifrit; her mother's elder sister. 'Gwinifrit the loud'. The Aunt who insisted at every family occasion upon declaring at the top of her voice that;

'I don't mind the fact that my favourite niece is a lesbian! I've nothing against them, live and let live, after all it only leaves even more rampant ass for we straight gals'.

Of course Senifer's mother, her Aunt's sibling would stay away as she always did for to her;

'Homosexuality is an abomination. Two sexes came out of the primordial soup and it was meant to be that male lay with female and not with other males and female should not have coitus with female, it was unnatural and unhealthy and if all female's did it then the race would be doomed to extinction!

The bitter irony was that Senifer wanted her mother to be with her in her hour of grief, while, if Aunt Gwinifrit wished to stay away then that was fine.

Three more Tuica's and the numbness began to kick in. She and Reen had enjoyed seven marvellous years together, something some people never had, never knew such a depth of passion and devotion. Her mother and even Gwinifrit could not be expected to understand that. Now she was a widow, for they had been ceremonialised at the Legal Offices of Crocea, where same sex contracts could be sworn out for three shillin. She could be a merry widow, she knew that Reen had been worth at least seven thousand gold shillin, a sum that Senifer could not spend in a lifetime. Added to that what would Cydoniamech Industries settle to keep the matter out of court too?

After another couple of Tuica's, Senifer fell into a deep, yet troubled sleep on the lounge sofa.

TWO

WHAT WAS THAT pinging noise? She was trying to sleep and her head ached. The sound went on and she opened her eyes, it was as though her eyelids were made of emery paper. A darting pain lanced through her head and then settled to a dull ache at the back of her skull. With difficulty she pulled herself out of the warm embrace of the couch and went to the door, activating the view screen.

It was Clement! What was the time, how much of it had she spent in a drunken stupor? She activated the entrance mechanism and waited for her brother to walk into the apartment.

"Hi, Sis, by the holy hours of the new Church of Mars, you look dreadful. Have you been drinking"?

"Hello, Bro, thank you for doing this for me and yes I got bomberated last night. What was I supposed to do, just sit around weeping"?

"Fine", he decided dropping his holdall in the hall, "I'll go and make some Ausonia coffee, while you go and take a long hot shower and then let the water run cold for the last few minutes, see how it brings you around".

"When was the last time I told you you were the best Bro any girl could wish for"?

"When you had a total distort with Reen and got yourself thrown out and had to spend a few days at our place", he smiled sadly.

"Yeah, we did sort of have a few spats didn't we"? She remembered them fondly for a second.

"Spats"? He echoed, "More like non atomic wars, but you always seemed to agree an armistice in the end".

"What can I tell you, we fought well and loved well, on balance the good outweighed the bad and now...............and now............she's; gone"!

A torrent of tears gushed form Senifer and Clement held her for a good two minutes before saying,

"Come on now, she wouldn't have wanted this, she always looked on the bright side, go and get that shower".

Mumbling thanks, she went into the bathroom and stripped off the hastily thrown on slacks and frock-top she'd thrown on before the med-squad had arrived. Climbing into the shower she turned on the precious water, that would last for only seven minutes before the automatic cut off turned it back off again and began to shampoo her short dark hair, that she wore cut into the nape of her neck. The first time she had come back from the hairdressers with it cut so her mother had told her she looked like a boy.

Her looks were elfin, that was to say her features were quite sharp and even though she had been given the opportunity to augment in her teens, she had refused. Preferring to be elfin, slim and flat chested. How she had looked had never bothered her and she certainly had never entertained the notion that she could have attracted the like of Reen Glynfandell.

Drying herself quickly, head pounding, she went into the bedroom, their bedroom, for the first time and avoiding looking at the bed, selected a long floral frock that made her look waif-like with her slender frame. It suited her mood however and she drifted into the kitchen where the aromas of coffee and scrambled eggs greeted her.

"By the up and down and all that's in between my ruddy cranium is blasting", she complained to Clement, who promptly went to exactly the right place in the cupboard and shook out two Panadease for her. She took them with a sip of the coffee and seated herself before one of the plates. The crockery was white with royal blue banding, Reen had chosen it, saying it was utilitarian, whilst also being quite elegant. She had the most exquisite taste.

"Get that into your skinny guts and by the time you're done your head will be fine", her brother promised.

He seated opposite and downed twice as many eggs, apologising, "I'll go shopping in a bit otherwise I'll eat your apartment to a desert"?

"Take my thumbstik then, I can't have you coming here and helping me and expect you to buy your own supplies".

"I don't need to, you're coming with me. Don't think you're going to wander around in here all day and get yourself all maudlin".

"That's right, Bro organise me as usual".

"Someone has to. When we get back I'll change the bedclothes and then get in touch with an interment company".

"I've an email in my pad, some firm called amusingly Shadrack, Shadrack and Boot".

"I've heard that name somewhere before, was it in a Shakespearean play"?

"Don't think so, but it was in some play or other, written by an English guy in the late-middle times".

"Well I suppose it was bound to turn up again sometime. Might just be a coincidence or perhaps they're secret 'Sons of the Desert"?

"You and your early-middle monochromes, do you still watch that stuff, the thin one and his rotund partner"?

"Sure do and they still make me laugh. So you've eaten now, and your headache should be gone, we need to start putting a wake list together".

"Do we have to already"?

"We only have to do it once and I'll ping everyone once Shad, Shad and the other one get into gear".

"Do we have to invite Aunt Gwinifrit"?

"Wouldn't be a wake without her, you know she insists on being at all contracts and wakes".

"Can I have another Panadease then"?

Save them for when Gwinifrit does her wake speech, this one should be a zonker"!

They used Clement's pad and made a short list. Thankfully it was not a gigantic family and they hardly knew anyone on Reen's side. Of course it would be sad that their parents would not attend. Their mother would also expect their father to stay away and for peace and quiet, he would.

Then it was time to go and get some shopping, for Clement, despite all his great qualities was not a slim Jim by any stretch of the imagination. Once they had ordered a mountain of food to be delivered that afternoon, they pinged Shadrack, Shadrack and Boot. They turned out to be most professional despite their bizarre appellation and assured Senifer that no autopsy would be done on the body if she did not wish it.

"I don't want her cut into", she stated firmly, even when Clement tried to coax her into considering a law suite against Cydoniamech; for without evidence such would prove futile.

"I don't need more money", she was adamant, "And I certainly don't need any more upsetment. Reen goes into the blessed fire whole, just as she lived her life".

Clement gave up then, for cremation would certainly make any possible claim against the company who had created the P.A.P. nonsense.

That was the sort of sibling he was and he did all the organising and pinging, while Senifer did her best to stay cheerful, but sometimes the inactivity was the worst of all. The company she worked for as a graphic artist told her not to return until she felt mentally strong enough and privately she wondered if that would be ever. She had no need to work, had not really had since meeting Reen if she wanted to be a kept woman. Now it was different though, she was the wealthy one, she could find something more fulfilling than working for someone else.

Senifer first became aware that a couple of days had passed when Gholina showed up. Unlike the rest of the proposed wake she could not be expected to find accommodation in Zephyria when her husband was staying at Twenty three Kingsite Flats. The couple took the second bedroom and Gholina did her best to remain as unobtrusive as possible. That had always been her problem, she had grudgingly tolerated Senifer; because she was her husband's homosister. It never got warmer than that, the relationship remained cool. If Senifer were honest with herself, that was alright with her too. Gholina had a similar build to her husband, in other words leaning toward obese, this was something the waif-like Senifer could never understand, surely it was greed? It was easy enough to keep trim, one simply only ate what they needed. If fat people remembered their mouths were bigger than their ass holes then no one would be fat.

Clement was a rock though and yet he had a rim of fat around his midriff that was bigger than a flitter curtain. Perhaps he took some strength from it, who knew? She was always glad of him in the various crises she had suffered in her life though so big cuddly Clement was alright by her. Pity he was married to a blimp and they had contracted for seven years!

The preparations were conducted with admirable swiftness by all and before she knew it Senifer found herself putting on a black trouser suite with white roll neck blouse, she added a black wide brimmed hat and looked at herself in the long mirror.

'Gwinifrit is bound to say it', she reflected, 'But for once she'll be spot on, I do look like a man'

The limo-flit arrived and inside it's elongated rear the coffin Clement had selected while she was busy leaving everything to him. It was made of conti-lichen, the preparation when burned, then made excellent fertiliser. Reen would like the notion of returning to Mars and helping some vegetation to feed upon her.

Even travelling at a crawl they reached the Crematorium very quickly for in Zephyria almost everything was close together. The instant Senifer climbed out of the hearse she ran straight into Aunty Gwinifrit.

"Come here love and let me give you a hug", the dominating harridan requested.

Senifer was almost crushed in a meaty embrace.

"I'm so sorry for your loss my dear, I've always said I've nothing against you and your kind, you know, nothing against it at all. Me and your mother have argued about it, but she won't get me to stay away, no one thing I always do is attend every family matter. Would it help if I was to sit with you Senifer, you know, being as your mother and father have not graced us with their presence"?

"That's awfully sweet of you Aunty, but I'm with Clement and his wife, so that's taken care of".

"Who's conducting the er...service, or do you still call it that when it's not a man and woman relationship".

"Several of us are going to get up and say a few words, including a cousin of Reen's side. It will all be very tasteful Aunty.

"Oh, right well when do you want me to do my little eulogy, will someone give me a signal or something"?

"The service is for Reen, Aunty. You hardly knew her really, it's very good of you to offer, but it's all taken care of".

"I see, I'll just take my seat behind you then and listen to what others have to say", Gwinifrit sounded put out by the decision not to let her be included and Senifer thought to herself, 'Maybe that will keep her quiet for a while, if she sulks'.

She took her own place and Clement began the civil service.

He was four minutes into it when the event took place that no one present would forget as long as they lived!

A knocking sound could be heard followed by some dull thudding issues!

Clement hesitated, began to continue and then the knocking was heard again.

He fell silent and everyone began to glance about them.

Suddenly Gwinifrit jumped to her feet and cried out, "It's coming from the coffin! There's someone in that coffin that isn't dead"!

Everyone began to cry out at once and as a result no single person could make themselves heard. It was Shadrack junior that finally had the presence of mind to produce a screwdriver. Together with Boot, he pulled the coffin away from the oven door and farther back on the conveyor, then he began to undo the screws from the conti-lichen lid.

The sound dropped as the gathered mourners collectively held their breaths, how could the bodies have gotten mixed up and who was inside the one that had nearly been consigned to the flames?

The last screw came out, with difficulty the two undertakers prised the lid open and almost instantly a figure in an all white funeral gown, pulled themselves to a sitting position. Aunt Gwinifrit exclaimed,

"By Beelzebub's burning arse"!

One of the Glynfandell's screamed and fainted clean away.

THREE

THE DOOR TO the apartment pinged and Senifer rose from the table very quickly, "I'll get it you two finish your lunch". She asked her brother and sister-in-law, for she had only pecked at her own and found eating almost impossible given the events of the last week. Of course she was expecting someone anyway, someone from Cydoniamech Industries, since her solicitor had sent emails to them the night before.

She activated the tiny screen beside the front door and the colour drained from her face, she let out a slow gasp of air, then pressed the button that would unlock the door.

A woman of her own age entered and the two of them stood gazing at one another in stunned silence.

Finally the other woman found her voice, "Hello Senifer".

"Ariata! Is it really you"?

"I hope so".

"Reen told me you were dead, killed in the rocket accident of forty two".

"She was mistaken then, but you did not check, did not look it up on the net"?

"I erm....had a sort of break down, I was out of things for a while.... depression. Reen brought me here to Mars, to recuperate and I ended up staying. Why didn't you try and find me"?

"When you left so suddenly and with Reen, I figured that was what you wanted to do, I was not about to start pestering you. So is it Reen that brings me here"?

"You're not from…….."

"Cydoniamech Industries? Yes I am".

"But I thought you were going to enter medicine"?

"And so I did. Now on the engineering side of things, Cydoniamech Industries pay me well and I still get to see patients".

"You mean ones that have had problems"?

"Not usually, I'm usually involved in the transplant side. This is a very unusual case Senifer, the industry has sent me out to learn what went wrong".

"Oh, I can tell you what went wrong, Reen died that's what went wrong"!

"If the P.A.P. had totally failed, then there would be extensive or complete brain damage, is there brain damage Senifer"?

"You tell me, come and see her", Senifer's tone had grown frosty.

"The P.A.P. must have kept ticking over so slightly that it escaped general practitioner's tests, feeding enough blood to Reen's organs to keep her, in what would appear to be a catatonic state, for some reason it then rebooted just in time".

"She was nearly burned alive", Senifer told her abruptly as she opened the door to her lover's room. Since the near mortal spasm the two of them had slept separately, for Reen was still hooked up to an array of diagnostic equipment.

The duo entered together and Reen opened her eyes, her mouth twisted in disgust, "What's she doing here"? She demanded.

"You mean, Ariata, who you assured me was dead"? Senifer barked.

Ariata took hold of Senifer's arm, "Not now, wait until she's stronger".

"Get out of here, Skub and don't come back into my house again", the sick woman hissed.

"I'm from Cydoniamech Industries, Miss Glynfandell, and the correct way to address me now is doctor Skub. I am here to do some tests on your plantroniumprismatic atomic pump, but tell me to leave again and I will go".

"Go and get me some lichen-coffee and two Panadease, will you Senifer, while this quack starts with her questions and proddings"?

"What will you have Ariata"? Senifer asked as she turned to go.

"What will you have Ariata" Reen parroted with scorn in her tone, "Can't you wait for me to die, so you can be back with her"?

"An Earth coffee if you have some please", Ariata returned calmly, "And don't worry this sort of behaviour is not unusual in someone who has suffered such a medical catastrophe".

"Don't talk about me as though I'm not here, or already dead, do you hear me Skub"? Reen raged and Senifer left the room as quickly as she could. When she got back to the kitchen Clement observed,

"You look like you've just had a shock, Sis, everything alright"?

"Reen is still being hateful", his sister admitted, "I just keep hoping it will pass and she can get better".

"That woman, the one from Cydoniamech Industries, she looked sort of familiar, should I know her"? Gholina mused.

As she got the coffee Senifer tried to sound casual, "Doctor Skub was at Uni the same time as Reen and I".

"Skub", Gholina repeated, "Not Ariata Skub?! Weren't you two............"?

"Very good friends just before Senifer came to Mars", Clement came to her rescue.

"Before her mini breakdown then", Gholina was like a dog with a bone. "That was also just after that terrible rocket accident; remember".

"The luxury pleasure tour of Mars, the Moon and Callisto", Senifer said, there was no use in trying to hide anything from her sister-in-law. "I thought doctor Skub was on that rocket".

"So did I", Clement returned then, "If I remember rightly.......".

"Reen told me and I told you that she was", Senifer picked up the coffee cups, "She lied to us all and we never thought to check".

She turned to leave and Ariata suddenly appeared in the doorway, "I'm done for today", She began, "I've readings to analyse when I get back to the offices. That coffee smells great though, could I have it before I leave please"?

"Come in Ariata, remember me"?

"Of course Clement how are you"?

"Good thanks, you look good too".

Gholina glared at her husband and then asked, "I'm Gholina, Clement's wife I met you a couple of times too".

"Of course, at Lanco's party if memory serves me right".

"That's right", Clement enthused, "What a wild time that was. We all had a snort full that night, remember".

Gholina asked, sardonically, "Do you still do snufz, Ariata".

"It's forbidden by my employer", Ariata replied carefully, "We have regular drug testing and if we get two positives, that's the end of our career's with Cydoniamech".

"How is Reen"? Senifer asked, "Technically, I mean".

"The P.A.P. seems to be functioning perfectly at the moment", the doctor told her, "Her psychological state is not good, but then she's had an horrific experience. These things take time".

"I'd better go up and give her this lichen-coffee and her Panadease", Senifer apologised, "See you later; Ariata".

"I'll show her out when she's finished her drink", Clement offered.

Senifer went up the stairs and into Reen's room.

"There you are! Finished necking with the good doctor already, have you"?

"I was just getting coffee for you", Senifer countered, her lover's state of mind concerned her greatly, "Clement and Gholina have not left yet so she's talking to them".

"You're still in love with her aren't you? Unlike your feelings for me, that died with my body"?

"That's not true", Senifer gasped, "You know I love you Reen".

"But you hoped I was dead. Hope even now that I'll die again".

"How can you say these things, I've given you no cause to think I wish you dead, Reen. Perhaps a psychiatrist might be able to help"?

"Oh you'd like that. Get her to declare me insane and have electricity tear through my brain. Well forget that, there's nothing wrong with me apart from this useless pump in my chest. Now give me my Panadease and then get out".

Senifer passed her the tablets and the drink, "I'll come and see you in an hour", she promised.

"Don't bother", her lover returned, "Go and be with her, while I re-write my will on this net programme I've found on my pad. That'll fix you, you can be with her and poor again, you won't get a penny or a single share in my companies, how does that sound"?

"I never wanted any of your money Reen, that's not why we were together, you know that".

"Just get out now"!

FOUR

"YOU WANT ME dead", Reen spat for the hundredth time several days later. Senifer had stopped answering her. She carried on making the bed, while her hateful partner was seated in a high backed chair.

"Would you like to go out today"? she asked instead, "All the tests say the P.A.P. is now operating normally.We could go to the synthetic beach at Ascraeus Lacus lake. You'd like that wouldn't you"?

"Push myself too much you mean, get the pump to pack in again"? Reen was critical. "Would you like that Senifer? Or if it didn't pack in you could take me out on the Lake and push me overboard and claim it was an accident"

"If you don't need anything I have some matters to attend to downstairs", Senifer returned frostily.

"That's right, find some excuse not to be with me, get out then, so I don't have to look at you any more".

Senifer drifted down the stairs in a miserable sort of trance. She stopped at the holographic cube of the two of them together, their smiles seemed to mock her. The Roxbrough painting, entitled 'La Ascraeus Lacus în Seara Umedă' (the wet evening street of Ascraeus Lacus) that they had bought from the Romanian art dealer who owned a gallery there. The one that had been Reen's favourite for so many reasons now tormented her too. She would take them both down again in a while, leave the Scalla and two Fiorento's, they could stay up, they had been Senifer's choice and she would always find them magical.

She decided to go for a walk and then into the arcade in Zephyria, once the wind and sand became too much. Anything to get out of the apartment, for since Clement and even Gholina had gone back home, it had become a prison. Reen did not seem to be getting better when it came to her moribund state. Her body was recovering, but not her mind. The street was practically deserted, few Martians walked due to the constant sand storms, that varied from mild irritation to those heavy enough to threaten breathing. The single main cause of flitter failure was clogged filters. It was less windy than usually that day though and the weak and diminutive sun was breaking through the pink clouds taking much of the chill away.

Senifer had put stout boots on her feet which were somewhat incongruous to her printed frock, which reached down nearly to her ankles. Over this she had thrown on a black duffel and the hood kept all the sand out of her now growing hair. It was currently in the page boy style, for she had let her usual close crop grow out. The tall slender pseudo-glass doors of the Zephyria arcade slipped open when she pressed the plate and she was mightily relieved to pass inside the atmospherically and filtered building, with it's expansive array of shops that offered almost anything one could buy on the whole world.

The majority preferred to shop off the net where the choice also contained Earth and moon products, but many women still liked to touch and feel and try on first and that was the market the arcade aimed at. It therefore came as no surprise that the ratio of female orientated products was seventy five percent. Hardware and tools were few and far between, to see a goodly range of those one would have had to travel to Tempe or Tharsi.

Senifer went to the first coffee shop she came to a settled down to a Tharsicoff which she had recently switched to from her previously favourite, Ausonia coffee. The more recent choice was very strong and bitter and one only took it black, but it had the most caffeine in all the choices and she was becoming a bit of a caffeine junkie. She bought a crossword puzzle pad and stylus, one of the new cheap disposable variety and seated herself down to enjoy a couple of those plus perhaps three cups of Tharsicoff, before taking a look around the recent fashion designs. Part of her mind was shopping, part of it research for a return to work.

"Senifer Treadby is that you"? A male voice interrupted her thoughts. She glanced up to see a tall slim young man with the customary long hair and beard. He wore boho shirt and loons and brown pseudo-leather loafers. His hair was kept from falling over his face with a plaited leather thong at the ends of which were beads and feathers. He could therefore have been one in thousands on Mars and Senifer had no idea who was addressing her.

"I'm Treadby", she admitted, "But I don't recognise you sir, I'm sorry".

"Oh, I've changed quite a bit since university", he admitted, I didn't even expect you to remember me as we only saw each other in the refectory and the lounge occasionally. I was more a friend of Ariata Skub, than anyone else".

"Ah, just a minute you're not Ereggo Yhanes are you, the chap with the buzz cut who shaved every day"? the thought made Senifer smile.

"I admit to being guilty", he confessed, "And having no defence, throw myself on the mercy of the court".

"Reg from Regio they used to call you, because you were from Protei Regio, right"?

"Almost, it's Phrixi Regio, but yeah, I was Reg, whether I liked it or not".

"And who are you now, then. Get a coffee and come and tell me"? Senifer was glad of the company.

He waved a waiter over rather than going to the counter and asked for a Phrixitea, then responded to her question as he took the seat opposite hers,

"I guess I'm more Yhanes than anything, Senifer, because of what I aspire to".

"And what might that be, Ereggo".

"I'm trying to be an artist, in the school of Roxbrough, Scalla and Fiorentino".

"I have at least one of each".

His mouth hung open, "You tease me, of course, Senifer".

Call me Sen", she smiled, "And I'll call you Yhan. In actual fact I have two Fiorentino's".

"Wow, you must be very successful, what did you end up doing"?

"Graphic art for a big company, on the design team. I remember your stuff now I think of it, I liked it".

"You're very kind, no one else did though did they, especially our lecturers".

"They weren't there to like or dislike our efforts but to help create our own innate abilities", Senifer reasoned.

"So what brings you to Zephyria…..er, Sen. I always thought of you as a big city girl"?

"I sort of drifted in this direction and then got the job that keeps me here", Senifer found herself lying, did she not even want to mention Reen? Did she not even want to mention her homosexuality. Perhaps she thought it might strangle a new friendship that seemed to be in bud, a new friendship that she needed to blossom to replace all the lost love in her life.

"So Yhan, do you have a special person in your life"? she found herself asking him, for that would have been another obstacle toward a friendship.

"He shook his head and returned speculatively, "You"?

"No". The lying was becoming easier.

"I sort of always thought………", he began.

"What did you always think", she smiled, knowing he would not dare mention it over coffee.

"That you wanted to be unattached", he changed it to, "You know, no interest in hokking across with a guy"?

"And you were on the button with that, I wanted to concentrate on my degree and didn't want any distractions".

"Quite, quite, the same with me". That made her chuckle, Ereggo had been a wallflower who had no chance of much any way. Quite a few of the girls and about a third of the boys had been non-augmented, but even so that left Ereggo with little chance, he was just too much a shrinking horslyp.

"So why the arcade at this time of day"? Senifer changed the subject.

"The arts shop, I'm after canvas seconds that I can repair and make good as new, then I might eat this week or I might not".

"Gosh that sound sort of romantic in the artistic sense", Senifer enthused, "But I guess on a more practical level it makes you one of the poorest men on Mars".

Ereggo nodded with a sort of ironic smile on his face, "You put the pigeon in the hole Miss".

On a sudden whim she rose and instructed, "Come on, let's go to that art shop right now".

"We'll be sort of early", Reg from Regio gasped, "The stockroom won't have....."

"We don't need the stockroom, we're going to buy undamaged canvas, Reg".

"I can't, the price of......."

"I didn't say you. I said we, as in the two of us, now then where's the shop"?

Sputtering after her, he never the less told her what she wanted to know and Senifer, with purpose in her step for the first time in weeks, strode off in the indicated direction.

"Stop", Reg gasped hurrying after her, "I can't let you do it Sen, a guy can't let a young woman pay for stuff for him, it just isn't right".

Senifer turned, "Not even for a commission of sales"?

"What do you mean"?

Senifer smiled, "I'll buy you some blank canvas, if you agree to give me twelve percent of what you make when the picture sells".

That caused him to stop and give the notion a consideration, "So you're sort of like a sponsor, with interest in my work"?

"I am a sponsor and I am interested in your work" Senifer told him, "Do you agree"?

"Twelve percent's no good, I'll agree twenty five though"?

"Fifteen".

"Senifer come on, how much do you think they're going to go for, agree twenty five and you have a deal".

"You might suddenly have a better audience if some of my contacts in the art industry see what you produce"?

"You'd do that for me, Sen? Why"?

"For fifteen percent as I've already said".

"If you agree to twenty five percent I agree to let you be my agent".

"Twenty"?

"Twenty three percent or I walk away quickly and you don't know where my studio is, Sen"?

"Alright", people are starting to look. We have a deal". She held out her hand and they shook, it felt slim and fragile, even in his delicate artistic hands. The curious thing was they held each other for just a few seconds longer than was necessary and then self-consciously he let hers go.

"Now are we going to the art shop, or are we going to stand here looking at each other like a couple of drombies"?

FIVE

"YOU'VE BEEN WITH her", Reen spat and the amazing thing to Senifer was that she was in the kitchen on the ground floor as she spat the accusation out.

"Her"?

"Don't play games with me Sen, don't be a kun, you know Hades well whom I'm referring to. Tell me you've not been with her and the two of you aren't cooking up some scheme to get rid of me so you can be together"?

"I have not just spent my day with Ariata Skub", Senifer told her lover sadly, "To the best of my knowledge she isn't even in Zephyria.".

"Liar", Reen moaned sadly, suddenly going ashen. "You wanted the cremation to be the end of me, well I'm sorry to disappoint you, but it wasn't was it"?

"Reen you look like you've done too much coming downstairs, let me help you back up to your bedroom and get some lines back in".

"More Snufzmorph, yes you like me snufzed out of my cranium don't you? It gives you the chance to go out with her".

"You can have some Panadease instead if you want, but you should take something".

Suddenly Reen's anger and jealousy turned to self pity, she began to weep, "I'm sorry I lied to you about her, but I did it so I could have you to myself, I did it because I was in love with you".

"I know that, Reen", Senifer did her best to sound forgiving. "I've told myself that a thousand times since I learned the truth".

"If I was you I wouldn't see it that way", came the honest confession, "I'd be angry, I'd want me dead too".

"No one wants you dead Reen".

"Maybe you're telling the truth, maybe you are, but what about her, Sen? What about her? If she doesn't fix the P.A.P. I will die. Then she can have you all to herself".

"Ariata Skub has taken a medical vow, Reen and she's a professional, she would not risk her career at Cydoniamech Industries over your care, can you not believe that"?

"I didn't change my will", Reen suddenly declared. "I started to, but I love you too much".

"Our being together has never been about the money", Senifer told her and she meant it. "I have my own career and………..."

"You'll be alright when the P.A.P. fails and I'm dead"!

"It's not going to fail", Cydoniamech won't let that happen. If they thought it would then you'd be in the General now, having it replaced, so…..".

"But that's why they won't replace it", Reen cut in, "Because she's told them it's working alright now and when it fails you'll be together".

"She's not a liar. It is working alright now. Now come back to bed and let me get you some supper, what about some lichen-whole wheat crackers and some scrambled eggs and a nice cup of Lichentine"?

Reen allowed her to take her arm, but as they headed toward the stairs she muttered, "If only it wasn't her, if only it were anyone else that was monitoring it"?

So Senifer then did the only thing she could think of to calm her partner; she lied!

"She's not single, Reen, she lives with someone. So you see your fears are groundless".

"She's in a partnership! Casual or contracted"?

"Contracted", Senifer thought if she was going to lie it might as well be a whopper.

"Who? Who too? What's her name"?

Senifer reached and then decided, "Her name's Cally, she's a beautiful redhead, so I'm told".

They were half way up the stairs, "What if the fault can't be detected though"? She wanted to know, "What if it's still faulty but Skub can't find the fault"?

"The detection equipment is very thorough", Senifer assured as she helped Reen into the bed.

"But what if it isn't and it happens again"?

"Then the doctors will be more thorough a second time, they'll know what they're looking for. But it won't happen again".

"But if it does and the doctors miss it again? What then"?

"Do you realise the chances of that, they are practically zero".

"But they're not zero. They're not zero, Sen, and I won't be dead and they'll burn me Sen, they'll burn me alive"!

"Then I will arrange for burial the next time. It's exorbitant, but if it'll give you peace of mind".

"Buried"! Reen was still in mental distress, "Buried alive instead of burned alive you mean. Why do you want to bury me alive"?

"No on wants you to be buried alive, Reen, me most of all. If you are buried though, instead of cremated and the tiny tiny chance happens and you come back to life, you can have a transmitter placed into your coffin. You could summon aid and be rescued".

"Yes"! Reen's eye's glowed with fanaticism, "Of course that's the answer, a coffin with an oxygen tank inside and a transmitter. I want that Senifer! I want you to order one for me and it be brought here, to the apartment. I want to see it for myself, so that I can relax. Once I've seen it, once I know it's here and I can't be buried alive and not get help, my mind can rest easy. Will you do it at once, will you"?

"Of course, if it gives you peace of mind, darling", Senifer had to force herself to use the final term of endearment. For she realised at that moment that the woman before her was not the Reen she had loved. Some mysterious and essential quality that had made Reen the person she was, had gone. In some strange and bizarre way, Reen had died and the woman who had come back to life was her no longer!

SIX

"I LOVE THIS one", she told Yhan honestly enough. For some of them did nothing for her at all.

They had become Yhan and Sen and had been seeing one another for three weeks. Then Yhan had suddenly grown confident enough to ask her up to his studio. The place was typically a single man's. There was clutter everywhere and cups and glasses all over the apartment, that needed washing up. At least he'd thrown the cartons, that ready meals came in, into the bin, but that was overflowing and the inner bag needed replacing.

Then there was the acrylic paints that had been mixed into various palates, used tubes in a pile at the side of a multi coloured easel and canvases stacked in rows under one of the windows, A window that the sill could have used a duster, or perhaps be swiffened, for it was heavy with sand from the surface of Mars.

"Do you open the window Yhan"? She had asked him in astonishment.

"I have to! The caretaker of this place keeps the thermostat set to high for my comfort level, so I have let some heat out from time to time.

"Would it upset you if I …sort of cleaned up a bit".

"It looks alright and I know where everything is, but okay, only don't throw anything away will you, it's all good stuff"?

"Do you have some cleaning fluids, and where is your Swiffematic"?

"All in that alcove over there, behind the door, you just press it on the right hand side and it pops open. What do you want me to do, I can help you"?

"No, you'll get under my feet. Go and get a few groceries, do you want a list"?

"I think I know what I need, I'll not be long".

"No need to hurry".

She was half way through cleaning the place up when she realised what she was doing, 'Holy Buddha on a stick', she cursed in her mind, 'I'm nesting! We're friends and that's all, we meet for Lichencoff three times a week and talk about nothing important. I've never mentioned Reen. He's never made a pass at me, I'm pretty certain he knows I'm H.S. everyone knew at Uni, so what am I doing here'?

When she was done the apartment he called his studio looked fully ninety percent better and when he returned he shouted from the doorway,

"Excuse me have you seen Ereggo Yhanes, miss? He lives in this block somewhere in an apartment that's not as nice as this one".

"Try and keep it like this now Yhan", she chuckled and then her face grew suddenly quite serious. He misconstrued the reason for it and promised he would and she shook her head,

"That's not it", she said, "It's me".

"You, you've done nothing, Sen"?

"Yhan", she began taking the groceries out of his arms and placing them on a now clear and clean work surface in the kitchen, "You do know about me don't you"?

"What do you mean"?

"You do not about my, ah, preferences"?

"Sure, we've talked I know about lots of your likes and dislikes. You're not going to tell me that most of my work's crudage are you"?

"No, you drumbat I mean that I have no interest in hokking across with a guy, you were on the button with that, it's no longer because I want to concentrate on my career and don't want any distractions".

"Sen I know, you're H.M (homosexual) right? Sen I just like being your friend, I don't have any other expectations, don't worry"?

"Well that's just it", she began uncertainly, "I'm not sure I want you to have no expectations".

He took a step back and looked very thoughtful and then helpfully said, "Oh"!

"I think it might be a good idea if I went now", she began to look for her handbag and another bag she'd put some small purchases in. For his part he remained unmoving, unspeaking, making certain he did not say or do the wrong thing.

'This is crazy', she thought as she picked up her things, 'He obviously thinks of me as this way and has no interest in me anyway'. So she forced herself to ask him, her face suddenly flushing red,

"If I wasn't the way I am, would you ever be interested in a plain little creature like me"?

"But you are. Don't worry Sen I won't ever make you feel uncomfortable, I'm just very grateful for your friendship and I don't expect it to ever be any more. We can stay buddies, right"?

"That's not really answering the question".

"Oh, alright. Well, Sen, when I look at you I don't see a plain little creature, I see a slim delicate person who takes an interest in me and my work. I see a good individual who has a kind and generous heart and as a whole package I find it very attractive. Now how long do you want me to go on for, before your head starts swelling"?

She laughed at that and then the smile suddenly evaporated and she asked, "Do me a favour will you, give me a kiss".

"A kiss"?

"Yes it's when you press your lips….."

"Sen I know what one is. You don't mean a friend kiss do you? You mean a friend kiss"?

"Yeah".

He walked slowly forward, took her slim shoulders in his hands and bending down to her height kissed her very gently on the mouth.

"I have to go", she said suddenly then.

"That repugnant eh"?

"No", she reported at once, "No, that's why I need to leave and puzzle this one out, it wasn't bad at all, quite the opposite".

SEVEN

REEN WAS IN the lounge seated on the sofa. She looked better, much better than just after the failure. Senifer tried to sound cheerful,

"It's great to see you up and about Reen, you look so much better today".

"Where have you been"?

"Shopping like I said before I left".

Her former lover sniffed the air, "You smell of boar, are you on the slide Senifer, have you been frenging a man"?

"You can smell Eau de toilette" Senifer marvelled at her olfactory sense. "I bumped into Ereggo Yhanes of all people. Do you remember him"?

"Bumped into or bumped ugly bits"?

"You know Reen, you're really rather course when you put your mind to it aren't you"?

"You're growing tired of me. You wish I was dead, you wish it so much that you're prepared to lay with a man and ask him to kill me, that's what it is isn't it"?

"I've told you before, I don't want you to die, Reen. I have to say, furthermore, that your endless self pity and moribundity is beginning to fracture my nerves".

"Fracture your nerves", Reen laughed, a harsh brittle sound. "Maybe you should consider some lubie's then, maybe it's time you were on some medication - Sen"?

"Lichencoff"? Senifer asked as she poured some water into the kettle. Hoping the change of direction would misdirect the other woman.

"Camomile tea please", Reen returned form her position in the lounge, "Soothing, for my fractured nerves".

Senifer let that one go and told Reen, "Yhan showed me some of his work, you should come and look at it, there might be something you'd like for the apartment".

"What's the point of buying new things when you're not long for this world", Reen countered, "And my interest in boar is not as intimate as yours Sen. What's it like then, touching a male member, having one inside you"?

"For the love of the sweet baby Jewish prophet shut your filthy mouth will you", Senifer then cursed and though she meant it with every fibre of her being, she managed to keep her voice low.

Silence from the lounge while she made the drinks. As she went in with the cups, it was to see Reen crying quietly. She put the drinks on the pseudo plastic protective top of the Loigue faux twenty third century table and forced herself to put an arm around Reen. Her shoulders had become hard and bony there was no flesh on them, she had lost kilogrammes since the health hazard.

"Sorry darling, but your endless accusations aren't really necessary and they're beginning to wear me down".

"You're going to leave me. Leave me to die alone"?

"Not how I feel right now, but if you keep pushing, then it will become an option".

"To go to Ariata, or to Reg of Regio"?

"So you do remember him. No Reen; not to go to anyone darling, just to get away from you"!

Reen collapsed into her arms sobbing, "Please don't, please don't leave me"?

"Then it's time we got you help". Senifer decided. "Professional help, Reen. Ariata is coming a couple of hours and I'm going to ask her for the name of a good psychiatrist. Will you see one, Reen"?

"Only if it's a woman, I won't see a man, I'm not into men like.......", she went quiet.

"Now that was a first step", Senifer encouraged, "You were going to make another of your twisted accusations and you cut it off, I'm proud of you for making that effort".

"So you'll stay with me"?

"We are going to take this one day and then one week forward in units", Senifer used the well worn platitude, "Just keep trying, Reen and agree to see someone, no changing your mind, do you promise"?

Senifer felt the movement of Reen's head against her own slim shoulder, "Right then, it's time for a shower, wash your hair and put on a bit of slap ready for Ariata's visit, I want her to see how much progress you're making. Go on, go and get ready".

Thoroughly kowtowed for the moment, Reen went to do as instructed and Senifer let out a sigh of relief.

By the time Ariata arrived Reen was seated once more in the lounge and looking better than she had for weeks.

"Come in doctor"? Senifer requested being careful to keep her voice formal, "While you're with Miss Glynfandell can I get you a drink of something".

If her demeanour confused Ariata she was careful not to show it and she returned,

"A cup of Lichencoff would be lovely, thank you. So Reen how have you been and how are you feeling today"?

"As well as can be expected considering I've a defective unit in my chest, where my heart was", Senifer heard Reen return. Which was fair enough. Ariata was a representative of her firm and the retort was totally justified.

"I can only apologise on behalf of Cydoniamech once again", Ariata responded as if by rote, "And assure you that subsequent tests have not revealed any malfunction since then. I need you to go to the hospital now you're feeling better, for a thorough check, just to make certain it was not a thrombosis that caused the ah situation".

"You'd love to find that wouldn't you? Get your firm off the hook"?

"I sincerely hope that the tests would prove you healthy Reen. Or if you had a problem it would be easily fixed, but that's the point we've come to now you're stronger. There's no reason to delay, if you are otherwise vital I can make a ping right now and get you to the General this very afternoon"?

Senifer arrived back in the room with the drink.

"What do you think, Sen"? Reen wanted to know.

"It's your decision, Reen and your's alone", Ariata cut in, "If you agree, it would be me taking you, although obviously Senifer can accompany you if you wish".

"I don't want to accompany her", Senifer said firmly, "Reen and I need some time away from one another and I would also like you to get her appointments to see a psychiatrist. We've previously discussed it and it would help Reen's state of mind to have some therapy".

"Oh"! Ariata was clearly surprised, even though she had witnessed some of Reen's spat's in the past.

"Well yes I can do that if Reen herself requests it. Do you request it Reen"?

Reen nodded her head, hollowly she intoned, "I've had some depression, therapy might help. I don't want to lose Senifer".

"Alright then", Ariata was back to business, "Let me do some tests on the P.A.P. and then make a couple of calls".

Senifer went into the kitchen and waited until the tests and calls were done. Ariata then joined her, careful to close the door behind her.

"What's been going on between the two of you", she asked.

"I've made certain she had enough food and was taking care of herself", Senifer replied carefully, "Anything else is the psychiatrists area of expertise isn't it"?

Ariata looked shocked, "Well; yes, I guess. I was asking more as a friend. Are you alright Sen"?

"Just a bit sick and tired of Reen's moaning and accusations, but otherwise physically healthy, thank you for asking".

"I'm not so sure you're telling me everything, but as you say, it's none of my business, but I see a change not just in Reen, but in you too".

"Your primary concern is the patient though is it not Ariata"?

"Of course, forgive me if I seemed to be prying".

"I accept your apology", Senifer returned a trifle too quickly, "Now, if you're going to be with her until this evening I've plans for the day".

"Of course", Ariata sounded crest fallen, "I'm sorry if I've delayed your plans".

Senifer left the room, strode through the lounge without a word and went up to take a shower. She dressed quickly in the prettiest frock she owned, over which she threw an aged woollen cardigan and then her coat. Snatching up her purse she went back downstairs.

"Where are you going"? Reen asked, "Just in case we need to contact you"?

It was a reasonable request,

"West to Pavonis Lacus, if you need me".

"Pavonis Lacus"! Reen seemed to rouse herself from a stupor, "You mean to see...."?

"Yes", Senifer agreed without feeling the need to make any excuses, "To see my mother"!

Letting herself down the rear steps she went into the garage and took the cover from one of the flitter's there. The blue Pifco 250. Just one of the vehicles Reen owned, but which she had told Senifer she could use any time she wished. She activated the electronic doors of the garage and then thumbed the keyring and let the driver door sigh upward to allow her entry.

The interior of the Pifco smelled of new leather and rubber mats. The odometer showed a pathetic twelve hundred kilometres on it. She checked the battery, it was in extreme green, the water was full. The other readouts were beyond her understanding, but when she thumbed the ignition button, it read her print and the engine rumbled into life. Senifer was only an occasional driver, but the flitter was luxurious and practically drove itself. In fact if she so desired, she could have fed in her mother's I.P. and the flitter would have taken her there. She wanted to pursue the physical act of driving however and let the flitter ease out and onto the A15 and then to junction seven and the A23 that would take her west to Pavonis Lucas.

It was a typical day on Mars, cold, windy and sandy, the sun peeping out through the sand swirls occasionally and trying to turn the sky a lighter shade of flesh colour. On the road was a constant layer of grit, despite the constant sweepers that highway maintenance sent up and down twenty hours a day. Just off the road on the hard shoulder, the rust was thicker, but it created a natural barrier for those who lost control of their vehicles. Of course that was only if they speeded. Flitter's rode ten centimetres from the surface, their skirt almost touching, but not quite. An accident was more likely caused by clogged filters, which was a constant threat unless the flitter was serviced regularly.

Senifer had no need to worry on that score, the Pifco had been serviced and then put in the garage, it could not have been cleaner. When Reen had gone anywhere she had always used the big black Morphy-Richards.

"So after a while she put autocab on and turned on the stick player, she listened to some Everon while the flitter cruised at a constant one hundred and twelve point six five kilometres per hour. She was almost nodding off when the Pifco pinged giving her the opportunity to enter Pavonis Lacus on manual drive, or input I.P. for autocab to take her to her destination. She roused herself and took the octagonal wheel.

Within ten minutes she had passed down Walpole Street and then left to Pitt Road and finally over the junction and left to Peel Avenue and number twenty three and her parents sub-surface twin story, the top one of which was at ground level. When the engine died it took her quite a while to build up the courage to climb out of the flitter, but when she did it was to see her father standing in the front doorway on the pseudo planking porch.

The minute they saw one another, he waved and it was just what Senifer needed to take the next step.

Glinfer Treadby cried out, "Whoa stranger, it's good to see you, come and give your Dad a hug"?

Like a little girl Senifer ran to him and did just that. After a pause he held her out at arms length and declared,

"You look well and you're growing your hair, it looks nice. Why the visit, not that I'm not delighted to see you, there's no trouble is there"?

Clement had kept his word and kept the problems of Reen to himself. What surprised Senifer though, was that Gholina had too.

"Do I need a reason to visit you Papa", she asked then.

"No. Of course you don't, come on in, your mother will be stunned up side the head when she sees you".

"I'll bet she will", Senifer said. Her relationship with Senta had been difficult to impossible since she had come out.

"Senta darling look who's here", Glinfer called, and a florid woman wearing a floral apron suddenly entered the kitchen and smiled,

"My, Senifer. This is a surprise, come on in the best room and sit down while I get you something to drink? Would you like some lemon, or do you want something hot"?

"After a dusty drive I'd like nothing better than some water thanks Mama".

"I can't give you water", Senta returned, "If you don't want anything hot have lemon".

"Water will be fine really".

"The lemon is really nice, you'd enjoy it"?

Glinfer could stand it no longer, he laughed "Sen have lemon".

Laughing they went into the lounge that her parents still referred to as the best room, even though there was no other room on the ground level.

Senta came in with three glasses of lemon and Senifer took one and took a sip, her mother had been right, it was good.

"So what have you been up to"? her father wanted to know.

"Nothing worth reporting Papa, though I have started to sponsor an artist".

"Do we know her work"? her Mother asked, they had all always been interested in art.

"I don't think he's sold even one piece yet. He's from University, I might have mentioned him before, Ereggo Yhanes. I'm trying to get an exhibition for him, with my firm, though some of his work is not my taste,much of it is".

"So it is a man"? her mother latched on to the fact like it was very important.

"Yes and my sponsorship would make me a percentage if I could get anything of his placed. I've bought him a few items, canvases, paint, that sort of thing, but nothing I cannot afford to lose".

"And you knew him already"? Mother again.

"We attended some of the same lectures, I bumped into him in Zephyria a few weeks ago and it started from there".

Senta then said seriously, "If you called because you were wondering, then we know, Senifer, your Aunt, my sister came to see us".

"Good old Gwinifrit", Senifer observed with some bitterness, "I'll give her this, she's consistent".

"So how serious is it"? Glinfer asked, "She said something about her being declared medically dead and you actually got to the funeral before…."

"Her name is Reen", Senifer tried hard to keep her temper. "Anyway you don't need to worry about her any more, as I know you have been doing. We're no longer a couple".

"You've split with her while she's ill"? her father sounded incredulous, "That's a bit callous, Sen".

"She's physically fine now", Senifer found herself justifying to him, "But her attitude toward…, toward us, has taken a sharp change, I cannot put up with how she's behaving any more. She's getting help form a psychiatrist and then I'm going to move from my current post at work and ask to be relocated. That's what I came to let you know".

"So you're going to a new post and you're going to be be without any friends", her mother responded.

"I hope I'll still have Clement, his flitter can get him anywhere in the southern kingdom in a few hours. He's talking about getting on of the new air-flitters once they become wisely available. Clement won't let me down".

"Like we have", Glinfer finished for her.

"I never said that".

"You didn't have to", Senta returned with a trace of bitterness. "Look Sen, I know my decisions have been hard on you, but while you're in a city on your own, with only Clement to call, we'll always be; I'll always be happy to receive a ping from you".

"Alright Mama thank you, I will ping".

"And what about this Ereggo, where does he fit into all this"? her mother wished to know.

"I haven't figured that out for myself just yet", Senifer returned honestly.

EIGHT

WHEN THEIR DOOR pinged, Clement and Gholina expected various friends and colleagues to be without, but, not in their wildest imaginings would they have guessed who was on the other side that evening.

"It's your sister", Gholina gasped looking at the tiny inspection plate.

"She's got a name, Lina", her husband complained, "Well don't just stand there with your mouth open, let her in".

Senifer came into their kitchen and she looked different in many ways. She now had shoulder length hair, held in place by a lovely pink clasp. Her face was carefully and femininely made up, she was dressed in a lovely pink flowing frock that extended down to her ankles and even her duffel that was over it was in beige, rather than the black or blue she used to favour.

"Senifer"! Gholina gasped, "You look fantastic"! and the woman meant it. "Come in, we were just sitting down to a hot pot, would you join us"?

"I'd be delighted", Senifer agreed, another first, she had never shared anything with Gholina, but there again the other had never offered before.

"I'll get another glass if you'd like a white wine", Clement added after giving her a hug, "It's from Earth, from the country of California".

"I'd love some, as long as I'm not intruding"?

Clement glanced at Gholina who smiled, "Don't be silly, you're family, how could it be an intrusion"? Clement grinned like a Cheshire cat.

"So what brings you to our neck of the dunes? Not that we're not glad to see you, Sis"?

"I'm taking a trip and you were on the way", Senifer lied, "And I wanted to get some advice off Gholina, after dinner".

Gholina stopped serving the hot pot in shock and then resumed carefully so as not to spill anything,

"Anything you think I can help with Sen, I'd be glad to give you the benefit of my deep and expansive wisdom".

Senifer laughed at the joke and Gholina smiled in pleasure, Clement continued to grin, he could hardly believe his ears and eyes. They seated and began to eat,

"This is first class Gholina you must let me have the recipe' when you've finished dispensing your pearls of wisdom", Senifer said around a hot mouthful.

Gholina actually simpered, "It's not real difficult, I just add a few herbs and spices to a pretty regular concoction".

"Well that must be the secret then. I like your top by the way, where did you get it"?

Gholina leaned forward and confided, "Nice isn't it and I actually got it from Primarnia, only twenty nine sestersius"!

"You're kidding right, it looks far more expensive than that, it's so elegant".

"Not as elegant as your frock Sen, that's truly lovely".

"I can get you one, it was a freebie from a rep, you're a ten right".

"You mean it".

"It's as good as in the courier system".

Clement was in heaven. He had always hoped his wife and sister would get on like there were doing at that moment. So when they shooed him out of the kitchen and told him they would do the dishes he agreed without so much as a murmur.

"You sit and tell me what's it about, while I wash the dishes", Gholina asked. Senifer responded,

"No way, Sis, I do my share".

Gholina froze, looking shocked.

"What is it, what's wrong"?

"You called me Sis".

"Oh. I'm sorry I didn't mean to……".

"No, no, it's alright. In fact I liked it….., er Sis. You know I was an only child, so I never had a sister before".

"Well you've got one now", Senifer told her and when she hugged Gholina, the other woman did not shy away from the intimacy.

"Okay, let's get these dishes done and see how Clement's holding up, he's probably in shock ha ha ha ha".

The two of them laughed together and Senifer finally came to the point,

"It's about men, Sis".

"Men? Well I know them. I know one especially well so what do you want to know about the strange beasts"?

Senifer had the grace to redden, "I've gotten sort of fond of one, if you understand what I mean"?

"Fond"? Gholina grinned, "As in fond, fond"?

"As in triple fond", Senifer laughed, then grew serious. "Gholina; Reen and I are over, we've been over since she died. I've waited, waited for her to get better and now after six months I figure she's strong enough to leave".

"And you want to move in with a guy"?!

"No, not right away. Well maybe. Oh, I don't know".

"Well as long as it's clear in your head", Gholina observed sarcastically and they laughed at her humour.

"I like this guy, I mean a lot. But if I tell him I'm moving out of the apartment, he might just ask me if I want to crash at his place till I get somewhere of my own. I don't want to get somewhere of my own, before I leave the apartment, because then….."

"He wouldn't ask".

Senifer nodded, "If I move in with him though, he might make a move on me".

"And you don't want that"?

"I don't know".

Gholina grinned, "You don't know, so you might want him to. Senifer the little homo, might want some boar"?

"Funny eh"?

"No, not funny, just perhaps a bit hard to take. I mean do you really know what you're doing Sen"?

"No".

They laughed and Clement poked his head around the door. "Are we going to watch a quad-vid or something, or are you going to natter in here all night"?

"We'll be in soon, Sen's staying the night is that alright"?

"Sure; great", he disappeared again.

"I was going to drive back this evening".

"Nonsense you know you're always welcome here, now this business with the guy, tell me exactly what you want to know"?

"Well I guess I know what happens and that's scary enough, but I want to know, what they like, you know so nothing comes at me like a big surprise"?

"Oh. Well…..".

NINE

REEN LOOKED UP from her pad. Though she was up and about, her pallor could still have been better. The trouble was she never got any sun. Plenty of Martians were pale, but Reen never got any sun.

"Oh hello! It's, no don't tell me it'll come, your name's...."

"Nice to see you cracking jokes darling, how did this week's therapy go, you seem to be making progress"?

"Will you sit please"? her tone was reasonable so Senifer joined her on the couch.

"May I know where you've been for the past three days"?

"I did mention it Reen, work for the firm, some images for the front of Marsexy magazine. I had to go and direct some tri-vid for the usual girl who's on vacation on the Moon. Don't you remember"?

Her former lover's brow knitted in concentration and she admitted, "Sometimes some of the hypno sessions leave me with tiny bits of drop out, I'm sorry Sen, it's not up here any more", she tapped her temple.

"Well that's where I was Reen. In the new MAG there's one of them new flitterods, you know the three wheeler they're developing for the adolescent market, a sort of super stable bike for use in the Mars outback".

Reen tried to look interested, but it was plain she had none what so ever in flitterods.

"Would you like a drink"? Sen rose, thinking to offer a hot cup of something, but Reen nodded.

"Please can you get me a small Lichengin and lichtonic, with a twist of lime, there's some in the fridge".

"Oh, sure, bit early isn't it"?

"What does time matter to someone who doesn't get out much any more".

From the kitchen Senifer called, "Well you have everything here don't you, what do you need to go out for. It's not like you need to go to work or anything".

"I've told you, neither do you, but you keep on with that post at your images company".

"I enjoy the job Reen - here".

"Thanks, please sit, I want to talk about a few things"?

Senifer looked momentarily apprehensive, but she seated herself and they both sipped their drinks for a moment, "Okay then, Reen you have the floor".

"Do you still love me, Sen"?

"Oh, what a ridiculous question"!

"Is it"?

"Reen, I thought the therapy was really helping you make positive steps just lately and then you go and come out with something like that".

"Let me ask you another one then, do you wish on balance that I'd died that first time months ago".

"No of course I don't, what do you mean, 'that first time', as well"?

"Oh, I just feel it will happen again, you know? Call it woman's instinct, female intuition".

"I think you're being silly. You seem calmer, but you're still moribund, Reen".

"Where as I think the scales are beginning to fall from my eyes, Sen".

"Really and what great epiphany are you about to experience".

"That you and I are over and I need to accept that. You can stay here as long as you want, Sen, but eventually, you will have to find somewhere else. Oh and my will, I shall be changing it, but properly with a solicitor, when I get around to it".

"This high drama does get rather tiresome you know, Reen", was all Senifer said.

"I don't think I'm being melodramatic, Sen, in fact a horrible calm has gripped me right now".

"That will be the blue lubie's, have you taken too many"?

"You want me dead, Senifer".

"Satan's unholy bowel flush not that again"! Senifer gasped and rose to leave the room.

"If it's not true, move back into my bedroom this evening, our bedroom as was and I'll forget about the whole thing, I'll accept that it was all paranoia on my part".

Senifer hesitated, she thought about the notion and realised with horror that the idea of doing so filled her with dread, a dread close to revulsion! Carefully she said,

"Alright Reen, but not tonight, I've important things to do with work, set out just how I want and I've work to do on it, give me to the weekend".

"I will, for now just kiss me", Reen decided.

Senifer leaned over and kissed her briefly, neither woman felt anything at all.

TEN

"**I** WANT TO go away with you", Senifer said as they lay together, the aftermath of their love making still keeping them warm, even though the studio was cool as usual.

"And it has to be very soon and you have to do something for me".

Reg raised himself up on one elbow, "Leave Zephyria, what permanently"?

"Yes, an new start, for just the two of us, a new start and a new Planet".

"What back to Earth, I've never been to….."

"No, not Earth, Venus. I want to start some designs on Venus and I want you to paint Venus before anyone else gets the same idea".

Reg considered this bold move and said reasonably, "But neither of us in actual employment and no wage coming in, how long do you think we'd last before the money ran out"?

"Reen's wealthy and right now I'm the recipient of her will".

"Well yes, but there's two things wrong with that Sen, she didn't die and if you and I go to Venus, she'll change her will".

Senifer rose and took him in her arms and whispered in his ear, "That's why she has to die before we leave, Reg".

Despite himself he shivered and considered that, "How do you propose to get her to cooperatively pop off at the convenient moment".

"Well I've thought about that one", Senifer said. "She's died once, so it wouldn't be especially suspicious if she managed to do it again. I've also thought of a fool proof way of doing it".

"You're talking about murder, Sen"!

"Yes that's right, she's very very wealthy Reg and never actually enjoys her money any more, whereas, we can use it to realise our ambitions".

He was silent for perhaps five seconds before asking slowly, "How fool proof"?

"The apartment was one of the first built in Zephyria, because of that it has airlocks at the doors as you know. For when Mars was first settled it had no breathable atmosphere. So the cellar still has the old oxygen/nitrogen pump down there".

"Yeah but it's redundant as there is air on Mars now"?

"That's obviously right, but when the airlocks are locked at night no air moves in either direction and it gets slightly warmer in the apartment. If the airlocks stayed locked for days it would actually get more difficult to breath".

"You propose to lock Reen inside for days on end, that seems pretty risky to me, all she needs to do is use her pad and…..".

"No, that obviously won't work, Reg. Just think about a pump for a second, what can a pump do, apart from pump air into the apartment"?

He grinned in the semi darkness, "Extract! You propose to lock her bedroom and take all the air out of it. Again though what about her pad"?

"I'll make certain it isn't in her bedroom when she retires, she'll asphyxiate and everyone will assume the P.A.P. malfunctioned again. Once she's dead we pump the air back in and a medical examination will conclude that she stopped breathing".

"I'm not sure about this, Sen, I mean can we hope to live with ourselves afterwards"?

"I can, she should be dead anyway, only technology kept her alive. A hundred and fifty years ago she'd be dead now, dead and burned to ash. You have to decide if you're in this with me or not, Reg. If you want to come with me to Venus or if you don't".

"I want to go with you to Venus".

"Then you have to be in it with me, it's the only way, we have to do it together, so that we have to trust one another, so that turning the other in, would result in the death penalty for both of us".

"Do they have the death penalty on Venus", he joked. "When do we do it"?

"Tomorrow night, she's hung around long enough and she's thinking of changing her will, we have to be quick and we have to be decisive".

Reg held her and kissed her, felt the warmth of her pressed against him, "I'll do what ever you want, Sen, I don't want to lose you".

ELEVEN

"WHAT YOU'RE GETTING here sir is a real mean machine", the salesman who could have been advertising toothpaste told Clement. "Three hundred brake horse power on three wide super tough Durelli wheels. This isn't your powerful flitter, this baby actually touches the surface of the road. With the rear wheels being so close together it's more stable than any ancient motor bike, that the clubs still use on Earth, but with all the tactile benefits of feeling the wind against your face. Now I know what you're going to say what about the dust, but the visor has filter's and a high impact, fully polarised surface. Added to this the proximity alarm system and auto braking mechanisms and it's as safe as the best flitter's on the road and only four nine nine point nine nine for a limited period only".

"That's five hundred shillin", Clement pointed out.

"It is indeed sir, the best five hundred you'll ever spend and we even give you the sestersius change. This awesome Zanusi Roadtrike 300 can be yours today, your insurance and tax for your flitter covers it and we'll even give you a tank of water to put into the steam system, absolutely free. The micro-pile is guaranteed for seven Martian years. So the only thing you'll probably ever need to change is the odd tyre, what with the roads being what they are".

"What about the helmet and suit".

"Well this is really your lucky day sir, because we just happen to have both on special for the last day today".

Clement shook his head, "If I buy the Roadtrike, I want a suit and helmet thrown in".

"I've got to make a living sir, you can't really expect me to let you have a ten shillin suit and seven point nine shillin helmet for nothing. You don't mean it do you"?

"If you want to make the sale today, that's what I want for the money and my thumbs good for it", Clement was obdurate.

"Alright let me have a word with the manager and I'll see what we can do".

Clement waited, twenty minutes later he was speeding down the road on one of the very first Roadtrike's on the planet, the Zanusi Roadtrike 300 was an excellent man-toy and he totally loved it from the second he had climbed onto its narrow, but formed saddle. He had the true impression of speed, the ground rushing beneath his feet, the tyres kicking up great cloud of dust behind him that he could see in one of the handlebar wing mirrors. The machine had six gears, under his right foot, the clutch being under his left hand, he pushed it to its limit and broke every speed limit on every road he hurtled down.

He got to the apartment at twenty one seventeen and thumbed the buzz plate with a gloved hand. There was the customary delay while the occupant inspected who was without and the airlock hissed open, Senifer was standing there in a night gown her face was drawn into an expression of loss and grief.

"Something's wrong", he observed, all news of his new purchase forgotten, "What happened, Sis"?

"It's Reen", Senifer told him, "This time the med-squad are even more certain she's gone for good"!

"Can I put my machine in the garage, it's got an entry code but it's new and the dust......".

"You're staying"?

"Sure, I've still some days owing at work and they'll be fine about it, looks like we need the services of Shadrack, Shadrack and Boot again".

"Put your machine away, I'll raise the doors from in here. There's something else though Clement, Reg is here he's staying with me too, but we'll both be glad of your help with all the arrangements".

When Clement entered the kitchen it was to see a tall slim young man with the customary long hair and beard. He wore a boho shirt of black with fawn horizontal stripes and and orange loons. On his feet were brown pseudo-leather loafers. His hair was kept from falling over his face with a plaited leather thong in black and royal blues, he was drinking a cup of herbal tea

"You must be Clement". He said, holding out his hand, "I'm very pleased to meet you, everything I've heard about you is good".

They shook.

"Same here", Clement returned with warmth, as Senifer entered the room, "Drink, Bro"?

"Please, I'll have what ever Reg is drinking".

"Clement has just bought himself a Zanusi Roadtrike 300", Senifer told the youth who replied,

"Wow. Really, you must be one of the first, I've seen them on the net, they come in at about fifty five hundred don't they".

"Actually I got a right deal, four nine nine point nine nine and free suit and helmet plus a full tank of water and a seven year warranty on the micro pile".

Reg whistled, "Sweet, I'd love a ride".

"You can come pillion any time, but not at the front, she's my baby", Clement offered.

"I understand. I'll take you up on that offer too, soon, er, Clem".

"I have to ask now", Clement grew serious, "Where is the body right now"?

"Hospital morgue", Senifer returned. They've done all the biological tests and it's definite, Ariata has also done everything to check the P.A.P., there's nothing wrong with it".

"Again"! Clement was incredulous. "It has to be faulty! Are you going to sue"?

"Once the funeral's over, I'll see how I feel, right now I want her buried so we all can have proper closure".

"I have to say you're handling it well this time, Sis".

"Well it wasn't such a shock after what happened seven months ago and the way she was for that time, well, it's almost a relief really".

"Okay then, I've some people to ping, tomorrow I'll get busy and we should all be done in three days. It's interment this time isn't it"?

Senifer nodded, "The special arrangements are the tank of oxygen and the transmitter, I'll have the receiver of course".

"She can't be catatonic again, surely"?

"Never the less those were her wishes and I intend to see that they are carried out to the letter", Senifer replied.

Clement got busy, the same guests were called and all other arrangements were made, Reg helped Clement with some of them, while Senifer put the apartment on the market,

"I can't stay here, according to the will it's mine anyway so, it has to go", she had said.

When the funeral came around Aunt Gwinifrit had found a great deal of the wind taken out of her sails when Ereggo was constantly at Senifer's side. She could have gone into a loud diatribe about bisexuality, but was shrewd enough to know her niece had just become a very rich woman and you don't upset someone if one day you might benefit from being close to them.

Clement lead the service and on this occasion they then went outside to a special and rather exclusive site where real nyloplanyon headstones were situated. The coffin was lowered into the ground by a special machine and various members of the congregation threw flowers into the pit before the machine began to fill it in.

Once they got to the wake, which was in the Zephyria Grande Hotel, Senifer announced to everyone that she had obtained a post with her firm that would enable to her to set up a brand new office in Artemis. She and Ereggo were going there as soon as they had tied up a few loose ends.

"Artemis", Gwinifrit had echoed, "Another new town, where is it dear, up in the north"?

"It's west of Ember Caves Aunty", her niece had promptly supplied.

"Ember Caves is on Venus, Sis", Clement noted and he looked greatly saddened by the news.

"Well Artemis is a new build", his sister told him, "A frontier town if you will, it's an exciting prospect, Bro. Don't worry about seeing me, there's Skype and you can visit twice a standard year, more and more rockets are going from one world to another as the cost goes down".

"I see you've got it all worked out then", he replied sadly and even Gholina looked a little saddened by the news.

"Yes", came Senifer's firm reply, "Everything is going just how Reg and I planned it"

TWELVE

T HE ROCKET WAS gleaming silver in the light of the midday sun. Senifer and Ereggo were nervous and excited in equal degree. It would be the first time either of them had been off world.

"You float-age", Ereggo asked for the twentieth time.

"I'm mega-float-age, everything's fine, we're wealthy and we're free, we've a long and brilliant future ahead of us, Reg", Senifer stated with a certain amount of satisfaction.

"Yeah, I guess you're right", he returned, his conscience bothering him for the hundredth time.

"There's no guesswork involved, Reg, come on get over it, we got away with it and she was not a happy woman, we did her a kindness"

"I just worry about Cydoniamech". He told her, "With it being a burial, a rare burial for Mars, they may decide to dig her up, at any time".

"And they'll find what"? Senifer smiled coldly. "A - P.A.P. with no discernible fault and a withered up corpse. So what will they learn, quick get your passport, it's check in".

Ereggo did as instructed and they passed into the waiting lounge, it would soon be time to board,

"You're thinking that once we're off world, we'll be safe aren't you"? she guessed.

"We'll have Venuser diplomatic immunity", he returned.

"But we won't need it", she assured, "But I guess you'll relax in about thirty minutes or so".

"When we're over half way to Venus", he corrected, "Officially in Venuser space, then the Constabulary cannot touch us. The Beadle of Venus will not want to".

"You know she's dead right"? Senifer almost savoured the feeling. "We've heard the last of Reen Glynfandell".

Down in the red dust of the planet however, in a poly-carbon crate the plantroniumprismatic atomic pump still had a residue of atomic power. It was enough, following dormancy, for it to compute a tiny amount of energy sufficient to produce a self diagnostic. It did so, even though it had been supplying indeterminable energy sufficient to oxygenate Reen's brain, avoiding fatal damage so great, as to render the patient brain dead. The diagnostic told the poly-carbon chips that the pump was still operational if required, the bio-readings told the computerised mechanoid parts that the patient was not beyond resuscitation.

It produced an electric shock to the body and the pump increased it's activity. Three beats a minute went up to ten, the heating unit began to increase the temperature of the blood flowing through it, the beats went up to twenty per minute. After an otherwise interminable period the beating of the pump had increased to sixty five b.p.m. Reen Glynfandell awoke into a black box of specific dimensions and knew she had been buried alive.

She screamed!

No one could possibly have heard her, the pump increased it's pace. Eventually she began to calm down and realised the oxygen in the coffin was swiftly being used up. Gropingly, she felt for the slim tank that would increase her life expectancy to twelve hours. She placed the mask over her face and forced herself to breathe normally. Then she found the simple transmitter. All it consisted of was a simple box with a tiny toggle switch, she threw the toggle and waited. The digging would start soon, then the sound of screws being unscrewed, then for the second time in her life, Reen Glynfandell would cheat the grim reaper.

"What the burning arse of Satan was that" Ereggo demanded in shock at the piercing tone that issued from Senifer's hand luggage.

For her part the girl's face drained of all colour and she announced in hushed tone, It's the frenging transmitter, I don't koofing believe it, she's done it again".

"What? What are you talking about Sen"?

"Her! Reen! She pressed the transmitter".

It took Ereggo a few seconds to process that information and then he finally and desperately suggested,

"It might have gone off on it's own, it might be a fault of some sort".

"The fault is ours Reg! Reen is still alive, the koofing toggle on the unit could not have depressed on it's own".

"Perhaps something moved", he tried to suggest, "You know, inside the coffin, something shook the body and it fell onto the transmitter".

"Moved"? Senifer was sardonic, "Moved under ten feet of Martian dust, what could possibly have ruddy moved except for her"?

"Well, I don't know maybe she had some sort of rigour mortis spasm. You know, like when a chicken runs around with it's head chopped off"?

"She didn't move for four solid days, Reg. No, there's only one possible explanation, the frenging P.A.P. has brought her back; again"!

The rocket departure was then announced over the public address system and the other passengers began to que for entry into it.

"What are we going to do"? Ereggo demanded illogically, "We're so close Sen; so close".

By way of answer Senifer took the tiny speaker box out of her bag and let it drop to the floor. Then she suddenly stamped on it with every ounce of her being. Abruptly the beeping ceased.

"There"! She said in satisfaction, "There's no further signal now, come on, we're going to Artemis".

Ereggo was speechless for several second and mutely joined her in the rapidly diminishing que, then he said rather woodenly,

"But she's not dead, Sen, Imagine the horror; trapped in a sable box, the air running gradually out, waiting for someone to come and then, the realisation that no one is going to; horrible"!

"It will all be over in less than a day", Senifer decided aloud, there was not the hint of remorse in her voice. "While we have a lifetime of luxury and satisfaction ahead of us on Venus".

He followed her, wondering at the person she had become. They went out briefly into the cold air of Mars and then up the steps of the gantry as the rocket sighed and sizzled. As then bobbed their heads down to enter the rocket, Senifer half turned to him,

"It's over now Reg, everything ahead of us will be pleasure filled".

The rocket lifted off in the year three thousand two hundred and forty nine, August twenty third, exactly four days before the outbreak of Venflu, that would kill everyone on the planet except for the Biotron!

---------------- fin ---------------

FROZEN IN A DREAM

Violent - silent scream
Frozen in a dream
(and now that you hear)
Empty roads and silent streets
Where we fell on to our knees

Reed - Booth

ONE

THYLES MATIS HAD only been built twenty five years and was as far north westerly as it was possible to be on the red planet. It boasted the lowest temperatures that mankind had thus far managed to colonise. It had been constructed for the ice miners and their families and everyone that lived there was connected to the mine one way or another. So on the fateful day when the Post Office come bank was robbed it was the biggest most talked about event in the history of the town; eventually! Not only that but the list of suspects responsible for the robbery was mighty short, a list of no more than one.

The mine belonged to *North Martian Consolidated*, and the bearer bonds that were in the post office at the time were printed by them, by way of the payroll for the month. The sole custodian of the place was Travador Myn who on that fateful morning, was just stacking the bonds into the bank safe, having received them from Marsecure but twenty minutes earlier. He was a grizzled ninety eight year old, but he was also the most trusted and dependable post office custodian on all Mars. The day up at Thyles Matis began like any other, with a cold dawn and an even more frigid wind gusting down from the north pole. The frigid quiet was rudely shattered when a tremendous explosive bang rent the air and the lock on the airlock of the post office come bank, was blasted clean away.

Myn was not slow to react, in fact for his years his reaction's were nothing short of remarkable. Swift as he was though, he was not quick enough. A lone tall gangly figure; his face covered by a crash helmet with polarised visor burst in. He was in a gang of one, no one else took part in the raid. Before Myn could pick up his own blaster, which was only a snub nosed pistol, the intruder let off a cruel second shot with a long blaster rifle. The report took a huge chunk of flesh from Myn's shoulder, but as he began to black out from the pain, he had just enough time to see the initials carved onto the faux mahogany stock of the tremendously destructive weapon, B.D. There had been no call for cooperation nor surrender, the enmity that the shot demonstrated was total and uncaring. The consequence could only have been thought out before hand and that conclusion arrived at and accepted. If murder was to be committed, so be it!

Over in the town's victuals market, Fren Adone' heard the commotion and as was her nature, began to dash toward the post office to see if she could help. The wind was whipping up the sand and particles of ice, as it usually did in Thyles Matis, visibility was not at a very high level. Consequently all she saw as she dashed from one establishment to the other, was a lone figure suddenly burst from the crime scene jump onto the getaway machine and roar away on a road-trike. Fren to her credit did not even stop to consider the consequence of her valour, her speed did not diminish in the slightest as she dashed into the post office. As a result, she found Myn before he had bled to death and was quick to ping the town doctor, who luck would have it, was not down the mine that morning. Max Tintagel, the town's lone practitioner of medicine snatched up his bag and jumped into his flitter. Twelve short minutes later he was bending over the injured nonogenarian and applying a synthetic pressure bandage, the actions of both turned out to save Travador Myn's life. The post master would be forever in the doctor's and Adone's debt.

By the time anyone had the chance to gather their wits and call the town's Beadle, it was all over bar the shouting and the shooting so to speak. Hoddington Brownsword received the ping and straight away went to the weapon's rack for his long needle rifle and dashed into his own flitter, but though he was at the post office in five minutes, he was twenty five too late. He could not have responded any quicker, nevertheless the perpetrator was long gone and so were the bonds. He rushed into the post office and the first person he encountered was the very one who had pinged him,

"Hello Fren, what's happened here"? Brownsword demanded urgently.

"The payroll Hodd, it's gone and poor Travador nearly bled out".

"Bled out"?! That was even more unusual, "Knifed you mean"?

Fren shook her head, "Shot".

"I'm guessing the doctor beat me here then if he did not lose all his blood. Where is he"? the Beadle demanded,

"He's resting at the minute Hodd and I don't think he's in much of a state to talk, he lost quite a bit of blood", replied a voice from the doorway, it belonged to Doctor Tintagel.

"Fren was just telling me, but how did he lose it, what was the weapon"?

The vast majority of shootings on Mars were the result of needle gun discharges, so for someone to bleed copiously, it was an event. Max Tintagel tried not to sound too conclusive, but he was bound to reply,

"Blaster rifle, and it had a mahogany stock, Myn told me that important detail before he fell asleep, I've given him a sedative"!

"Might that stock just have had initials carved into it"? the Beadle wished to know, already knowing and dreading what the answer would be.

The doctor nodded, but said no more, forcing Brownsword to ask, "What initials Max"?

"B.D.", the doctor went to the sink and began to wash his hands, the water ran red and not from Martian sand. "Could have been stolen Hodd, you won't know until you go out to the D'nab house".

"I suppose it could have been", Brownsword reasoned, "But it would be something of a coincidence. When it comes to keeping law and order in Thyles Matis I don't believe in coincidences".

"What are you going to do Hodd"? Fren wished to know.

"There's only one thing to do", Brownsword told the two of them, "I'm going over to the D'nab house and ask a few questions".

Nash D'nab was Thyles Matis' self proclaimed important citizen, according to him nothing happened in the mining town that he did not know about and nothing happened that he did not sanction. His lone son Bolet was ironically the town's hot head and ne'er do well and a constant source of embarrassment to his father. Nash loved his son though and Brownsword could not count the number of times he had talked the Beadle into looking the other way when Bolet had gotten himself into hot water.

This was something different though. Armed robbery was a shocking step up even for an arrogant hothead like Bolet. The only trouble was Nash would stand between Brownsword and Bolet no matter what the crime and they both knew it. Both of them and the doctor too.

"I've not seen Nash for a while", Tintagel observed, in the most casual tone he could adopt, "Mind if I come along and keep you company Hodd"?

There was a gleam in the Beadle's eye as he noted in a gruff voice,

"I don't need nurse maiding, Max".

"And I never said that you did", the good doctor replied, "But Nash could do with a physical check up and if you give me a lift, it will kill two birds with one stone".

"What about Travadore"?

"He's well out of it for now and if anything changes Fren can ping me. There's nothing I can be doing here".

"Then I suppose we'd better get Fren's store locked up so she can stop here with Trav and then set off".

The doctor nodded. Pleased to be part of the subsequent investigation.

It was snowing as they exited the post office and went over to the Beadles black and white flitter. The officer responsible for keeping law and order in the mining town cursed under his breath, snow would cover important tracks. He threw on a heavy waterproof and then went back outside. He made a careful inspection of the red ground before it turned into a white gleaming carpet that allowed no one to see beneath it.

"What are you looking for"? The doctor called through his open doorway, on the passenger side of the vehicle.

"Tracks", Brownsword muttered almost to himself. "Why didn't Myn know for an absolute certainty who shot him? Was the assailant wearing a road-trike visor by any chance"?

"Why yes", the doctor was impressed, "But how did you work that out"?

"Tyre marks on the ground out here. Two spaced around a tighter pair in the centre, only a road-trike makes those markings and that's not all, one of the front tyres has something stuck in it, a sharp piece of gravel at a guess. The gravel leaves a deeper indentation in the ground".

"Bolet has a road-trike and the only other owner of such a vehicle is the local vet up here in Thyles Matis", the doctor noted obviously, for it was common knowledge.

"But only one of the Roadtrike will have that front tyre with the piece of grit stuck in the front wheel".

Brownsword climbed into the flitter sending rivulets of melted snow everywhere. The doctor fastidiously tried his best not to get his own duffel soaked by it.

"Only thing is the vet doesn't own a blaster rifle Hodd. Especially one with the initials B.D. carved into the stock".

As Brownsword gunned the flitter to life he replied, "Blaster guns can be stolen though Max. On the other hand if young D'nab's road-trike is out front of their house and it has a bit of gravel stuck into the front tyre......".

He had no need to finish the sentence.

The flitter drove easily over the snow, for it floated on it's curtain ten centimetres above the ground. With the windscreen wipers going the Beadle drove at the same speed as usual, the roads around Thyles Matis were nearly always empty of traffic.

The house of the D'nab's was an impressive building of pseudo-nyl bricks, slotted together like the ancient Lego, but then with the outside coated with a special protective waterproof resin that let no moisture through at all. A second wall was then constructed inside it and the chamber betwixt them loaded with insulating fibre. It was the most insulated building that could be constructed at the time. The snow had thankfully stopped by the time the two men climbed out the vehicle. It never snowed for very long on Mars, there simply wasn't that much water vapour in the lower ionosphere. The Beadle made a careful search of the ground and sure enough there were tyre tracks in the red rust. Tyre tracks that showed that one wheel had a piece of aggregate stuck into the rubber. A damning piece of evidence then. Brownsword made a note that the last set of tracks, as far as he could judge, were in a northerly direction and then he looked up.

For they had only reached the front railings, when a huge bear-like figure of a man came out the house and met them half way. Nash D'nab was the foreman of the mine and also an individual of no compromise, many of the local populace feared him. Brownsword was not one of them.

"What's this deputation all about then Hodd"? Nash boomed. Noting keenly that the good doctor was in the Beadle's company.

"Been a bit of trouble down at the post office, Nash", the Beadle began, "This and next months bonds for the payroll have been stolen".

D'nab shook his head, "That's not good, some of the boys wait for their bonds every month you know that, I expect you'll want me to tell them".

"That's not necessary", Brownsword replied in his easy drawl, "As Beadle of Thyles Matis, the duty falls on my shoulders".

"So you just came out here to warn me then eh"?

"Bit more than that, Nash. The kid who did the job was carrying a blaster rifle with a mahogany stock and the initials B.D. carved into it".

The doctor meanwhile was surveying the surroundings, but could see no sign of a road-trike. Brownsword had not really expected it to be outside the house.

"You'd better come inside then", D'nab said a certain menace in his tone, "I'll check Bolet's cabinet, see if it's been broken into".

The trio walked gratefully into the warmth of the D'nab kitchen together. The owner of the property offered the visitors nothing, but merely demanded,

"Wait here, I'll go take a look in his bedroom".

"He's not going to take this too well when it hasn't been busted open", Tintagel breathed to the Beadle.

"*If* it hasn't", Brownsword returned reasonably. Even at that stage, with the circumstantial evidence they were gathering, he hoped that the younger D'nab would have nothing to do with the crime.

They watched a trickle of condensation dribble down the double glazed window, situated near the kettle and Brownsword deliberated whether to crack one of them open, when D'nab returned,

"Hard to tell, but it looks like the lock's been forced and then relocked", the foreman told them.

"Mind if I take a look, Nash"?

D'nab glowered, "My word isn't good enough for you, Hodd? It's been good enough for you in the past. What are you hoping for"?

"Nothing to do with whether I believe you or I don't, Nash", Brownsword returned reasonably, "But if it has been forced then it's technically a crime scene, and I have to dust it for prints. I'll get my kit out of the flitter".

"Just a minute, Hodd", D'nab demanded, "You know the only prints you're likely to find on that cabinet belong to my son and he isn't a robber. He may have been a real live wire a couple of years ago, but he's never been dishonest".

"I'm not suggesting anything at this stage, Nash", Brownsword continued on in his lazy drawl, "And I wouldn't be looking for Bolet's prints, just some that have no right to be there, that's all".

"It would seem to me that my word should be good enough for you Hodd", D'nab was beginning to sound angry and perhaps a little frightened. "You, who I was in no small part responsible for getting into the position of local Beadle".

"Don't go letting your skirt touch the ground, Nash", the local official responsible for keeping order in the town requested, "I'm going to dust that cabinet, with or without your permission".

The two men stood eye to eye for several seconds and then D'nab cursed,

"Go and get your kit then damn you, I really would not have expected this sort of suspicion from a true friend".

While Brownsword was gone, D'nab demanded, "And what are you doing here anyway doctor, come to patch up some imaginary bruises"?

"Hodd asked me to come along, sort of like a deputy if you will", Tintagel lied.

"Oh I get it", D'nab was sardonic, "Like Wyatt Earp and Calamity Jane"?

"That's actually very funny", the doctor laughed.

"Well it's the only thing about this farrago that is", the foreman scowled. Brownsword came back in and went to go upstairs,

"*I'll* lead the way, Beadle", D'nab commanded even though Brownsword had been a guest in the house many times in the past. "And you stay where you are, Jane"!

The Beadle and the doctor exchange a glance but said nothing.

Brownsword followed in docile fashion, but satisfied that he had faced down the mine foreman on this particular issue. He dusted the cabinet and ran the reader over the powdered surface, it bleeped it's completed survey and compared the imprints with those stored in Thyles Matis data base and then the Martian National data base.

The Beadle glanced up at his acquaintance, who was craning his neck to see the device's tiny screen.

"Only Bolet and your prints on here, Nash".

"So the thief wore gloves", the foreman concluded at once. "You can see the lock's all scratched and tampered with"?

Brownsword looked at the lock through slitted eyes, true it was somewhat battered, but it only looked harshly used to him.

"Where is Bolet, Nash"? he asked.

"What are you going to do"? D'nab demanded.

"What do you think I'm going to do? Ask him some questions, like where he was about an hour ago, for one".

"No need", D'nab returned quickly. "Because he didn't rob the post office, I give you my word on that, Hodd. Are you going to tell me you doubt my word"?

"Now that's not what I'm saying, or what this is about, Nash", Brownsword returned carefully, eyeing the other's clenching fists. "But I've got to do my job and to do it properly I have to ask Bolet a few questions".

"But you don't", D'nab was obdurate, "Because I've just vouched for him, he's not done anything wrong".

"If you don't tell me where he is, Nash, I'm going to have to go and look for him myself, also I take a dim view of you trying to pervert the course of my investigation".

"Investigation"! D'nab barked, "Don't make me laugh, this isn't an investigation it's a man hunt and you suspect the wrong man".

"Are you one hundred percent sure of that, Nash. One hundred percent"?

D'nab's shoulder's seemed to slump, he tried, "You can't take him in, Hodd, not my boy, since Jereme passed he's all I've got".

"The law is the law, Nash. Without it what do we have but chaos and anyway nothing's been proven. All I want to do is talk to him".

"I don't know where he is"! the mine foreman confessed then. "He should be on the morning shift over at face 'B', but they pinged me just before you pulled up to tell me he hadn't turned in for work. When I saw Tintagel, I thought something had happened to him".

"I'm going to look for him, Nash. It's the only thing I can do".

"Not alone then and you can send the good doctor back to town, I'm coming with you"!

"You aren't going to stop me, Nash".

"You said you wanted to talk to him, so we'll go and talk to him".

The two of them went back downstairs and Brownsword told Tintagel what had been decided,

"You can go back to town in my black and white, Max", the Beadle said, "Nash and I will go out in his Rovflitter".

The doctor looked doubtful and hesitated but, he was assured by a simple tacit nod and climbed into the official law and order flitter and after Brownsword had retrieved his pad, drove steadily away.

"He's a good man", the Beadle said to D'nab.

"Yes, of course he is", came the neutral reply.

"So where are you going to start? How in Hades do you know which direction to take"?

Brownsword told the foreman of his observations regarding the tracks around the property, the piece of aggregate that would indicate where the robber would be headed.

D'nab said less belligerently than he had been until that moment, "I can see how you're coming to the conclusion that my boy is mixed up in this somehow, Hodd. I don't really blame you for your suspicions, but I *know* my lad and he would not shoot a fellow human being. Who ever stole the rifle, must have made his getaway on Bolet's trike. That's not such a stretch is it, I mean is it"?

"Not at all", the Beadle agreed, for the sake of peace. "So drive very slowly and let's hope the snow holds off. I'll keep an eye on the tracks and with luck they'll lead us right to the rider".

As he turned on the engine, Nash D'nab said quite calmly, "If it leads us to Bolet there will be a simple explanation I'm sure, Nash. One thing you need to know, if there is no explanation, you're not taking my boy to the gaol-house".

"If he's as innocent as you are convinced he is, that won't happen will it? Hoddington pointed out. "Let's leave it at that until we have the answer, alright"?

D'nab eased the Rovflitter forward at little more than twenty four k.p.h. The tracks lead them north, there were no further towns between Thyles Matis and the pole, nothing but frigid ground, then the glacier and perhaps the odd observation outpost, where the only shelter was the occasional temp-hut.

D'nab noted, "We go any further, Hodd and the only thing we're going to find is the Chasma Boreale".

"I seem to remember the Norwegians doing a survey up here around forty six and leaving a station this way, Nash"?

D'nab nodded, "You're right they called it Hvit Håpløshet, white hopelessness, you think who ever robbed the post office is going to stash the bonds there"?

"Well I doubt he's going to hide them at the pole, Nash. There's one other possibility though, one I don't want to consider and that's the one that is he heads into the pole to hide his tracks and then comes out again in a different direction".

"Well if he does you'll just have to make a ping to Fabreri Sinus and bring the constables in on the thing".

"Not what we want is it"? the Beadle asked.

"Well as I know it ain't Bolet, who did the robbery, then I couldn't really care less, Hodd. The main problem I have is the loss of the bonds. North Martian Consolidated are not going to be very happy at what you let happen in your ward. I'll do my best to keep you your job, but.........".

Brownsword realised D'nab was enjoying his current conjecture, but was happy to let him talk on. It still meant they were on the trail of the perpetrator, if it turned out to be Bolet and he thought it would, then his problems would begin afresh.

The Rovflitter reached the edge of Mars' northern glacier and D'nab stopped the vehicle.

"Now what"?

"Have you some snow shoes in this crate"?

D'nab nodded, asking rather obviously, "You're going on on foot, after a road-trike"?

"I intend to", the Beadle admitted. "It seems to me, Nash, that the trike won't have gotten very far on this snow and ice. If we continue north, toward Hvit Håpløshet, I'm guessing we'll soon find it abandoned, or we'll find our perpetrator. If you don't want to go any further, I'll thank you very much for your help and let you go back to town".

D'nab shook his head almost at once and pulled up the hood of his parka, over his shock of still black hair.

"I'll get you some snow shoes and a compass, I've a stove in the back there and a pan, we can at least make some Lichencoff. You'll carry the rucksack, right"?

"I will and I'll see you remunerated from the local Beadle fund for the rental of the gear, Nash".

By way of answer D'nab merely grunted and began rummaging in the back of the somewhat untidy vehicle.

They set off grimly, a few minutes later. The wind contained less sand at this altitude but instead it lashed their faces with hoarfrost, needle sharp ice crystals that had formed on Mars pole by direct condensation at temperatures well below freezing point. This was a harsh, albescent, unfeeling landscape that rivalled anything the Earth had to offer and they knew they could not stay, could not survive long.

Then the white unit appeared as they squinted through the lashing turbulence. By it's tell-tale shape they knew it was the road-trike covered with hoarfrost, before they were close enough to touch it.

"The water in the tank will have frozen", Hoddington cried over the noise of the blasting they were receiving. Like all vehicles on Mars the engines were super powered steam devices powered by micro-pile batteries, thus *green* and non polluting to Mars' atmosphere.

"Whoever is in front of us cannot have gotten far", D'nab thought out loud. I'd guess Hvit Håpløshet is only about two kilometres further north, he'll be holed up in the cabin.

Hoddington Brownsword agreed, the only thing he did not agree on was the identity of he, whom they sought.

"It might be a good idea for me to take it from here, Nash", he suggested, "After all if you're so sure it's not Bolet, what's the point of carrying on"?

"And if the robber's holed up and waiting for you with a blaster rifle, you think you can arrest him alone, without getting your fool head shot off"?

"That's none of your concern".

"Hades on fire it isn't, I want the bonds back where they belong, otherwise there's going to be Beelzebub to answer when my boys find out they aren't getting paid".

Brownsword grinned, "And that's your chief concern is it? There isn't some tiny part of you might admit the possibility that we're chasing Bolet"?

"If we are, he'll have a good reason for being up here, Hodd and you aren't going to shoot him until I find out what that is".

"And if he did it, Nash. Oh I see you get angry at that, but what if your boy's gone rogue and robbed the post office, what then"?

"Then *I* take him in. I'll give him to you once I find out what he's up to, *alright*"?

The Beadle nodded and they began to trudge grimly toward Hvit Håpløshet and at least one answer.

"Hodd"? D'nab asked over the howling wind.

"Yes"?

"We're going to take him in alive aren't we"?

"Of course, I've stun level needles in my rifle, level one. Have you just thought it might be Bolet"?

"It could be I suppose, after all we don't know where he is, he should have gone to work this morning. He was always a bit, well, you know defiant. I'm hoping he's gone looking for his rifle or perhaps his road-trike and unlike us gone in the wrong direction".

"Why wouldn't have pinged you, let you know what was happening"?

D'nab's confidence seemed to be dissolving by the second, he shrugged his huge shoulders and admitted,

"I've been very strict with him. Had to be, as his only parent. He might not dare tell me his rifle was missing, or…….".

"Or he did the robbery"?

D'nab nodded, "Or it was him, yes. We had a real bust up night before last, he owed some money for gambling debts and wanted me to bail him out and I wouldn't".

"So he might just have come to the conclusion that the bonds at the post office were a solution for his quandary"?

D'nab nodded again, "He said he'd get the money some way himself. We nearly came to blows, it was the worst argument we'd ever had".

"Let me guess", Brownsword concluded, "You've not really had civil words since"?

"That's about the size of it, yes. Look; up ahead the Hvit Håpløshet station".

"Well we've got to get some shelter in case he opens up with that blaster of his, you edge around that drift to our left, I'll approach from the front".

"You'll be right in his line of fire if he decides to fire"!

"That's right", the Beadle agreed solemnly, "But that's my job Hodd, now go before I decide to change my mind and swap us around".

"You're going to shoot him aren't you"?

"Level one, Nash, and it's better than him shooting me, now go".

D'nab rushed away as fast as his snow shoes allowed him. Brownsword was just waiting for him to get the meagre cover when a blaster going off sounded and the Beadle dived to his right. He heard the sound of hissing snow and ice as it boiled away. The frigidity of the pole soon took it back down to water though and it would soon be ice again. Had the blaster hit the Beadle's flesh, it would not have been so self repairing.

"Hodd"! D'nab shouted, "We ought to go and get more help, we aught to return to Thyles Matis".

"No"! the Beadle decided, "He'll get away, I'm going in cover me".

Before Brownsword could regain his feet however D'nab shouted and jumped to his feet,

"Bolet, it's your father! Come out and we'll sort this, no one's died yet, don't make it worse than it already is".

There was another blast from the hut and D'nab was thrown from his feet. The Beadle rushed forward while the shooter's attention was on his new target and made it to the front of the hut. He instinctively crouched low and another blast tore part of the wall away just above his shoulder. Up and firing in one swiftly continuous motion, Brownsword heard the grunt of the enshrouded figure within; heard him collapse. The needle had done it's work.

The first thing he did was not to check the identity of the runaway however, but to call after D'nab. His huge figure climbed to his feet and strode slowly toward the station. He held his injured left arm steady with his right. The cold had already frozen the blood on his sleeve.There was an interminable few seconds while the two men just looked into each other's eyes, neither speaking, asking nothing of the other. The only sound was the shrill keening of the ever gusting wind.

Then D'nab seemed to make a decision for the both of then, his eyes closed and he nodded his head. Hoddington Brownsword turned and went slowly into the dimness of Hvit Håpløshet. He looked slowly down allowing his eyes to properly adjust, he was still looking at the back of the fallen youth's neck when footsteps proclaimed the arrival of D'nab in the cabin too.

"He's not dead is he"? he asked the Beadle. "I don't think he recognised my voice what with the sound of the wind and this snow blanketing everything otherwise he would not have……..".

"Nash, it isn't Bolet"!

"Are you certain", the injured foreman stared into the dimness, his eyes already dulled with pain.

"I'm as certain as anyone could be, Nash. This kid isn't even Caucasian"!

"But if it isn't Bolet then where can he be"?

"Who knows? After the bust up he might not have felt like telling you about his girlfriend; yes the one you don't know about. Or he might be down at the pool hall or gambling, or looking for his rifle. We'll find out when we get back to Thyles Matis".

Brownsword took some nyloplanyon wraps from his uniform and tied the youth's wrists together.

"I'll have to drag him, you see to it that arm doesn't bleed to much. Do you want to stay here and wait for me to send someone out for you or are you able to walk with me"?

"If you don't trot and you've got the pack and that kid to drag, I think I can keep up with you, Hodd", D'nab grinned despite his pain.

"You and I will walk back together, the foreman and the Beadle of Thyles Matis".

---------------------- fin ----------------------

CRADLE OF LIFE

He would hope that, left to itself, the slight spark of life which he had communicated would fade ;that this thing, which had received such imperfect animation, would subside into dead matter; and he might sleep in the belief that the silence of the grave would quench for ever the transient existence of the hideous corpse which he had looked upon as the cradle of life. He sleeps ; but he is awakened ; he opens his eyes ; behold the horrid thing stands at his bedside, opening his curtains, and looking on him with yellow, watery, but speculative eyes.

Mary Shelley.

ONE

HEPPENDINE STAX WAS seated behind the most ostentatious desk of genuine real Earth wood in his equally opulent office. He was a wealthy man. Indeed he was a very wealthy man. More to the point Stax had so much accrued riches that he did not even know how much he was worth himself. None of Stax vast value had been inherited either, all he had, he had gathered and meticulously hoarded by the drive and strength of his own endeavours. He was the managing director of several powerful companies on the corporation driven Earth, he had a place on the board of over ten more and he owned fifty one percent of several more. All that and he was only ninety seven years old.

At the tender age of eighty six his heart had given out, but he was promptly fitted with the best mechanoid nuclear powered replacement and deciding to maybe take things a little easier had emigrated to Mars, for the sake of the lighter gravity. His entire family had emigrated with him. They had dared do nothing else, he was not immortal and one day, after his demise, the will would only remain favourable to the faithful. Such was his reputation that he was invited to become a member of Mars Elite Club.

The Elite Club had met on a monthly basis for a few years and had consisted of the five most influential men on the red planet. One had finally died however, while another had been one of the pioneers to settle Venus and the remaining three were looking for equally lofty replacements. Stax fit the bill to a tee and joining, he completed a quartet with no lesser luminaries than; Grandios Vul

Grande - Soil Man of Mars; Lord Aubrey Saint John Willow - of Yorkshire; and Chief Constable Heiter Starhoven - Mars Constabulary.

Stax had met the other three members of the Elite Quartet on three occasions and found he looked forward to their monthly gathering with mounting pleasure as time went by.

Seated behind his desk Stax poured himself a white port (of the very finest quality) and smoked one of his 1in2 cigars, those illegal mixture of fine Cuban tobacco and Snufz one of the most controversial substances mankind had ever witnessed. The combination of the two was sending him into a state of self hypnosis and meditation, when the pad on the shining surface of his desk pinged, abruptly fracturing his aberrations.

"Sorry to disturb you, H.S." his P.A. apologised, "But there's a young man out in the outer office here and he is most insistent upon seeing you"?

"Does he have an appointment"?

"Actually no, sir, as I know you'll be aware, for we went through your diary for today but an hour ago, didn't we"?

Stax gazed at his favourite canvas losing himself for the moment in it's intricate patterns and colours before returning dreamily,

"Send him away then, no appointment is what, Ston"?

"No appointment, is no appointment, H.S".

The pad went dull and Stax returned to his cigar. He glanced about his office with an appreciative scrutiny at the wonderful things contained there in. In addition to the array of canvas', were some first edition books of not inconsiderable value, two Mazioki violins (although he could not play himself), one of the daggers used to assassinate Julius Caesar (genuine) and two nails from the cross of the Jewish prophet's crucifixion (not genuine but priceless). The contents of that very room was therefore beyond calculation.

Suddenly rudely interrupting his self congratulatory reverie, the exquisitely panelled door burst open and a young man blustered in, Ston hanging futilely around his neck in an attempt to dissuade him in his current course.

"What is the meaning of this"? Stax asked quite calmly, he rarely lost his temper, since his heart replacement.

"Ston call security at once".

"Give me a few seconds to explain please", the intruder begged, "I've tried to make appointments with you and been frustrated at every turn".

"Just a minute then Ston", Stax was intrigued, "Let's see what this young rapscallion has to say for himself"?

"Sir", began the youth, straightening his clothing that the scuffle had made a-rye, "I am Naros Vatin".

"Ah", Stax recognised the name. "The Naros Vatin who claims to be a suitable suitor for one of my grandchildren, Marionna Stubbsinge if I'm not mistaken"?

"Yes, sir, I am in love with Marionna and she reciprocates my feelings in full".

Marionna was the daughter of Stax' own daughter who had married his solicitor's son some years previously, they had produced two children and she was the female of that union.

"I deduce that you have come to request her hand in contract, which is only obtainable with my consent. Well you know the answer to that, Vatin, so good day to you young man".

"Why is your reply in the negative sir, when I'm sure your granddaughter has told you of our commitment to one another"?

"How much does your freight company gross per month, Vatin"?

The enquiry took the young man by surprise, but after a few seconds he estimated,

"Three thousand shillin sir, but why….."?

"And after tax, insurance and other overheads what do you clear"?

"I would hazard to guess around a third of that, when all overheads are paid".

"One thousand and that would mean two fifty per week then. Do you expect the granddaughter of **Staxovstok**, the heir to countless wealth to live on such a paltry sum while she waits to receive her inheritance"?

"Two hundred and fifty shillin per week is far more than many happily do Sir", Vatin debated, "And Marionna would happily be one of them if you gave us your blessing for a union".

"Well I do no such thing", Stax was able to say with a certain sadistic satisfaction. "So that concludes our business; permanently young man, you may leave and goodbye".

Vatin did not leave however instead he asked, "I ask you to reconsider, sir? Come and see my freight business and then decide if it has the expansion potential I know to be the case. Why we could even end up business partners"?

Stax had no delusions that it would impress him, but the mention of the magic word business sent a tingle down his limbs and he entertained the notion of absorbing this young popinjay's business into his own vast empire. So he replied,

"Very well, Vatin, I will do that, make me an appointment with Ston here and I will see you then, now good day to you".

TWO

"IT'S WELL ORGANISED", Stax agreed having seen all that Vatin had to show him. "And your housekeeping's in good order, Vatin, your pad records similarly so, however".

"However Sir"?

"However, the entire operation is too small, you need to expand or you'll be taken over by one of the larger concerns. If you continue to grow, I'll regard your proposal once more in five years time".

"Five years"! It seemed like a lifetime to a youth who was smitten with a comely young wench, "Sir, that is too long".

"Then I offer one other choice", Stax began a steely glint in his avaricious eyes, "A takeover. Amongst my concerns is a freight business too, ***Frontier***, agree to a merger with the sale of fifty one percent of your stock to me and I will look at your request again".

"You want to buy me out"?! Vatin was alarmed rather than delighted, "But I've put nearly nineteen hours a day into the building of ***Vatintransit***, and if I agreed you would control all major decisions from the sale onward".

"Of course, I know this", Stax smiled mirthlessly, "That is my offer, Vatin, take it or leave it"?

A voice suddenly cried out from above them on the warehouse's mezzanine, "It's going *look out below*"!

Stax had not the reactions nor the agility of Vatin and he froze, but the young man dived toward him and the two of them fell to their left. The crate;

the banding of which had snapped as the forked lifter had disturbed it, crashed downward and almost missed them both.

Almost.

Not quite, the metallized corner caught Stax a glancing blow at the side of his temple. With it's velocity and mass it was enough to be later described as a *'tragic and freak accident'* Vatintransit being exonerated of any blame in the death of the business magnate!

Not that Stax possessed the where-with-all to be aware of any of this, for he was stone dead and for an indeterminate period he knew nothing but total sable, nigresense.

THREE

S TAX SUDDENLY FOUND he had the ability to think. All was still devoid totally, of light, but he was self aware.

'This is very disconcerting', his first reflection was, *'Where by Lucifer's singed tail am I'*?

There was little chance of an answer, he was therefore astonished when he did in fact receive one,

"You are in limbo, Heppendine, do not become alarmed, I am here to explain what is happening"?

"I'm not alarmed", the magnate replied and his voice sounded strangely in his ears, *"But I am disconcerted. Why am I in limbo, what has happened"*?

"This will take some getting used to, but you were killed by the crate that struck you, you are dead"

Stax considered this for a few seconds and then asked, *"So why limbo, am I on the way to the great reward, if there is such a thing"*?

"You are in a waiting zone while I decide where I am going to make your next stop. Are you not curious as to my identity"?

"I suspect you're either an angel or a demon"?

The other made a wheezing sound of amusement, an alien chuckle, *"No, Heppendine I am a Viriligan"*.

Stax had heard the use of such a nomenclature; he dredged his memory and came up with the right one first time,

"*Those huge green reptiles that we've seen images of, on the tri-vid. You're one of those from Proxima Prime*"?

"*Nyjord*", the Viriligan corrected, "*We prefer General Darn's name given to the world and yes I am one such creature. I have the capability of traversing vast distances of space with my mind alone. I also possess the aptitude to place your mind into the body of another creature, a second existence if you will, a reincarnation*".

"*I don't want to be reincarnated*", Stax complained, "*I want to be reanimated. If you make it that the accident did not prove fatal for me I will make you wealthy*".

"*I am already wealthy*", came the response, "*Oh, I may not have the lucrative collection of items that you possess, but I have something far more precious*".

"*Oh yes*", the magnate returned, "*And what might that be....Viriligan*"?

"*Karma*"!

"*The cosmic principle, according to which each person is rewarded or punished in one incarnation according to that person's deeds in the previous incarnation. You have existed before in another form*"?

"*Indeed and before we go any further you had best give me a name, it will make our tour easier*".

"*Tour, what are you talking about*".

"*The name first Heppendine*".

Stax considered, something short and to the point he thought and decided, "*Very well as you are, so shall you be named; Frank*"!

"*Frank it is then Heppendine. So let me explain what is going to happen next. I have to decide whether to reincarnate you into the body of one of my fellow herd, that would be if you passed the dissertations by the highest grade, or....*"

"*Dissertation? A lengthy, formal treatise, supplied by whom*"?

"*Why your friends, or family or business associates of course. You did not let me finish however. If you fail to come in at superior grade and only register average, then you will be placed into a Hăprioarăăm*".

"*I don't want to be placed into anything*", Stax complained with futile inevitability, "*I want to return to Mars*".

"*I have not the power to recreate life I'm afraid Heppendine, that would be the working of one far more sophisticated than I. So let me get back to the point of how I am able to help you. If the comments of your peers and friends only record an intermediate level then you will be reincarnated into a Hăprioarăăm*".

"*What by Jupiter's impressive beard is one of those*"?

"*Think of it as a doe and you will not be far short of the general characteristics of the creature, it lives on Brahma. Unfortunately though placid and harmless it has the unenviable distinction of being the staple diet of the Usultragruli*".

"*That sounds fierce*"? Stax began to be interested despite himself, it did not look like Frank was going to bring him back to life.

The Usultragruli is a creature that would exist if a geneticist of Mars were to combine the DNA of a tiger with a brown bear, suffice to say it's a fierce-some carnivore. Finally we come to the third possibility, that you will record a series of poor testimonials, in which case you will be reincarnated into the Nyjordic Slime-worm".

"Stop right there"! Stax demanded, *"I don't want to know about a slime-worm, I don't want to know what it eats, or what eats it, I'm 'not' going to record poor testimonials"*

Well Heppendine, only observation will reveal whether that expectation is optimistic or not so let's go".

Before Stax could utter another word in the inky blackness of limbo, light appeared and it was pink and they were on Mars. Stax felt no cold, not the warmth of the sun either, it was as though he was standing in a huge tri-vid presentation, as though he was one of the principal players. Indeed he was a principal player in a far more important play, the subject of which was his effect on others and the fate it would thus decide for him.

"Can I buy a superior grade reincarnation and cease with this rather facile charade"? He asked and his voice was at least returned to what he perceived as normal.

"Your wealth is worthless Heppendine", came the response, "Even if I had a use for it, which I don't, you no longer have access to it, in fact you're totally bereft of funds now".

Stax gazed at the source of the reply, the voice came from a young woman! She was of average height, slim, lithe in fact and had not displeasing features. Her hair was an average sort of brown, but curly and at her shoulders, her eyes were brown too and possessing of wisdom.

"You did not tell me you were female"! the former owner of great wealth gasped.

"As a Viriligan I am neither and both male and female, it's difficult to explain. The presentation you see before you now is the person I was before my fatal flitter accident. It's convenient while we converse among your acquaintances and family".

"I think perhaps I'd better give you a more suitable name, or will you tell me what your name was before you died"?

"It was a long time ago much has happened since then, I chose to forget my human name, Heppendine".

"Then I must call you Francis".

"Francis, Frank, it makes no difference, Heppendine, the important stuff starts now. I must begin your assessment, whom would you have me start"?

Stax began to seriously consider just what was indeed happening to him. He was dead, that much was certain. The important thing now was to have

Francis witness superior grade testimonials from his colleagues and friends so that his reincarnation would not turn out to be a living hell.

"I would have to name my banker, Warren Leafhound then. He manages my accounts. If he wasn't impressed by what I had accrued then I don't know who would be".

"Then we shall see", Francis reflected. "Don't be alarmed at the shift of position on this world it will not take long and don't try and converse with the living, it's not possible, they can neither see nor hear us. We on the other hand can hear what they have to say, especially about you".

Before Stax could ask anything a dizziness gripped him, the plain they were standing upon shimmered and vanished and the interior of Protorutus bank swam into focus. Two older and stately looking men were in the manager's office in conversation. One was dressed in all black, the other, shorter and bald, in browns and greens.

"Ah", Stax recognised the duo at once, "Leafhound and Stubbsinge, my solicitor and the father of my son-in-law".

"Let's listen to what they have to say then", Francis suggested firmly.

"….the news on the net regarding the crew of the Искатель-Seeker who have successfully landed on Hyderabad. Calling the landing site Samara"? Leafhound was asking his associate.

"Yes", Stubbsinge agreed, "Rather surprising considering how long they were missing. No doubt an explanation will be forthcoming in subsequent transmissions".

"I wonder if they will encounter the Viriligan", the banker seemed fascinated by the prospect.

"I suspect the Viriligan will play their part in the Iskatel-Seeker's drama", the solicitor agreed, as he sipped his lichen-wine. "I've mainly come to ask you about Stax' accounts today though Warren, have you a rough idea how much the grizzled old boar was worth"?

"Hard to put an exact figure on it", Leafhound admitted, "His stocks and shares change value slightly on an almost hourly basis, but an approximate estimation would be in the region of half a million gold shillin. Not that the family will be waiting for it, he's provided for them quite comfortably, so the reading of the will is not desperately urgent".

"You see"! Stax observed to Francis, "I provided for my family, that makes me superior level for sure"! The girl hushed him with a finger to her attractive lips.

"Not at all", Stubbsinge agreed, "In fact most of them will be relieved the old goat's gone"!

"What"! Stax gasped.

"Yes", Leafhound confirmed, "Old Heppendine knew how to accrue wealth, but when it came to personal relationships he was a pauper".

"A grasping old blackguard I'd have said", the solicitor added, "He never cared who he had to trample, how many lives he had to ruin to get what he wanted and to gain monetarily, I'm certain you're right Warren, it's a relief he's not around any more. I certainly won't miss him".

"The ungrateful little twerp"! Stax expostulated, "I made his firm what it is today and let his son have my daughter's hand in marriage and that's what he thought of me as a result! I'd have expected better from Leafhound too, the bank was a tuppenny ha'penny outfit before my account went into it".

"I think that makes your current rating substandard, Heppendine", the Viriligan/Girl observed sadly, "Where too next"?

"Losaplin. Jolin Losaplin my old friend of many years and bridge partner". Stax decided and no sooner had he pronounced the words than the bank vanished and an opulent hotel room swam into focus. Seated together were three men, all of mature years, all dressed in expensive finery that proclaimed their obvious good fortune and wealth.

"That's Jolin, seated in the chair", Stax explained. "The other two are our bridge opposition and team. The industrialist Dublimo Dak and his business partner Skel Tiledrago".

"Listen to them then and see if they exonerate your reputation Heppendine", the female figure suggested.

"No bridge tonight then chaps until we find a new fourth hand", Dak was saying.

"A shame", Tiledrago added, "But at least we won't lose any money tonight, Dub".

"That's true the number of times we won two games, only for Jolin here and Hepp to get more points in the third and take the rubber", Dak observed.

"There was a reason why we were so lucky", Losaplin confessed guiltily then, Stax was cheating, dealing from the bottom of the deck, I'm surprised you never noticed it. I intend to give you back every sestersius you lost".

"Ah, Jolin, we knew he was doing it", Tiledrago told the surprised partner then, "But who argues with someone as powerful as Stax".

"And the old rascal always insisted we play for money", Dak chuckled.

"Yes", Tiledrago agreed, "All that money and he still wanted more, was prepared to cheat his friends to get it. How pathetic does that make him"?

"I've calculated the amount I owe each of you and am going to make bankers drafts to the correct sum", Losaplin informed them, "As to what Stax has taken, well, you won't be seeing that again will you"?

"He was a pathetic piece of lichen to do that to us month after month wasn't he"? Tiledrago persisted.

"Yes and we the only friends he had. Still rumour has it he's good to his family at least. It's all water under the *bridge* so to speak". Dak punned and the other two laughed along

Francis turned to the stunned Stax,

"A greedy grasping cheat", she said, "I'm afraid your level is just about as low as any that have been assessed Heppendine. I hope your family can raise it a little"?

"They will", Stax promised with chagrin, "The family all loved me, you'll see". His confidence was beginning to be shaken however and he asked desperately,

"Do many of those you select end up as slime-worms, Francis"?

"I cannot give you an honest answer to that Heppendine, because I do not know".

"Do you know if everyone who dies on Mars is now subject to this scrutiny and resultant reincarnation"?

"We choose those who interest us for one reason or another".

"And for those not chosen, what is their destiny, their fate"?

"You seek the age old answer for mankind now", Francis noted, "Even if I had that I would not give it you, there are some things that are best remained unanswered and unanswerable".

"I ask for a reason, perhaps oblivion is better than being a slime-worm, perhaps better than being a Hăprioarăăm or even a Viriligan".

"I would not know, I do know the simple joys of being the latter, but I'm not allowed to tell you what they are".

"Not allowed by whom"?

"The herd for one, the cosmic balance for another".

"Is not the latter nothing more than an abstract concept". Stax had grown introspective.

Francis smiled, "I think it's time we were on our way Heppendine, come, a chance to see your family one last time".

The friends and the hotel shimmered and swam into nothingness and Stax found himself in the living room of his rather magnificent home on Mars. Seated in the company of his wife was the wife of Leafhound. They were animated and in conversation, Missus Leafhound was asking,

"So you are widowed Palmer, how are you getting on with that, do you miss Heppendine"?

"I am constantly aware of his absence", Palmer Stax admitted, eyeing a slim Easter island tall head wood carving on her occasional table, "His presence is in many of these magnificent items he acquired over the years. Do I miss his living presence though, no I don't"!

Missus Leafhound nodded, "Heppendine was not an easy man to get along with but you must have loved him, after all you married him".

Palmer nodded, "Yes I loved him once", she admitted, "He was dynamic, ambitious and dashing in his youth, admirable qualities in a suitor. He changed gradually though, he became avaricious, obsessed and he brooked no defiance from anyone, including me. In the end the only way we could get along was when I did everything he wanted. I'm sorry he is dead, but I shall become a merry widow".

"What will you do"?

"I will travel. Firstly I want to see the swiftly growing cities on Mars. The new and magnificent architecture that is springing up at Schiaparelli, Lowell and Olympus Mons. I hear the royal palace of King Rövalaát's of South Mars is magnificent and that of King Iyhyt's of North Mars will be every bit it's equal or maybe even better when it's completed. Once I have seen as much of this world as anyone I will go back to Earth and visit the capitals there. The new palaces of the American kingdoms will be particularly worthy of interest".

"That sounds like a simply marvellous plan, but one that you can only realise because of Heppendine's money", Leafhound pointed out.

"You're right of course" Stax was relieved to here his wife admit, "He was certainly not a bad man, just too driven in the end and yes I will miss his humour and his arrogance, it caused me to laugh many-a-time".

"Amusing arrogance", the Viriligan noted, "That's not exactly upper level recommendation, but it's slight improvement".

"So I've made Usultragruli meat, how comforting", Stax was not cheered.

"I never said that", Francis noted, "Have we done Heppendine or is there more, what about the granddaughter that wanted to marry"?

"Marionna"! Stax brightened, "Of course, my favourite member of the family, my loving granddaughter. Yes we must see if she gives me a worthy testimonial"

"Very well Heppendine", the Viriligan agreed, "But then we will be done, I have no desire to hear more from those who knew you, my enthusiasm is spent".

Thinking of all his rivals in business and what they would say about him, Stax admitted bleakly,

There is no one else, Francis, Marionna is my last hope and if my last hope fails my fate will not be a pleasant one will it"?

"That's something you waited too long to think about Heppendine", the Viriligan pointed out, "Remember I mentioned the cosmic balance, the balance has a way of equalising all that happens in the galaxy".

As she told him this the room that he had spent so long creating and was now of no use to him rippled and slowly dissolved to nothingness and it was gradually replaced, as a much more humble dwelling swam into focus.

Heppendine knew before he even turned and saw who was facing his granddaughter that the property belonged to Naros Vatin.

"We seemed to have come full circle", the magnate said as he glanced about the place, he was getting quite philosophical due to his recent experiences, "I cannot honestly expect the young man in question to have much of a good word for me".

Francis merely smiled and looked keenly at the young couple.

Stax for his part was surprised to see some rather good canvases on the walls of the lounge, "I wonder where he got them"? he said to Francis, not expecting an answer, but the Viriligan told him at once, "If you mean where he bought them then the answer is nowhere, he painted them himself, they are his own work"?

Stax looked at them again, keenly and despite himself heard him say to Francis, "They are actually very good and the brushwork indicates a rather gentle touch and pure spirit".

"Maybe it's a shame you could not have gotten to know him better", Francis observed and then both their attention was taken by the conversation taking place.

"It seems sort of ironic that something tragic had to happen, in order for us to be together, Mari".

"You think grandfather's death tragic", Marionna replied.

"That's a pretty awful question", Vatin gasped, Of course it was a terrible tragic accident! How can it be described otherwise"?

"He was not exactly kind to you", Marionna noted, "And he made mother's life miserable at times, when she was alive".

"Miserable how so"?

"His rigid ways, the restrictions he imposed on her".

"And yet he sanctioned 'her' marriage, to your father and the happy result was you darling". He went over and took her gently in his arms and kissed her on the forehead.

"As to his attitude toward me, he was protective toward you sweetheart and I sensed he was beginning to warm to me the longer we were together. It was a terrible shame that banding snapped when it did, I tried to save him, but I was too clumsy".

"Yes, right", the young woman made the scornful affirmative sound like she did not believe it for a second.

"Marionna"! he was aghast, "You do believe it *was* an accident don't you"?!

"It came at a rather convenient moment", she told him suddenly serious.

"Marionna if you think there's even the slightest possibility that I'm a murderer, then leave now and never try to see me ever again"!

"Okay", the young woman was suddenly placating, "I believe you when you say it wasn't planned, Naros. I'm sorry I even entertained the notion. You know grandfather was not a popular person though, any one of a number of people would have acted in a very different way".

"I saw his good qualities", Vatin returned. "He provided for everyone dear to him and protected them in a way that he believed was right. His success in business was a positive quality, who wants to fail in their financial endeavours. I wish he were still alive to happily consent to our contracting".

The scene faded and Stax found that for the first time in his existence he was at a loss for something to say. He had finally found an ally in the least expected of places and it moved him greatly.

"Well", noted Francis quietly, "A testimonial from someone you barely new carries a very high tariff Heppendine. I'm pleased to tell you that it has; at the eleventh hour raised your level to superior, congratulations".

"I am going into the head of a huge green reptilian creature that has six legs and twin tails", the magnate asked.

Francis nodded, "You will graze in the grasses of Nyjord and learn the mental disciplines of telepathy and teleportation and if you prove a good student, a great student, one day you will be the one who sees if one of the newly deceased deserves reincarnation".

"I'm ready then", he agreed and meant it, "In fact it will be the beginning of another great adventure. I just have one last question before I say goodbye to you"?

Francis smiled her knowing smile and duty fully asked him, "And what might that be Heppendine"?

"The obvious one of course, I've seen the images transmitted from the far away planet. The tri-vid of the Viriligan and their most shocking characteristic by far is the fact that they possess two necks and two heads on the end of them. So what I want to know is, when I go to my new body, who will be in the other head, who will I be spending my second existence with"?

Francis broke into a huge grin and her reply was, "Can't you guess"?

------------------- fin -------------------

THE MULE

Mind heals all sickness, Mind Reforms,
Mind makes the sinner free,
Mind bursts the bonds of false belief,
Mind melts mortality

Willis Vernon Cole

ONE

THE NAME OF the hospital was Yorkshire General, it nestled in the heart of that county in the country, the Empire of which, was the greatest on Earth. As such it boasted the very best nurses and the most skilled and compassionate doctors. It was a bustling busy place always throbbing with the tide of human flesh that burst through it's doors twenty four hours a day.

Doctor Phin had not slept for twenty straight hours and he was just considering going off duty when Lessie Portmantle was rushed into A.& E. There had been an emergency call from the Yorkshire Regal Hotel, the young woman had taken an overdose of blue Lubies. The tranquilliser when administered in sufficient dosage could be fatal and the bottle found beside Portmantle's bed had been empty. The good doctor began to pump out her stomach and also had the where-with-all to call security. Once out of danger, the young woman would have to be guarded until the Psych department had a chance to evaluate her state of mind.

Phin walked down the albescent corridor on his way to the locker room, exhaustion gripping every muscle and sinew in his body. Should he actually attempt to return to his apartment on his road-trike, tired as he was? Or would it be better to simply go to the bunks supplied for such doctors and get several hours sleep; before journeying home for a shower, clean clothes and a good hot meal? As he was debating this, the tall muscular figure of Spencer Tasker intercepted him,

"Trouble Doc"? his voice was a rich baritone, matching his appearance quite aptly.

"Not really trouble, if you mean my pinging for one of your men earlier", the good doctor replied, "Just a suicide attempt, came in about half an hour ago; needed someone to keep an eye on her for a while".

"Got it", Tasker noted, "I'll go down and check on things while she's in recovery. Say you look absolutely bushed, on your way home are you"?

"I was just debating if it was safe to ride, or if I'd be better trying to get some rest here. You know how it is though, if I stay someone will ping me and then I still won't have a change of clothes, a shower, or any food".

"And the traffic out there is mad today", Tasker added. "Say Doc, I owe you favours enough, I've an idea, why don't I get one of my team to take the handlebars, you get on the back"?

"And how's he going to get back here".

"I'll get an ambulance to swing past your place when it's in the right area, they shouldn't have to wait too long".

Phin stopped to consider it, "You do owe me a few favours".

"Yes I do, so let's be safe rather than sorry, eh Doc? I'll have someone at your road-trike in the basement by the time you drag your sorry ass down there".

"Thanks Spencer", the doctor agreed and despite his fatigue increased his pace. The last thing he wanted was someone to ping him whilst he was still in the building. He reached the western lift and thumbed the button for 'G' (ground floor). Dully watched it slowly descending from seven through six and so on till it rang and the metal doors slid open. No one was inside, great, he thumbed 'B' (lower-ground floor) and it set off in it's continued descent at once.

The doors opened and the frigid draught of the late autumn Yorkshire temperature flapped against his scrubs and caused him to shiver. Should he return for his riding suit? It would mean going back to the ground floor and the locker room? On the other hand the ride would only be fifteen minutes or so and the front rider would be shielding him from most of the draft. He could always get a shower to warm him through once he got home.

He decided not to risk going back and even put his pad on auto-answer, which would give and receive a reply message, without anyone knowing he was anywhere near it. He could see as he strode briskly down the dim concrete sub surface structure, the bowels of the hospital, that a figure was already at his trike. The light of the exit was behind the figure, throwing it into sharp relief and he noted that the security officer was female!

As he got closer he began to judge that it was not only a shapely female in riding leathers, but one with long flowing hair the colour of honey. She must have heard his footsteps for she turned and smiled in greeting asking,

"Doctor Phin"?

"That is I" Phin assented, "You're one of the new influx aren't you, I don't think we've met".

"This is my first month", the girl agreed, she really was lovely, "Name's Jentine".

"Surely you trust me with your first name Miss Jentine".

Her smile grew even broader and she grew even lovelier, "It's Flis and now you have the advantage over me, for I don't know your first name"?

"But you do", Phin chuckled, "My first name *is* Phin, most of the junior doctors use their former nomen, it's become something of a trend here at Y.G".

"Where's your coat or your riding gear"? she asked as they shook hands. He noted that her fingers were devoid of rings, but then that was always suggested by the hospital anyway.

"My leathers are in my locker. Had to make a quick getaway, but I've an old sheepskin jacket and my helmet in these two panniers".

"Let's go then, I'm on the clock, Tasker runs a tight ship".

Phin took his keys and unlocked each pannier to get at the indicated apparel. Then he climbed onto the saddle behind the already mounted girl. He took a firm grip on the pillion handles.

"They aren't as safe as putting your arms around my waist", she called through her helmet.

Phin did as directed and discovered that under the slim outline of the leathers there was a lithe muscular torso.

"Get in tighter", she called and he thought to himself *'delighted to oblige'* and grasped her firmly, pressing himself into her back. The trike roared up through the exit at around eighty point five k.p.h.something Phin would never dare do, but somehow he trusted the girl's skill and did not feel alarmed. Then they hit traffic and he began to feel the girl's warmth passing through to him and he actually fell asleep!

"Hoy, doctor, wake up, is this you"?

Phin looked groggily up, sure enough they were in Huntingdon, 3 Briar Drive. The apartment complex rose above them for twelve stories.

As they both climbed off the trike, Jentine asked, "I'm not going to have to carry you up there am I, which floor are you on"?

"I'll make it", he smiled, "You'd best come up for some tea while you wait for an ambulance, I'm only on the third floor".

"Lead the way then doctor doctoreye".

"What does that mean"? Pin asked.

"Nothing, just joking" the girl grinned as her helmet came off and her lovely hair cascaded over her quite wide shoulders.

They took the stairs as the lift was in use and Phin noticed how easily the girl vaulted them three at a time.

'Fit as well as decorative' the bachelor doctor noted mentally. He pressed his eye to the reader and the door clunked open, the lock was the newest of retinal scans type, totally secure in fact.

While he strode to the kitchen and thumbed the drink maker she began to take off her leathers, for the room was temperature controlled at a comfortable nineteen degrees. Phin stood in the doorway and watched the lithe Amazon strip off the suit.

"I suppose you're used to watching girls undress eh, doc"? she joked.

"Only when it's medically necessary", Phin smiled. "So what's your story Flis? What's a girl like you doing in security"?

"A girl like me"?

"You know one with other obvious attributes, why did you decide to enter a potentially dangerous occupation"?

She did not answer right away but was looking at his pride and joy instead a magnificently vintage sound system with a valve amplifier.

"I was into martial arts in my teens", she told him absently as she touched the smooth gold fascia of the amp. "Sort of had to look after myself when the boys began to tease me for my height".

She was tall at a hundred and eighty three centimetres, only just short of him by four centimetres.

"Is that actually stereo"? she wanted to know, looking at the cherry wood monitors in either corner of his room.

"We only have two ears", he told her, at the machine which promptly dispensed two waxed paper cups of hot beverage, "Do you want yours' sweetened"?

"Please; one. What do you listen to on it then, with your only two ears".

He handed her the then sweetened Yorkshire tea, "Sit down and I'll play you something". He turned on the stik player and amplifier.

"Thank you; there's no sound".

"You have to wait five minutes for the valves to warm up", he explained.

"Why not simply get yourself a three sixty point one unit surround sound"?

"The material I like was written for stereo reproduction", he told her, "You'll see in a short while".

"I'm keeping you up, you look all in".

"Once it's playing I'll go and have a shower, then I'm off to bed", he promised, "I can trust security to let themselves out and lock me in can't I"?

"Of course", she chirped, "And thanks for the hospitality, Doc".

Phin pressed a rather quaint arrow shaped button on the player and the soothing tones of Field's First Piano Concerto began to emit from the monitors.

"Oh, Doc, that's delightful, you may well convert me to ancient stereo", she admitted.

He went for a hot shower and when he came back the music was still playing but she had gone.

TWO

WHEN DR.PHIN AWOKE and glanced at the bedside chrono he saw he had slept nine hours straight. He pushed back the bedclothes and strolled into the room on the way to the kitchen, more than ready for some breakfast. There was a faint scent in there still, a mixture of toilet water and hair spray. It caused him to smile, he fancied that if Flis Jentine was not seeing anyone at the moment, he might well like to get to know her better. He hadn't asked for her Skype though and that faintly annoyed him.

While his breakfast was in the hyper-wave he activated his pad and keyed in the records of patient Lessie Portmantle. The lab report was completed and he was most curious to see what it revealed about the attempted suicide. He was instantly alert to some of the readings. Her blood had only the amount of *'Somnoease'* that indicated she had taken one tablet! What she did have though, in considerable quantity was Snufz!

The bottle had been empty, but it had been emptied to look like she had overdosed. He cast his mind back to the stomach contents, it had been unusually clean,but he had presumed at the time that most of the sleeping tablets had been absorbed into her system and so had given her an injection of stims and left it at that. After all, when he had left her, pulse and blood pressure readings over her cot had been quite normal, even though she had not woken up.

She had never been asleep though!

It was all some sort of charade! The chance of her being comatose on one Somnoease' was next to zero.

Why had she submitted herself to a rough stomach pumping and stayed in an apparent coma? Phin was intrigued.

He pinged the hospital and asked for security, Tasker's image swam onto his mini screen,

"Hey, Doc, you look much better", the security man observed.

"Thank you, I feel much better", Phin reiterated, "Listen Spencer, is that patient Portmantle still under guard"?

"Yes, sir, she hasn't moved all day".

"Good, keep a close eye on her for me till I get back there, I want to have a word with her"!

He was distracted then for a second, by one of the brand new air flitters passing his third floor window. It was a beautiful shade of orange and had sleek fairing of chromed flashes on it's wing bumpers. Phin wandered how long it would have to be before some sort of floating markers were used to indicate lanes. Otherwise an air crash was going to seriously increase his workload.

The air flitter was just cruising around and he guessed a potential customer was giving it a test flight, there was also argument as to whether an ordinary hover flitter license would be sufficient to allow someone to cruise at eleven metres from the ground and it wouldn't be long before the Japanese giants would come up with an air flitter that could cruise considerably higher.

When the badge of the air flitter caught his eye however he was surprised to see it was a Craiova, the resurrected Romanian car industry was now expanding into flitters and air flitters and it looked as if they would beat the Japanese, Czech, and German companies to the punch.

Deciding to leave shortly Phin just pinged the net news before he set off for another shift, the length of which he could only guess. The Indian-Scandian war had ended and a peace treaty signed the day before. King Darren II had proclaimed it a great day for celebrating peace on not only the sub continent of India and the continent of North Europe, but all over the world. Austazealand had been swift in their response to their monarch and the Prime Minister had added her wish for the same.

On a graver note Zulushire had warned Swaziland that further incursions into their eastern borders would result in an extreme response. While in the far east the 'police action' of the Komsomolosk Army had resulted in the shooting of several Wakkanai rebels who were intent upon passing themselves off as immigrants.

'So', thought Phin, 'It's business as usual, with good and bad news; let's get to work'!

He used his spare helmet and the coat of the day before and beat the traffic by going in early, although even at that early time the roads were beginning to clog, perhaps the new cash incentives to resettle Venus would help a little, the truth was there was just not enough room on planet earth for twelve billion people.

Phin had considered the thought of the twin to Earth himself, the plague was over and the few Biotrons were now desperate for human companionship as the Venuser seemed very dour and naive. He was not sure if he could stand the long nights and days however, day after day of darkness seemed particularly miserable to him.

'Anyway, I am happy at Y.G.', he thought in conclusion and then reached the hospital itself. This time he made it to his locker and took out a fresh set of scrubs, then he went to his pad to find out where Lessie Portmantle had been warded. He was on a mission, determined to get to the bottom of her little mystery.

THREE

"MISS PORTMANTLE, OUR records of you are somewhat sketchy, would you be gracious enough to tell me what happened yesterday"? He asked her, when he had travelled to her ward.

"I got into York a couple of days, from Preston, looking for a job", she responded, "I've no friends nor family here in Yorkshire, I can't understand what happened, you say I was found by room service".

"Yes", Phin confirmed, "Seemingly unconscious".

"What in tar do you mean by *seemingly*, I never called for an ambulance you know, I'm not here by choice. Do you have the authority to start questioning me".

"Stop the nonsense", Dr. Phin said coldly and evenly. "While you're here and I'm your attending I have every right to ask you whatever I think pertinent to your case"?

"And I have every right to refuse to answer", the girl replied defiantly and contrarily.

"I'm looking at your results Miss Portmantle and you only have sufficient sleeping drug in your system to induce a light sleep, you didn't overdose did you"?

"I was depressed and couldn't sleep, now you're putting me on the spot I can't remember how many pills I took or didn't take. I'll be on my way then; if you don't mind"?

"I'd like you to stay overnight for observation", Phin decided then, "If you did only take one pill and had a reaction I need to discover why and what caused your unconsciousness, I have to be thorough, will you stay another day"?

"If that's what you recommend, sorry for being snappy earlier".

"That's understandable under the circumstances, you rest and I'll drop in to see you later".

He went to seek out security officer Jentine for more than one reason.

FOUR

"**I** CAN'T UNDERSTAND her attitude, she's defensive and secretive" he told the striking figure of his new acquaintance.

"She's up to something, I'll talk to her in a little while, she'll give herself away and then I'll let you know".

"I'll put you in my pad, then Flis. Oh and just in case, can I have your home e-mail do you think"?

The attractive girl smiled, "Why Doctor you're not thinking of fraternising with the non medical staff are you"?

Phin flushed but proceeded, "If you'd like to go to dinner some time, it would be my pleasure to take you to a nice restaurant"?

"Are you asking me out Doctor"? She teased and waited while he squirmed, "Well when you send me an invite I'll give it consideration".

Her pad suddenly pinged and after reading it she became serious, "There's a Mister Portmantle in reception, Doc, asking to speak to his cousin's doctor".

"Will you accompany me to my office and sit in on the meeting please".

"Certainly, Doctor, lead the way".

Moments later they were ready to see what Mister Portmantle had to say,

At his secretary's permission the man entered the office. The duo did not know what they had been expecting, but Portmantle was not it.

He was dark and heavy, almost fat, with two days stubble on his chin and he had eyes that roved every inch of the office. If Phin could choose a single word that summed him up, it would be furtive!

"I've come to collect my cousin", he began without preamble, "She ran away from her parents house here in York and they're very worried about her".

"She told us that she wasn't local, Mister Portmantle. I'm sorry to have to tell you she's under observation until tomorrow at least", Phin told him.

"Well in that case I've a back pack for her with some clean clothes and toiletries in, may I give them to her"?

"Alright", Phin conceded, "But you can only stay for ten minutes, she's supposed to be resting, she had her stomach pumped last night and a shot of antipostat".

"Of course Doc, you're the boss".

When the man had gone Jentine was on her pad sending a message to the security officer outside her door,

"I'm not sure about her, nor his package, but I didn't think we had the right to go through it, my chap will keep an eye on them when it's handed over".

"*Your* chap"?

"Oh, didn't you know I'm Tasker's deputy and he's not in today, so I'm in command of security".

I'd better not keep you any longer then, thanks for keeping Portmantle under observation, if anything interesting transpires, please ping me".

"I will", she smiled, "I have your work and home mail addresses"!

FIVE

FOUR HOURS LATER Phin was busy and had almost forgotten about the mystery when his pad pinged.

"I'm in your office, Doc", the image of Jentine informed him on Skype, "I need to talk to you a.s.a.p".

"On my way", Phin was happy to be seeing the decorative security girl again. As he entered his office he asked,

"Is it about Portmantle".

Jentine nodded, "I did a check on that cousin of her's. No such cousin exists on record. Not only that but since his visit she's been happier and talkative with the nurses, a different person they tell me".

"Your man see anything change hands"?

"No but it could have been hidden in a seam of her clothes or anywhere really and he couldn't exactly stay in the room with her".

"So what is your deduction, Holmes"?

She smiled at the joke and then grew serious once more, "I reckon she's a *Snufzhead,* doc and that guy, he wasn't a family member, he was a mule".

There was a knock on the door, before Phin could react to the deduction, it opened and in strolled Orgo Nem, the hospital head dispensing chemist,

"Orgo"? Phin asked, "What're you doing here"?

"What do you mean, what am I doing here, I got your ping to come and see you", the chemist replied.

Phin was suddenly alarmed, "I didn't send for you. How many of there are you today"?

"I'm on my own till noon, but don't worry I locked the place up......."

Jentine was already out of the door as Phin told Nem, "The dispensary is on the same wing as a patient of mine who may be an addict, come on"!

They raced to follow the lithe and admirably swift security officer. The polished floor could be treacherous though and they had to move quickly but safely. When they finally caught Jentine it was to find the dispensary still locked.

"Whew thank goodness that was a false alarm", Orgo Nem gasped, fighting to regain his breath.

"I'm not convinced", Jentine told them then, "Open it up, Or....what was your name again"?

"Nem, Orgo Nem", the dispensing chemist told her as he fed the correct combination into the key-pad.

They hurried inside and he looked around, "Nothing seems out of place".

Phin breathed a sigh of relief but Jentine was still not satisfied, "What's in the locked cabinet over in the corner"?

"The heavy duty drugs, doctor's signature only", Nem supplied.

"Snufzmorph"? the girl asked.

"Among other things", Nem began to look nervous again.

"Open it up"! Jentine barked.

"Now just a minute......", Nem began.

"Open it Orgo, you'll get your signature the instant you hand me the pad", Phin told him.

They waited while Nem went through the process of feeding in yet another code to get the cabinet to open. Phin watched Jentine's finger's hovering over her pad,

The cabinet was totally empty!!

Phin's finger's danced on the pad and throughout the hospital a dull siren began to drone, "I've put the hospital on status:- Red", she told them, "We're locked down, no one gets in or out, till my men have searched everyone and everywhere".

Phin was impressed with the girl's efficiency considering that she was new, her training must have been very thorough.

"How much was in the cabinet Orgo"? he asked the chemist.

"Plenty, but how did she get in, there's three hundred shillin of Snufzmorph gone not counting the other stuff".

"Take a full audit", Jentine snapped, "Right this minute the hospital is under security supervision and command. Cut on the streets that stuff is worth much more, though it's not gone yet and it's not going to be".

She hurried out of the dispensary, no doubt to supervise the search, Phin returned,

"Do as she says Orgo", then he hurried after her.

"Are you going to ping the constables"? he asked the girl.

"Only when we've got them in our custody", Jentine promised, "The place is sealed now, Doc, the only way they can go is up. Good job code red locks all the windows too or a third member of the gang could have just picked anything or everything up off the street".

"You think there's a gang of them"?

She nodded as they rushed into the lift. Jentine hit the button for 'R' roof, she was no doubt playing a hunch, but Phin trusted her instincts implicitly. They waited, breath bated as the lift took them upward. It went to the very top of Y.G. and opened out onto the roof, which was flat.

"Get behind me, Doctor", Jentine instructed as she drew a needle gun.

"Miss Portmantle", Phin cried, "Please come out, the place is sealed up tight and security is armed, come out and we can talk peacefully"?

"Doctor Phin"! the girl cried desperately, "Be careful, he's got a gun"!

A figure jumped from behind a cowled vent, but the instant he appeared Jentine fired and he looked astonished and then crumpled to the surface of the roof, a blaster slipped from his nerveless fingers. Jentine went over and took the blaster away as Phin approached the girl.

"Thanks for the warning. Now come here, you're too close to the edge".

Jentine lifted a package, "The drugs are back in our possession", she told him with satisfaction.

But Phin was watching the girl and with a desperate fling, she left the roof, to plummet down toward the paved street below. He raced to the edge and looked down, Portmantle was spread eagled on the cold hard surface, a warm pool of red slowly growing around her shattered form.

"She was an addict", he said as he rose to his feet, "Probably not her fault, we should feel some sympathy for her".

Jentine grabbed the folds of the mule's clothing and began to drag him toward the lift, her sympathy was not so sensitive it seemed. Once they were back inside, the lift descending, she tie wrapped the still paralysed form of the cousin.

"He was in charge of her", she was almost thinking aloud, "The filthy pedlar won't have used the stuff himself, merely praying on and controlling the weak".

Phin nodded, "She didn't look much older than twenty maybe twenty two, her life was wrecked before she even began to properly live it. If she hadn't jumped, I could have helped her, there are drugs that......".

"Forget it Doc Phin", she stopped him, "It's the most insidious and unstoppable drug that there's ever been, she was doomed from the first moment she snorted her first hit".

The lift opened and two of her men took the pedlar, who was just beginning to stir.

"*Now* it's time to ping the constabulary", Jentine said.

SIX

THE CRAIOVA SLIPPED through the overcast Yorkshire air with powerful ease, Jentine leaned over the side, through her open window and stroked the smooth paintwork,

"Didn't you think of getting this repainted, Phin"?

"I like orange and anyway other air flitters will see it coming", he chuckled, "You seem to be getting over your fear of heights"?

"Well if there's an accident, at least a doctor will be instantly on the scene", she smiled.

"This doctor would like to be on the scene quite often in the future"? Phin chanced.

"Well I don't know", she laughed, "I mean you're a bit flash aren't you, Doctor. Dinner at a fancy restaurant and then on the second occasion a flight in your brand new flitter, you're trying too hard to turn a girl's head".

"Now wait a minute", he objected in mock indignation, "I thought you said dinner was just dinner, so that makes this only our first date".

"Not even that really, you invited me to a test drive is all".

"I've *bought* this"! He objected then, "Traded in my road-trike for it"!

"Oh yes, to avoid having to have any more lifts from poor old security officers", she laughed.

"Seriously though", he told her, "The traffic is getting so bad in the morning that I had to get up here to get to work on time".

"It's alright if you can afford it and have you a special licence, because if not I'll have to tie wrap you and interrogate you".

"In that case I unfortunately have to tell you that I do have one of those new air-fitter licences, but you can still tie wrap me any time you want".

She smirked and said, "Maybe I will, doctor, in the future, maybe I will".

VIRTUAL REALITY

re·al·i·ty (rē-ăl′ĭ-tē)
n. pl. re·al·i·ties

1. The quality or state of being actual or true.
2. One, such as a person, an entity, or an event, that is actual: "the weight of history and political realities" (Benno C. Schmidt, Jr.).
3. The totality of all things possessing actuality, existence, or essence.
4. That which exists objectively and in fact: Your observations do not seem to be about reality.

adj.

Relating to or being a genre of television or film in which a storyline is created by editing footage of people interacting or competing with one another in unscripted, unrehearsed situations.

Idiom:

in reality
In fact; actually.

Farlex Dictionary

ONE

"THIS NEXT PATIENT is a very sad case", Doctor Redring told his new understudy, "And the worst part of it is, it might not be the last we see with this peculiar psychosis".

"Oh, really", Doctor Bilton was intrigued, "With only such an, as yet, tiny population, Doctor"?

"It's the very conditions of Venus which are at the heart of the case", Redring replied as he unlocked the room, which was in fact, a very comfortable and furnished cell. It eased open and Redring went inside,

"Good morning, Home", he greeted the man - seated at a table, on a hard chair.

"Ah Ambassador, I'm glad you've come to see me", the patient, Home began, "We need to discuss my return to Yorkshire, the court will be missing me".

"It's his day for being king of a future country on Earth", Redring whispered to the younger psychiatrist, louder he replied, "Yes your majesty, unfortunately the formula you gave us for the fuel, has not proved to be successful".

"Then I must return to the real world and study this problem", Home sounded naturally disconcerted.

"The real world"? Bilton echoed.

"Yes", Home was deadly serious, "I know what you Tarvians believe but it's not true, *this* is a virtual reality world. I feel for you all truly I do and I'm certain you believe you're real. In fact, I guess you *'feel'* real, but you are the virtual race of Tarvia and only in the virtual universe do you actually continue to exist. Now though, I must return to reality and re-check my formula, good day to you; gentlemen".

With that, Home climbed to his feet and went over to a couch, he closed his eyes and said no more.

"What's he doing"? Bilton asked.

"He has gone into the real world", Redring told his understudy.

"I get it, he thinks that virtual reality is real and we are some sort of computer game", Bilton deduced, "But there's no hood, nor visor, how can simply sitting with his eyes closed take him to some sort of sound and graphics"?

"That's the psychotic part", Redring told the fellow practitioner of medicine, "He claims that he's no need of a hood nor any other equipment, because he's installed one into his own head. The supposed device then became the real existence, the real world a fantasy".

"And has his head been scanned, is there anything in there"?

"Some small pieces of metal and a lot of scarring", Redring informed, "It's as though there was a foreign object in there at one time and some clumsy surgeon removed it. Or when I say surgeon it might have been a butcher for the mess he left behind".

"Could he have used local and tried the removal himself"?

"Who knows? The point is the removal did not stop the fantasies, nor the belief that this world is the virtual world and the one he goes into, the real one. I don't even know which came first, did he have the device or what ever it was, removed because he suspected what was going on, or did he have it removed because he thought we would cease to plague him"?

"His real life must have been pretty unpleasant for him to become this psychotic", Bilton offered, "What does his family say about it all, doctor"?

"His wife has gone back to Earth and refuses to answer any of my pings", Redring returned, "And let's face it, the last person we are going to get an accurate account from is Rale Umberto Home".

"Rale Umberto Home", Bilton repeated, "Is that for real? I mean what where his parents thinking; R.U.Home"!

"Even more ironic when you consider his present condition", Redring observed, "Are you ready for a spot of lunch Doctor, before we look at the next patient"?

TWO

T HE SKY WAS as dark as an inkwell when Home came in, his clothes sodden. It was a usual Yorkshire August and the rain came and went and then came again. In Byron Avenue, Quenda Home was cooking her husband's evening meal, another culinary masterpiece, no doubt.

"You're dripping *all over* the hall carpet Rale", she scolded in the tone of voice that her husband found to be most piercing and very unpleasant.

"What can I do, it's pouring out there"? he attempted to defend himself. Mistake.

"I told you, take an umbrella, but oh, no! You don't listen to me, that's the trouble Rale, you never pay *attention*"!

"I pay attention about sixty percent of the time dear, but my span is unable to concentrate on the endless flow of diatribe that constantly *dribbles* from your mouth".

"Oh yes that's right", she began, "Start in on me when I've been slaving in this house for you all day. You are an ungrateful *beast* at times, Rale, ungrateful that's what you are"!

"So that's your day sweetness", Rale felt that a certain level of sarcasm was called for, "Thank you for asking how *I've* been".

"You call playing with toys all day work do you"?

"I'm an electronic engineer love of my life, I don't play with toys. I'll go and change before dinner, don't put it out until I'm back in the dining area, please"?

Rale flounced out the hall considering to have won that round.

When he got back down to the dining room however it was to be greeted by a cold dinner on the table, in his place. Grimly he did his best to hypo-wave his tea back to hot, eat it, before retreating to his man-cave. Once inside with the door bolted, he breathed a sigh of relief and went to this antiquated but useful computer tower.

On a table beside the electrical antique rested a headset with visor and headphones, Home placed the virtual reality helmet on his head and escaped from the real world for a couple of hours. Once tired of that he turned to his electronic bench and began work on his newest project, the miniaturisation of certain components. This involved several minutes at a stretch of backbreakingly bending over a huge magnifying glass and the use of tiny tweezers and the needle point of the smallest soldering iron that was manufactured at the time.

He could only work on his project for so long each evening, before the muscles in his back began to bunch and cramp and he knew it was time for bed. He trod warily down the stairs in his slippers, holding the handrail to lighten the load on the creaking stairs. The building was three hundred years old and the pine had been raw when the stairs had been built. The sap had dried out of the planking used, centuries past and beneath the underlay there was significant room for movement. The slightest noise would disturb his harridan of a wife and a fresh tirade of reproach would begin. So he had to make no sound.

He longed for a new build, one where the materials were all synthetic and so much more practical. As he possessed little charisma though, he had been passed over for promotion many times and being the only bread winner, was not particularly well off. Indeed his hundred year mortgage still had half a century to run. This was typical life in the teaming county of northern and north eastern England oft referred to as Onglia, by the net-press, while the mid-lands was called Saxonia and the opulent south, Londridium.

The place was teaming with coloured and eastern-European originated descendants and if anyone failed to make it in the south, they moved north, where wages were poor, but processed food was cheaper. Due to these factors, seventy two percent of England's two billion, lived in the north! Half of a tiny country, housed a sixth of the entire world's population. Of course it was understandable given the birth control measures in China, the reduction of Syria, Iran, Iraq, Saudi Arabia and Yemen to radioactive dust. With global warming most of Africa had been reduced to desert, so these changes had forced the world's twelve million to move into the habitable areas left and with arable land at a premium, the skyscrapers continued to go higher and the congestion of the cities grew worse by the decade.

Once Home had lived on the fourth floor of Byron flats, he still lived in the same rooms, but now the walls sides had been strengthened three times, as Byron flats became Byron Towers. Firstly extending upward to six floors, then eight and finally twelve. The old beams inside had stood up to it because they had been injected with the newest *nylocrete*, but the stairs remained as they always had, along with the floorboards.

Home slipped into the kitchen and switched on the tea-maker, a waxed paper cup fell into the dispenser and the hot beverage began to pour into it, all he had to do was add sweetener. He heard a *meowing* on the stairs and the cat flap yawed upward to allow Genghis to enter.

"Now then matey, how are you today"? Home asked him, he much preferred talking to Genghis, over his wife, the cat never answered back. He remembered when they had gotten the animal and he had told Quenda that he had decided to christen the creature Genghis.

"Genghis Cat geddit"? he had laughed. She hadn't, her reply shortly afterward, when he had attempted to reply was,

"Oh, well I don't think Mister Khan at the net-news parlour would approve of you calling a cat after him".

"His first name is Rajeel you stupid woman", he had raged, she had further infuriated him by adding,

"Then the cats name doesn't make sense; Genghis Khan instead of Rajeel Khan".

The cat rubbed up against Home's leg and he bent to scratch behind it's ears. Genghis began to purr in instant pleasure while Home wished he had not asked his back to bend again that evening. Having sipped his tea and spent a half hour with the cat on his knee, Home bid him good night and sneaked up to bed, sliding in beside Quenda with the minimum fuss. On balance it had been a good evening.

THREE

TWO DAYS LATER Home was very excited to read a blog from a micro-engineer in Chaplynka, the Ukrainian had claimed to have finally created the first working nano-bots. Fortunately for Home, the scientist, one, Aleksei Tsvyk seemed to speak excellent standard, for Home's Ukrainian was zero. He quickly typed a message to the man, asking him several pertinent questions regarding his work. Then he continued on with his own. He was halfway through some research himself when a message pinged to him in reply and it was clear that the other knew his field. If his claims were true it was the breakthrough Homes had been waiting for, the answer to all his own problems with miniaturisation.

He turned to his programmer, *'Light Cowboy'*, who for months had totally refused to give Homes his real name and to add insult to injury had told Homes his own nomen was not actual.

"Have you seen this Boy"?

"Home! Are you home? Really? How many times have I told you it's Light, or even Cowboy when only the two of us are here, but never Boy"?

"About the same number as I have asked you, your real name", Home sighed, "Now have you seen this, or not"?

"Show me"?

Home passed the programmer his pad and after a few minutes Light Cowboy whistled,

"This could be our ticket Homes my dear chap. With my new V.R. Programme and your synaptic plugs a reality, we could give everyone V.R. without the need to wear a headset, ear-buds or anything".

"Refresh my mind again about your new virtual reality programme Boys"? Home was equal to the task of making the other's name into a plural, in a crude attempt at literary irony.

Light Cowboy sighed, "I told you, I'm maybe six month from having an interactive V.R. programme that doesn't need a pad, a stick or anything. Well when I say anything, I mean with the exception of shaving parts of your head and attaching sensors to your skull. If you can get the sensors down to probe size though, then one can have such tiny devices inserted in the brain and play V.R. with no equipment at all. Then, the next step is for me to make the programme self-learning and you can have any fantasy you want, just by turning on your probes"!

"Synaptic plugs", Home corrected, " installed between the synaptic structures that permits a neuron, or nerve cell, to pass an electrical signal to another neuron. By placing the plugs in position we can then make the neuron behave how we want them to, with your V.R. programme. Give them learning capability as well and voilà we have fantasies becoming real in a person's brain whenever they have the times to create them.

"There's just one snag to all this"! Light Cowboy warned then.

"You mean you think Aleksei Tsvyk is going to be another one of those scientists who only predict the creation of nano-bots"?

"Well that's for you to decide, you said he answered the right questions, if you're satisfied, I'm satisfied".

"Then,…."?

"Electrogineer Inc; they smell one hint of what we can do, will do, my friend, they'll slap a patent on it and get their solicitors' to make sure we never see a Venustersius of one of the most exciting breakthroughs in V.R. since Sinclair created the ZX Spectrum".

"What will we do then"?

"If Vysk checks out, or whatever his real name is, there's then only one thing we can do, pack in our jobs"!

"What"?!

"Quit, call it a day, jack it in, tell them to stuff it…..".

"I know what it means in words, Boy, but what are we going to do for money? You're okay being single, you probably having savings and can manage on……"

"Hold up there Tonto", Light Boy steadied Home, "I have overheads too, I'm not rolling in Venushillin, but you and I can be and we can still leave Electrogineer Inc".

"Pray do tell"?

"By leaving Earth"!

"Floating away as we float our shares so to speak"?

"That's not funny, no, look at this"? Light Cowboy then passed his pad for Home to read, Home tapped the screen and read:-

Workers Wanted!

Are you a skilled or semi skilled worker and fed up with the pay your current employers are paying you? If so then we have a fabulous opportunity to offer you. We will give you triple the pay; yes you read it correctly, triple your current salary to come to Venus and do exactly the same job for three times the money! Interested? Please ping venusgovernment@solarmail.venus We will tell you once you have filled in our simple to use application form, if we want you, if we do, the adventure and the new life can begin in as little as two months. All costs to be settled by us and free settlement in one of our new luxury bubbles on day-side.

"Venus"! Home exploded, "They've just had a deadly plague there, no wonder they're begging people to go".

"There's a vaccine now, Are You Home? Do you think they want folks to go out there to trip and die on them? They're wanting to repopulate, to live beside the Venuser and the Biotron and just think R.U. they won't have heard of V.R. half of them. That's a virgin market as rare as one you could find next door to a whore house in Turkey"!

While Home winced at the analogy, he was forced to admit that the plan did have certain attraction, but then he thought of all the obstacles that stood in the way of realising such a bold and impudently courageous move, they were all called Quenda!

FOUR

A T THE SOUND of her scream Home was forced to admit, "I can see you are greeting this proclamation with less than abundant enthusiasm, Quenda"!

"You never even consulted me! To be asked to up sticks and leave Yorkshire is one thing, but this isn't like moving abroad to say the German Empire. This isn't like being asked to an American country, this isn't even like being asked to move *down south*"!

"That's right Quenda", Home agreed, "It's more exciting, it's a trip through space for one thing and then settlement in one of the new bubbles that are being built in the English sector".

"I'm *not* going", she tried then.

"Well that would be a waste of a passport and inter-planetary visa, but if that's how you feel...."

"Wait"! She exclaimed desperately, "You'd leave me *behind"!*

"The job's taken, light of my life, with Electovene Industries, triple pay and the permission to work on private projects without interference from the company at any time, but with option on any stocks that may be created thereof".

"You think you'll have time for private projects, what about me, what am I going to do"?

Home smiled, he knew she was weakening, "They need office personnel, you used to type, remember when we met you were a....".

"We're married now, why do I need to work"?

"You don't have to, but you're bored Quenda and there will be even less for you to do on Venus than there is here".

"You should have consulted me first, before making such a disruptive decision".

"And I would have told you that the pay was triple, the interference from the new company on my private project was less. Then we would no longer be struggling with bills, other overheads and the problems of overcrowding here. We can take Genghis too, I've already cleared that, he'll be the first cat on the planet, the local news-net are going to do a little story on him".

"That's just dandy then, a story on the ruddy cat but no mention of your long suffering wife".

Home resisted the temptation to point out that if one of them was long suffering it was actually he and not her that had done most of that over their years of struggle, but he did not think it the right time to make that point.

Instead he noticed that part of the kitchen vinyl was pealing in the corner and began to critically assess his surroundings. There was only one word to describe their abode; shabby!

"A new apartment in the English sector Quenda, built just for our arrival. If you think about it it's exciting".

"Will we take my mother's bedroom suite"?

"No, too heavy, just a few underclothes, everything else is going to be supplied by the company at zero cost; **zero** cost honey, no debts, no mortgage, we'll live like a king and a queen"!

"Oh yes in the dark for six months of the year".

"One hundred and twenty one days and then the compensation for that is one hundred and twenty one days of daylight".

"I've heard *hellish fire*"!

The satellite foils cut most of the sun's heat and light to Earth tolerable levels. A huge planting project is being undertaken by the companies that are settling there. In a couple of years it will be like southern Spain, I'm looking forward to it".

"So where are we going then? Ember Towers where the plague started"?

Home shook his head, "The new English settlement that they even let 'me' name and guess what, I've called it Byron! It will be connected to the other English bubbles by rail, they're just finishing those, you'll be able to visit the Russian site of Venugorad and Nusorgorad and even get, by connection, to the Kansas bubble of Star Spangles if you want".

"Why do I want to go to them if they're full of foreigners"?

"Because there's going to be an International Women's League for you to join, the Poles and Romanians are going back out in force and there's talk of a German and Scandian bubble going up soon. Venus will be the new frontier Quenda and you and I can be a part of it".

"Well I won't like it", she warned, "But I'll come, I don't want our flat neighbours thinking I can't hold this marriage together".

Home raced up stairs and messaged Light Cowboy by email, then he decided to write to Aleksei Tsvyk as well, he went on *emachat*;

> *Home:- are you there aleksei?*
>
> *Tsvyk:- I am, Home, are you definitely signing with Electovene Industries?*
>
> *Home:- yes, it's solid now the email goes off in the next few seconds, so will you come to Venus with us?*
>
> *Tsvyk:- I said I would if you two were going and Electovene Industries have offered me an attractive package to leave Ukraine…a lovely apartment in the Venugorad complex also, we will be able to commute.*
>
> *Home:- yes there is a rail bubble that will be finished by the time we get there, the whole network will be completed.*
>
> *Tsvyk:- Our combined project will take V.R. to a level previously undreamed of, it is an exciting prospect*
>
> *Home:- and hopefully a lucrative one, if the cowboy can create the programme he promises he can. Right, I have to go and sign up, text you on the morrow, good health comrade*
>
> *Tsvyk:- Good health my English friend.*

Home signed off and simply sat at his desk in deeply speculative thought. The scheme would succeed, it must succeed, he thought about it and wondered how could anything possibly go wrong?!

FIVE

"**I**'M VERY NERVOUS" Quenda admitted at the very last minute. They were seated in the shuttle that would take them up to the Космическая шина the Russian rocket that was the next to blast off to Venus.

If they were lucky they might even see Aleksei, for he would be on his way to Venugorad as another Electovene Industries employee. The rocket was large however, the Russians had enjoyed many years of space exploration and since the American states had all gone independent were only followed by Germany, Poland Romania and England, although in the last seven years the Chinese were pushing to take a place in the top five.

Home took his wife's hand and it was a measure of her timorous response to blasting through Earth's gravity and atmosphere, that she did not shy away from his touch. The first ten minutes were the worst. When the initial g-force jolted them all in their safety hammocks and the pressure continued until they were free of the upper ionosphere. Then there was the weightlessness and the continual course changes until shuttle Copernicus safely docked with space rocket Космическая шина. A dull thump told them the two had safely locked together and they were given explicit instructions on how to use the hand rails to float toward the airlock.

The instant they passed through it, their weight sharply returned, they were inside the outer rim of the huge spinning central ring of the Космическая шина. It's rotation just right to emulate one gravity. Space hostesses and hosts showed them to their arranged seats and they were reunited with Light Cowboy, who had flitted to Constanța once he had given their former company notice, for a few days holiday, before taking the shuttle from Lumina both in Romania.

Keen to show off the prowess the hypno tapes had bestowed upon him he greeted them, "Salutări, prietenii mei mă bucur că ați reușit, cum a fost zborul dvs. de navetă"?

"Very funny Mister cowboy", Quenda brooded, "You know we don't speak Romanian"!

Home however returned, "Dimpotrivă, din lumina vieții mele, am făcut un hipno-curs și am înțeles perfect Light Cowboy".

The Cowboy burst into laughter and Home had to hurriedly explain to his wife, "He asked if we had a good shuttle ride and I replied that I understood what he had said as I've taken a hypno course in Romanian too, for quite a few of those who we will be working with will be Romanians and Poles".

"I expect you've learned ruddy Polish as well then smart ass"? Quenda fumed.

"Ale oczywiście, jak nie wszyscy Polacy mówią standardowo i podobają im się w ich języku", Home grinned and swiftly added, "They like it if you exchange a few words in their mother tongue".

"Well they should learn standard like all good Yorkshire folk", Quenda retorted, "So if you two are going to jabber in that gobbledygook once we've achieved space velocity, I'm off to find my suite and go to bed".

"Your suite", Light Cowboy smiled, "This is space now Quenda, you'll get a bunk and very little privacy, there's no wasted space on a rocket".

"Thunderation, this is going to be fun", she gasped and closed her eyes as if to dismiss the pair of them.

Home could not remember the last time he had enjoyed himself quite so much. He leaned over past his work colleague and looked out of the porthole, the Earth was already receding into a small blue marble, what a magnificent sight as the stars began to shine. Home was entranced by the nigrescent blanket of space, the twinkling lights that were distant suns, as they had been some years ago. For space was so vast that even light took centuries to traverse it.

"How's the programme coming along"?

"It's not easy, there's a lot of work to do, but I'll have it finished by the time you and Aleksei will have the nano-bots ready for you. Are the synaptic plugs in your schematic"?

"I can tell you they are", Home was pleased with himself, All I need now is the tiny workers to create some of the truly minute circuits and we'll be ready to place some into a living subject".

"I've been contemplating that phase" Light Cowboy mused, "I'd like to volunteer to be the guinea pig"?

"Too dangerous if things go wrong", Home decided, "The programme might even need some tweaks and alterations. Whereas, once the probes work, my part in the project will be finished, therefore it should be me who has them inserted into his brain".

"And which surgeon are we going to approach to do the operation"?

"There's already one of note living in ember caves".

"A Venuser"?

"No a Biotron".

"So you've got every little thing worked out. Shall we go and see if we can find Aleksei"?

With the cold fusion engine of the Космическая шина, the journey only took ten hours and most of that was spend in acceleration and deceleration. Then they were forced to once again transfer to a planet-to-orbit shuttle. It turned out to be the Isaac Newton. They had found the Ukrainian and were all allowed to sit together for the first drop into Venus' thin atmosphere. One that was gradually increasing by the day. The Isaac Newton knifed through the ionosphere as though it was warm butter and the landing was exceptionally smooth. Once they were on the tube train that was taking them to Byron, Quenda demanded,

"Hypno-tapes are incredibly expensive Rale, did you use some of our small nest egg to afford them"?

Light Cowboy looked uncomfortably on, as Home replied without preamble,

"I did, an investment for the future sweetness, once our project is complete I'll give you a pile of nest eggs".

"You had no right to use it without consulting me first".

"And yet the account was in our joint name with either to draw".

"We should have discussed it".

"And you would have said no. My way we avoided the usual unpleasantness".

She was about to say more when Light Cowboy interjected, "Incredible, we're here look"!

Quenda was derailed in more than one sense of the word and a company flit taxi was waiting for them as they walked awkwardly toward it. Their gait slightly lighter than they were accustomed to. Each of them were ten percent lighter than when they had commenced their incredible journey.

The flit-taxi was more for splendour than necessity, for their apartments were only four minutes from the rail tube. Everything was close together on the newly built bubble. They were informed by the driver that Light Cowboy was to be in single apartment one hundred and fourteen while the Homes had a double, number twenty three.

Light Cowboy and Home were given their codes to unlock their respective door's and the driver handed them their holdalls', with their entire Earthly possessions.

"It's across the way Sir, on the second floor of yonder tower", the driver informed Light Cowboy, while, he merely pointed up two levels to Home and said, "You are just there, welcome to Venus, the company will be pinging you very soon".

He was gone before they good decide whether he should have been tipped, although neither of the men had any Venushillin, which was the unit of currency in the English sector.

"Well, then, I'll go and throw my bag into my new cubby hole", Light Cowboy chuckled.

"What are you calling it that for"? Quenda wanted to know at once.

"There'll not be a great deal of space in our new abode", Home told her, "It'll be bijou, but brand new, sweetness".

"Bijou"! she was scornful, "That's your description of pokey isn't it"?

"Exquisitely elegant and tasteful, That will be our new love nest", Home could never be outdone by his wife when he was in a good mood.

"Well it will certainly be larger than our nest egg, that's for sure".

She turned and lead the way, leading him to wonder what had happened to the woman he had married.

When he joined her in the apartment block, it was to realise with some satisfaction that she did not as yet know the code to unlock the place, with the care of unfamiliarity, he keyed into the pad 555-home-23-vene-Ind and the door hissed open.

"How many character was that"? Quenda demanded, "It'll take forever to get in and out of this place".

"Twenty", Home's mind was keen, he had not made a point of counting them, "Better than getting our few possessions stolen".

"What possessions, we only have what we're standing in practically. Oh, by thunderation, look at this….this; cupboard"!

Home rushed to the only window and gazed through the thick plexi glass to the horizon beyond. There were pools of some sort of liquid, from which, huge clouds of vapour were rising. The terrain was mainly sun blasted ground with the occasional rock that was pitted and eroded by the alien atmosphere. Home found the vista terrific and exciting,

"Come and look at this"? he asked. Quenda was not listening though, she was still examining the tiny interior of their new abode.

The empty doorway did not lead into an entrance hall but straight into the small main room. At one wall were two let down folding chairs and a similarly designed table. The room was 'filled' with a two seater sofa and a brand new but old fashioned three dimension plasma was screwed into a facing corner, the screen looked to be about five hundred and fifty centimetres wide if that.

Quenda went through an arched hole in the other corner, there was no door in it. Home followed her. The shower stall was to their left, then a sealed chemical lavatory, that at least had a door. The narrow passage had another arch to the right which lead to a bedroom that just accommodated a double bed (standard size, no one used standard size any more). If one went beyond the arch there was a room with a laundry machine a freezer and a hypo-wave and that was all their abode consisted of!

"We can't live in this"! Quenda exploded.

"We can and we will, until something more expansive is offered to us", Home returned firmly, "It smells new sweetness, not of damp and mildew, the walls are all delicate powder blue and nyloplanyon, they will maintain easily. The floors are all faux mahogany but actually also nyloplanyon, it won't take you longer than ten minutes to Swiffematic-down".

"But there's no room", Quenda almost sobbed, "What am I going to do all day, stare at a wall I can reach out and touch"?

"We have our pads, we can ping and we can keep in touch with anyone we want, you can read, watch films, listen to music; or…..".

"I could find some part time work", she finished for him, "That's what you want me to do isn't it? Earn some money for components for your mysterious project with Cowboy"?

"Whatever you earn, you can keep for yourself, I will be earning enough money for everything else".

"Well I guess I'm going to have to make a go of living in this bubble then", she noted in resignation.

"Yes", Home added, "You are"!

SIX

T HE SURGEON CONSIDERED Home's request with scientific curiosity,

"It would not be a procedure that would be sanctioned by any medical body that I belong to Mister Home", he finally told the electro-engineer.

"But it would not be fatal, even if it failed would it"? Home added, "And call me Rale, Doctor".

The surgeon gave it some more consideration, he did not offer his own name, neither first, nor surname, for in truth he had never possessed either.

"No it wouldn't kill you, nor would it damage your brain with metal objects this tiny, how was the creation of such managed"?

''*Good'*, thought Home, *'He's curious'*

"Nano-bots", he replied honestly, "They're prototypes of the Russian scientist Aleksei Tsvyk, currently working out of Venugorad".

"And the programming, who created that"?

"Light Cowboy, in Byron. Why do you stay in Ember Caves when it's the Romanian sector, Doctor"?

"This has always been my post since I came to Venus, I'm happy here and my apartment is seven square metres larger than the single units in the English bubbles. I had an offer to relocate to 'Under Sands' but declined it for that reason. Have you had a chance to visit the three new German bubbles by the way? They have the very latest of facilities and some lovely apartments. If you can afford the rent you should have a look at Polsitze for you and your wife"?

"Maybe I will, doctor", Home had no thoughts along those lines, but he was not about to disagree with the surgeon on any point.

"So; the procedure, will you do it, please? I can go to seventy if you will"?

"Seventy Venban or seventy Venleu"?

"No, no no; seventy Venushillin"!

"Ah, well then....come here tomorrow, go to theatre one and wait for me, be there at fourteen fifty hours and have your head shaved".

"All of it"?

"I know what you're thinking, the entrance will be small, but you will have a curious bald spot and it will be hard to keep it free from infection. Easier to take the whole lot off, I hear it's coming back into fashion with those who have male pattern baldness anyway".

"You're not going to paint my head purple are you"? Home joked then.

"No", the surgeon seemed to take the enquiry seriously, "Brown, like iodine".

The next day passed swiftly and Home grew nervous as well as excited. He was determined to go through with the procedure though. One Terran day later he was on the surgeon's table his head shaved, just as instructed. The surgeon, without preamble, picked up a syringe and injected his head.

"When I start drilling you'll feel some pressure but no pain. As you will already suspect I'll drill five holes, to insert five tiny probes into your head and then finish up. Approximately an hour after you've left me, the programme should start to become available to you. If you feel any discomfort what-so-ever you must ping me straight way, now, are you ready"?

"I'm as ready as I'll ever be, Doctor", Home told the Biotron.

The drilling commenced and it felt exactly as he had been instructed. He could smell strange aromas but felt no pain. Sooner than he had suspected, the surgeon told him,

"The probes are in, Home. I just have to finish up now".

"Are you screwing the bits of my skull back into place"?

"No, they're too small, I'll be using surgical glue and then put the tiny scalp flaps back in the same way. Once your hair grows, nothing will be noticeable at all".

In less time than expected once again, the surgeon laid down his tools in the tray and told Home,

"It's done, stay still and rest for a couple of hours, than I'll check in on you and if you feel alright, you can go. See you in two hours, I'll let the Cowboy in now".

The surgeon exited the small operating theatre and the programmer entered shortly afterward,

"Hi metal-head, how's it going", the younger man quipped,

"Get out, you've not been sterilised", Home joked back.

"But one day I want to have little cowboys".

"Then you shouldn't be in here".

"Seriously. I understand it went well, exactly as the surgeon expected"?

"I guess so, I can't wait for the plugs to go on line, you've set everything automatically"?

Cowboy nodded, "You'll be back in your apartment and suddenly feel them activate, from that point on a mere concious effort will take you to V.R. and then it's up to your imagination as to how the themes play out. I'm going to ping Aleksei now and let him know all went well".

Home lay still and waited. He had anticipated this moment for months and he could wait a little longer, the last thing he desired to do was give in to impatience and ruin the project.

"That's done then, the ping's off. I'll get back to work, no sense in us both losing a day's pay. I'll come and see you this evening, okay"?

"Sure, I might take a nap, I fell sort of dizzy and tired, see you tonight".

Light Cowboy let himself out and within minutes Home had drifted off to sleep.

"How do you feel"? the surgeon asked, waking him an indeterminate period later. "I let you sleep for three and a half hours, you should be able to sit up now".

Gingerly Home hoisted himself to a sitting position, realising he felt normal, he swung his legs to the side ready to stand.

"Careful", the surgeon cautioned, "Dizziness may still effect you for forty eight hours, although your additional rest will not have done any harm".

Home slowly took to standing and to his delight, "I'm good, Doc"!

"Then you can go home, the programme should be available to you any time from now".

The two shook hands and Home carefully left the theatre. He was concious of putting one foot in front of the other, his every move pre-thought. He strolled to the rail tube and climbed on the Ember Caves to Byron express. Within the hour he was entering his apartment.

"By the holy shrine of the Hall of Whispers, what have you done now, Rale, where's your hair"?

Home smiled to his wife, "I got tired of the grooming and this is my new look. I gather you don't like it"?

"You look like a convict, don't expect me to be seen out with you until it grows back"!

That's a good reason to keep it like this', Home thought to himself. Instead he replied,

"What are we having for tea my dear"?

"Whatever you get, I'm tired and don't forget I work now too"!

"Very well I will go and whip us up some culinary delight", he slipped into the kitchen and then.......

Zing!

The probes came on line. Home did nothing to activate them for the moment, he forced himself to make dinner and eat it with his harridan. He waited for her to go to have her shower before he thought,

'Right; V.R.'

The result was disappointing. He was still in the cramped apartment, could still hear the noises of Quenda showering. Just a moment though, he had instructed the V.R. in no way, so what did he expect. What should he do first? Baby steps, Cowboy had instructed more than once. No use trying for a serious adventure until he was much more practised. So he looked around the room and decided the plasma was not big enough,

'Right then expand to a thousand centimetre's', he mentally commanded and before his very eyes the screen grew until it was the size he desired!

It worked!

V.R. with no apparatus of any kind!

Home was still seated in his place on the sofa gazing at the new large screen when Quenda came into the room in her robe,

"What the......! Rale, when did you get that? Can we afford it"?

"You can see it"?

"The three'D', it's a different one, of course I can see it".

"How is this possible", Home thought aloud.

"It's possible because you've gone and spent some of our money again without asking me", Quenda complained.

Then it hit Home, he was in V.R. this was not his wife, it was the Quenda he expected to come out of the shower, one who would behave exactly as he had expected she would. He was in a virtual world. He did not especially like it though, but he could improve it, improve it as long as his imagination could supply the details.

Should he stay and play, or return to reality and wait for Cowboy to visit so he could tell him the great news of success? Home was a conscientious man and so he thought,

'V.R. off'.

The set returned to it's usual dimensions and Quenda asked,

"I'm going to have an early night if that Cow friend of yours is coming, do you want a cocoa before I go"?

"Please dear and thank you".

He had only just received it, was carefully sipping, when the door pinged. The inspection screen showed who he was expecting and he thumbed the release,

"Howdy pardner", Light Cowboy stepped inside, "Have you some good news for lil' old me"?

"I'm not talking to you unless you stop with the Texas twang this instant", Home chuckled, but the mirth gave him away.

"It did didn't it, it frenging worked"?!

"It worked. Let me get you a drink to celebrate, what will you have"?

"Venvod if you've got it, it's the only local spirit that doesn't taste like scheisse".

"Two Venvod's coming up".

"So what did you do"? The drinks unit was only several centimetres from Home's elbow, in fact in his quarters' everything was at his elbow.

"I imagined that plasma twice it's size and it grew to exactly that"!

"Yes and then what"?

"Quenda came into the room and chewed me out".

"But she wouldn't have been able to see it"?

"The V.R. Quenda".

"You V.R.ed your wife the same as your own wife?! If I had V.R. I'd be married to Zillian Verna".

"Zillian Verna the famous and beautiful tri-vid film screen actress and centurairess"?

"Hey if you've V.R. you aim high, Homeboy. So what happened then"?

"You don't understand, Cow, the probes ran along the same lines as my thoughts, just as you'd programmed them too. Quenda was perfect just down to the last detail, the probes had taken her from my memory and put her in the running programme".

"Well, of course I knew I could write the thing really", Light Cowboy tried to sound casual about it and totally failed, "So then what happened"?

"I turned it off to wait for you, I'll try something else tomorrow before work".

"How soon before we can apply for the patents".

"I see no reason for delay you can fill our the on-net forms right now if you want".

Light Cowboy left the apartment two hours later deliriously happy and already planning the spend of his first thousand shillin.

Home could not sleep however, he was too excited, too vital with the adrenaline rush. So he seated himself in the place that was dedicated to him on the cramped sofa and......

Zing!

The room was perfect in every detail, it was so exact that if he had not know he was in V.R. He would have believed himself to be in reality. He thought about what he would like to do with the programme. The cramped quarters, what if he decided he wanted them bigger, but how much larger? He imagined a room five square metres larger. The room shimmered for a second and then it was actually how he had envisioned it. He got up and walked around, there was no join on the floor where the *extension* began, it was as though the room had always been that size, those dimensions.

This was better than anything he could possibly have anticipated. A V.R. programme that actually existed inside his head. It was like….like actual fantasy, with no gadgetry to put into place, the only limiting factor was the user's imagination. Home tried to imagine the retail price of such an instalment and it was totally beyond his grasp; but it would be pricey. Yet people would buy it, in fact they would clamour for it. It would be more attractive than e-books, evids, others music, because with V.R. anyone could be a composer, a musician, or just about anything they desired.

It would put an end to disability, Snufz addiction, crime…..

One could run without legs, fly without a plane, get high without actually taking anything, murder without killing anyone, steel without robbing, the list was endless.

Home went to the window. The vista was a scarred grey with pool of acidic content, from the pools noxious vapour rose, Home did not like it. He imagined away the pools; they vanished! Next the scarred and pitted rock and rubble was replaced with grass, clouds appeared in the blue sky, trees sprang up from the horizon. It was like painting with his brain; except that unlike any painting he could have produced this was totally lifelike. If he didn't know better he could have gone outside.

Or could he anyway?

Surely his V.R. self could stroll in Venus' pleasant meadow without actually physically moving from his seat!? He thought,

'V.R. off'

Sure enough he was still on the sofa at the exact same spot. Yet his virtual self had been standing at the window. That meant he could go outside, but only in the V.R. vista of course.

Zing.

Back at the window he imagined a door, to it's left, after all there was plenty of room for it. Home opened the window and gingerly walked outside suffocation and burning acid did not suddenly grip his chest. The vista had no aroma though, nor any discernible temperature that he could feel. It was like an unfinished scene, so….He imagined the smell of fresh air, the hint of grass, the warmth of the sun and it came to pass.

It made him feel like a god!!

SEVEN

"JEEPERS YOU LOOK rough", Light Cowboy observed, "Too excited to sleep Homey"?

"Actually yes", Home admitted, "I used the V.R. again".

"Was she sweet"?

"If you manage to get your mind out of the gutter for once, I'll tell you about the Venus I created".

"I'm all ears".

Home told him about the scene he had created and how he had entered it.

"We'll go to the patent office in our lunch break then".

"Good idea", Home responded, but as it was to turn out; it was not!

He could not wait for his shift to end, so he could do some more experimenting. Usually he was happy to be at work, but that day it was just an inconvenience to him.

He rushed home on the tube train and entered the cramped apartment. Quenda wasn't home, good! He could enter V.R. for a while, before she arrived.

Zing.

The apartment was back to being spacious and filled with fresh rather than recycled air. For a few seconds Home simply enjoyed the change, it was great to get away from the diminutive dimensions of the abode he shared with his wife. Then he thought of the possibilities that awaited him, what did he want?

He imagined Quenda entering the apartment and the door opened and in she stepped,

"Hello dear, you're glad to see me", he said to her and Quenda smiled and replied,

"Yes of course I am darling, how was your day at work"?

"Stressful", he told her, "As always my love, but I endure it for us, because the pay is able to provide us with what we need".

"All I need is you darling", Quenda returned and came over to him and kissed him on the cheek. Home looked at her critically and then made a few *'improvements'*. The lines on her face disappeared, her hair was no longer going grey but shone with lustre and vitality. She grew a little shorter for he liked petite women, her bosom that had been beginning to sag grew pert and slightly fuller, her waist tucked in slightly, her ass became taut and nicely rounded. Quenda's eyes changed from muddy brown to a beautiful shade of azure, her nose slightly smaller her lips slightly fuller. Home looked at her again and desired his wife for the for the time in months.

He rose to his feet and took her in his arms and her body pressed to his as they kissed passionately on the mouth.

"Let's go in the bedroom", he breathed.

Her immediate reply was, "I want you, now"!

They tore off their clothes and coupled noisily, he marvelling at the soft smooth tautness of her skin.

"Do you know what I want you to do first", he asked her huskily, ready to go again. It was something she had *never* done for him.

"Of course darling, I'm glad to please you in any way I can", she murmured as she kissed him on the neck, then the chest, the stomach and then did what he had been eagerly anticipating.

After but a couple of minutes, he could feel his excitement mounting and he instructed, "Come up to me now, I want to be inside you".

It was sensational, she rode him like a lusty horse and even though he was close she obliged him by a moaning climax just before his own. They lay panting together and then when he had regained his natural breathing, he suggested,

"Let's get in the tub together".

"Our new tub in delicate avocado with the gold taps, you wait there while I run the water. It will cost for that much you know sweet heart"?

"We can afford it", he grinned.

They bathed together, delighting in one another's bodies, for he now had a fantastic six pack a wide chest and narrow waist, the thick black hair on his chest intrigued her and they did it a third time and then washed again.

The two of them dressed one another in their nightgowns' of decorative and immensely expensive samite.

"You go and get your strength back, while I get dinner my love", she suggested and he returned to his sofa and thought,

V.R.off.

The tired ageing saggy Quenda entered the cramped apartment and informed,

"There's lichen-fish fingers in my bag, are you going to get some dinner on or sit there like a useless lump all evening"?

Sighing, Home rose to do as bidden.

EIGHT

H E WAS ONCE more being examined by the surgeon, the operation had been two days hence,

"No ill effects at all".

"None, Doctor, nothing negative".

"Your serotonin levels are incredibly high, you've been enjoying yourself; a lot"?

Home smiled, "That's about the size of it, yes".

"Well try to ease up a bit", the surgeon frowned, "The human body does not appreciate anything done to excess, Rale. If you push in any direction, too far, some unpredicted consequence will result".

"I felt great, Doctor, stop worrying, your work was first class".

"You're not listening to me, Rale. Go easy for a few days, whatever you are doing is creating an unnatural imbalance in your brain, you don't want that, I can't predict what would happen if you went too far with this thing, but it would certainly be deleterious to your well-being and possibly your sanity. You can't mess around with the brain"!

"Yes, Doctor, right; thank you, can I go now"?

"Of course, but come back in a week, I want to do some more tests".

"More tests, why"?

"I wish to constantly monitor you for the first few weeks of this…this, transition. You have become something that you were not before, you have changed the entire balance of your mind and body, there may be side effects that we cannot, as yet, anticipate".

Home sighed, "You've got it, Doctor, thanks again". He hopped off the table and landed rather heavily; of course, he was in reality, he wasn't the athletic muscular Rale Umberto Home, but the middle aged, running to fat, Home.

He decided to walk back to the apartment, rather than take the tube train, there was a deep pavement at the side of all tracks for those who felt athletic. Home began to walk down it and then, he decided to have some fun…

Zing.

There were three of them! The tall blonde youth, the short dark middle aged one and the fat shaven bald twenty something. None of them were wearing a pleasant expression on their drawn features. Home imagined the petite red headed girl suddenly at his side. She gripped his arm, in trepidation,

"They don't look like regular and sensible citizens Rale", she noted. "You'll protect me won't you"?

"Of course Traycea", Home returned in his manly baritone, flexing his muscles to ready themselves in case of sudden violent activity.

They drew closer to one another the group and the couple, the lanky youth cried,

"Okay grandpa, we'll take your money your valuables and your girlfriend".

"Wwwhat do you want with me"? Traycea stuttered in fear.

The same youth grinned maliciously and glanced at his bald comrade in crime, "Cutter here has a hobby, he likes forcing nice ass to do his bidding, if they don't then he lives up to his name, isn't that right, Cutter"?

Cutter, for his part merely gave a lop sided grin and drool ran out of the corner of his mouth.

"Be not alarmed", Home said to the girl in dramatic prose, "None harm shall come to thee, this I fore-swear".

"If and it does please you sir, I will be grateful you have my word upon it", the girl returned in the same style.

"Did you not hear me chum"? Lanky wanted to know then, "Make with the cash or I'll let Cutter do some work on your miserable hide"?

Home removed the hand of the girl gently from his arm and took a couple of strides forward and then stopped.

"This is how this grim little scenario it going to end", he announced to the trio of would be robbers and rapist, "You're going to turn around and disappear around the first available junction. If you do that you get to continue your miserable little existences without harm nor injury. The alternative will not be pleasant; for you that is".

The lanky blonde who had done all the talking asked, "Are you for real? We're kitted up and ready to rumble, moron, what do you have"?

From his beautifully embroidered boho shirt of finest linen Home produced a pen.

"I have my pen".

As one the trio laughed loudly, the short dark one, whom Home decided to think of as Shorty suddenly produced a length of piping and asked Lanky in a squeaky voice,

"Let me break something, it always softens them up".

Cutter however drew a hunting knife and asked in a mean growl, "Or I could carve something rude into his chest".

"No, no boys", Lanky denied them, "Don't forget, he's got a pen"!

They laughed uproariously once again and then lanky grew suddenly quite serious,

"Fun over, this is your last chance dumb-ass start emptying your pockets and pass your girlfriend to us, or you will not like what happens next. You can write that down with your pen if you want ha ha ha".

Home stood his ground, his breathing regular, every muscle in his body taut and ready for action.

"Alright we've wasted enough time", Lanky decided, "Shorty, break something".

Time seemed to slow down (mainly because Home had decided to go into slow motion) Shorty slowly strode purposefully forward raising the pipe. With an expert jumping kick, Home's foot crunched into the would be assailant's chest flinging him back into the other two with bone breaking force.

Lanky began to draw a snub nosed blaster, but then Home pressed the clip of his pen and a thin blue beam of pure laser energy slashed through his neck. The beam instantly cauterised the wound and Lanky's head tumbled to the floor and came to rest at Home's feet. There was a look of horrified astonishment on the head's crude features and the body meanwhile slowly fell into an unfeeling heap at Cutter's feet. With a roar of enraged animalism, Cutter launched himself at Home and a second karate kick snapped the wrist of the hand that was holding his knife. He fell, whining, to his knees.

"There will be no witnesses", Home said simply and taking hold of Cutter's head he cleanly snapped his neck like a chicken's. Home was turning back to the girl before Cutter had even crumpled to the concrete of the pavement. The girl rushed forward and was in his manly, muscular arms as she breathed,

"You were magnificent Rale, How can I ever demonstrate how grateful I am to you"?

"I have a few ideas", Home grinned lasciviously.

Two hours later, totally sexually sated, Home thought,

V.R. off.

He remained in the bed with the girl! The scene had not changed, disconcerted he thought again,

'V.R.off'

The scene shimmered to nothingness and he was back on the pavement of the tube, totally alone, as though time had been frozen. Something of a risk, he must make sure in the future that he only turned on the V.R. when in a safe location and environment. He went home.

Quenda entered the apartment, "Do you ever do anything useful when I'm not here"? She demanded, "Have you swiffened, or put dinner on the go, have you done anything except go into one of those staring useless ponders of yours"?

"You usually bring tea with you so how could I hypo-wave it and anyway it might be cold before you got home, you arrive at different times".

"The boss wanted me to do some extra work for him", don't get off your useless ass, I'll do it", she complained bitterly.

Later that evening when he V.R.ed, he strangled her to death and enjoyed the way it made her twisted features turn purple and her never ending, nagging tongue loll uselessly out of her mean mouth.

NINE

"YOU, HOME"? THE office boy asked bluntly.

Home eased the crick out of his back, put his hands to support it and asked, "Who wants to know"?

"Boss wants to see you"! and then he was gone.

"Hey Cowgirl", Home called to the next bench, "The boss wants to see me? What's his name"?

"Go through that door over there and down the corridor it's the third door on your left, marked Spoorharp", his friend and co-inventor told him.

Home rose stiffly to his feet and went down the described route. He had never been so far into the bubble before and thought the grey paintwork totally unnecessary, what was wrong with leaving the sides transparent? He stopped at the door marked Xior Spoorharp Mg and knocked on it, even though it was wide open. Behind a desk covered in electronic parts and computer pieces was a slim, grey haired man with a less than happy look on his angular features.

He looked up from his pad, at the sound, then asked,

"You Home"?

"I am".

"Come in, sit down, close the door behind you".

Home did as directed and faced the manager once more.

"I've been monitoring your work, Home and have recommended you for a pay rise starting immediately". Spoorharp told him.

Home responded, "Thank you sir, how much extra will it be if it's alright to ask"?

"Excuse me"? Spoorharp asked, "Have you been listening to me, Home? You look exhausted, why don't you get a good night's sleep? I'll repeat, your work is good but there's not enough of it, now what's this about your extra nonsense"?

Home came to full alertness with a jolt. Had he absently mindedly turned the V.R. on?

"I'm working on a new circuit for air flitters Mister Spoorharp". Home said desperately.

"I know what you're working on, Home", Spoorharp grumbled, "I monitor your output on this console here and you're working at a crawl. Electovene Industries pay well and are therefore entitled to expect quality results, now if you're having a problem with the circuit you're working on you should come to me, so that we can discuss it. Are you, Home"?

"Having a problem"?

Spoorharp inhaled sharply and decided in a moment, "I'm going to send you to the company doctor, for a check up. He'll see if you are having any adverse reactions to being on Venus. I don't want you to worry, it's to help you, so that in turn you can produce for us. I'm putting your torpidity and confusion down to a physiological matter. There will be no mention of this in your file".

Home mused, *'I could snap your neck like the dried up twig of a dying plant'*.

Spoorharp's face drained of colour and he asked, "Are you threatening me, Home"?

"I beg your pardon", Home asked he was beginning to feel a rising panic take hold of him, he did not seem to be in control of the situation.

"You just threatened to strangle me", Spoorharp gasped.

"Who did"? Home had thought it, but he hadn't thought it out loud.

Or had he?

"Right, Home" Spoorharp decided, "I'm putting you on paid sick leave until the doctor sees you. You've done some good work for us and I'm sure you're very capable, but there's simply not enough of it and I now know why".

"Why what Mister Spoorharp".

"Why you deserve every penny we pay you", Spoorharp smiled.

'V.R.off', Home thought in desperation, but it was not on! He asked numbly, "Just what do you want me to do, sir"?

"Get your stuff cleared off your desk for the time being and go home…er, Home. You'll be pinged when to come in to see the doctor. Or you may have to travel to a specialist outside our company. Now I don't want you to worry, no one can help getting ill and it's nothing to be dismayed about, right that's it for now".

Home got up to go, but Spoorharp halted him with,

"Just one other thing, Home"

"Yes, Sir"?

"Yes, that's right, off you go and get some rest, good man".

"And the other thing Sir"?

"Forget it, I'm not going to put it in your file".

"Not going to put what in my file Sir"?

"The threat".

"Threat"! Home was dismayed, "Have you any idea who could have sent such a thing"?

Spoorharp looked sympathetically at Home, "Home, get off to your family, or whom ever it is you billet with and get some rest".

"I live with my wife, Sir"?

Spoorharp frowned and glanced down at one of his pads, there was nothing on it about Home being married, but he let it go,

"Alright then, get on now, there's a good chap".

However, Home had leaned forward and read his personnel file on the pad upside down,

"That file says I'm single", he gasped, "But when I filled in the application I put several details about my wife".

Spoorharp began to look slightly nervous, slightly afraid, he responded,

"I know you did it's a computer error, Home. Don't worry, I'll see you once you've been to the doctor and you can tell me all the discrepancies, alright"?

Home looked at him in a most peculiar fashion and seemed to be trying to access some sort of memory, but thankfully he slowly stumbled from the office in a daze. Spoorharp immediately pinged personnel, one of the clerks came on the screen before him,

"Ah yes Spoorharp here, I'd like to make an appointment for employee kwv559-Home, to see the company doctor please. I've just sent him home on full pay until we can assess him, he looked totally exhausted".

"Tiredness is not in the Doctors' remit", the clerk noted unhelpfully.

"It was nervous exhaustion", Spoorharp returned curtly. "Make the appointment, tell the doctor when you do, that the patient seemed to be having trouble concentrating and was illogical and delusional at times".

Before the clerk could argue further he cut the connections, "Ruddy clerks", he muttered, "Give them a tiny bit of power and they become megalomaniacs over twenty four"!

Home wandered down the corridor and tried to make sense of what had just happened. Spoorharp did not seem a logical man, one minute he was congratulating him and making him an offer of more money, the next he was saying his work was not up to scratch. Then to cap it all, he wanted Home to see the company doctor. Company shrink more like!

Still if he wanted him to go home on full pay, that was certainly alright with him, it would give him more time to escape reality. As he was clearing his desk, Light Cowboy asked,

"What's going on"?

"I'm on sick leave, active immediately".

"But there's nothing wrong with you".

"That manager thinks there is and he's just told me to go home. Going home is what I'm going to do".

"Well then get some rest", Light Cowboy told him, "You do look up side the middle".

"Ping me later if you want", Home said and picking up his brief case, promptly left the factory.

He was just inside his apartment and taking a second to relax on his sofa when the door pinged. He groaned, climbed to his feet and looked at the inspection plate. A tall attractive young woman in a combman uniform was standing without. Home pressed the button that unlocked the door from the inside.

"Can I help you"?

"Inspector Gray, Sir, calling in response to the ping earlier, can I come in Sir"?

"Certainly Inspector", Home had no idea what she was talking about but did not want to find out in the corridor of the plaza.

"Sit down Inspector, can I get you a cup of Ven-tea"?

The woman seamed to sag, "That would be very welcome, Mister Home, one sweetener if you please"?

"In one stride Home was in the tiny hole that was the kitchen and dialled up two teas, as one of the waxed cups was filling he asked,

"To which ping are you referring, Inspector"?

The young woman glanced at her pad, "Ten thirty three hours E.S.T. (Earth Solar Time) Mister Home regarding the absence of your wife, Quenda Home".

"I beg your pardon, Inspector, but I don't understand"? Home handed her the first cup to be ready and before she replied, Gray took a sip of the hot beverage,

"Aah, that's welcome Mister Home, thank you, it's been quite a day, this is the first drink I've had".

Home collected his own cup and took a seat on one of the kitchen chairs which he had dragged into the arch way.

"You said something about my wife's absence", he said incredulously, "She'll be at work I didn't......."

"We checked with work Sir", Gray cut in, looked down at her pad, "Shadrack and Boot Sulphuric Acid Recycling, they confirmed she's not been in for the last two days. You must be in shock, understandable, probably made the ping when you were deeply distracted".

"I don't think...." Home began.

"Is it me or is it hot in here Sir"? Gray cut in and she rose form the sofa and began unbuttoning her uniform shirt.

Home looked on stupefied, "It's the same as usual, eighteen degrees, but I can......".

The shirt fell from Gray's shoulders and she turned to face him, her bosom was quite impressive.

"You must be missing her", she said in a soothing voice, "Missing the sort of things a woman does for her man".

"I er.....", Home's was beyond comment as the inspector unclipped her brassiere and the resultant display was pleasing indeed.

He just had the presence of mind to think.

'V.R. off'!

The topless inspector was still there though and then in his arms and then her mouth on his, hungrily and questing.

'This does not happen to someone like me', he thought as she took his hand and fell on the bed with him.

V.R.off! V.R.off dammit!!

Then her hands were undoing his boho pants and her hands were on him in a very intimate area.

'This is not real, the probes are doing their own fantasy and I can't stop them'

When she took him into her mouth though, he did not want the V.R. to stop. Not for a while!!

TEN

HOME AROSE FROM the bed and went to shower. He let the hot water wash away his guilt and then turned the jest to icy cold. It was only when he got out and was drying himself that he realised that the shower was sonic! Water being at premium on Venus! He returned to the stall swiftly, the shower was totally dry, yet his towel was damp. Feeling somewhat shaky he looked at the bed, which was made and of Inspector Gray there was no sign!

It was time to see the surgeon and Light Cowboy, the probes had to come out before he completely lost his grip on reality. He was hungry so he hypo-waved some chilli con carne'. He seated himself in the two seater sofa and waited for something to happen, the last thing he wanted was for the plugs to start firing without his mental command.

He waited.

Nothing seemed to be changing, nothing was moving so he pinged Shadrack and Boot S.A.R. the connection was made voice only,

"This is Rale Home, can I possibly speak to my wife please"?

"Sorry Mister Home you've missed her, she's left for today, she should be with you any minute now".

Thanking the female voice he cut the connection. So Quenda wasn't missing! Never had been missing therefore, then the whole Gray thing had been the probes. Home filed that, he then thought he knew what to expect, what was real and what wasn't. He was wrong!

The door opened and Gray walked calmly into the apartment as though it was the most natural thing on Venus to do.

"Hi sugar", she said and leaning forward to kiss him her blouse billowed slightly,

'Well those are the breasts I think I remembered' he thought.

"Have you eaten yet or were you waiting for me"?

"Can I just ask you what you are up to, Inspector"? Home asked politely.

"Not yet tender-stuff, we can play the cop and the robber later, right now I want something to eat and a nice cup of Ven-tea. Once I've had a shower we can decide who wears the cuffs tonight"!

She strolled into the kitchen and put something in the hypo-wave.

Home slowly joined her,

"Inspector Gray, do you actually think you live here"? he asked and the whole time his mind was screaming,

'V.R.off! V.R.off! V.R.off! V.R.off! V.R.off! V.R.off! V.R.off! V.R.off!'

"Don't be impatient tender-stuff, let me have my tea and a shower first alright"?

"What is my exact name", he asked her.

"Rale Umberto Home and you are guilty of annoying your wife. Now come on, let me get to the table"?

"What's my date of birth, Mz Gray".

"It's March twenty third, thirty one ninety seven, you're fifty three years old".

"What was my mother's name"?

Gray hesitated over a mouthful of food and then answered "Ionwi. If I get one wrong, do I have to wear the cuffs"?

"Then Home realised that of course she would know the answers! He knew them and the plugs could read his thoughts, his memories, everything about him. So he changed his line of reasoning,

"You look about thirty to me Inspector, what are you doing with someone twenty odd years your senior".

Gray laughed, "Who knows how love works out tender-stuff, I've always gone for men rather than boys. Have you planned tonight's viewing on the net, or can we watch something I like for a change".

"What would you do if Quenda walked in right now"? he asked her then.

"How do you know about her"? Gray suddenly frowned, "You didn't do, it did you"?

"Strangled her you mean, yes, I confess it was me".

"Right tonight, when the fun begins, you're the one who's wearing the cuffs, I know you'll have read it on the net-pad".

"I never got her background though", Home persisted, "Who was she with, here on Venus"?

"She was a spinster, Rale. Now come on let's little Rale and little Denton watch the tri-vid for a while".

"Your first name's Denton"?

She laughed, "You're still wearing the cuffs".

He could not think of anyway out of this constant spiral down into a world that was not real. Perhaps his sanity would be saved if he simply let the events play out until he got to the surgeon, yes that was it, just go with the flow, like travelling down a river, in a boat.

Another night in bed with Denton Gray was not such a nightmare anyway, so he said,

"Denny, you watch what you want tender-stuff".

"Denny….Denny, I like that Rale, you should start calling me that I never liked Toni".

Somehow he made it through the evening and then at bedtime there was plenty of compensation for his dilemma. The next morning he was on the train platform for the first express to The Central. From there he would change and get another train to Wintership Simics-Fel and then after a second change would be on his way to Ember Caves. The trains were very fast and much quieter than any other form of transport since they had gone electric and replaced steel rails with nyloplanyon. He was in the huge Romanian bubble just before lunch and then had to wait for an appointment in the surgeon's general practice.

Finally he walked into the room at fourteen fifty five E.S.T.

"And what can I do for you Mister….Home"? the surgeon asked after having consulted his memory bank.

"It's me, Doctor, Home! It wasn't more than a few days ago that you operated on me".

"I'm afraid that's not possible", the Biotron replied, "I would have remembered you"!

"I was in one of your theatres'", Home persisted, a feeling of grave misgiving starting to grip his bowel.

"The brain surgery, look my hair is still short, look where you drilled my skull". Home tilted his head for the surgeon to see, the site of his procedure. After nothing more than two seconds Home heard him say,

"This is certainly not my work, Mister Home. What on Venus did you have done in such tiny apertures anyway"?

"The synaptic plugs, Doctor, for the V.R. system"?

"Synaptic plugs? V.R? Do you mean for some sort of virtual reality"?

"Yes the one Light Cowboy wrote the programme for, the one Aleksei used to create his nano-bots".

"Mister Home, the procedure you are describing sounds beyond the law to me and certainly would not be conducted by a member of the medical profession. Now if you would kindly leave my surgery. I have other patients and I would suggest you do not come back here, otherwise I will be forced to contact the combmen, regarding your bizarre activities"!

Home looked at the surgeon in disbelief, but then saw the earnest look on his face and could see argument was going to get him nothing but possibly arrested. He rose and abjectly left the med-cent. What was he going to do now? The plugs were taking over his mind and he could not go to a doctor about it?

The only people left to him were someone who insisted on calling himself Light Cowboy and a Russian who was in Venugorad. He looked at the rail network, all the way back to Byron was closer. In more of a daze than contemplation, he made his return journey and got back to Byron at twenty thirteen hours that evening. When he opened the door of the apartment, he did not know who would be waiting for him.

It was Denton Gray, but she did not looked pleased to see him, more like nervous!

"What's the matter, I had to go all the way to Ember Caves and back, that's what I've been doing". He was used to apologising to a spouse, but his absence was not the reason for Gray's change of mood, she asked him,

"Last night, Rale, you mentioned you strangled Quenda Fillial, I thought you was joking obviously, but during our investigations into the case today, it turns out you did know her".

'Of course I knew her, she was my wife', he wanted to scream at his virtual wife, but that would not have helped his position in the constant running nightmare he was enduring.

"How did I know her then"? He asked. For he was genuinely curious.

"Yes, Rale you may well try to play the innocent now, but it's too late, we have surveillance footage of you, among many others, visiting her in her place of residence.

"To do what ? I don't understand"?

"To do her you ruddy, dirty, swine"!

Before he could get over the shock of imaging his former wife as a whore, his virtual wife was demanding,

"What's the matter with you, Rale? Wasn't I enough for you? I know we played games and stuff and I tried my best to please you always, but what were you doing with her? Did some sick sort of sex game too go far? Or are you evolving into a murderer now"?

"I could try and deny this", Home said leadenly, "But I no longer know what *'this'* is, what *'I'* am, what the world of Venus is all about. I don't know who or where I am Denny".

"Well there's not enough evidence to arrest you yet, Rale. You can't stay here any more though. I've packed the bag in the bedroom for you, I suggest you go and ask if you can sleep on your Cowboy friend's floor for the night. I will be filing for dissolution of our contract in the morning".

"You've decided I'm guilty"?

"You are guilty Rale, perhaps not of murder, but you're ruddy guilty. Please take your bag and go".

As he was half way out the door she observed, "And to think I got a transfer to this night-time world just to accommodate your job preference".

It was madness, a stranger was throwing him out of his own apartment, for sleeping with his wife. He felt like his sanity was being nibbled at and it would not take him long before he became unhinged.

He pounded on Light Cowboy's door, taking it out on the nyloplanyon instead of waiting for it to open and having a go at the programmer. After a pause it opened and Light Cowboy complained,

"Hounds in Tartarus, Homey why don't you beat the blasted door down"?

Home strode past his friend and ran straight into the single seater chair, "You live in a hamster cage", he complained, "Where am I going to sleep in this tiny rabbit warren"?

"Sleep, what's the matter has she thrown you out ha ha ha"?

"Inspector Gray has thrown me out, for sleeping with the red light lady of the night, one Quenda Fillial", Home told his friend. Then he waited with bated breath. To his considerable relief the Cowboy explained,

"What? Run that past me again"? and after Home had, "Who is Gray and what's he doing in your apartment and Quenda as a comfort girl, no offence, Home but that's pure fantasy".

"You want fantasy"? Home began, "Pour me a large Venvod and I'll give you a superb fantasy tale".

His friend poured two drinks and Home then told him of the events, as he had perceived them in the last forty eight hours. When he was finished Cowboy was silent for several seconds and then he asked,

"So Gray's a girl and she's tender meat and you sort of ......".

"Will you act your age for just a minute, Sillycow"? Home fumed, "We've got to get these plugs out of my brain".

"Sure sounds like it, only one part of your tale I can take exception to is mention of the Biotron however. You're in virtual, if you think the most famous surgeon on Venus, survivor of the great Venuser plague and defender of the Venuser themselves, drilled your skull and stuck probes in your brain"!

Home sighed, "That might be so, I don't exactly know what is and is not real, any more, so if not the surgeon, then whom"?

"Metal Phlude of course".

"Phlude"! Home exploded, "You let… sorry *we* let, the dim kid from the foundry, drill holes in my skull"!?

"He was the only one as'ud do it", Cowboy chirpily agreed, "He did a pretty neat job as far as I could see".

"You were in a theatre with him? I hope you were gowned and masked"?

"What theatre? He did it in the foundry before the night crew came on, though strictly speaking they're the other day crew being as it's been day now for……."

"I don't believe this", Home cut him short. "I let dim Phlude drill holes in my skull and stick bits of metal in my *brain in a* FOUNDRY"!

"Hold your horses", Cowboy tried to soothe Home, "Here have another drink".

"Yes", Home agreed miserably, "I'll hope it has some sort of antiseptic property against my impending sepsis".

"It wasn't like that", Cowboy defended, "He'd swiffened the floor of all swarf and metal drops and he washed his hands in Germosud. You could have eaten your dinner off the press bench".

"I think the plugs are still working", Home groaned, "I'm still in some sort of mad mechanical loop of your devilish programme".

"Look, Home" Cowboy began gently, actually using his right name, such was the demand, "We'll get somewhere cleaner for the extraction and….."

"There isn't time, they've got to come out" Home barked, "And they've got to come out tonight! Ping, Metal Phlude and get him to clean up the place and we'll get over before the night shift gets there".

"He couldn't do it in time and anyway he might not have any more of that Snufz he gave you before the last operation".

"Frenging butterflies in a killing jar"! Home cursed, "I took Snufz as well"?!

"You had to have the buzz or the pain would have been too much", Light Cowboy explained.

"This is like an episode of Frankenstein", Home muttered miserably.

"Well then why don't we get him"? Cowboy wanted to know. "Is he on Skype? Home"?

"No, Light, he's not on Skype, just ping Phlude and ask him to get over here and give me a large Venvod, in fact give me a very, very, large Venvod"

"But what about this Frank Stine, can't he come and….."?

"Ping, Phlude"! Home demanded and reached for the Venvod bottle.

"Leave some for sterilising the wounds, Home", Light Cowboy cautioned.

ELEVEN

FROM THE COMFORTING shrouds of inky oblivion, Home was forcibly dragged. Upward, upward toward light and the worst headache he had ever experienced. He threw himself downward again and this continued for an indeterminate period. Finally, he could stay in the darkness no longer and he slowly cracked his eyes slightly open once more. Agony lanced through them into his head and an incessant pounding in his temple began. The room was far too bright, the silence far too loud, but then he heard the noise of movement. Add faintly antiseptic smells and the muted conversations and he knew he was in med-cent.

He remembered the waking nightmare, before! After screaming himself hoarse, he had blacked out. Phlude had turned up at Light Cowboy's closet-come accommodation and it was evident from the start that he had almost as much alcohol inside him as Home. He had thought to bring his *surgical instruments* though. As he lifted them out of the tool bag, Home saw a standard Rolls-Royce two speed hammer drill, a centre punch, some nip nosed pliers, a claw hammer and a tube of Rolex super glue!

It was a measure of Home's intoxication, that he did not call off the *delicate surgical procedure* at that point. Phlude proceeded to pour Venvod over the instruments while Light Cowboy had a hissy fit at the mess he was making and the surgical fluid he was wasting! Good quality surgical fluid that could have alternatively gone down the Cowboy's own neck.

Satisfied that the medical centre was ready to commence, Light Cowboy seated himself on Home's chest as a precautionary medical measure. The chief surgeon then declared,

"I'll af to use da ole punch to get da bits of bone out da holes what are blocked up".

Thinking not to distract him, by underlining his grammatical errors, Home remained silent

The highly delicate action would involve the hole punch and claw hammer. After the second *tap* Home blacked out and was then in med-cent. A nurse was suddenly bending over him, she had that wafting and erotic mixture of starch and bleach that turned many a stout young man's head to lustful thoughts.

"He's coming out of it doctor", she breathed and then moved out of Home's current tunnel vision.

The doctor was tall, dark haired his nose quite sharp his features drawn, he had a days stubble bluing his chin,

"How do you feel, Mister Home"?

"I've a headache the size of Byron, Doctor, can you give me anything for it".

"Certainly, nurse two cc's of snufz-morph, please"?

"Yes Doctor", a saucy voice confirmed.

"Where am I please, Doctor"?

"You're in med-cent".

Home asked patiently, "Med-cent where Doctor"?

"Oh, right your disorientation is that bad? Med-cent in Tophead, I'm Doctor Redring, general surgical is not actually my normal field, but we're still stretched pretty thin while the recruitment campaign continues".

He pressed a hypo-dermal spray to Home's arm and the pain began to subside almost at once,

"Better", Redring asked.

"Getting there", Home felt the fog lifting from his vision and focus coming back, the nurse was as pretty as she sounded.

"So. What happened, how did I get here, I remember nothing"? Home went to put a hand up to his head but Redring cautioned,

"Don't touch your head for the time being, Mister Home, it's sterile now, you know". He took a breath and warned, "You might not be entirely happy by events, if Mister Light's account of matters is anything to go by".

"Mister Light", Home echoed sarcastically, "I'd like to turn mister Light's lights off, what did he tell you Doctor"?

"That you wanted the computer parts out of your brain"!

The bed seemed to disappear beneath Home and a huge maw of panic wanted to gobble him up and then spit him out as a mangled mauled mess.

"The synaptic plugs are still in place"? Home heard a voice ask and then realised it was his own, had *he* just spoken.

"Synaptic plugs"? Redring echoed, "Very interesting I had not heard them called that before, what was their medical purpose, Mister Home"?

"They were not put in place by anyone with even a hint of medical experience, Doctor. Indeed it's a miracle they went in the correct locations at all".

"Those being; of hearing and other perceptions like, touch, taste, vision, etcetera"?

In growing alarm Home asked, "And they weren't taken out, that means I don't know if I'm even here".

"You're in med-cent my dear fellow" Redring tried to ease Home's agitation, but just in case his assurances were falling on deaf ears he added,

"Nurse two cc's of Lubie".

"Strength, Doctor"?

"Better make it blue"!

Home remembered something the doctor had mentioned almost in an aside and asked, "You told me you were not in surgical, Doctor, what is your field of expertise, if you don't mind me asking"?

"Why it's psychiatry, Home, now get some rest my dear chap and we'll talk again later".

Another hypodermic hissed into Home's arm and he drifted gently into an untroubled slumber. It was devoid of any dreams and an indeterminate period later he awoke and found the nurse near his bed.

"Hello Mister Home, how do you feel now", she asked, "Ready to make the voyage do you think"?

"Voyage nurse, what voyage"?

"Back home, sir"?

"You mean to Earth? I do not wish to return to Earth, I just want to get the plugs out and …." he had absently touched his head and found he had a full head of hair and there were no puncture wounds in his scalp.

"Where are they? The plugs and how can I have hair already, some new sort of procedure that none outside the medical profession know about yet".

"Please do not get yourself agitated again Agent Genstrean the Transmuter will be available very soon. Now keep quiet or you will ruin the mission at this late hour".

Home groaned, the plugs were still in place, of course they were and he did not have a full head of hair, he was in V.R.!

'V.R.off! V.R.off! V.R.off! V.R.off!' Home thought like some sort of religious mantra, but nothing seemed to change.

The nurse suddenly came from around a wall with a curious looking device on a castored trolley. For some reason it did not quite look like a medical contrivance to Home. It had a huge conical snude with wires coming out of the larger diameter of the cone, these fed into a large pad. The nurse instructed him hurriedly,

"Stay still Genstrean and good luck"? He saw her tap various symbols on the pad and thought,

'What a bizarre imagination I've got, what are the plugs going to drag from it next making up the next fantasy'?

The med-cent shimmered to nothingness and he found himself momentarily surrounded by absolute blackness. Yet he could see himself, his hands before his face, it was not as though he was in the dark, but rather that which surrounded him was devoid of light. It had no absorptivity either though, it was just simply nothing!

No sooner had he began to be intrigued by it, than it was replaced by the gradual fading in of a strange scene indeed. He found himself in a vast hall, the walls of which were silvery grey and swept up in fluted columns to a great spiralled roof several metres above his head. He glanced down at his body and discovered he was dressed in some sort of toga held together by hidden magnetic strips. He was just examining their clever action when a very tall and slender woman with ascetically set features hurried from around one of the columns and halted before him,

"Genstrean, it's so good to have you back, how are you? Are you still disorientated, it will take a while for it all to come back to you, that was the deliberate nature of the drugs"?

"I'm afraid dear lady I did not understand a single word of what you just told me, so I cannot imagine where the plugs got this nonsense"?

On the woman's slender wrist was a small pad held in place by a strap, as she hurriedly tapped it, Home said,

"That's a simple but clever idea, once I'm back in the real world I'll have to patent that. I'm not going to make anything out of the plugs that's for sure".

Another woman appeared, this one less severe looking, she was blonde and slim, and quite attractive, she looked at the severe looking woman and asked,

"You sent for me Duchess".

"Yes, doctor, it's as suspected, he has Tarvian-psychosis. He might even still believe he's one of them, we need to bring him back to reality before you can debrief him".

"Will you come with me please, Genstrean", the decorative blonde asked.

"I'm, Home", Home replied.

"Yes you are, Genstrean that's good you realise that, now this way please"?

Home chuckled at the mistake his name was causing and went with her, no sense in trying to buck the plugs, he could not fight the images that were being shot straight into his brain.

He followed the elegant and pale doctor and she lead him to a large furnished room that looked nothing like a hospital ward. The room was decorated with cream coloured velour drapes that hung from the high ceiling, at one side was a deeply studded white leather three seater sofa, which the doctor indicated he be seated in. Doing so with a wave of her elegant hand.

Home took a seat and smelled,

"Are you making this of real leather"? he asked

"I'm sorry, Genstrean"?!

"The sofa we're sitting on, is it supposedly of real cow hide"?

"It is real leather, Genstrean".

"Why Genstrean, what's the significance of that"?

"Genstrean is your name, agent Genstrean of Measborough Dike".

"So this is Yorkshire", Home laughed, "I never saw a building like this in Yorkshire".

"But you did", the doctor argued, "You just don't remember it, but with my help you will, I will help bring all of reality back to you".

"Reality"! Home echoed, "I would love to get back to reality, but I don't figure on that until I get the plugs out of my brain".

"Genstrean there are no plugs, we used the transmuter to send you to the virtual world the computerplex has created, the Tarvians aren't real, they only exist in the programme. Until we can figure out how the programme can be successfully turned off, hundreds of sad sufferers will continue to suffer the resultant psychosis, just as you bravely volunteered so to do, in the name of research. Now, I am Doctor Hyphon and I am going to help you with reorientation. Firstly do you want anything? Food, drink a cigarette, you surely will not want to sleep will you"?

Home thought, *'Okay let's play for a while and see where this leads, what else can I do'?*

"I'll have a Venvod then please, Doctor".

"I'm sorry I've no idea what one of those is, was it a hot beverage, a soft drink, or something alcoholic"?

"Venvod is a shortening for Venus Vodka", Home explained, "Have you Vodka, Doctor, I don't mind which nationality"?

"Of course, one Russian Vodka coming up".

She walked over to what looked like a wall, waved her hand and said, "Dispenser, two small Russian Vodkas".

"Impressive", Home noted, "Voice activation, glad I imagined that".

Two elegant glasses suddenly appeared in a recess, part of the wall had silently slid to one side. Hyphon lifted them out and passing one to Home resuming her place at the opposite end of the sofa to him.

"Let me give you some information your Maj….er agent Genstrean", she stuttered.

"Your Maj"? Home echoed, "What were you going to say then, doc"?

"Oh dear", Hyphon sighed, "This will get me in trouble with the Duchess when she learns of my mistake. Too much too soon, will you tell her you remembered yourself your Majesty"?

"The duchess being the rather severe looking lady we encountered a few moments ago"? Home deduced. The doctor seemed delighted,

"Yes that right, Sire, the Duchess Tula your aunt".

"So I'm an agent and a royal, the king in fact"?

"You were the king, who became an agent to help those of his people who were suffering from addiction to the programme, the virtual reality world of Tarvia".

"So this is the real world is it", Home smiled, "And everything I remember of my entire lifetime as the elector-engineer Rale U. Home was something cooked up by the programme. The programme that can be entered by means of the transmuter".

"This is incredible progress, your Majesty" Hyphon beamed taking everything he said at face value.

"Do you remember anything else, agent Marva for example, who is still in the programme and sent you back to us".

"The nurse"!

"That's right, she is posing as a nurse, in Tarvia".

"So where am I king of"? Home asked

"Oh, you don't remember that"?

"Refresh my memory"?

"You're king here, in the real world, on Earth in Yorkshire, you are the king of York".

"Yorkshire is a sovereignty"?

"It is, ever since the devolution of Northern England into the separate, former counties, in fifty three".

"That would be thirty two fifty three"?

"No, Sire, thirty three fifty three, the time line is not the same in Tarvia, remember"?

"It's so easy to forget", Home smiled sardonically. "Do go on"?

"Well, do you remember your family, your fiancé"?

"Fiancé"?

"Yes Princess Denton of Leicestershire".

"Now that you mention it I do remember Denton yes"! his double entendre was totally wasted on the good doctor.

"Would you like to meet her, she has been most concerned for your safety while you were in the programme"?

"Why not"? Home was actually beginning to enjoy himself, "Wheel her in".

"Wheel her in? She's not incapacitated in any way, your Majesty".

"Sorry, an aberration, bring her in then Hyphon and when just you and I are present you can call me simply Genny"!

"I would not think to be so familiar, Sire".

"Then I make it a command", Home laughed.

The doctor rose and hurried out of the room, she returned after only a brief interval with inspector Gray in her company. The princess Denton had no doubt been waiting without, eagerly anticipating a chance to be reunited with her fiancée.

"Good my lord", Gray began, "How go-est for thee, I have been sore vexed and in a state of great trepidation whilst thou hast been in the nefarious programme".

Obviously flowery speech was a characteristic of Leicestershire in this reality.

"Princess Denton, you look well", Home replied, "As am I and all the better for seeing you".

Gray seated herself beside him and kissed him chastely on the cheek, "What is thy prognosis, Doctor", she asked Hyphon.

"He is making startling progress", the doctor actually curtsied as she spoke, "I have expectation that he will be himself in but a few short days".

"Those tidings gladden my heart, dear sweet Majesty"

"Fabulous", Home agreed with all the sincerity he could manage, which was in fact infinitesimal.

'Oh well, it this is to the fate the plugs have in store for me it could have been much worse', he thought, although the destiny of his actual body was of some small interest to him too.

There again surely Light Cowboy would not just let it starve and he could not imagine he would get far with a comatose Home. For he believed he had been in the current V.R. since he had awoken from his botched operation. Not that it was any longer possible to tell one way or the other.

"Before lunch would it be possible to bathe, change into other clothes"? He asked his intended.

"What so ever thou dost desire, my sweet Prince", his intended returned. He could not have imagined better in a fiancée.

He was shown to his apartment within the palace and it was nothing short of his wildest imaginings. All was once again heavy drapes, they seemed to be the current fashion; of royal blues and deep oranges tied back with gold ropes hung on huge bronze hooks. The overall feel was quite old fashioned, but then Home was also, so it was not surprising that this fantasy world had taken on the characteristic.

The walls were adorned with ancient oil paintings, depicting horses and antique weapons added to the wealth of yesteryear. He went into the bathroom and threw off his quite grimy overall of the day; how long had that day been?

The bath was a huge white enamel container with enormous clawed feet clutching balls of brass. He turned on the dolphin shaped taps and the hot and cold water poured from their open mouths. In the place of liquid pumps of depilatory and cleansing liquids there was a glass bottle of shampoo and an enormous keg of soap.

Unpractised with the open razor he decided to let his beard grow, after all king's of yesteryear tended to wear beards. Having shampooed and soaped himself from head to toe he climbed out and dried himself on an enormous bath sheet of thick white cotton. There chanced to be a full length mirror before him and he looked at V.R. king Genstrean.

He was pleased with the figure he saw. Lithely muscular, with a six pack of abdominals, thick black hair on his head, chest and legs. A handsome man, a royal figure. Naked, he strode into the bedroom and opened the door of a huge double wardrobe of carved and polished walnut, that resided next an impressive four poster bed covered in thick silk sheets of royal blue.

The clothes were the sort he would have imagined of course. Pantaloons that buttoned just beneath the knee, long white socks that left just the knee showing, doublets of deep blues and mulberry embroidered with silver thread.

He threw one on and then drew a white waistcoat over the top of it and he cut a dashing figure when he returned to look at his reflection once more. He cleaned his teeth with a brush and some white gritty paste instead of sucking a dental tablet. Then he brushed his hair and chose some black leather slippers with gold buckles on their tops.

Feeling much more his own part, he descended the massive winding staircase and went once again into the room he now thought of as the drawing room. Gray was still there and she was reading. Not a pad though, but a book of paper pages in a leather binding and the pages looked to be made with genuine wood pulp!

"Would you like to show me around the palace", he asked her.

She started, looked up from her studies and smiled at him.

"T'would be an most exceeding pleasure, my sweet Prince", she affirmed.

Together they trod down lengthy corridors decorated with grand tapestries, looked into rooms with tall multi-paned windows filled with furniture of various timbers and upholstered with materials from Earth's past and now Earth's future too. Then Gray asked him,

"Would my Prince like to see without"?

"Outside"?

She nodded either feigning not to notice his odd aberration or simply accepting it due to his past trial and tribulation.

So she lead him onto an expansive veranda and he was stunned at the vista of South Yorkshire, for it was magnificent!

Gone were the ancient high rises. Replaced by lofty fluted building of towers and spires. The buildings seemed to be built from either stainless steel or chrome and shone and glittered in the sunlight.

"This be thy realm my king", the girl told him and he saw how impressive it was and he wanted it to be exactly so.

"Yes", he agreed, "Indeed it is and soon it will be one that I will share with thee my dearest" and he found he had no desire what so ever for it not to be.

TWELVE

K ING GENSTREAN HAD been in
Yorkshire three physiological months
when he felt suddenly queasy. He gripped the rail of his royal carriage, just as he
was waving to the thronged masses. Those who had come to witness the royal
wedding that would forge an alliance between Yorkshire and Leicestershire and
effectively annex Lancashire.

Then…..

Gniz!.

'No'! Genstrean screamed in his mind, *'I don't want to go back in the transmuter,
what vile rapscallion and enemy of the throne has done this to me, I belong here in my
kingdom'!*

He found himself on a low and rude cot and the instant the scene
shimmered into actuality a padded door opened and a tall, dark haired figure
entered and looked at him sympathetically. The man's nose was quite sharp
his features drawn, he had a days stubble bluing his chin, he wore a white lab
coat, it was doctor Redring.

"Thank the stars and moonless world of Venus, we got you back, you've
not injured yourself in here, Home"?

Genstrean looked dazedly at the doctor, unable to fathom quite how he
had returned to…..to what?

A world that held far less happiness in it, than the one he had been in for
the last quarter. He had not tried to enter the transmuter, it must have been
the Tarvians!

He examined his position. Had he tried to forget the past and yet ended up in the programme on Venus with a complete set of false memories provided by the enemies of the crown.

They did not wish to help his subjects They did not wish any to be cured of programme psychosis. They wanted them to believe Yorkshire the programme. These individuals were not human, they were as Hyphon had maintained, Tarvians? Venus was the Tarvian's world, only people lived in wondrous Yorkshire? Did they think him incapable of knowing their insidious plot?

"How couldst I have harmed myself varlet (he had picked up some of the Leicestershire vernacular during his courtship) when the room be padded. By who's authority dost thou imprison me"?

"Imprison"?! Redring gasped, "You're not in a penal facility, my dear, Home, but a sanatorium".

"A building for the housing of the mentally infirm, sirrah, I'll have you know I am fully compos-mentis, of sound mind and sound a body as any in my realm".

"Ah the realm", Redring seemed to understand something, "The realm you've built for yourself in V.R. the fruit of your much more than average imagination Sir".

"Thou hast failed to prove thy case Sirrah", Genstrean then told the physician, "The Tarvian world be not real 'tis nought but a virtual reality"!

The doctor seemed to find the statement difficult to refute and with good reason, for how could he?

"In your world do you have the synaptic plugs driven into your brain"? he finally asked.

"Good Sir physician the transmuter be evidence enough to prove *my* case?

Redring considered that point and found the mere existence of a non-existent machine impossible to deny.

"Do you not miss this world"? he asked in desperation finally.

"My dear Sir Tarvian, in the real world I am the king.

Newly married to a young and comely princess of a neighbouring realm. My subjects love me, the kingdom is wealthy, spacious and clean and I live in a palace, with more personal wealth than I can spend in a thousand lifetimes.

We Yorkists call this world the land of the Tarvian which is a word with the same sort of definition as your word pleb, to whit; an ordinary person who has low social status. Now you ask me which world is real to me and which one is not. What would you answer"?

Redring promised, "We will not let this body perish, we will care for it and maintain it, that is our way, even if we are Tarvian. You will receive the occasional visitor, but the visits will be infrequent and will diminish with time. I do not think there is anything more I can do for you, Home"?!

Genstrean nodded his silent agreement to the spoken deal, then requested, "Please close the door on your way out, good doctor".

It closed to, with the cushioned swish of deep padding.

Zing!

SUPERNAL WILL

MY future will not copy fair my past
On any leaf but Heaven's. Be fully done
Supernal Will ! I would not fain be one
Who, satisfying thirst and breaking fast,
Upon the fulness of the heart at last
Says no grace after meat.   - Elizabeth Barrett-Browning

ONE

THE LONG DISTANCE train had just travelled approximately half the circumference of Mars. It ground to a halt in the very north of the small, cool world. Kunowsky was a bit more provincial than Thurtrum was used to and expecting. He shivered under the light sleet that fell on his uncovered head. He was used to indoor stations with canopies of plexi-glass. No matter, promotion was promotion and his new post would be a coveted one, head cashier.

To take it up he had left the bosom of his mother, the protection of his father and cut the apron strings. Hebes Chasma was way too far south to make commuting a sensible proposition. So he had pinged an estate agent up in the town he now trod and arranged a meeting for a showing of a small bachelor apartment. It was quite a risk, but at least he had seen the tri-vid's and had a pretty good idea what to expect.

If he hated it when he got there, he could always book into a low cost boarding house while he looked at alternatives. He saw Missus Smine whilst still half a street distant, her latest liposuction was well overdue and the bright scarlet parka she wore made her look like a walking danger sign. To his horror she recognised him and began waving and crying greetings that he was too far away to hear. He might have been, but half the neighbourhood was not.

He quickened his pace, his gait made awkward by the bulk of his holdall and rushed to cut the distance between them in the shortest time possible.

"You have to be the young man I've was contacted by Skype", she enthused, "Mister Thurstone isn't it"?

"Thurtrum", he corrected her for the thousandth time, and spelled it out for her.

"Oh dear", she protested, "All my padwork is wrong now, still it's the same difference isn't it no matter how you spell it. I won't have to change any of the forms will I"?

"Yes you will. For you see one of them is my name, while the other is not. I hope you see the difference Missus Spine"!

"Smine", she corrected automatically and then laughed, "Oh! I see what you mean, you had me there didn't you"?

There and **only** *there',* he thought and asked her, "Are we near the property Missus Smine"?

"Oh! Yes, It's up above these shops actually, there are four bijou apartments and the vacant one is number three. I've got the combination, but when I've given it you, it might be a good idea to change it, you never can be too careful you know".

"Shall we then"? he wondered and she finally lead the way. At the side of the shops was a combination steel door, the code for which was only six digits but it was better than nothing. The door swung open and a series of stone steps took them to a fire escape top. Going through an open archway, the four doors of the apartments were in two rows of two, either tide of a short passage.

Missus Smine took a card from her pocket and keyed in the ten digit code for apartment three, she then pushed the door open and let Thurtrum enter ahead of her. The entire apartment was painted from top to bottom in white, which Thurtrum supposed was a safe bet. There was a lounge, kitchen/utility room, bathroom and bedroom. None of the rooms were larger than one person could expect.

"It will look much warmer when the furniture comes I expect", Missus Smine said, "Have you a bed coming or do you intend to furnish from lodgings and move in when it's done".

"If I've organised things correctly everything I need will arrive between now and twenty hundred hours".

"Oh! So you knew you were going to take the place"?

"It's cheap and close to the bank, those were the critical factors".

"Oh! Well, here is the pad-page I need your thumb on mister *Thurstum* and the bank agreement and then I'll leave you to it".

"All of which I'll gladly thumb, once you've corrected my name on each one", he said and waited while she did, before agreeing to anything.

Within the hour, after some frantic pinging the deliveries began. He breathed a sigh of relief once the bed was in, knowing he could manage without almost anything else. He was just using the tea-machine for the very first time when a female voice called,

"Hello".

Thurtrum walked into the lounge and almost collided with one of the most striking blondes he'd ever seen.

"Whoopsy sorry", he flushed, "Can I help you Miss, what have you in your flitter-van"?

She smiled and her face was made beauteous by the expression, "I'm not delivering, silly. I'm from number two, across the hall you know. Saw someone was moving in and wondered if they'd like a hot drink"?

"That's neighbourly of you, Miss"?

"Just call me Farli", she held out her hand and they shook, hers was delightfully frail and soft feeling in his own.

"Oh, you have lovely hands for a man", she said, despite his observation in that area, "Are you an artist of some sort"?

"Hardly I work in a bank", he laughed, "What do you do"?

"Let me get you that drink and we can talk some then", she suggested, Had she just avoided an awkward question?

"I've just set my new machine making a cup, let me change the digit to two".

"Sure thing", she agreed readily, "One sweetener please"

"Ah, problem".

"That's fine not bad for having only been in the place three hours, I'll just nip over the hall and get one from my pad".

"Surely you're sweet enough", he said and she laughed and went to her own apartment, while he cringed and asked, "Surely you're sweet enough is that the best you can do"?

She came back momentarily with a sweetener and a tea spoon, holding it aloft, she explained, "Just in case the cutlery hasn't come yet".

"It has actually", he grinned, "But if I stole that, it would grow by one hundred percent".

"You've only one spoon"?

He nodded,

"And one knife and fork, but of course this is sufficient because I've only one mouth. I was on a budget and it was only so elastic".

"What will you do for the house warming"?

"There isn't going to be one, I'm desperately waiting for pay day and anyway I only just arrived in Kunowsky, who would I invite, I've no friends"?

"Well you have one now", she smiled and it was quite possible that he fell in love with her at that very moment.

TWO

THREE MONTHS LATER and the job was just beginning to be routine for him. The manager had his eccentricities, but then he *was* English. As far as Thurtrum was concerned he knew where he stood with Mich Smotumu, it was alright to call him by his first name, but never to forget he was the general manager.

The apartment began to look more like a home. He had just enough furniture for himself and a single guest, which left the place looking deceptively spacious. There was only windows in the bedroom and for two months he found he could easily sleep with the light that came from the road, when it was dark. Then one day when Farli was over for a cup of beverage, she wandered into the bedroom before he could notice and cried,

"Vant, you've no curtains at your bedroom windows".

He rushed past her and began to make the bed, embarrassed that she had seen it unmade.

"I can sleep with the street lights they don't keep me awake", he told her.

"What about if you've nothing on", she smiled.

"I undress in the bathroom, turn off the light and then walk into here and get into bed. If it's light outside you can't see in because this room is quite dim anyway".

"What if you're not alone then"? she asked and laughed uproariously when he turned a deep scarlet. "Poor Vant, not gotten lucky yet in Kunowsky. Here if you've been paid let's go shopping for some curtains"?

He had a healthy bank balance by that time, head cashier commanded a decent salary, but she always seemed to be impecunious and to make her feel better he pretended to be in similar straights.

"Well I don't want anything too gaudy", he protested, whilst being delighted at the idea of being seen out with her. What if people who saw them, thought they were a couple? How round-side would that be?

"What do you mean, I have superb taste"? She pretended to be wounded and laughed then by adding "My curtains are a lovely shade of bright yellow with huge marigolds printed on them".

"Now I know you're exaggerating", he laughed and then suddenly asked, "You are aren't you".

"No of course not come and see for yourself".

Thurtrum went quite pink and spluttered, "No that's fine, I believe you".

"What's the matter Vant", she asked quietly, "Scared I'm going to rape you"?

"Come on", he dashed for the door, "Let's go shopping for beige curtains".

Laughing delightedly she dashed after him. That particular expedition cost him far more than he had anticipated, she persuaded him to buy curtains in midnight blue, a 360.1 sound system, several ornaments that were not even to his taste and several canvas', half of which were to his taste (which she hated) and half of which were not (which he hated). It should have been a pertinent message, but it wasn't, by that time he was infatuated with her.

Once everything had been delivered and installed in the place they sort of decided together (she decided and he agreed) on location, she told him,

"Instead of somewhere you sleep, it's now looking like somewhere you live" and she kissed him, on his lips and he kissed her back. Then they began to kiss one another, first with enthusiasm, then with passion and as was inevitable, they ended up in his bed. He marvelled at the smoothness of her skin, the suppleness of her feminine curves and enjoyed her eager participation.

Finally she told him,

"I have to go to work now, my shift starts in an hour".

"Get showered here and fetch some clothes and I'll run you into town"? he offered wanting to spend as much time with her as possible. She frowned and holing him close admitted to him,

"Vant, I work at the Blue Papagal in Obraznic Lane".

"The topless bar"! he gasped, "What do you mean, do you....what do you do there Farli"?

"Wait tables, it was all I could get, I have to pay my rent don't I"?

"Wait tables.... what do you mean exactly Farli"?

"I mean I'm a topless waitress in a sleazy bar, is what I mean", she disentangled herself and made to leave. He could not believe it was her who was getting angry.

"Don't leave like this, cross with me"

"I don't need your disapproval".

"It's not that, it….."

She came back to him, stroked his hair, "It's what then"?

"It's jealousy and I know I have no right to feel it, but I do, the thought of other men ogling your; ogling you and thinking; well we both know what they'll be thinking".

"Do you want me to give my notice"?

"Your notice? You mean leave and then, then how would you: You mean, you could…."

"Move in here and you could keep me until I found something, something that better met your approval"?

His heart leapt at the prospect, to have her with him every day, to *have* her every night.

"If I said yes"?

"If you say yes; then I will".

"Then I say yes Farli". He could hardly believe it. They made love again and then both showered and he drove her into the Blue Papagal in Obraznic Lane and she handed in her notice. Three weeks later she moved into the apartment.

A month after that she began looking for somewhere larger and reluctantly, although he was happy where they were, he let her select something more central, more spacious and more expensive.

She shopped like mad to outfit their new apartment, she never seemed to find the time to look for alternative employment. His bank balance slowly dripped down to almost zero, but he was deliriously happy. They moved and he hoped the spending would curtail and it did for a while, but then he asked her to contract with him for five years (periods were eighteen months, three years, five and ten) and her agreement entailed more frantic shopping for outfits for a party and for, just about everything else.

His bank account went into the red, then it went into red alert!

He found himself in Smotumu's office one morning,

"You wanted to see me Mich"?

"Yes have a seat Vant, I'll get straight to the point. One of the clerks have brought your account here at the bank to my attention. Now I know you've recently had a great deal of expenditure with your engagement, moving and then the contract party and civil service, so I'm not especially surprised that you've run up a sizeable over-draught".

"Yes Mitch, I'm hoping it will calm down and then I can….."

Smotumu held up his hand palm toward Thurtrum, saying, "There's no need to explain, I understand, only the thing is you'll pay twenty three and half percent on an over-draught Vant, while, if I offer you a personal loan, the rate drops to six and a quarter".

Thurtrum blinked, "That's very good of you, I never expected; well, thank you".

"I've been watching your progress here at First National and I'm pleased with your diligence and hard work, so much so, that I'm letting you have the second swipe card to the vault, Vant. This will mean some late night's for you, but it also comes with an extra fifty a month".

Thurtrum could see it was a win, win situation, he got the rise, Smotumu got to slope off every evening leaving him to see to the day's business.

"I really appreciate this Mich", he gushed and rushed home that evening to tell his new and beautiful wife.

"So you'll be left in charge of all that money"? she noted, there was a curious ring to her tone of voice.

"Yes", he did not notice, "It's a position of great responsibility and with the extra whazumahs I can pay off the over-draught".

Three years later the over-draught was even bigger!

Events had spiralled out of all control and things were about to get a whole lot worse!!

THREE

S MOTUMU'S OFFICE WAS very modern; all chrome, glass and stainless steel. He was a man with a modern outlook, a man who liked change and opportunity, a man who loved Mars. Mich Smotumu was the general manager of the First National, the largest and most successful of the Banks of Mars and his office was in Kunowsky.

There was a knock on his door and Smotumu looked up from his pad,

"Come in", he cried. It swished open to allow Head Cashier Thurtrum entrance,

"You asked to see me Mich"?

Smotumu did not have time for grand titles and his staff all referred to him by his first name.

"I've just been looking at net news and another safety deposit box owner here at the bank has passed on. I've already had a communication from the family telling us they have no idea of the code. You'll have to ping that man of yours and ask him to undo it for us".

"Of course Mich, I'll get right on it".

"And as before, watch him like a hawk you know I don't trust him".

Thurtrum smiled and let himself out. The head cashier knew just how much 'his man' Spider Hourglass could be trusted and it was not a great deal, no not much at all. Getting back to his desk in the main office of the bank he picked up his pad and pinged the one time convict.

Hourglass features swam into focus.

"Hello again Spider", the head cashier began, "Your I.P. indicates that you're still stopping in Lomonosov, I've another comparatively easy job for you".

"A safety deposit box that no-one has the combination for"?

"Just so, when can you get here"?

"I can be there in an hour", the former resident of Mars' Correction Facilities told him, "I'll see you then".

Hourglass cut the connection and pondered, what was becoming a poorly, not so lucrative sideline for him, that of legitimate locksmith. It gave him pause to consider the immortal topics of life, death and time. It was not the easiest of work that First National had commissioned him for and some of the sixteen digit combinations took some time to crack. Especially the Alucard-Krankenstein's and most of the safety deposit boxes in the vault were of that very manufacturer. It was the living that had used them and the dead that brought him to them and the time he took to open them.

He asked himself not for the first time, why he had taken the job in the first place, it was certainly not for the shillin. He knew though, he really knew the reason when he examined his emotions clearly, he just liked being in the vault, close to all that money.

Hourglass ran from his apartment in the boarding house at Lomonosov and dived into his flitter. The ever present dust was a nuisance to him and he hated it with a passion. He turned on the stik player and gunned the engine, the sound of the machine and the sound of Deep Purple's Machine Head filled the confines of his Sanyo 140hp vehicle.

It was a modest flitter, but had been in his budget when he had bought it. It got him from 'A' to 'B' and today that was from Lomonosov to Kunowsky.Well within the time he had allotted himself to get to his destination, he was pulling up outside the bank. Another dash through the thin, dust laden atmosphere and he was inside it's rather opulent walls of modern materials. Hourglass found the overall effect sterile, but there again perhaps banks were not supposed to be places of cultural stimulation anyway.

He walked over casually to Thurtrum's desk,

"Ho Vant how's it hanging", he always took particular delight in watching the head cashier squirm at his over familiarity. Thurtrum hated him to do it in front of the staff he supervised, so of course Hourglass did it even more.

"This way", was all he hissed in reply.

Spider simply added the ten shillin he was going to get for the job, to his diminutive bank balance and yawned with ennui. Then he saw the pretty little cashier that had caught his eye previously and winked at her, she proceeded to flush in a most attractive way.

"What's her name", he asked Thurtrum. The head cashier merely grunted,

"There'll be no fraternising with the staff, Spider, if you please".

He lead the safe cracker through the enormous circular and severely armoured doorway of the bank's vault. Spider could smell the money, no wonder they called it filthy lucre.

It was only the work of twenty minutes to get the safety deposit box open, the shortest time he's ever cracked the sixteen digit code, and then Spider left the bank, knowing a draft would be going into his own account almost instantly. He was not keen on how Thurtrum had stood over him the whole time though, it was as if the head cashier did not trust him!

Two evenings later he got another ping from Thurtrum and it was out of hours!

"What's up at this time of the day"? he wished to know.

"I've been watching your er, work", the head cashier said hesitantly, "I don't think you're entirely honest and that may work to our mutual benefit".

"What are you trying to say Vant"?

"Spider how would you like to make a thousand silver shillin. On the proviso that you then emigrated to Venus"?

"I'm listening Vant"?

"The bank has just won the account of Red-U-Can which as you'll know is the Mars branch of a massive company on Earth. They plan to commence their account by depositing two thousand silver shillin in our vault".

"The main vault, that houses the safety deposit boxes"?

Thurtrum nodded, "The vault that has a twenty four digit code and a swipe card too".

"Another Alucard-Krankenstein. The code is capable of being cracked by an expert, but to get a forgery of the card is virtually impossible", Spider told him.

"So I've been told, however there are two cards to the vault, Spider, Smotumu has one and guess who has the other"?

"The head cashier".

"I like my Martian tan", Spider replied, "And you get pretty pale in Correctional Facilities, believe me I know".

"You're talking about getting caught", Thurtrum scoffed, "But we'll get clean away hours before Smotumu comes to open the bank in the morning".

"I'm not your man, Vant", Spider returned, "I've only just got out of the slammer and I have no desire to do another stretch", and before Thurtrum could say any more, he cut the connection.

He had forgotten the whole conversation a week later when there was a knock on his apartment door once again in the evening. He looked at the inspection plate and almost whistled, a statuesque blonde with everything in the right place was standing on the other side of his door. Without further ado he opened it,

"Mister Hourglass"?

"I don't believe I've had the pleasure"!

"I've made a special trip to find you, may I come in"?

Spider stood to one side and as she wafted by he enjoyed the view and the aroma of a very desirable women. She looked around his humble dwelling and there was no emotion on her face, good, she accepted it for what it was; temporary.

"Can I offer you a drink", Spider asked hospitably.

"Certainly, anything strong", she slid down onto his beaten couch and her skirt rode up to reveal the best pair of legs he'd seen since; ever.

Once two Marspirits were in their hands he asked her,

"What have you come to see me about; Miss"?

"Call me Farli".

"Alright Farli, what do you want with me"?

"My full name is Farli Thurtrum".

"I see".

"I have a Honda Skirt 250 outside, would you like to go for a night ride".

There was more than one answer to that question, but Spider chose,

"Sure once you've finished your drink, I'm all yours".

They drank up and she lead him down his stairway to the street, following Farli Thurtrum was an experience in itself and Spider's imagination was doing handsprings into various possibilities. The Honda was a deep red and very sleek, just like it's owner. She slid into the driver side and shot off the minute Spider had taken the passenger, she drove quickly, just as he had expected.

"Where are we going Farli"?

"The new lake at Passionata, it's not far".

"West of this place and Kunowsky, what's going on Farli"?

"I thought we could take a moon-lit dip, Phobos will be up in the sky and the new robot lifeguard and spy saucers look after anyone who's not a strong swimmer".

"Alright sounds fun and then you're going to tell me what's going on right"?

"Of course, how can there be any secrets between two people who've seen one another naked"? she crooned and that was the clincher for Spider.

She made small talk as they zoomed toward the destination and he was happy to answer in kind.

At the rocky beach, as dawn was then painting the sky a beautiful mixture of pinks, blues and crimson, she threw off her clothes before him and rushed into the very gentle waves. Spider was not far behind her and they swam while the metal lifeguard patrolled the beach. It had all been created for just such purposes as this, importantly, it was all free.

Farli then swam to the shore and lay on the beach totally naked and without any sort of conscience at all. While Spider let his own body dry by the meagre warmth of the distant sun he demanded,

"So Farli Thurtrum come closer".

Without any guilt what-so-ever they made love on the sand and then dressed slowly.

"Vant has been stealing from the bank for some time", she admitted finally.

"I see", he smiled "And you are the carrot that is supposed to convince me to break into the vault and get the Red-U-Can deposit"?

Farli gave him a crimson smile, her teeth white and even, her bosom (which was impressive) pointed in his direction so that the memory of her, with him, was keenest.

"I don't care about him", she told him then, "But I've known about it from the beginning and that makes me an accessory".

"I'm guessing he spent some of his ill gotten gains on you as well didn't he"?

She nodded, "So you see if you rob the bank it gets me out of a spot as well as him. Then you and I can have many more pleasant assignations".

"Starting with lunch at the Super-Alimente"?

"Alright the swim and; the other thing has given me an appetite".

FOUR

"I HOPE YOU'VE not been waiting too long", she breathed heavily, the overall effect was to make her low cut frock of greens and browns an even better choice.

"I've only just arrived", Spider admitted glancing at his silver wrist chrono, they were both only tardy by five minutes.

After they'd ordered Spider asked,

"Farli, when did you first decide you wanted to get Thurtrum out of the way permanently"?

"I beg your pardon"? she laughed, but the sound of it was hollow and insincere.

"Murder him and make an awful lot of cash in the process"? He watched her carefully, "The thought has crossed your mind, just like it's crossing mine now. You admit you've lost your feelings for him, so you find a nice man who can open the vault for you and get rid of the baggage at the same time".

"I'm not sure I……".

"I open the vault, throw your husband into it and lock him inside. The manager finds his body in the morning, he's died of suffocation and the two of us make off with two thousand while he gets the blame, it's a good scheme isn't it Farli"?

"Clever", she smiled, "And according to *your* plan all I have to do is get you to fall in love with me"?

Spider nodded, "For which, you are well acquitted, my dear Farli".

After that first lunch Spider saw more and more of Farli Thurtrum and it was very pleasant doing so. One afternoon as she was lying beside him in bed, her gorgeous hair draped over his pillow, the smell of perfume and sex heavy in the air, Spider got up on one elbow and said,

"I'm going to do it".

They kissed passionately before he told her, "One thing though Farli, if you double cross me, I'll......". he let the sentence hang deliberately,

"Cross you"? she was incredulous, "I love you Spider".

"Are you telling me what you want me to hear, or do you mean it. I mean you loved Thurtrum once didn't you"?

"Oh I don't know, I just think now that I thought I did, but the truth is I didn't and the truth is I do love you".

When she was gone, he pinged her cuckolded husband, Thurtrum swam into focus on the tiny screen,

"We'll do it tomorrow night. Make sure you're still in the bank at eighteen hundred and don't forget the card".

Thurtrum looked surprised, "You've changed your mind, why and why do we have to do it so soon after I've only just found out"?

"So you don't have time to think of some way of ending up with the entire amount Vant".

"We're partners in this, why would I double cross the only man who can make it into the cash"?

"A thousand does things to a man Vant", Spider reasoned, "He gets a thousand easily and then starts to thinking he might make that thou, two".

"Half is all I want, that's our agreement".

"Then be there and when I say, or the whole thing's off"

Spider cut the connection and then pinged the head cashier's wife, "It's all set", he told her once they were connected.

"Spider"? she asked, "How long will he last? I mean how long will the air in the vault take to be exhausted".

"Why, are you getting cold feet"?

"No of course not, it's just that, well I was wondering that's all".

"Ninety minutes, maybe two hours at the most".

"And by that time we'll be on a rocket for Venus"?

Spider nodded, "The constables will find his body just how Smotumu discovered it and conclude he was going to take more than the two thousand he already had and the door swung shut on him. We'll be free and clear".

"Surely they'll think he had help, an accomplice"?

"And I have a pal who's getting out of Argentia Planum Gaol tomorrow and will bank draft him with a few hundred, directly into his own. His name is Londmo Sloom and he's already got a record which includes doing banks.

When the Constabulary are searching around for likely suspects who've just come into a bit of cash, they'll see the sudden influx in Londmo Sloom's account and conclude exactly what we want them to conclude".

"I'm worried something will go wrong".

"Why don't you come back over right now and I'll put your mind at rest"? *'And your body'*, he thought.

"I can't", she decided, "If he suspects we're in on this together, then it will all go wrong. No, I have to stay here tonight".

"Alright then, have that super fast flitter of yours outside the bank tomorrow at eighteen fifteen but not before, ready to make a fast drive to the rocket launching port at Mare Amphitrites".

"Where are we going"?

"To Scouring Plains in the English sector and a life of luxury".

FIVE

THURTRUM WAS JUMPY from the start, "How long's this going to take"? He demanded. "I've got the card".

"This is a twenty four digit Alucard-Krankenstein", Spider said somewhat obviously, to the head cashier, "It's not like opening a tin of beans, Vant".

"Well don't waste time talking then, get on with it", came the unfair response.

Spider pulled a electro-stethoscope from his bag and bent down to commence the delicate work. Thurtrum paced. The safe cracker ignored the distraction and heard the second correct digit click into place. It took him a Martian world record, to get the lock to slid back and he then began spinning the huge spoked wheel while the head cashier swiped the the reader. It yawed open totally silently.

The unlikely duo rushed inside, on the wall opposite the safety deposit boxes were the unlocked cash containers. Spider saw the light from the overhead L.E.D.s suddenly catch in Thurtrum's eyes and observed the glint of naked avarice. While the head cashier was hastily throwing the piles of money into his holdall, he carefully picked up a bag of silver shillin from a nearby counter.

"That's my half", the head cashier gasped, half turning, his face and head glistening with perspiration. The bag of coins caught him square on the temple and he crumpled to the floor like a wet rag. Spider filled the second bag and then heaved them up, stepping carefully through the lip of the doorway.

"So long loser", he said to the unconscious man, "I've got all the money and I'm porking your wife"!

As he slammed the door shut with dramatic pleasure however, rather than with careful stealth, the sudden vibration set off the banks trembler alarm! The sound was absolutely deafening. Klaxon's blared considerable decibels and the whole of Kunowsky heard the unholy clamour.

Spider bolted for the flitter, threw the bags in before him and slammed the door down.

"Go"! he declared.

As Farli gunned the engine and tore off, she demanded, "What happened, something go wrong"?

"I tripped some hidden alarm, he'd not told me about", Spider lied, "Not to worry we'll be at the rocket port before the constables work out what's happening".

Farli Thurtrum drove like a woman possessed, which in truth she was. They left the flitter in the long stay red zone of the rocket port and made their way into the vast arrival area.

""Now what do we do with all this cash", the thought seemed to occur to her for the first time, "What if we're chosen to have our bags checked manually"?

"It's not illegal to take currency off Mars", Spider told her, "We can put a few hundred in our clothing, walk it through. The rest we leave in a safety deposit locker here at the rocket port".

"What use is that, we'll be on a different planet and one that uses different money"?

"The banks on Venus will give us a decent exchange rate for what cash we take off Mars". Spider told her. "The rest; we make occasional business trips back here and take back a bit at a time".

Farli grinned, "You've thought of everything, what now then, a drink at the port bar"?

"Every possible outcome", he boasted, "Yes, let's go, I could do with a stiff one - that holds itself up".

"Five drinks in each and they were both uncoordinated and the time had been whiled away. They staggered to passport control holding each other up, as best they could. As they were queing Farli's features suddenly drained of colour.

"What's up babe, are you going to throw up", Spider wanted to know.

The beautiful blonde pointed up to the huge crystal display above the next gate, the one that was to take them to Venus.

Spider read the texton that ran beneath the images of First National at Kunowsky.

Head cashier, Vant Thurtrum was found inside the vault and has, as yet no explanation for the missing amount. How did he come to be on the inside of a safe previously locked by the general manager, Mich Smotumu, earlier this evening? Smotumu said in an interview with the constabulary, "There has been a discrepancy on the balances for some time, but it never occurred to me that my head cashier could be involved in the matter". Inspector Litseinik of the Mars Constabulary was unavailable for comment, although it seems Thurtrum is being held so as to help him, with his enquiries.

"They found him alive", the sozzled Farli muttered.

"Of course, with the alarm going off he never had time to use up all the air in the vault. He can't have informed on us though, otherwise why haven't we been picked up? I don't get it what's he holding out for"?

"He must still love me and figured we'd be dealing him in later"? The drunken wife murmured, illogically. "Imagine that, he's still in love with me".

"We might get on the rocket yet then, but there's one thing for sure".

"What's that"?

"He'll crack eventually and when he does they'll trail us to Venus".

"So what", she chuckled, "They won't have any evidence, we don't have a big percentage of the money on us".

"No, but they'll keep an eye on us and a trip back to Mars and any attempt to get at the cash and we'll be nabbed for sure. All we've gotten away with is spending money for a couple of months".

Farli looked thoughtful and then tried to brave out the devastating news,

"We'll just have to manage along like other couples do then Spider, we'll have each other".

"Of course babe; good of you to think positively", Spider managed.

Farli Thurtrum was a beautiful and desirable woman though and Spider was not an especially special looking man, he did not even have regular height. How long would it be before she tired of him?

'She used to love Thurtrum and now she loves me', he thought, *'But for how long'?*

SIX

"I DON'T KNOW how many times I have to tell you the same story, inspector"? Thurtrum replied for the umpteenth time. "I was doing the books and two figures suddenly rushed into the office and hit me over the head with something, once I came to, I found myself in the vault, they'd obviously used my card, but one of them must have been a safe cracker, because I was not the one who opened it".

"What do you think Mister Smotumu", Litseinik asked, "If Thurtrum here was one of the gang why was he on the wrong side of the vault and our enquiries prove beyond a shadow of a doubt that he has no connection to this Londmo Sloom what-so-ever".

"I'm sorry Thurtrum but you're fired", Smotumu said and then, "Without physical evidence of either actual or electronic kind you cannot hold him anyway can you inspector"?

Litseinik shook his head, "Who-ever got inside that vault left no D.N.A of their own and as for Thurtrum here, his would naturally be all over due to the natural course of a days business".

Smotumu nodded tacitly and Litseinik said,

"You can go Thurtrum, but if you suddenly come into a pile of money….. Well, don't".

Thurtrum rose with as much dignity as he could manage and exited the office and then eventually the station. It was dawn, but he was not sure of the date, the sky was a dull pink as the weak sunlight began to penetrate the darkness.

His mind boiled. Betrayed and abandoned. That was not the end of it though, he would not rest until he had found them and then.......

His imagination failed him, He looked up at the beautiful dawn sky, the pure white light of a rocket taking off was leaving a wonderful line across the canopy, he wondered briefly where it was headed.

HIS KEYS WERE RUSTY, AND THE LOCK WAS DULL - SNAPPER: OF THE YARD [HE ALWAYS GETS HIS MAN]

Saint Peter sat by the celestial gate:
His keys were rusty, and the lock was dull,
So little trouble had been given of late;
Not that the place by any means was full,
But since the Gallic era 'eight-eight'
The devils had ta'en a longer, stronger pull,
And 'a pull altogether,' as they say
At sea – which drew most souls another way.   Lord Byron

ONE

IT WAS THE most famous Police Station in the solar system; Scotland Yard, which still resided in London, England, English Empire, Earth. The current Chief Constable was one Duncullis by name and he was secretly proud of the superb record that had been established under his command. Crime was down, in all it's various guises, detection was up and the city of London was once of the quietest places in the English Empire.

So when Duncullis received a ping on a highly secure channel and discovered it to be all the way from Venus, he was naturally disturbed, the incident was unexpected and the one thing Chief Inspector Duncullis did not like was when something he had not anticipated; happened. Intrigued he tapped the connect icon and the features of Chief Constable Tweem of English Track, The Central, English Sector, Venus. His heavy jowled features' swam into focus and he growled,

"Duncullis, how are things at the Yard"?

"They could not be better, Tweem, what about over there in English Track".

"Good, no problems here, with the exception of one, that is, you remember Inspector Quorum"?

"How could I forget the nephew of His Majesty"? Duncullis began to get a very bad feeling about the nature of the ping.

"Well it seems our Inspector up here has gotten a nasty dose of home sickness and I was forced to report it to His Majesty".

'I bet you were! I bet you couldn't wait to get rid of the frenge up' Duncullis thought to himself. Instead he asked,

"Well that's obliquely interesting in a mild sort of way, but what makes you take time with sub-space net time to tell me"?

"Well", Tweem began, with a malign glint in his eye, "I don't know where His Majesty got the notion but, he suggested that instead of just bringing Quorum home, it might be nice for an officer exchange to take place. Sort of use the incident to give two valuable members of our respective forces inter planetary experience".

'Yes you sephrance, I wonder where His Majesty did get that notion', Duncullis thought, he replied,

"I'll post up a request for a volunteer then, Tweem. Let you know if an officer comes forward".

"Well it's not just an officer I want", Tweem had the temerity to pursue, "Not for a valuable Inspector like His Majesty's nephew, but like for like, Duncullis. I want an inspector as part of the deal".

"Now you listen here, Tweem….."

"You're not going to suggest that His Majesty's nephew wasn't valuable are you, Duncullis".

"Well; of course not but…..".

"His Majesty had only heard of one of your chaps, Duncullis and that was…..".

"NO"! Duncullis roared, but Tweem simply waited and then continued,

"Inspector Scannell"!

Inspector Vernon (Snapper) Scannell was a legend in his own lifetime at Scotland Yard. His record when it came to crime detection was unsurpassed. He could have risen, comet-like through the ranks, had he so desired. Scannell got the biggest thrill from catching the perpetrator however and had refused several times to be taken from the front line.

Now Tweem had manoeuvred the king into agreeing to swap his own incompetent nincompoop of a nephew with the police officer with the most impressive list of convictions behind him in the history of English crime detection.

Duncullis was beaten and he knew it. How could he persuade his Majesty that his own nephew was an imbecile? One that should never have even made constable never mind inspector. If he went to the king and asked him to change the name of the man he was losing, that would not sit well with the crown either. He did the only thing left open to him,

"If it takes me years I'll get you back for this Tweem", he cursed and promptly cut the connection.

Inspector Scannell himself was more philosophical,

"I see, well maybe they have some interesting cases for me to work on".

"Unsolved cases that none of the obtuse officers up there can solve more likely", Duncullis was not mollified in the slightest that his best officer was quite prepared for the exchange.

"I've never been off world, it will be an experience", his inspector observed, with his long time habit of always seeing the bright side of any given situation, "I had better go and pack my ten kilogramme luggage".

"Try to act in such a way as they want to send you back as soon as possible", Duncullis instructed, thinking of his figures.

A mere thirty hours later Scannell was seated in shuttle Churchill and waiting for take off. He found he was enjoying every aspect of the entire adventure.

"Everything alright, sir""? a pretty stewardess asked him

"Capital, thank you", the man known as Snapper assented, having gotten the moniker from the very early days when metal cuffs were still in use. Many was the penetrator the inspector had snapped the bracelets onto, on their way to the Yard's cells.

He settled back in his cot and savoured the escape from Earth's atmosphere; the docking with the Polish built Przestrzeń Rakieta and the enormous g-force at the massive cold fusion propulsion system launched them on their way to Earth's sister.

He used the time in space to catch up on his reading, including hypno-learning programmes in Romanian and Polish. Then the shuttle Gladstone came up to dock with the Przestrzeń Rakieta to take them down to English Tracks and his new assignment. He took his last look at the stars, the brilliant bright bauble that was responsible for making all life in it's system possible, before making his way to the airlock. Beneath the shuttle was Venus, strangely mute of colour since the massive array of foil that encircled it. It blocked out so much of the fierce sun that was impossibly close, were it not the case. It was said that in another decade genetically modified plants would be propagated in special humus, brought to Venus at tremendous expense and the beginning of Terra-formation would have commenced.

The trip through the incredibly thin and still poisonous atmosphere was brief indeed and Snapper exited the airlock and had his first experience of life under a massive complex of plexi-plas. He had no need to take a train to the offices of English Tracks, for they were situated next door to the rocket port. He walked carefully in the lesser gravity and presented himself to the desk sergeant and then on to his interview with Tweem.

The first thing he noticed about the man was his heavy jowls, unusual when so much corrective surgery was widespread.

"You sent for me Chief Constable", Snapper began. He noted the look of triumph on the other's flabby features.

TWO

"I'M REALLY PLEASED you decided to keep this splendid house at Ember Caves Gibnie", Crom Highbrow told his new wife.

"Well you always loved Ember Deeps, Crom and in truth, I would have found it very difficult to part with. It doesn't bother you that I shared it with Chaut"?

"How could it, he was my dearest friend", Highbrow noted, "And I was so pleased for him when he met and married you, although I found myself loving you too, as time went by".

"But you never gave me a sign, no hint of how you felt"?

"How could I, he was, as I've already said, my oldest and dearest friend. No, I resigned myself to seeing you happy with him and was glad for you both".

"Well now you don't need to suffer so, darling and Ember Deeps is ours, rather than mine".

"Put your arms around my neck and then punch in the code then", Crom Highbrow commanded with a smile and he carried her over the threshold of one of the original properties to be built on all Venus.

"Good evening Missus Crimso", a voice startled the pair of them.

"Oh, Missus Trime"! Gibnie flushed, as Crom let her down to her feet. "I didn't think you'd still be up, you shouldn't have waited for us, the reception went on far longer than we anticipated. Oh, and it's Missus Highbrow now".

"Congratulations to both of you", Trime murmured before adding, "I've cleaned through and turned back the sheets to air, do you have any luggage or anything to…."

"I can deal with anything else Missus Trime and thank you", Crom cut in, "You go and get your sleep now".

"Yes sir, thank you sir, welcome to Ember Deeps. You'll find the place polished from top to bottom the only place I've not cleaned is the…."

"We're very tired Missus Trime", the blushing bride told her then, cutting her short, "We're going to our room now, goodnight".

"Of course ma'am, good night", then she was gone.

"What a queer fish", Crom chuckled.

"But very hard working and cheap", Gibnie told him, then blushing asked, "It's time we were retiring too Crom. You know Chaut was a good husband, I never thought I'd find true happiness again especially as you were his dear friend, you're making me very happy Crom".

The next morning the new master of the house noticed certain items about the place were missing, he asked his wife,

"Gibnie, what's happened to the canvas of you and Chaut, that was hanging on that wall and the lovely tri-v cube that you always……"

"I got rid of them", she cut in simply, "There's no need to remember anything about that time in my past now".

"But I don't mind them", he offered, "I don't think….."

"Well I do!" she cried and the look of shock on his features must have motivated her to an explanation. "I just want to concentrate on my life with you now Crom, you must see that, I'm Missus Highbrow now and that is what is uppermost in my mind and my aspirations, to make you the best wife that I can, do you understand"?

"Of course", he took her in his arms and the incident was soon forgotten.

He was in commodities and the market was vital, Venus was being repopulated and the Biotron and Venuser were also in need of all sorts of product. The former lone occupants of the world were discovering their new senses and with those discoveries came new demands.

Chaut worked while ever there was a need for his presence at the markets and that meant a good deal of the time. Before he was aware of it, much had developed on Venus and there were changes in his domestic situation too. One day he took Trime to one side and ask her in conspiratorial fashion,

"Did you know the first master of this house; Trime"?

"No sir, I was engaged shortly after his demise, but I can tell you the first master had some wonderful items about the place. Then one day Missus Crimso as was then, ordered me to get rid of all his things. I'd almost completed the task that first night when you arrived Sir, now it's as though he never lived here, it there anything else Sir"?

"No, thank you Missus Trime".

As she was walking away she muttered to herself, "I'll never forget the look on Missus Crimso's face as she ordered me to dispose of everything, get it out the place or destroy it, she said, I don't care which".

"Trime"! the voice froze the domestic to the spot, "What are you dithering about, bothering my dear husband, have you nothing better to do with your time this evening"?

"I've dinner to hypo-wave", Trime apologised and hurried away as Gibnie called after her,

"Get on with it then and stop wasting your time and my money".

"Is there any need to talk to her like that, darling"? Crom tried to reason with her, "These aren't Dickensian times after all".

"I pay her to work not to tittle tattle with you, Crom and who ever Dicken is; he would do well to treat his staff as exactly that, staff, not rumour mongers and gossipers".

"Rumour"? Crom echoed, "I have no idea what you mean, darling"?

"Go and get your shower, you smell of med-bacco and cheap cologne", Gibnie snapped leaving her new husband to gaze after her with a mixture of alarm and upsetment.

Once again he threw himself into his work and the resultant monetary reward was something of a consolation. He could not understand the swift change in his wife's attitude to everything however, so he resolved to do something about it and booked a weekend break right over the other side of Venus in the holiday resort of Athena in the Polish sector. The place was a health spa, come luxury accommodation come restaurant of the highest calibre,

"I've booked us a relaxation weekend in Athena, darling", he told her that evening.

"How nice", she returned in reserved fashion, "But do we need a break Crom"?

"Well I could do with one and I thought it would be nice for the two of us to spend some time together, this property has a sobering effect upon you Gibnie, perhaps we really should consider selling up and finding something newer, new properties are becoming available all the......."

"No"! Her reaction was totally out of all proportion to his suggestion and she found it necessary to apologise, "Oh, I'm sorry darling, I didn't mean to snap at you. You know you might be right, we could do with a weekend away, I'm going to have a look at what to take right now".

So it was settled and they got on the train at the very next weekend and went to the holiday spa of Athena. The vista of Venus was changing all the time as the sulphuric acid was being 'harvested', processed and shipped to the rest of the Solar League of Planets. It was leaving the surface of the scarred world a strange sort of mustard shade in certain areas. In others the rock was as ebon as space itself, and then there were the yellow and almost green shades. It was not at that time an attractive landscape at all, but it was an ever changing one and one that man would one day make far more vital, just as he had with Mars.

The two of them spoke little as they enjoyed the express train journey, the clear sides of the tube allowed them to see more of the planet in the two short hours than they had ever seen before. As they got off at the other end, onto Athena platform, Gibnie said,

"That was very pleasurable Crom, I'm so glad you booked this now". It was as if by getting her away from the dreary old house, a veil of melancholy had been dissipated from her, one that clung like an invisible shroud to her body and mind, but almost tangible for all that.

"I am looking forward to the weekend in no small degree", he enthused, "I feel it will be a lovely break for us Gibnie a real treatorini"!

It proved to be exactly that.

They had massages, pedicures, swam in the pool (heated) of real water, steamed in the sauna. In the evening they dined on finest Polish cuisine and their conversation was light airy and amusing, just like it had been when they were seeing one another before the marriage. Crom dreaded it ending, but two twenty four hour periods ended and then as they were half way home, the twilight gave way to darkness the darkness that would last for one hundred and twenty one days, or roughly half of Venus' year!

The nigrescent blanket seemed to have a dampening effect upon Gibnie too and she grew sombre once more, staid and impatient and not easy to communicate with. Of course that phenomenon was not peculiar to Gibnie as it turned out, there were only a few very strong minded humans on Venus who could stand the length of the long night and not get depressed to one degree or another.

Missus Trime took Crom to one side the first opportunity she got,

"She's gotten rid of every piece of evidence that Chaut ever lived here", she told him leaning into him so that he could smell the mint on her breath.

"Probably to make me feel more at home", He countered.

"If you say so Sir", she muttered clearly disappointed with his reasoning.

The sombre nature of the old house settled on them both, like a melton cloak.

"Here are your keys", Trime handed them to him one day, "All except for the cellar door, the reinforced one".

"Why would she let me have all the keys save one"? he asked her.

"Perhaps you'd better ask her that", was the reply from the domestic with dark inference.

The first time they got a visitor, Gibnie had gone into town, there was only Crom and the domestic in.

"Is this the residence of the Crimso's"? a rather serious individual wanted to know.

"Yes", the domestic agreed guardedly.

"Are they home"? asked the man.

"The master of the property is in".

"The master"? the man sounded surprised, "By that you are referring to Chaut Crimso"?

"No Sir the *new* Mister Crimso so to speak; Crom Highbrow".

"I see", the man made a note on his pad, "Would it be possible to talk to him, my name is Scannell".

"Come in then Sir", Trime bid him enter.

"Thank you", the airlock closed behind him.

"Scannell you said, Sir",

"Inspector Scannell of Scotland Yard".

"Scotland"? Trime echoed, "The country Scotland"?

"No, Scotland Yard the combmen station in London on Earth, I'm a visitor to Venus, for the time being".

"I'm Crom Highbrow Inspector", Crom had been listening in the entrance hall. "Please come into the lounge, can I offer you something to drink"?

"I'd love a cup of English breakfast tea if you have some", the combman smiled.

"Missus Trime, please fetch the Inspector some breakfast tea", Crom asked the domestic as the two of them took a seat. "What can I help you with Inspector"?

"I was actually hoping to speak to your good lady wife, Sir", the Inspector said, "Is she going to be out for long"?

"She's gone shopping Inspector; so you see I have no idea how long her absence will be. Perhaps the matter is something I know something about, what is it pray"?

"I can always give you some details Mister Highbrow", the combman said, "It's a matter of some delicacy, but I'm sure between us gentlemen it will be fine".

"I'm intrigued, Inspector, please go on"?

""Are you fully aware of the details regarding Chaut Crimso's death".

"Yes Inspector I am", Crom was happy that it was a question he could answer, "The tube wreck between Ishtar Commons and N/Gen Branch, Chaut Crimso was on that tube, the wreck was so bad that some of the bodies were too damaged to make positive identification possible, even with DNA analysis, there was chemical burn, the tissue was too degraded. Nothing of poor Chaut was ever found".

"Poor Chaut; you knew Mister Crimso, knew him well"?

"He was my best friend of some years inspector, I was the best man at he and Gibnie's wedding".

The inspector was making hasty notes on his pad with an electro-stylus, which he obviously favoured over a finger nail.

"We only actually have the then Missus Crimso's word that her husband was on that very tube express".

"And you are suggesting that she was not telling the authorities the truth, or you would not otherwise be here, would you inspector"?

"It's just that the insurance company who insured Chaut Crimso's life for four hundred silver shillin are not entirely sure that the tube carried Mister Crimso to his death".

"And yet Gibnie had a ping from her husband, telling her he was on his way and was about to board the tube. The ping that showed it was from his very own I.P".

"A pad which she had access to surely, as his wife. Tell me Mister Highbrow, did Gibnie Crimso ever made any romantic overtures toward you, before her first husband was reportedly killed"?

"None inspector, absolutely nothing, I assure you".

"You don't seem surprised by my line of questioning though do you? Neither surprised nor outraged"?

"Does that make me fall under suspicion of being an accessory? If indeed there is need for an accessory in a supposed crime dreamed up by the insurance company"?

"I'm sorry Mister Highbrow, I know my questions have by their nature seemed indelicate".

"You're just doing your job inspector. I do have one question however, if Chaut Crimso was not aboard the Ishtar Commons and N/Gen Branch tube, then where is he now"?

"I think he's dead probably, Mister Highbrow and as to the whereabouts of the corpse, then Venus is quite a large planet isn't it"?

Crom showed the inspector out shortly there after and was racked with misgivings until his new wife finally returned to the old house of Ember Deeps. Gibnie saw at once that her husband had something on his mind,

"What's the mater with you,"? She demanded holding a new frock up to her slender form.

"I had a visitor while you were out, a visitor who wanted to speak to you about Chaut".

Gibnie showed no emotion, "Really"?

"Yes he was all the way from Earth, Scotland Yard in fact, his name was Inspector Scannell, he wanted to know if Chaut was really dead".

"Well of course he is, he was killed in the tube accident, you remember it as well as I. Let me guess, the inspector thinks I may have cheated the insurance company, that Chaut wasn't on the train at all".

"That's very accurate indeed, Gibnie, has he a case to pursue"?

"No! Before you ask, the house is mine and the estate was too, all that I have I deserve, Crom. I tend to suspect you don't believe that to be the case"?

"You are my wife now and I love you Gibnie, I believe what you tell me and we need speak of this rather sordid matter no further", Crom said, but he could not shake the doubts he was beginning to feel and a few days later he got a ping from one Della Crimso, whom he had met at the wedding of Gibnies' to her first husband.

Dear Mister Highbrow, I don't know if you know this but Chaut was on his way to visit me on the day the tube crashed. I have never had any time for his wife, now yours and I make no secret of it. She is a greedy and manipulative woman and cannot be trusted. I am sorry if this ping distresses you but I can honestly tell you that my brother was afraid of your wife! The reason I am messaging you is to ask for some images of my dear departed brother. I am not prepared to ask your wife, but perhaps you still dare! I hope you believe my brother was on the tube that day. I'm not so sure! Two days before he was supposedly on that tube, he pinged me to say he had changed his mind and would not be visiting me after all! - Della Crimso.

"There's a Missus Highbrow to see you inspector", Snapper's secretary told him on the com.

The eyebrow's of the combman rose almost off his forehead, "She's come, here, voluntarily!? Very well, please let her come in"?

Gibnie Highbrow was exactly what Snapper Scannell had been expecting. Slim, coolly attractive and immaculately dressed in the very best non-working apparel the meagre selection of Venus fashion carried. She even wore a beret with a small black mesh front that covered her eyes.

"Come in Missus Highbrow, please have a seat", Snapper began smoothly, "How can I help you"?

"By leaving me and my new husband alone, Inspector", she came immediately to the point. "Crom relayed the details of your conversation with him and it did not help our new relationship in the slightest, so it stops and it stops today, do I make myself abundantly clear, Inspector"?

"I have no difficulty understanding what you're saying Missus Highbrow, but unfortunately the decision is not mine to make, the investigation was given me by my Chief Constable, following the petition to him by Venusure Life".

"Then please tell the Chief Constable that I wish to see him. In his office, right now"? Gibnie Highbrow was not used to waiting, when she desired something.

"He's a very busy man Missus Highbrow, such alacrity is not really realistic however…..".

"Never mind that", she cut him mid sentence, "I'll find his office myself".

She rose fluidly and went to the door without hesitation, as she opened it, she said, "Goodbye Inspector, we'll not meet again"!

Snapper smiled, he would not bet on it.

THREE

TWENTY MINUTES LATER Snapper's pad pinged and he was surprised to see a two eleven appear on the screen; murder! Intrigued he tapped for the details and rose to leave his office, as he walked past his secretary he asked,

"Is there a patrol flitter available in the bay, please"?

"Yes, Sir, came the immediate response, "Ready for the two eleven that's just come in, do you want a constable to accompany you? I gather you're on the case"?

"First available will do", Snapper agreed, "Have him meet me down there, which flitter is it"?

"Twenty three Sir, the blue Jet250".

Snapper took the stairs, he moved swiftly and confidently in the slightly lower gravity. He was excited despite himself, at last a case he could get his teeth into. The Crimso affair had bored him to tears, but it was not over yet, he could always run two cases though when one of them was only insurance fraud.

A young uniformed constable was waiting beside the Hewlett Packard when he arrived at the bay. He held up the activation button to show he had the flitter's starter and lock. He was very tall, thin and red headed.

"Inspector Scannell, I'm Heatput", he told Snapper.

"Do you want to drive"? Snapper asked, doubting the constable would have had the opportunity to drive a Jet250 much before. He was rewarded by a huge grin.

"You know where the Vincenti Mansion is"?

"Yes Sir, over at The Citadel in the Romanian quarter, we should take the A15 south and then split off at junction….".

"You drive then".

Scannell wanted to read as much as he could about the scene before they arrived. He climbed into the passenger side as Heatput let the door swing upward and then settled down to study his pad.

The Jet250 roared into life and Heatput sped off with some alacrity,

"Let's get there in one piece, Constable"!

Scannell began to read the preliminary and salivated and smacked his lips at the prospect of the investigation.

"Do you know who the victim of this crime is, Heatput"? He asked the constable. Replying before the young combman had time to answer, "Karlyne Vincenti, second cousin to none other than the mother of Prince Darren, who will one day be Darren III of England".

"Little wonder they wanted Snapper of the Yard on the case then, Inspector".

Scannell was impressed, "You've heard of me"?

"Yes, Sir, everyone at the station is excited by your arrival at English Track".

Snapper continued to read and it made an absorbing preliminary. One of the retainers of Vincenti's had found the decapitated body of her lady-ship in the lounge with none other than five witnesses/suspects, all denying any wrong doing or knowledge of how her lady-ship's head had become severed from the rest of her body.

In next to no time (or so it seemed to the daydreaming Snapper) the Hewlett Packard Jet250 flitter sighed to a halt outside an enormous stately home, residing beneath an even more gargantuan bubble. Heatput whistled,

"The Vincenti's must be worth a few shillin", he noted

"None of that once we get inside", Snapper cautioned, "Decorum at all times, Heatput".

"Yes, Sir", the chagrined officer agreed, as another combmen vehicle pulled up. This was the C.I.F. the criminal investigative forensic boys . Two men got out, one was wearing the most ridiculous ill fitting toupee Snapper had ever seen. The rim of hair around his obviously bald head, was grey, while the hair-piece was a corn hued blonde!

"Do we know either of them"? Snapper asked Heatput.

"The guy in charge is Harmoan", Heatput told him and then grinned, "The guys call him Wiggy behind his back.

"I see, so that fine head of hair is not his own then"? Snapper quipped.

"It isn't anyone's, Sir", Heatput chuckled, "Looks more like the straw you'd see on a horse's stable floor".

"What's the watch word, Heatput"?

"Decorum, Sir".

They went over to the two C.I.F.

"Do you mind if I go in and have a look around before you start, Inspector"? Snapper asked the wearer of the false piece.

Harmoan nodded, "No problem, you know not to actually touch anything don't you, Inspector"?

"Of course".

Snapper and Heatput went through the man airlock, which was standing ajar. The entrance hall was as elaborate as the building's exterior. Vincenti must have paid a fortune for the place, evidentially he would be one of the wealthiest men on all Venus.

There was not a square centimetre of wall space that was not covered with expensive art work, every surface contained very expensive ornamentation, the furniture and floor coverings were also exorbitant, but the single biggest expenditure by far must have been the bill Vincenti had footed for getting all of this priceless collection from Earth, Mars and the off Moon sculptures, to Venus.

"If this is the entrance hall what must the rest of this mansion contain", Snapper said to the young constable,

"Yes, there's certainly some bric-a-brac cluttering the place up that's for sure" Heatput agreed, evidentially not a connoisseur of fine object d'art.

At the doors of the hallway a confused looking combman, was relieved to see them,

"Is one of you Snapper of the Yard"? He desired to know. "My sergeant posted me here until your arrival, the witnesses are still in this room, behind me".

"Snapper", Scannell confirmed for him, "Do we know how come they didn't just scatter and leave? How is it they were contained so conveniently, all in the very place the murder took place"?

The local combman smiled and told him, "When you see the size of the deceased's butler, whom it seems was devoted to his mistress, you'll know why no one could escape, Sir".

"Alright, we'll take it from here then Constable and in future it's Inspector Scannell to you and your sergeant, understood"?

"Yes Sir", the constable quaked, while Heatput grinned, then he added, "It's used as a term of affection Sir, your reputation is legendary".

"Okay, off you go now", Snapper told him, but did not look especially displeased. "Right constable, use your pad on vidrec, I want everything carefully recorded in 2HD at the very least, understood"?

"This is a Russell-Hobbs 64gig pad - come P.C. come entcentre, Sir, you'll have the lot in tri-vid".

"Alright then, but watch where you put your great flat feet, we don't want Harmoan getting his hair off at us do we"?

Heatput laughed at the sardonicism of his inspector and replied that no, he did not.

Snapper opened the door and made his entrance. He could not have been happier no matter what the occasion.

The instant they crossed the threshold a huge individual barred their way, "And you are"?

"This is Snapper of Scotland Yard", Heatput replied ahead of the inspector, "You must be the butler".

"I had that honour Sir, your name if you please", he held out an enormous spade-like limb that they realised was his hand,

"Constable Heatput".

"Slanin, Sir, at your service. You'll find nothing touched nor contaminated. Over there, that sorry collection of individuals are the ones I discovered in this room, when I found my lady; dead. I can give you names and occupations, but am unable to tell you which of them was the murderer".

Snapper gave Heatput his opportunity, "Carry on Constable".

"I'll vid each as you name them, Slanin", Heatput told the butler and walked over to a seated group of attractive yet miserable looking young women. Heatput started on the left, aiming his pad at a delicate looking redhead.

"That's her lady-ship's florist Mel Kobor", Slanin told the constable.

They proceeded through the five of them, Somica Tweezle the hairdresser, Despa Sondenheim the chauffeur, Trounce Ingamaa the dog groomer and finally and ridiculously named Rikie Rik, her lady-ship's audio consultant!

Snapper looked at the corpse and removed head that had rolled a little further away from it. Even at distance he could see a pencil beam blaster had performed the decapitation, the two wounds were perfectly cauterised shut, there was no blood on the Persian rug both rested upon.

He returned his attention to the young women,

"Ladies one of you must have seen who killed her lady-ship, save us all a great deal of time and nuisance and simply tell me now who it was, I am Inspector Vernon Scannell".

The florist said, "We all had a pencil beam blaster, Inspector, but only one was supposed to carry a charge, as it turned out, none of them did".

Snapper gave the redhead his undivided attention, "You all had a pencil beam blaster"?

Kobor nodded grimly.

"Heatput, get Harmoan in here, ask him to take a blaster from each of the ladies and put them in evidence bags", while the constable rushed out of the room to do as instructed, Snapper told the miserable group,

"So you're all accessories to murder ladies and not only that you're harbouring a killer, this won't go well for you".

"Mel told you the truth, inspector", said the short, wiry, dog groomer, Ingamaa, "None of our weapons' fired, all of them were without charge".

"Very well, you're all at least guilty of conspiracy to comit murder, before I split you up and question you separately, who organised this bizarre tryst".

"Tryst, Inspector"? Slanin echoed,

"An appointment to meet at a certain time and place, especially one made somewhat secretly, in this case to commit murder most foul. Can you go and get five officers in here and then organise five rooms for individual interviews, please, Slanin, I'll watch the ladies. C.I.F. should be in here in a moment anyway"?

The butler gave a tight nod and hurried off to accomplish the task, he struck Snapper as extraordinarily efficient. Snapper tried one last time to wrap up the case swiftly,

"Ladies, obviously one blaster did have the charge necessary to commit the act of homicide, for we have a corpse! Who's your ring leader"?

Sondenheim, an unusually tall and dark haired woman told him then, "None had the charge, Inspector, we were duped. Told one of us would kill her lady-ship, but would not know whom it was until the weapon actually fired. That was how we were all involved in the tryst, as you call it".

"If the blaster's were all charge-less, how did her lady-ship's head happen to fall from her neck"? Snapper asked without humour, "And as regards being duped, by whom may I enquire"?

Before he could get his answer however, the door opened and in strode Harmoan, the edges of his hairpiece flapping with the speed of his entrance,

"Touch nothing", he barked superfluously, "Sergeant get those weapons bagged and tagged".

Snapper turned to the butler, "Are you ready to start escorting the suspects to separate rooms Slanin"?

The butler nodded and aided by what looked like two footmen, began to do just that.

"Where are they going"? Harmoan demanded, "I haven't take fibres, other evidence, I want DNA and I want….."

"Your men can go with each of them and do just that, I don't want them conferring any further", Snapper told him.

"Wouldn't it be better to take them all to your station"? Harmoan wanted to know then.

"You carry on with your collection of evidence, Inspector", Snapper soothed, "We'll cooperate with you in any way we can".

Heatput grinned, Snapper of the Yard did not need telling by anyone how to conduct his investigation, Harmoan was flogging the very dead horse that had supplied the material for his thatch.

FOUR

"ARE YOU RECORDING Heatput"?
"Yes Sir, all going onto the pad".
Snapper turned his undivided attention to the attractive redhead the slim Mel Kobor,

"Now I understand someone or something is stopping you from being completely candid with me Miss Kobor, so let's examine what I already know. Then we can take it from there and let's hope we get some answers in these pleasant surroundings. Otherwise the rest of the interviews will be conducted perforce in combmen cells".

Kobor seemed to shrink a little at that unsavoury prospect.

"An agreement was reached between the five of you, to kill Lady Vincenti. The deal was that five pencil beam blasters would be handed out between you, only one of which had sufficient charge to do the, ah…task. So you gathered together earlier today and, as decided, fired in as complete a unison as was humanly possible. How am I doing so far"?

Kobor then delivered the first bombshell,

"Six of us originally, Inspector, but for a reason we don't know, Henrietta didn't turn up".

"Henrietta"? Snapper demanded.

"van Berg, her lady-ship's maid"!

"Heatput, go and get hold of Slanin, have him get a constable to accompany him and put Henrietta van Berg in another room. Oh, tell Wiggy about her too".

Heatput raced from the room and Snapper hoped that van Berg was still in the mansion. They waited, the girl nervously silent, Heatput arrived back breathless.

"She's gone! I've put out a C.U.B. (Combmen Urgent Bulletin) to have her arrested, when seen".

"Good", Snapper turned back to the florist.

"Why did each of you hate Karlyne Vincenti enough to kill her and where is her husband"? he demanded.

"Anders is on the moon on a business meeting", the girl supplied, "He's M.D. of Vincentinfo and one or two other companies".

Vincentinfo"?

"The Softwear giants, sir", Heatput supplied, "They probably supplied the Softwear for my own pad, it's a massive earner".

"Ping him", Snapper instructed, "Get him back to Venus soon as. Now Miss Kobor, my other question, why did you and the others hate her lady-ship"?

"Because she was a right kund", the girl cursed with a passion that took the two men by surprise. "Nothing was ever good enough for her, she complained at every possible opportunity. She verbally abused every person she ever commissioned to do work for her".

"But she paid well"? Snapper guessed, "So instead of quitting, you all decided she had to be killed"?

Kobor nodded miserably, "I wasn't even in charge of my contract, Inspector, I work for Venuflora, every time the bitch put in another request to have flowers decorate her rooms here I dreaded coming. She made what could have been a pleasant task, hard work".

"She had something wrong with her brain, Inspector", Somica Tweezle told Snapper at her interrogation, "She just couldn't find it within herself to like anything anyone did for her, she was vindictive and mean and her tongue was sharp and cruel".

"So you cooked up a scheme for one of her employees to kill her", Snapper concluded, "Kill her in such a way as none of you would know who was the actual executioner".

"It wasn't my idea, but I went along with it", Tweezle admitted, "I was glad to be part of it, I don't deny that".

"Who was the first to suggest the scheme, who thought up the mechanics of the homicide", the inspector asked not for the first time, but once again he got the same answer.

"I don't know really, we sort of developed it over a period of time".

"But only one of you could have got the blasters".

"I don't know, all I can tell you is who looked after them once they were acquired".

"The missing maid"?

Tweezle nodded.

Snapper had interrogated all five by then and it was always the same story. Vincenti was so hateful to everyone around her that they had all agreed she must be permanently removed from the mansion. Some of them even claimed it was for Anders Vincenti's sake. In fact Snapper sensed that at least two of the sextet, Ingamaa and the missing van Berg were secretly in love with Anders and were probably also motivated by sympathy as much as hatred.

Once he was alone with Heatput, Snapper began to muse aloud,

"We'll have to let them all go and keep them under our watchful eye, take what we have to Tweem, see if Wiggy comes up with something to help us".

"I don't get it", the constable groaned, "How was Karlyne Vincenti killed? Oh, I know she was decapitated, but how? No one in the room saw who did it, if Wiggy confirms the pencil beams are all out of power, it will be an even greater puzzle".

"Yes indeed", Snapper of the Yard agreed, "An even greater puzzle".

FIVE

CROM HIGHBROW WAS waiting for his wife when she finally got back to Ember Deeps.

"You're still up"? Gibnie stated somewhat obviously, "I was going to slip in and not disturb you, it's late".

"Yes" Crom was non committal, "Did you speak to the chief constable Gibnie"?

"I did", Missus Highbrow confirmed firmly, "There'll be no more interference form that meddling inspector from Earth, I've seen to it".

At her husband's expression she demanded, "You look sceptical, Crom, do you believe what I'm telling you"?

"Of course, darling", there was no sense in a heated exchange at such an hour.

"Good then the matter's settled, we'll not say any more about it Crom".

"There's just one thing, Gibnie".

"What one thing, what is it"?

"I've had a ping from Della Crimso. She claims that Chaut had sent her an email before the tube departure, telling her he had changed his mind and would not be going to see her after all".

"That's right", Gibnie was totally unphased, "And when he told me the same thing I spent some no small time persuading him to change his mind and go after all. Now you know what's been hanging over me all these months, I changed his mind Crom, in a way I was guilty of his death".

Crom was suddenly full of sympathy and rose to take his wife in his arms, "I'm so sorry, Gibnie. No wonder you seemed distant and withdrawn, little wonder you don't want the combmen asking stupid questions".

"We'll get past this Crom", she turned her face up to his, "And then we'll be happy", and they kissed and retired for the night. The next morning though, Crom had another surprise waiting for him.Trime dropped luggage onto the entrance room floor and told him,

"I'm leaving now, Mister Highbrow, the best of luck to you".

"Leaving, why"?

"It's when I go out to shop in the local precinct, Sir. The stares and the whispers, I've had enough".

"Whispers, about what"? He asked, but he already knew the answer.

"They're calling your wife the Black Widow, Sir. The rumour is that she killed Master Crimso for the house and the insurance".

"They, who is they"?

"Anyone who doesn't live in this house".

"You're letting gossip mongering get to you"?

"It already has, Sir, but not after today. I'm sorry, I hope you get a replacement really soon; goodbye".

Crom could not answer and the housekeeper left in grim silence.

He looked out of the front window, beyond was the dark street, neon lit to dispel some of Venus' eternal night. The whole scene depressed him and he pinged inspector Scannell.

> Highbrow - My wife is going out for the day. I am beginning to suspect there is something to the disappearance of Chaut Crimso but what can I do, how can I help you?
>
> Scannell - Once you are in the property alone ping me again and I will come out to see you Mister Highbrow, subsequent investigations into the DNA evidence left on the train does not add up. There is not enough vestige left to add up to the supposed people that were on that express. I personally am convinced that Chaut Crimso was elsewhere the day he disappeared.

Highbrow read the reply with increasing agitation, it was time to put the matter to rest one way or the other.

He did as directed and within an hour, was answering the door to the inspector and another combman, whom Scannell introduced as one constable Heatput.

"Please explain to me again about the train", he asked Scannell.

"There were ninety five bodies on the train that day according to DNA vestige, Mister Highbrow, "Snapper told him, "Ninety five different scraps of different DNA evidence. We have finally accounted for ninety six tickets sold, ninety five relatives of those who could not be initially identified have now been contacted, we are one ticket short in terms of scraps of DNA and that purchase was made by your wife, not her husband, as one would expect".

"So you think Chaut is hidden somewhere, on Venus, what about off world"?

"Not possible rocket passage is too well documented, Chaut Crimso is somewhere on this world and with the level of surveillance we now have in all areas, he couldn't be moving about".

"So his body is inert"?

Snapper nodded, "Inert as in dead and buried somewhere out there (he nodded toward the window). Or his corpse is hidden somewhere in the bubble system. Then again it is practically impossible to secrete a corpse anywhere that is covered by the high-def cameras that are festooned throughout the public places of Venus. It only leaves one place, Mister Highbrow, this house. It's old, there are few cameras and it was convenient to your wife. How long will she be absent"?

"A shopping trip so I estimate most of the day".

"Then without a warrant, we need your permission to conduct a detailed search of these premises. Premises that now belong to you, in addition to Missus Highbrow"?

Crom took a deep breath and as he exhaled consented, "Do it, Inspector, let's put this matter to bed one way or the other".

Heatput went to start moving, but Snapper put a hand on his shoulder,

"Before we start prising things up or tearing anything down Mister Highbrow, do you have access to every area of this house yourself"?

"Yes of course", Crom returned incredulous at the question, "I've been in every room".

Heatput made to start again but then Crom added, "Well except….."!

Snapper smiled, echoing, "Except what, Sir"?

"Well it's not strictly speaking the house, but rather the cellar, there's a huge metal inlaid door locked, barring our way to the caves beneath this property".

"You say our way, Mister Highbrow, does that mean no one has ever been in the cellar since the house was bought".

"I don't know", Crom felt his spirits sink still further, "All I can tell you is I don't have a key for the door and it looks pretty tough".

"Heatput get one of the maintenance boys over here soonest"? Snapper asked, licking his lips.

The trio went for a drink and by the time Crom had made them and they were consumed, a burly combman from maintenance, he was at the front door. As Crom led them all to the metal studded barrier he asked,

"Try and make as little mess as possible please, this might be a red herring".

The newcomer nodded, lifted his high pressure bolt gun and fired it at the lock. There was a terrific tearing noise of ruptured metal and his burly hand pushed the door open. Crom surveyed it, a single ragged hole in the metal, no damage to the jamb. Snapper clicked on his high powered pen flash light and gingerly proceeded expecting the stone steps that lead to the concrete cellar. He carefully descended and then suddenly neon lights flickered on overhead in the cellar pit,

"Found the switch Sir", Heatput pronounced proudly, just before, "Jeepers creepers what in tarnation is *that*"!

The centre of the bare walled cellar contained what looked like a huge metal coffin on a castored trolley. From one end of the metal and glass contrivance was a series of wires and tubes that lead to a control panel situated on one wall of the cellar. Above these were two metal heavy duty three pin sockets, providing the whole affair with electricity.

"If I'm not very much mistaken", Snapper told the others with satisfaction, "We've just found Chaut Crimso and after all our speculation he isn't dead after all".

The maintenance man told them, "That's a cryogenic chamber! See how the cooling system includes a chamber with an outer wall and an inner wall, the chamber housing has the body inside; a wicking structure in thermal contact with one of the outer wall and the inner wall of the chamber; the delivery system is therefore spaced apart in relationship to the chamber and fluidly connected to the wicking structure for transporting a working fluid to and from it. Look at this magnetic resonance imaging system including the cryogenic cooling system".

"Hobby of yours is it"? Snapper asked with no small amount of irony.

"No, Sir, but I can tell you one thing, he's going to really need a doctor if you want to reanimate him".

"I don't understand what's going on", grumbled Crom who was shocked to numbness. "What's the purpose of doing this? Just for the insurance? And when was Gibnie going to thaw him out"?

Snapper asked, "Are the two of you about the same height and weight, by any chance, Mister Highbrow? Have you both dark hair"?

"I guess so; why"?

"Could Crimso with the right clothes, i.e. your clothes and a bit of makeup etcetera pass himself off as you"? Snapper was peering through the thick frosty glass of the chamber.

"You mean, the plan was to swap us over after a certain period and then escape somewhere with all the insurance, perhaps off world".

"You're way ahead of me", Snapper nodded, "Although I'm not so sure you would *be* frozen"!

"How much easier is it to kill someone when they don't suddenly disappear"? Heatput added his comment.

This caused a very grave expression to appear on Highbrow's features,

"Do you mean to tell me that Gibnie married me, knowing she was going to murder me"?

"We will not know for absolute certainty until we have questioned her, but that looks to be a reasonable assumption I'm afraid, Mister Highbrow". Snapper affirmed.

"Then I cannot wait for her to return here and see you tie wrap her wrists together, Inspector"! Highbrow said with a certain amount of understandable heat.

SIX

W ITH THE AFFAIR at Ember Deeps satisfactorily concluded and the Crimso's both behind bars awaiting trial, Snapper was free to read every scrap of information he had on the Vincentis before interviewing Anders, at the station, in his office.

"Let me begin by offering you my most sincere condolences and sympathy for the brutal demise of you wife, Mister Vincenti", Snapper began.

"Thank you, Inspector", the husband said no more and was not easy to read.

"I suppose you know we have all six suspects under surveillance and investigation now. Van Berg was apprehended at Polspitze rocket base in the German sector over in the west? It would also appear that she organised the agreement between all of them and her fleeing the scene makes it look very bad".

"And yet I do not believe Henrietta would be capable of committing murder most foul", Anders surprised Snapper.

The inspector had been most impressed with the cool and beautiful maid who was Romanian in origin and found her to be the strongest suspect, so he asked,

"Why so, Mister Vincenti".

"Because Henrietta is in love with me, she does not realise that I am aware of it, but I have guessed. Knowing this I doubt she would do something that would hurt me so".

"I see", Snapper had to admit to himself, there was a certain logic to that line of reasoning, love could be selfless, but equally so, it could also be calculating and cruel. "Then perhaps we should also rule out Miss Rik, because I believe Rikie Rik is also in love with you, Mister Vincenti"

The M.D. looked surprised at that revelation, "My wife's audio consultant, I doubt she could have been at the house more than ten times".

"Ten times to fit audio throughout the property, Mister Vincenti? Is that not inordinately excessive"?

"Well ah, Karlyne always had exact specifications in mind for any project she undertook, Inspector".

"Well, to those who look more likely rather than those who don't", Snapper went on, "Our investigations have revealed that it was Trounce Ingamaa who acquired the weapons and Somica Tweezle who bank rolled her until the others gave her the money back. In interviews since the ah,..incident Mel Kobor has been stridently least sorry for her part in the conspiracy. That leaves your chauffeuress, Despa Sondenheim, who is the most guarded of the women concerned. You live there Mister Vincenti; cast your mind back, is there any incident, any overheard scrap of conversation that you can recall, that might point me in the right direction"?

"I have already given that question much thought on the way back to Venus, Inspector and the answer is no. What I want to ask you though, is, how can five women be in a room with my dear departed wife and when she ends up, up.....".

"Take you time, Sir".

"None of them had fired a charged weapon! No one in that room had residue of energy on their sleeves from a weapon discharge so how can Karlyne have ...."?

"That is what we are attempting to determine, Sir", Snapper was as disconcerted as Vincenti.

"If no one in the room did the foul and bloody thing, then perhaps you should arrest everyone else on Venus"! Vincenti finally exploded in frustration and anger.

Then a flicker of inspiration suddenly lit in Snapper's eyes,

"That's it"! he gasped, "If no one in the room fired the shot, then the shot must have been fired......."!

His finger stabbed a touch pad on his desk and he sharply commanded his secretary,

"Get Heatput and Wi.....er, Harmoan in the garage in ten, please"? Then he turned his attention back to the startled widower, "Can you come to the house with us, Sir, you may have just hit upon something that could lead to us cracking the case".

"Yes, of course, but what…..."

Snapper rose swiftly from his desk and blurted, "No time to explain yet, it's just a theory, come on, let's get down to a vehicle"?

As the speeding vehicle raced toward the Vincenti residence the owner said,

"Now you do have the time to explain, Inspector".

"It was when you said about arresting everyone else on Venus, Mister Vincenti that it occurred to me. If the murderer was not inside the room when the foul deed was committed, then the only possible explanation was that the murderer was *outside* the room".

"Outside"! Harmoan echoed, "How could that be done, Scannell"?

"Mister Vincenti, I assume that just as in all other bubble residences, you have space suits, in case the bubble loses it's integrity and the air is lost"?

"Of course", the M.D. confirmed, "In case of emergency everyone has a suit they can hurriedly climb into".

"And then someone, in a suit could be at the window of the lounge and fire through it"! Snapper declared.

"That would take an unusual device Snapper", Harmoan noted, "A surgical laser perhaps".

Snapper nodded, "A surgical laser, precisely. A surgical laser that produces a barely visible single atomic beam that can cut through….., well we know what they can do".

"So if we search the suits"! Harmoan was ahead of the inspector.

"And such a device has a focusing setting", Heatput gasped, "So that it can cut through the insides of a patient without harming the outside. So it could go through the window without harming the glass"!

He pulled the flitter to a halt and the four men rushed inside. Harmoan insisted upon searching the suits alone, finally with a yelp of triumph, he raised just such a surgical tool in his gloved hand and dropped it into an evidence bag.

"Who's suit is that, Mister Vincenti"? Snapper asked, already knowing the answer. The M.D.'s shoulder's sagged as he admitted,

"Henrietta's".

Snapper turned to Heatput, "Go and arrest the maid, she should still be in the property, Constable".

"Yes sir", Heatput agreed and then, "But it was you who cracked the case, don't you want to go and do it"?

"Snapper of the Yard always gets his man, constable", Scannell replied with a wan smile, "And Henrietta van Berg is decidedly not a man"!

IMPIOUS

Oh, gently on thy Suppliant's head,
Dread Goddess, lay thy chast'ning hand!
Not in thy Gorgon terrors clad,
Not circled with the vengeful Band
(As by the Impious thou art seen),
With thund'ring voice, and threat'ning mien,
With screaming Horror's funeral cry,
Despair, and fell Disease, and ghastly Poverty. Thomas Gray

ONE

T HE SUN WAS low in the sky and the wind growing cooler as Patchric guided the quadri toward the town of Khmjn. Setting in the west; as it always did, Proxima was right in his eyes, for he was heading toward the Sea Of Bengal and the new settlement of the Khelac. He had been to Katowice to visit his grandfather King Darn and was now returning later than anticipated. Thankfully journeys across the land of Zentrum was swifter since the quadri had been domesticated.

The beast was a huge quadruped with cloven toes, numbering three on each foot, it allowed blankets to be draped over it's long back and once that was the case Khelac could guide it with pressure from their knees and tugging gently on the long brown hair around it's neck. It was thus the preferred mode of transport on Nyjord, being the only one at present.

Finally the first building of the new town appeared silhouetted by the setting sun and Patchric urged his mount to a slightly swifter pace. He was glad to jump down and go inside the rude hut, for the journey had made his back ache and a break in it was welcome.

"Patchric, you are returned", Klomar stated the obvious. He was the owner of the trading hut and stocked food stuffs, building materials and weapons. "What can I get for you, how is your hut coming along"?

"It proceeds", was the reply, "I have need of flour, some berries and the cleanest water you have, the rest I carry with me in this backpack".

"From the king no doubt? Well I have some boiled water and some sweet blackberries and the mill has just supplied me with flour so there will be no mites in it yet".

Patchric waited while Klomar got together his order. Outside the wind was getting up and he could hear rain falling on the hut's thatched roof. Most of the modern conveniences and supplies had been the developments since his grandfather had come down from the skies in the great silver tower from the distant land of Urs. Life was good on Nyjord and the Barabora had been driven from Katowice, Kozosse and even distant Kranga to the south.

"The smithy has just finished with the new iron from Katowice, Patchric, he's made a couple of beautiful machete if you would like to look at them"?

"Alright", Patchric agreed, "I could do with a machete, the fronds around my new hut could do with cutting back".

"Useful for defence too in case the Barabora are stupid enough to come this way", Klomar sensed a sale on the horizon.

"My thagomiser will deal with anyone who decides to trespass near my hut, Klomar, it has already tasted blood".

The machete was of fine workmanship, with a carved blue handle from the tough bough of a frond and Patchric asked,

"How much, for everything"?

"Twenty pebbles"?

The pebbles were made of jade and used as currency on Nyjord, another institution introduced by King Darn. They came in two sizes, pebble and bead, the bead being worth one tenth of a pebble.

"Too dear", Patchric began the process of haggling with the hut owner and trader, "I'll just take the supplies", and he went to hand the machete back.

"Just a minute Patchric, do be not so hasty, remember the uses a machete can have".

"Oh yes one could be for hacking a greedy trader to bits", the king's grandson jested.

Klomar blanched slightly at that, he returned hastily, "What would you say if I said I will accept nineteen and five"?

Suddenly the door hurled open and the now cold wind brought a frigid draft into the hut and no small amount of rain. A small hooded figure, with features hidden hurried inside and threw back the cowl.

Patchric stared, the girl was a beautiful Banteme maiden.

"Have you the sweetened egg bark chew"? she asked ignoring the variegated skin of the other traveller.

"Of course" Klomar returned cheerfully "One and seven".

"One and five is a fair price", Patchric interrupted loudly and then to cover his embarrassment, "And for my purchase eighteen and three. Here are twenty pebbles; there - you are......."?

"Miula", said the maiden taking the chew sticks, "Thank you......"?

"Patchric", he responded in Banteme.

"You speak the language of my people"?

"He is Prince Patchric of Katowice", Klomar supplied.

The door blew open again and Patchric went to close it, "It is getting heavy out there, have you far to go, Miula".

"A hut on the far side of Khmjn", was the response, "Not far I think, I've already walked from Byo, to the north, Highness".

"No need for titles here, Miula" Patchric told her, glaring at Klomar and testing the edge of his new machete with his thumb. Once again the trader blanched.

"I have the quadri, you can climb up behind me and I will take you where you want to go, for the darkness is here and you should not be out alone on the road".

"Who are you intending to visit"? the trader suddenly asked.

Miula only answered Patchric though, "I'll take the offer of a ride, the rain *is* getting heavy".

"Come then", the two of them braved the elements together. The wind was causing the rain to smite them in sheets and both threw up the cowls on their cloaks. Patchric took hold of Miula's heel and hoisted her up onto the quadri's back and then he hurled himself up in front of her.

"Put your arms around me"? He cried over the noise of the wind and rain, or you might fall off".

She did as directed and he marvelled at her slimness and lack of weight. Progress was slow as they began to encounter the odd isolated hut and after ten minutes in the driving rain Patchric shouted,

"I need to stop at this hut, it has the food for my beast here".

"Very well", the girl muttered unhappily, "We're getting terribly wet and I'm getting cold".

"Then I will summon all possible hast", Patchric promised and pulled their mount to a halt.

"Patchric", a voice cried from inside the hut and the prince of Katowice hurried inside, leaving the girl to stay mounted, or follow if she desired.

Khenu offered Patchric his arm and the two grasped it in the traditional Khelac fashion,

"How was the king", the trader wished to know.

"Well and my siblings, my father and my other family, all well. The mines are producing well and several Viriligan are constant companions of the Khelac and Banteme of the fortress".

"Good", Khenu seemed genuinely pleased to hear the tidings, "I have the frond seed for your quadri, no mould in it yet, here's the sack, will you give me fifteen pebbles"?

"I will Khenu, because it's a fair price", Patchric agreed. The door opened and Miula slipped inside.

"It's stopped raining", she announced to the hut in general, "But the ground is absolutely sodden out there".

"Oh dear" Khenu noted, "The well may have come up again if it's rained hard".

"Where have you been Khenu"? Patchric laughed, "It was a heavy rain for certain".

"What's this about a well"? the girl desired to know.

"The centre of the town is in a hollow and there is a natural well there. If it rains too heavily the centre becomes a great pool. We will only see how bad it is when we get there and star light is not enough for us to do so until we are close".

"I hear there are stars on the fortress, Patchric", Khenu exclaimed, "That shine with some magic power the lama calls electrodes"?

"Electrisit", Patchric corrected erroneously.

"Can we get on please", Miula interrupted them, "I am cold and I am hungry and I just want to get to the far side of this sodden town".

"Of course", Patchric was a little disconcerted by the girl's abruptness, but he had the manner to cover up his own annoyance. Once again he helped her up onto the quadri and making sure his panniers were evenly filled to maintain balance, vaulted up behind her.

It was now decidedly cold and damp and visibility beneath the cloud filled sky was poor indeed. Patchric let his mount walk the journey,

"Why is it going so slowly, can we not go any swifter than this"? Miula complained.

"My steed could break a leg, if any of the road has collapsed with the heavy downpour we had, it's very difficult to see when the huts are so spaced apart, the pace will pick up once we get nearer to the centre of town".

"How long will it take to get to the centre"?

"Just another kilometre".

The quadri suddenly let out a squeal of pain and almost stumbled. Patchric let the beast hobble to a halt.

"By the orb of Brahma"! the girl cursed, "Be this another infernal interruption".

"My mount has obviously stepped on something that has given him pain, I won't know how badly he's hurt until I get down in the mud and take a look".

The wind that had previously dropped slowly began to pick up again and it tugged at their sodden clothing making the chill factor most unpleasant. Overhead Brahma the green and blue giant could be seen occasionally as the clouds scudded through the black cupola of Nyjord.

Patchric slipped down the side of his mount and lifted up one foot at a time,

"Well, what has happened to the clumsy beast".

"Just a sharp stone caught in between his second and third toe on his right foreleg".

"Instead of telling me, why don't you pull it out"?

"It's not that easy it's lodged, I'll need to get my hunting blade and ease it out, it's in one or the other of my panniers so I'll have to search for it".

The slim young woman slid down the far side of the quadri and began walking,

"What are you doing"? Patchric called after her.

"I've had enough delay, thank you for the ride, good night".

"You should not walk out alone, come back, please", Patchric called, unwilling to go running after her, after all, if he caught her then what? Assault her to protect her, that would never do.

"Be careful then and good luck", he cried and began the search for his blade. It was a clumsy process as he could not put anything on the sodden ground as it had turned to mud. That meant he could not empty out either pannier in his search for the slim hunting knife, so he fumbled around and went by touch rather than vision, which was very limited under the night sky.

Finally his fingers found the cold iron of the blade and he pulled it free and then it was only the work of ten seconds to dislodge the stone. The quadri's foot seemed fine so he buckled up his panniers once more and vaulted back up and proceeded the way the girl had gone, when she had left him in the dark. Perhaps he would overhaul her and still be able to take her the rest of the way on her journey?

"Halt, warrior, there is hazard ahead", a voice cried out in the dark and Patchric pulled the quadri to a stop.

"What is the need to block my way"? he called without dismounting.

Two warriors approached and one had a guttering brand that cast meagre amber glows to their brown features, Patchric recognised the Prowadza (police man) Lunsor as the slightly taller of the duo,

"The centre of town is a lake, the well has spewed the water back up to surface, you will not get that way, if you are going toward the western edge of the town".

"I've already experienced a murderous night and it is not getting any better", Patchric moaned,

Lunsor squinted up into the night, trying to discern his features, "The prince of Katowice, how was the rest of your journey, how is the king"?

"He enjoys rude health Prowadza and I enjoyed my visit and my journey home until the storm".

"Well take a steady detour Prince Patchric and your home is still safe and dry, unlike the unlucky ones who live in the centre".

"Are they alright"?

"The lama Skirean has accommodated them all in the Temple of the Blue Moon".

"Then I will be on my way, good night Prowadza".

"Good night Prince Patchric".

Patchric got to his own hut, a better construction than any other and went into the black interior. He lit a fish oil lantern and made himself a light supper, ate it and then undressed and crawled under the thin blanket that was on his cot, he was asleep in minutes.

TWO

T HE NEXT MORNING was bright and sunny and the ground was steaming back to it's usual dry tracks when Patchric arose. He performed his ablutions in the latrine behind his home and then had breakfast. He was just finishing when there was a sharp knock at the door, he opened it to the lama Skirean and the Prowadza Lunsor, the latter was carrying an iron tipped spear.

"What can I do for the two of you this fine morning"? the tall Khelac asked of the duo.

"You must come to the temple" Skirean instructed, "There to answer certain questions".

"About what pray", Patchric asked.

"In the temple you will discover the nature of Lunsor's investigation", the lama said with a certain satisfied tone.

"Then I'll help you in any way I can", Patchric returned, curious as to the particular of Lunsor's enquiries, "Lead on".

He followed them to a wooden structure that dwarfed all others, even his own and the strange trio went inside.

"Come to the altar", the lama ordered.

Patchric had no desire to cross the most powerful woman in the town, so despite her abrupt lack of respect for his station, he did as directed, without a word. There was the heavy smell of incense and *leaf-blow* in the air. The familiar aroma of the Temple of the Blue Moon.

"Patchric, do you know a woman called Miula"? Lunsor asked him then and then reminded him superfluously, "And remember you are answering in the presence of the blue goddess"?

"Yes I met her last night and gave her a ride into town, well part of the way anyway".

"It is as Klomar said", the lama noted with certain glee, "You occasioned her and took her with you".

"It was during the storm and she was on foot, so yes, I occasioned her as you say, lama. Where is this leading"?

"We found Miula last night, on the roadside, strangled to death", Lunsor told him heavily.

Patchric was shocked and said nothing to the revelation.

"Sit down, Prince Patchric", Lunsor requested and the door of the temple opened as Patchric took a seat on one of the temple's benches.

With another of the Prowadza warriors was Khenu, Lunsor said to Patchric, "You traded with Khenu last night for food stuff for your quadri"?

"That's right", Patchric admitted freely, "Good morning Khenu".

Khenu nodded, "They were together lama, that is all I know".

"I could have told you this, if you had asked me", Patchric said with a rising unease.

Lunsor told him, "Together just before the girl's body was found, Prince Patchric. Do you want to tell the lama, in the presence of the Blue Moon goddess what happened between you and Miula"?

"I met her at Klomar's trading hut and offered her a ride into town, as the weather was foul and she was already soaked from the rain. We stopped at Khenu's so I could pick up some feed for my quadri, shortly afterward she decided to walk as the rain had stopped, that is all".

"Why would an unarmed maiden decide to walk through the darkness of a stormy night when a warrior had offered her a ride on his steed"? the lama sounded sceptical.

"Why would she even be travelling in the dark"? Lunsor added.

"That was her business and it remained private, as I did not quiz her"., Patchric was beginning to lose his temper, the inferences were obvious, he was the only suspect in the investigation of the Prowadza.

The door of the temple swung inward yet again and the next person to enter was Klomar.

"Good morning, Klomar", Patchric greeted the trader, but the other's mouth twisted in distaste and he did not return the gesture.

"Klomar", Lunsor began, "When Prince Patchric and the unfortunate maiden Miula met in your hut, did they know one another"?

"No". The trader returned and gazed at Patchric for some moments before declaring, "He was wearing a long cowled cloak, but under that I could see he had blue breeks, now he is wearing amber breeks".

"That is true what of it"?

"Why did you change your breeks from one day to the next"? the lama demanded, her eyes' glinting with malicious accusation.

"The other pair are crusty with mud". Patchric told them, "I got covered in the stuff when I was forced to take a stone out of my quadri's foot. Now I have had enough of this charade, what is the purpose of all these questions, do you think I strangled someone I had only just met? What would be my reason for doing such a senseless thing"?

The lama offered, "Perhaps there was no stone Patchric grandson of Darn? Perhaps your breeks got covered with mud when you strangled the maiden? Perhaps the poor innocent child would not exceed to the lustful demands of one who thinks he can have anything he wants just by asking, so he killed her with his bare hands".

"Perhaps you are a bitter, twisted old woman, who resented my coming to this town", Patchric flared.

"Let us all just take a moment to calm ourselves", Lunsor suggested, with a strange smile on his features. "Thank you for bearing witness before the Blue Moon goddess, Prince Patchric, you are remaining in the town overnight"?

"I live here remember"? Patchric did not feel calm, "And I am courting the girl Mostah, daughter of Mosten, a respected elder of this town".

He noted the look of distaste that twisted the grimalkin's weathered features and realised that she hated him because of it.

"Thank you for giving me the opportunity to bear witness before the goddess of the Blue Moon, but now I am going".

"Wait" the lama halted him on final time, she picked up a book from one of the benches. A paged grimoire held together by hemp twine containing leaves of pressed frond parchment, she held it out to him in her wrinkled claw,

"The prayers of supplication to the Blue Moon goddess, take them warrior and meditate on their wise counsel, they may be of use to you".

Was the crone being sarcastic? He could not decide and took the hallowed volume and even managed a stiff nod of thanks.

With that Patchric, prince of Katowice took himself out of the temple and went in search of his sweetheart Mostah, daughter of Mosten.

He found her beside the river Tchichi were it had swollen into a torrent, rushing back into the sea of Bengal, she was washing clothes and did not notice his arrival. The day was bright and warm and to Patchric, in his present mood, somewhat incongruous.

"Mostah", he said simply, saw her hear him, turn on her knees and then, not rise to her feet and come to him as she usually would. "Is something amiss, sweetheart".

Mostah frowned and still not rising but returning to her task asked, "That I do not know, Patchric, *is* there something amiss"?

So the wizened old witch had been to see his sweetheart had she?

"You have spoken to our lama"?

"She came to see me not long after the rising of the sun", Mostah admitted. Finally she rose uncertainly to her feet,

"It seems you are suspected of rape and murder, Patchric".

"Rape! I was not told the girl had been molested before she was cruelly done to death"?

"Did you need to be told"?

"Do you need to ask"?

Mostah fell silent and looked down at her feet, before finally confessing, "I need to ask".

"Then ask", he demanded and she approached him and asked him directly, "Did you rape and murder last night, Patchric"?

He looked her straight in the eye and told her, "Of course I did not, sweetheart. The Prowadza know I was the last who admits to being with her last night and they have no other clue as to who might be guilty of such a heinous act. The lama spurs them on because she does not approve of our courtship".

"Skirean does not approve of our liaison"?

"She does not. Why? Do you care"?

"She is lama; priestess of the goddess of the Blue Moon, I do not seek to gain her disapproval".

"And now you know you have it, what of us, Mostah"?

The girl hung her head, the end of her chestnut waves were damp with the waters of the Tchichi. Patchric lifted her chin with a gentle hand and kissed her on the forehead.

"I am innocent of crime, my love, but I fear the poison Skirean spreads could task me greatly, is your father in his house"?

"He is, what do you want with him"?

"I think it might be fortuitous to ask him to send a messenger from amongst his retainers, to get word to my father. He should know, of what, I stand accused".

"But you have not been accused".

"That is true", Patchric agreed, "But I fear I will be".

"I believe your innocence, for you have looked into my eyes and declared it".

"Yes, but not all will accept the same assurance I fear".

He left her to complete her task and walked quickly back to the house of Mosten and his family. The elder was seated outside the grand wooden affair, taking some sun and smoking leaf-blow in a carved frond pipe.

Elder, Mosten", Patchric nodded to the man who had his respect.

Mosten rose gently to his feet and returned the nod of respect, "Prince Patchric, Mostah is down by the river, washing clothes".

"Yes, elder, I have seen her, now I am come to see you. I need a favour".

Mostah frowned, "You are obviously aware of what you stand accused, are you guilty, Prince Patchric"?

"I am not".

"The lama has also declared you impious, is that why you carry one of her teaching tomes".

"I took it out of respect for her office alone, not out of any such for her", Patchric explained.

"Tell me what favour you need and if it be within my power, it shall be so"?

"I ask that your most trusted retainer be sent to Katowice, to tell my family of what is transpiring here".

"It shall be, do you wish any personal message"?

"I need the retained to depart at once and will not tarry him in any way".

Mostah turned to go inside the huge wooden house, "Then I am on my way, Patchric and he shall have my finest stead".

"Gratitude", Patchric replied and turning himself, went back to his own abode.

THREE

PATCHRIC OPENED THE door and this time Lunsor was on his own, "I have some more questions Patchric".

"Come in then and have some clean water, what do you want to ask me now, Prowadza"?

"Do you know Bilos the Crooked, who lives just at the edge of the hollow in the town's centre"

"I have seen him around and at gatherings, yes. He has a withered leg and walks with a stick. How is he of interest to you, Lunsor"?

"He said he was looking at the water coming out of the well and saw you last night, the girl no longer in your company, minutes only before we found her dead body in the mud nearby. He said you looked dazed and that your breeks were covered in mud, your hands as well".

I don't see the significance of this, Prowadza. I've already told you I got covered in mud taking a stone out of my quadri's foot, as to my dazed look, I was bone weary and in a rather unpleasant storm, how else would I have to appeared to anyone"?

"Where are those breeks, Prince Patchric, do you still have them"?

"Of course they are in the laundry area waiting to be taken down to the river".

"Mostah will still be doing your washing will she"?

"My domestic arrangements are not part of the investigation are they, Prowadza? What do you expect to find on the breeks except mud anyway. You told me the girl was strangled, so there could not be blood could there"?

"So you know she did not bleed"?

"I don't know anything about what happened to her once she left my company, now do not come back here Lunsor, unless it is to take me into custody".

"Very well then, I would be grateful if you would volunteer to come with me, Patchric. You see the girl's clothes were also covered in mud, torn and ripped from her body, but covered in mud and there was no blood anywhere".

"That's your case, mud"?

"Will you come quietly or do I have to get a group of armed Prowadza and return"?

"I need to make arrangements for my quadri if you intend to put me in gaol, Lunsor. You do intend to imprison the grandson of King Darn I take it"?

Lunsor nodded gravely, "I'll see the animal is looked after by one of my warriors and yes Patchric, I do intend to put you, the grandson of King Darn, in the goal"!

The gaol being a stout hut that a truly determined man could have escaped from, Patchric waited, He was fed and kept warm enough and when he demanded to know what would happen next was told a hearing in front of the whole town would be held in the temple two days hence.

"Someone from Katowice might not have time to get here by then", he told those who guarded him and this was met by either a shrug, or the remark that being from a high family would not save him from Khmjn justice. On the evening before the hearing however, someone did return from his home town, it was his aunt, Patchee, daughter of the sky traveller Wera.

She was allowed to join him in his holding room.

"Did you strangle the girl", was her first question,

"Do you really think me capable of such an act"? he asked the woman who had more striking variations in skin tone than himself. She then admitted,

"Of course not, but I had to ask, what is your defence, how can I speak on your behalf"?

"That there is no reason to think that I did do it, aunt. There is nothing on the girl that is mine, the evidence against me is simply hearsay and insubstantial".

"I will do what I can then".

"And if it goes wrong, will grandfather intervene"?

Patchee shook her head, her silvery hair bobbing around her shoulders, "It would cause a conflict between Khmjn and Katowice that neither could afford. You chose to live here because you fell out with your siblings", she reminded,

"Therefore you must accept Khmjn justice. The Barabora have been spotted just north of Byo, if we Khelac and Banteme began fighting, they would seize on the chance to attack the weakened victors".

"But grandfather has the needle rifles and the lightning guns".

"Yet not warriors in sufficient numbers to risk bringing the Barabora down on us".

"Then we will have to see how impartial the town's folk of Khmjn are"!

FOUR

"I SAW THE way he looked at the girl", Klomar said in the temple the next day, "I know how young men, young arrogant men are, what goes on in their mind when they see a young pretty and vulnerable girl. Not only that, he had murder on his mind, I feared for my own life when he knocked me down on price for a machete, it's a wonder he never chopped the girl up"!

"He has a sweetheart in the town though", Patchee objected, "You are only supposing all that went on in my nephew's mind".

"A murderous warriors filled with lust does not think about such things", Skirean said to the gathering. When he saw the poor creature, Mostah would not have been in his consideration".

The murmurings from this response, did not bode well for Patchric.

"Well it seemed to me that they knew one another, but the girl was nervous and there was nothing Patchric could do to keep her calm", Khenu spoke up when it was his turn.

"Nervous", Skirean repeated, "Fearing for her life perhaps and wanting to get away.

"Khenu cannot comment on that", Patchee objected.

"Why not"? Skirean demanded, "He was there and you were not, Patchric was not with his family, because he had quarrelled with them and that was why he came to live in our town in the first place".

"That has nothing to do with the events of the night we are talking about", Patchee said to everyone.

"It tells us Patchric was quarrelsome, so antagonist that he could not even get along with his own family", the lama pointed out.

"He was nervous and covered in mud", Lunsor cried when his turn to speak came around, "He looked like he had been down in the wet to me, possibly wrestling with someone".

"He has already explained that he had been in the mud to get a stone out of his quadri's foot" Patchee responded, "And to conclude he had been involved in some sort of struggle, is totally unfounded".

It was too late though, the inference was in the town's minds, objecting could not erase that image.

"Just give me a second to remember his exact words", Klomar said, "Oh yes, he said *'Oh yes one could be for hacking a greedy trader to bits'*, and I had to lower my price for fear of my life. So I am still alive, while the girl was the one who answered his lust for killing".

"Is it not true that you are being so vindictive *because* you had to lower your price and everything else you have suggested is simply in your greedy and twisted imagination"? Patchee demanded.

The lama cried, "Klomar has been a member of our town for years and should not have to be attacked so, simply because an aunt with royal connections turns up here to try and get her nephew off with murder"?

"When I found the body, it was still warm", Lunsor told them, painting a grim picture, "Me and my man had only just been talking to Patchric, so my question is, would anyone else have been out and about on a night like that"?

Bilos the Crooked rose awkwardly to his feet, leaning heavily on his stick and told the people in the temple,

"I was looking at the water coming out of the well and saw the prince that night, the girl was not in sight. That was only minutes only before the Prowadza found her dead body in the mud nearby. Patchric looked dazed and his breeks were covered in mud, his hands as well".

"We are going over the same ground", Patchee replied in exasperation, "The mud has already been explained".

Skirean croaked, "Not to the satisfaction of the good people of our town it has not. We go over the ground and every time it shows Patchric in and around the place where the poor girl was brutally raped and strangled to death. Only one conclusion can be drawn from all that"!

"A good quadri could have gotten to the other side of town in much less time than it took Patchric that night", one of the Prowadza told the town, "What was he doing? Was he taking a stone from his mounts foot as he claims, or was he having his way with a poor innocent half his size and then, when he realised what he had done, killing her so she could not accuse him of anything"?

"Both are equally possible", Patchee told them, in response, "But if you know my nephew as well as I do you have to believe what he claims, for he is of good sound character and would never hurt someone like Miula of Byo.

"She says that *because* she is his aunt", the lama cried out, "Even though all the evidence points at his guilt she bases her defence of her nephew on family position and privilege. Well such a connection does not allow one to get away with doing exactly what they want with others and the good people of this town will not let *anyone* get away with murder just because they are royalty. Justice is justice and should be equal for all".

"We have heard all the evidence and the good people of this town have found you guilty by a majority vote. You will therefore be taken from this temple tomorrow morning and stoned, until you are dead". Lama Skirean pronounced.

"You do not have the authority to stone the king's grandson", Patchee objected, but the lama persisted,

"The town's people of Khmjn do so by the authority of the goddess of the Blue Moon, which is higher than any man, king or otherwise".

Patchee came to see Patchric shortly afterward, "By the time I reached Katowice and told your family what is too happen, it would already be too late to save you. I am sorry Patchric, I did what I could".

His next visitor was Mostah, she had the presence of mind to be weeping, no matter what her personal suspicions were.

"Can your father intervene for me"? he asked her as he held her in his arms.

"Like your grandfather, the king, he has not the authority over a goddess", she sobbed her reply, "The lama is obdurate that the sentence will be carried out in the morning. I am so sorry Patchric, I love you, you know".

Patchric received another visitor that evening, and his identity was a surprise, it was Lunsor the Prowadza.

"One day, Lunsor you will discover evidence that will show I was innocent. You are a good Prowadza, when you do please posthumously clear my name"? Patchric asked of him. "Something will be uncovered, something that will make you think, something that you can take to the lama, will you do that for me at least"?

Lunsor's feature's were knotted in an enigmatic expression and Patchric felt obliged to say once again,

"I did not murder Miula. I will be stoned to death in but a few short hours, there is no reason for me to lie to you right now".

"I believe you Khelac", the Prowadza said coldly, "Not only do I believe you mongrel, but I am certain you are telling the truth. I will tell you why, only you and at this late hour when you are soon to be executed. *I* killed the girl myself"!

"What"?

"It was simple, I sent the other Prowadza to fetch food from Klomar's and while he was gone backtracked from your position. Then I raped the bitch and strangled her. By the time the other warrior returned I was just far enough away from the body so that we could stumble upon her together".

Patchric was lost for words and so the Prowadza was able to go on,

"She deserved to die, Prince of the Khelac, she was going to blackmail me or tell this town she was carrying my child; which in actuality, she was. I had taken a trip to Byo while you were in the bosom of your high flown family, she made eyes at me and let me do what I wanted and when her usual did not happen for two months she sent word by skreet* that she was coming here to expose me. I would have lost my post as Prowadza, my woman would have left me, I would have been ruined, so I did the only thing I could, I ended it".

"You tell me now, knowing I am going to die for your crime"!

"Well I could not tell the lama or confess in the temple hearing, if I had I would

* a small bird like a crow, used to convey messages - tied around it's leg.

be in your place now. The secret must remain between us and when you are executed in the morning, there will be only one, who knows the truth".

"You are wrong Lunsor, you should have not boasted to me", Patchric cried triumphantly, then called" Guard, guard, come to the door".

When the guard came he asked, "Fetch my aunt and the lama to this holding room please, there is something they must hear"?

Lunsor laughed, "They will merely see this as a pathetic attempt to get a stay of execution until your grandfather gets here and you use your privileged position to scamper back to Katowice. I will deny everything I've just told you, who do you think Skirean will favour, Khelac mongrel"?

He repeated that in various variations until the duo of requested women arrived in the holding room.

"What is this"? the lama demanded, "What do you want of me condemned man? Do you wish to finally confess your sins and beg the Blue Moon Goddess for forgiveness so you may enter Elysium instead of Tartarus".

In answer Patchric held up a small oblong stick, that he had removed from the pocket of his jerkin. With his fingernail he depressed a tiny stud and though tinny, the distinctive voice of Lunsor could be heard saying,

"It was simple, I sent the other Prowadza to fetch food from Klomar's and while he was gone backtracked from your position. Then I raped the bitch and strangled her".

"What trick is this"? the lama demanded.

Lunsor growled, "Sorcery, that stick is the work of Badrevil of the netherworld".

"No lama, it is not", Patchee insisted, "That is a recording device brought from the stars by those who came in the silver towers. It makes a faithful copy of what is said or sounds one makes and plays them back to those who know how to use it".

"Demonstrate it to me then here and now", the lama demanded.

"Say something now", Patchric requested after depressing two buttons on the stick.

"If this device proclaims me wrong, it will burst into flame and be destroyed, this I have sworn by the power of the goddess of the Blue Moon", the lama intone piously.

Lunsor sat heavily on the bench then, while Patchee played the oath back to the lama.

"Come", Skirean said to Patchee and Patchric then, "Lunsor will take your place, for he is the one guilty of the foul crime and he has condemned himself by his own tongue, in the morning he will be the one to suffer the penalty. Prince Patchric, I have wronged you, will you come to the temple with me and witness my request for forgiveness from the goddess of the Blue Moon"?

Though he did not believe in such superstition, Patchee nodded generously and agreed,

"Yes, lama, I will".

WHITE FLAME

When the white flame in us is gone,
And we that lost the world's delight
Stiffen in darkness, left alone
To crumble in our separate night;

When your swift hair is quiet in death,
And through the lips corruption thrust
Has stilled the labour of my breath --
When we are dust, when we are dust!   -- Rupert Brooke

ONE

"ISN'T IT LOVELY to get out of the town and by driving through the outdoor plains", Takom observed, "I get so tired of being cooped up in the airtight buildings".

"The dust can be a nuisance", Lorn observed, "But a trip out is nice and I've heard that Lake Passionata has become incredibly popular in the northern reaches".

"We should do this more often", Takom persisted, Ausonia is beginning to drive me to distraction, I wish we could move closer to the equator, where it gets almost warm at midday".

"But the wind still blows great clouds of dust everywhere", Lorn objected.

"Then why don't we move off world altogether", Takom glanced up through the transparent dome of the flitter's roof, surveyed the sun that was too small - when seen from Mars.

"You know why", Lorn yawned.

"But you don't love him", he objected, "I don't understand why you don't just divorce him".

"You know why that is too", she groaned through her ennui at the turn of the conversation, one that they had conducted many times before.

Gilliam Treet, was the husband of Lorn, he was also C.E.O. of Marstallations, Greengrow and Martian Future Projects Inc. As such his combined income exceeded twenty seven thousand per annum, in silver shillin and Lorn was used to living her life to an exorbitant standard.

"But there's more to life than money", Takom pointed out, "Like love and companionship".

"Companionship that is so much more pleasant when one can afford the little things in life without worrying about bills", she grinned.

"Did you ever love him, Lorn"?

She thought about her short, bald and bespectacled husband with his pot belly and his sweaty forehead and returned simply, "No".

"If he had hair transplants, laser surgery on his eyes and lost some weight, what then"?

"Still no"

"Why on Earth did you marry him then"?

"He was loaded and all I had was my looks and my body, the merger was mutually beneficial and continues to be so".

"Do you love me then"?

"You amuse me", she chuckled, "You're handsome, intelligent, tall, have a good body and know how to use it in bed, so I guess I do, what's love anyway"?

"It's the way you feel about money", he returned grimly, almost bitterly.

"Don't sulk darling it will give you wrinkles. When I think about Gilliam I almost draw a blank", Lorn observed, half to herself. "He saw me waiting tables in the Excellsior and asked me to dinner the following evening. Inside three months he'd presented me with a magnificent duridium ring with one carat diamond in it's centre and we were married three weeks later. Of course you know all that being D.C.E.O. at Martian Future Projects Inc".

"For which I flog my guts out for a sixth of the money he commands", Takom sulked, he was beginning to grow petulant.

"I suppose I might have grown fond of Gilliam, could have been almost content with him, if you hadn't seduced me".

Takom cast his mind back to their first meeting in Gilliam's office and remembered the signals she had given him. Signals he had acted upon as soon as he had the chance and *she* seemed to think the seduction had been in the opposite direction.

"So your feelings' for me have changed how you feel for him", he concluded.

"Perhaps, Takom, but it's not *always* about you, you know"?

She tormented him. His lust for her as a physical object, overrode all feelings of self worth and decency, once she started in on him in this way.

Then she suddenly changed tack, something else she was want to do and said,

"You've made all the difference sweetie".

He almost turned to her, to kiss her, but the road up to Passionata was only compacted dust and rust and he had to watch what he was doing at the wheel. They reached the lake. The magnificent artificial creation of man, on the formerly dry planet. The pathetic moons meant that the water was like glass and Takom stripped off and strode into it with gusto. Meanwhile Lorn huddled in a blanket on the cool rusty shoreline. He waded out and swam until he felt his limbs beginning to cramp with the frigidity of the water; so he turned back and then waded back out as quickly as he could.

Lorn laughed at the blueness of his lean torso and defined muscles and deliberately gazed at the front of his trunks. She remarked with heavy innuendo,

"Very very cold was it Tak"?

He laughed and began to vigorously rub himself dry with a coarse towel.

"Come here", her voice was husky with lasciviousness, "I'll find you somewhere warm to put it.

The cove they had chosen was very private so he let her tug his swimming pants down and she took him into her mouth.

Twenty minutes later they lay beneath the blankets both catching their breath from their mutual climaxes.

"That was like *'From Here to Eternity'*, you know the beach scene", he told her.

She shook her head.

"The pre-ancient film, with Burt Lancaster".

"Oh; one of those dreadful two dimensional things you watch on that strange contraption of yours"?

"A projector, yes one of those, one thousand nine hundred and fifty three it came out, isn't even in colour, well the original anyway".

"One thousand and something? Did they have electricity then"?

"Yes sweetie they had quite a few conveniences in ancient times", he smiled, she might be decorative and energetic, but Lorn was not really intellectually stimulating, especially to hold conversations with at times.

"So; Lorn, when am I going to kill him"?

He expected her to be shocked, possibly even horrified, but he had totally misjudged that issue, as so many before it,

"I don't care, just so long as I'm not home".

"Actually, it would be much better if you were. Listen to my idea; I break through the airlock, kill him, take some of your valuables and leave you tied up. Then I ping the constabulary from a mobile telephone and tell them I was driving by and heard a scream"?

"A mobile telephone, so they don't get your I.P."?

He nodded. She asked,

"So how come I cannot identify my assailant"?

"Masked, gloved, dressed in a black catsuit, what can you tell them? Plus the fact that you are tied up and robbed throws the constables onto the wrong scent. They are looking for someone guilty of manslaughter after an aggravated burglary went wrong, instead of your husband's murderer".

"Well you can't shoot him then can you, that looks too premeditated, too neat"?

"Why can't a burglar carry a gun"?

"A gun sort of speaks to intent, you want to throw them off the scent then you have to do something that looks spare of the moment".

It seemed Lorn was much nimbler minded when it came to homicide, than when discussing historical matters.

"So I've not to take anything in myself"?

She nodded, "It has to be something in the property".

"Does Gilliam have a blaster, or a needle gun"?

"Forget guns, they are in locked desk drawers anyway, it has to look like he surprised you. You could even turn the lights off on your way out and leave me trussed up on our bed, more comfortable for me while I'm waiting for the constables to arrive. I tell them we were having an early night, he heard a noise downstairs and went to investigate, then you burst into the room and tied me up".

"Can I rape you then"?

"D.N.A. sweetie, you can rape me some other time! So what about the eagle sculpture in the study"?

"You want me to bludgeon him to death?!"

"Not necessary, just cave his skull in".

"I'm not sure I can… I mean….."

"Well if you're not man enough maybe my next boyfriend….."

"Don't do that, don't threaten to get rid of me because I'm a bit squeamish about committing a brutal murder. What about the kitchen knives, I could stab him, I know I could do that"?

"Once again that's too organised, no Tak, if you're going to kill my husband for his money and my body, you'll have to crush his head in like a rotten egg".

"Must you be so; so graphic in your description of it"?

"It *will* be graphic on the night. Think about it, if you can do it, you can have the money and me, forever".

"I don't need to think about it, I just need to build up the courage and I think I know how".

TWO

WILEY AWOKE VERY slowly and it felt like the top of his head might come off at any second. He really must stop sampling the product before putting it out for his discerning clientèle. Automatically he reached for his cigarettes (the tobacco variety) and snapped the end of one to crimson life.

The racking cough that sent him into paroxysm served to get quite a bit of congestion out of his lungs. He went over to the sink of his one room bedsit and hawked up most of it. Then, as he was fastidious with personal care and hygiene rinsed his mouth out with Lichen-vodka and cleaned his teeth with his left forefinger.

Rat (he had forgotten his real former name) Wiley regarded the image in the mirror that stared back at him with bloodshot eyes. His skin the colour of a scarred and pitted battleship and an array of greasy hair that had seen a comb, but not that year.

He was not happy with what he saw, but until his gambling debts were cleared with Murdering Meffen, he had to continue his current sorry occupation. Rat sold Snufz on the back streets of Mars, or to be more specific the back streets of Yaonis Fretum. The latter was notorious for being the source of the drug in it's various guises and Rat was proud to be one of the chief dealers.

Wading through the detritus of a month's ready meals, he left his bedsit. One of the cheapest in the town and strolled along Polk Alley that flared into Jefferson Boulevard. The wind was cold, but not unbearably, but as usual it was filled with red dust, the rust of the oxidated planet.

He stopped to remove a carefully hand rolled 1in2, the cocktail of tobacco and snufz, it also happened to be the best seller on the streets at that time. His eyes darted hither and thither constantly, to make certain no combmen were about. Combmen was the colloquial term for constables, that had migrated from Venus and Rat Wiley did not want any of them combing the alleys of Yaonis Fretum, for him!

"Hey, Rat"! A voice wheezed behind the dealer, "Is the top above the bottom dude and are those sides pulled in"?

Rat whirled around momentarily alarmed, but relaxed when he saw it was Freebie Sellow.

"Don't sneak up on a wide boy like that, Freebie", Wiley chastised the snufzhead, "You're liable to get you're koofed-up brains blown all over the street".

"Relax chango* I'm not one of Meffen's boys", Sellow wheezed and began that silent chuckle that moved his shoulders up and down and ended in a bone rattling cough "Say chango do you have any medicine for a poor broken down homeless chango, living on the streets".

Sellow always referred to snufz, as medicine.

"You're not homeless, Freebie, you've got a squat over in Jackson Villas and I'm not a charity, your name isn't Freebie because you have the whahootis*²"!

"I'm not looking for a handout", Freebie straightened up and assumed a posture of what he thought was a respectable citizen of Yaonis Fretum, "I was merely enquiring if you might be carrying any medical samples"?

"Get out of here, Freebie and don't come back unless you have something in your wallet other than cockroaches".

Rat was looking beyond the chango and saw a hesitant figure in very well cut clothing entering the alley. His shirt which was white and cut in the cowl collar style of the day's fashion, was not in need of washing, he wore purple looms and his black shoes looked like they might actually be from a cow, leather! His haircut, for he chose to wear it not in the fashionable ponytail, but rather the square neck of the young executive, looked like it had cost more than Sellow had paid him in a year.

* Colloquial - world/gypsy/reggae man, friend, wide boy, man
*2 Coloquial - money especially in cash

Wiley did his best to straighten himself up and began to stroll toward the fashionably handsome, potential customer, striking as casual a poise as he could manage. The other seemed to half turn, he was obviously in two minds whether to proceed and Wiley knew he was a snufz-virgin and as green as the grass on Earth. He seemed to square his shoulders and find some resolve though and he continued to walk toward the dealer, who could feel the cold steel and reassuring barrel of a needle gun nestling against his ribs.

They stopped when about a metre apart, Wiley greeted,

"Hey chango, you meeting the man with the bill and looking after the little lady".

"I beg your pardon, do you speak standard"?

"That was street standard, Mister, but apologies, what can a hard working business man do for a processional executive like you"?

"Are you a drug dealer"? the man enquired, as though it was the most natural thing on Mars to come out with.

"Are you looking to get your damn stupid head blown off, Mister"?

"No"! The other paled visibly despite the warm of his thermal clothing, "I seem to have managed to offend you"?

"That's something of an understatement chango" Wiley told him, feeling comfortable in himself, the other man was clearly afraid of him. "I shall have to search you now for recording devices, you could be an undercover combman".

He began fumbling through the other's very expensive attire while the man stuttered,

"I assure you I have no connection with His Majesty's Constabulary in any way, Sir".

"So it would seem, so what can a chango do for a chango then"?

"I thought I had made my position clear, I wish to exchange illegal narcotics for folding shillin".

"You see now you are speaking a universal language with me, Mister, do you have a budget may one enquire".

The man smiled nervously at Wiley's use of irony, he admitted, "I thought I would like enough to fill say two reefers".

"Well the term is a little archaic, but I understand the gist of it, Mister, you're after the Solar System's most glorious gift to mankind: grey, lichen-weed, bud, dope, pot, herb, snufz-grass, the great smoke-pit. This wonderful lichen, when spliced genetically with yeast creates mental happiness. Rolled into a joint, blunt or packed into a bowl etc., mixed with tobacco it is the single most effective way to relax and be at ease, the best known to man. It can be smoked from joints, blunts, pipes, bongs, hookahs, one-hitters, bubblers and indeed just about anything".

The smart man looked stunned by the depth of Wiley's product knowledge, then he asked,

"So what are we looking at here"?

"Ah, the whahootis required to secure a successful purchase. Two little bags should do for you, Mister processional executive, so I require one shillin of His Majesty's coin of the realm".

"I thought it was easier to get than that, that I could get the amount I want for fifty sestertii".

"Did you now! Well let me ask you this green-boy, is it worth getting your head blown off for a lousy fifty sestertius, sestertii, sesterces or what ever you want to call half a shillin"?

The money was handed over, followed by the bags,

"Pleasure to do business with a classy gent, Mister. See you next Tuesday".

"I won't be coming back this way", the other promised.

"That's just about what they all say to start with and they all do, before they stop", Wiley grinned.

"What do you mean before they stop, why don't they stop initially"?

"I mean when they shuffle off this veil of tears, chango, why do you think it's called Snufz? Because you snort it like snuff, or because eventually it causes you to snuff it, put out the eternal candle, become a former human being"?

The man hurried away shivering slightly. Wiley looked down at the shillin in his grubby paw, what he could do with this morning was a huge fry up at Fat Mama Bluie's.

THREE

BAR HAD PARKED his flitter around the corner from the house and his head was buzzing fiercely. The very atmosphere inside the vehicle was enough to cause anyone to become intoxicated. He gripped the movement handle and hauled himself through the archway of the door and stood for several seconds on the pavement. Mars was spinning wildly around. He began to stumble toward the corner, unable to walk in a straight line.

As he managed to get himself three quarters of the way, a large blue multi-legged creature crawled across the pseudo-lawn and regarded him on stalked eyes. It could not be a spider, the eyes were not right, it was covered in royal blue fur and had six legs and then it opened a tiny mouth in it's thorax and said,

"You're trippin' to the moons baby, calm down and stick to the plan"?

"What do you know of my plan"? Bar felt ridiculous having an actual conversation with the bizarre creature.

A smaller beast suddenly scurried in front of the blue one and from the larger, a huge mucus covered tongue launched from it's mouth and the smaller creature gave some sort of heinous scream and then Bar heard the crunching of it's terrible death.

"Sorry about that", the blue beastie apologised as it munched, "But a *Deformatine* has to eat right"?

"Go away", Bar closed his eyes, "You're not real, you're not even there"!

The closing of his eyes made him lose his balance and he went sprawling onto the softness of the artificial turf. When he gasped and opened his eyes fearfully, he was greeted by two cat-like Deformatine, whatever a Deformatine was.

They regarded him with oval eyes that were bright xanthic with tiny green pupils.

"You wont do it", declared the larger of the two, "You might as well go back to your own place right now, loser"

"Don't be like that, Jeremat", the smaller Deformatine said reasonably, "He'll pull through this stage and then comes the euphoria and feeling of omnipotence".

"Shut your critter hole", Jeremat cursed back, "He's a poof, he'll back down, murder is no game for mincing left footers".

"Go do it", said the little one, but Takom Bar was disconcerted to see it begin melting before his very eyes.

He slapped himself with his own hand to try and snap back to reality and Jeremat suddenly burst with a bloody pop of guts and bits of sinew. Takom wiped his face and discovered that the film that he removed was colourless; sweat. He looked for vestiges of any creature, living or otherwise, only to learn that there were none.

Shakily he got to his feet and prepared to pull the lump hammer from his burglar's kit bag. Then it occurred to him, why make such a racket and possibly alert Treet of danger, when he knew the combination to the lock? Surely better to sneak in with the minimum of noise, catch him unaware?

He pulled on his gloves, pulled the black pseudo-plast mask over all but his eyes and pressed the keys in the correct order. There was the satisfying click of tumblers falling into place and he pushed the door open and eased into the hall. The only light he could discern was coming from the study. He knew his way around the property having been in it many times during afternoons of hurried and languid sex, dependent upon the circumstance.

This was the point of no return!

Bar could hear his own ragged breath wheezing inside the mask, the movement of the special fabric over his own ears and beyond, the sound of shuffling inside the study. He shook himself, took a deep breath and picked up the deadly piece of artwork.

Then he took the next step and then another, then he knew he would not turn back.

With deliberate violence he kicked in the interior door and through the eye-holes of his mask, saw Treet jump, the look of surprise almost instantly replaced by one of fear. Hands fumbling to get inside one of the desk drawers. Bar strode across the room and brought the eagle down with such violent force that one of it's wings broke off.

The dull crack of skull bone was as sickening as he expected. The corpse, for the blow had undoubtedly been instantly fatal, tumbled onto a Persian rug of inestimable value. Bar did not wish to examine his handy work in even the tiniest degree, he turned and strode to the stairs. Then he took a course of action that had not been discussed between the murderous pair; nor been part of an agreed plan. Fumbling in a pocket he pulled down his tights and pulled a condom onto his already stiffening member, for he was anticipating what he intended to do!

With the same kick that had ruined the jamb of the study door, Bar kicked in the bedroom door.

Lorn was on the bed dressed in a provocative negligee of brightest scarlet. "Oh, I heard the noise have you….."

His punch landed square on the left side of her jaw and threw her backwards, totally unconscious. As he turned her over and strapped her with duct tape, he could feel himself getting fully aroused. So this was what rape felt like to the perpetrator? He rolled her back onto her back, the livid bruise on her jaw line was still just a red mark, but it was already starting to swell and would look just right to the police.

Pulling out a knife, from a sheath on his belt, under his doublet, he cut the negligee from her being careful to also slice her skin a couple of times, as if done in lustful haste, which in truth it was. The silicone or oil-based substance, on the condom enabled him to slide inside her easily and he was so excited he lasted barely longer than two minutes, then he turned her over and buggered her. He left the condom on and would not remove it till in his flitter, it could be easily disposed of back at his own place.

Now he had to steal some cash and jewels. The Treet's had not been especially security concious and he stuffed some of both into his backpack and ran down the stairs.

His head had cleared, the added heart rate of his two orgasm's had flushed the snufz from his system. He vaulted to the flitter, and was on the 'A' road before he made the call to the headquarters of Ausonia Constabulary. The call was sound only, his progress through the streets of town would change his I.P. just about every other second,

"Emergency, Ausonia Constabulary, what is the nature of the emergency please"?

"I'm on Dorn Close in front of the Treet house", he lied, "I've just heard screaming and some crashing sounds, you'd better get out here quick"!

"Can you remain and tri-vid the property with your pad while the officers are on their way", the voice asked hastily,

"What…that……signal…..breaking", Takom kept covering his mouth with his hand as he spoke and then killed the connection.

He had done it!

Gilliam Treet was dead!

His wife brutally raped and their valuables stolen.

The Constabulary would surely conclude that aggravated burglary and rape had taken place!

FOUR

THE PATROL FLITTER sighed to a halt and two uniformed constables dived out. The night was chilled, filled with ubiquitous dust. Visibility was therefore not optimum, but despite that that were instantly alert. They saw the door was open and drew their blasters. This was practised procedure, covering one another as they rushed in turn forwards, bursting into the stately home of the Treets. When they reached the study seconds later, one of them was already using his shoulder pad,

"Unit Kilo474, we need the forensic squad out here at twenty three Dorn Close, also a detective from M.I.D. [Mars Investigation Department]. We have at least one body and are proceeding to search the rest of the property".

By the time inspector Hyde had arrived, the forensic squad were packing up and Lorn Treet had been taken to Ausonia Louise Gluck Memorial.

Hyde stopped for a moment outside the house and at the side of the flitter, to light his pipe (tobacco). His lighter refused to produce a flame,

"Have you got a lighter, Orkwell", he asked the detective constable in his company. Orkwell was just climbing out of the vehicle's driving side. He got to his feet with some difficulty, he could have done with shedding a few kilos. Hyde never mentioned it as he was thickening out himself.

"Yes Sir", Orkwell wheezed, the Martian dust did nothing to help his asthma. He passed over the device and Hyde puffed thoughtfully until the tobacco reached his lungs. By then a cloud of blue-grey smoke drifted around his trilby, an ancient head item that he wore to cover his thinning pate.

"The door's not kicked in, Constable", Hyde said between puffs. His junior trundled over and inspected the jamb using considerable care to touch nothing.

"No sign of a hacking device either, Sir", he concluded. "So we have aggravated burglary, involving violent death and rape and yet it looks like the perp was more a safe cracker by trade. If I didn't know Spider Hourglass was not on the planet....."

"You're sliding down the wrong lane, Orkwell", Hyde stopped his junior's train of deduction. "Hourglass is not capable of murder. We'd better go in sharpish and see the body before the forensic boys, bag, tag and take it away".

Orkwell lead the way, at top speed, which Hyde was not prepared to match, not because he couldn't just because he liked to see everything on the way. He bumped into Axel taking tri-vid images of the corpse.

"What've we got Stel"? he asked the forensic officer and colleague of many cases.

"Pretty straightforward Nigle', head bashed in with this broken ornament. Looks like it was busted doing the foul and heinous deed. Instantly fatal in my humble opinion but foren-patho will probably have to determine that for certain".

"The work of whoever was the intruder"?

"That would be a logical assumption at this point. Busts in does the husband goes up and roger-dodgers the missus senseless and then takes off with the goodies".

"Except that he doesn't bust in Stel, the door was opened, not broken down".

"Maybe they left it unlocked, inspector"? Orkwell mused.

"Unlikely! Once it gets dark, what sort of percentage of residents do that in this district"?

"Could have simply forgot to throw the combination"? Axel put in his contribution.

"Well find that out once we interview Missus Treet", Hyde mused. "I expect you boys have been crawling all over the place up there, anything we need to see"?

Axel shook his head, "It will all be on the holo-vid anyway. Rumpled sheets, bit of blood some condom lubricant, some slightly darker blood, that's about it now she's in Louis Gluck".

"Two different samples of blood, any chance she struggled and we've some DNA from our boy"?

Axel looked dubiously, "He seemed too organised for that, I think he would have taken the sheets if that had been the case. More likely the blood is from lacerations on Missus Treet when he cut the night clothes from her and the second sample will be vaginal, anal; or both".

"We need to catch this frenger before he does it again", Orkwell cursed. Axel asked,

"You think he will"?

The detective constable nodded his domed head, "Absolutely the blackguard likes it too much to stop at one"!

Orkwell's pad pinged then and he read the brief message, "The dead guys solicitor just turned up at the station, Inspector asking to speak to you, the detective in charge of his client's investigation"?

"His solicitor"? Hyde echoed. "Strange? What could he want, I'm not going to get the body off from being murdered am I"?

Axel and Orkwell squinted through the cloud of blued smoke, while Hyde continued to pollute the air. The junior officer informed,

"Seems he left an encrypted ping with his solicitor, one that was only to be opened in the event of a violent death, there may be some clues as to what happened here".

"I told you the intruder must have known the code", Hyde responded with satisfaction. "So he suspected he might come to an untimely end did he? I think we may have a case of murder on our hands gentlemen".

"And the wife"? Orkwell wanted to know.

"Collateral damage, along with the robbery, done to make it look like robbery when if fact it was murder. Right I'm going down to the station to see the solicitor, you go to the hospital Orkwell and see if the wife can tell you anything. I doubt she can though, otherwise the perpetrator would not have left her alive".

"Unless he heard the sirens, following the neighbours emergency call and didn't have time to complete the job"?

"Get some uniforms to canvas the area", Hyde nodded, "Though it doesn't take long to slit someone's throat, I suspect the wife will know nothing".

FIVE

"I'M VERY SORRY detective", Lorn told Orkwell an hour later, "But the assailant was wearing a black cat suit, and some sort of mask, he had gloves on too".

"Perhaps the kit will tell us something, D.N.A."? Orkwell murmured.

Lorn began sobbing again, "Thank the stars I was out cold when he committed those hideous crimes against me and violated me so. I don't know what else there is to say, detective"?

Orkwell patted her wrist in order to comfort her, but naturally she shied away from a man's touch at that moment,

"What about height, Missus Treet, did you notice if he was tall or short, was he broad and well built or skinny.

"Oh! Give me a second to try and think", then she convincingly lied, "I'd say he was shorter than average, maybe even very short and very very skinny, but wearing black I might be telling you all the wrong things"?

"No that's good Missus Treet", Orkwell made the appropriate jotting onto his pad.

Then he asked, "One last question and then I'll let you get some rest. Do you think it was robbery with assault, or did your husband have any enemies"?

"Gilliam! Enemies, why no he was very popular and very respected, no one would harm him on purpose. You say my dressing table drawers were all over the room, well my jewels were in one of the tiny top ones near the mirror, was one still containing a jewel inlaid box"?

Orkwell looked at the footage, then shook his head, "The box is gone ma'am, I'm sorry, can you give me an idea of what was in it"?

"My durinium eternity ring with carat diamond inlaid, my pearl necklace, a bracelet made from Callistonian oysters, my dress watch which was a jewel movement Pierre Garlone".

Orkwell whistled softly, "Mister Treet really splashed out on you, eh Missus Treet"?

"Well, detective, we were still in the throws of young and intense love, you know how it is"? She could see, Orkwell did not, but was rather enjoying the role circumstances had placed her into.

SIX

THE CRAMP STARTED at three in the morning, he awoke with the bed sheets wet with his perspiration. What was wrong?

Then it came to see him!

This one was a hideous mix of mustard and brown, a warted hide with seeping sores on it's back. It was sort of hunched, rather than standing on it's four legs, the only limbs that fur still clung too. There was a sickly sweet odour issuing from it, filling the room with the stench of decay.

"You're not real, go away, leave me alone". Bar muttered - before a fresh wave of cramps caused him to grind his teeth and no longer be able to talk.

"I think I'm real, I am self aware, so how can I not exist in reality", the hideous creature responded in a cultured and reasoning tone.

"Then what are you and how did you get into my apartment"? Bar found himself considering it.

"I know what you know, so I simply fed in the combination to your lock", the creature said, "My name is Mister Cuddles".

Bar tittered and was immediately aware that the sound he made was a combination of amusement and fear.

"You don't look very cuddly, have you been a tad under the weather then"? Bar still found the intellectual capacity to be sardonic.

"I'm a fellow snufz-head", came the reasonable response, "We share a common addiction".

"We share nothing then", Bar argued, "Because I'm not a snufz-head. I took it once to allow me to accomplish a rather unsavoury task, but that was all".

"If you mean foul and heinous murder", Mister Cuddles noted, "Homicide of a most violent and bloody type, why don't you say so"?

"I don't need the figment of my imagination to illustrate the fact, for; being part of my psyche, you already know".

"So you think I'm imaginary? Good, you still have some sanity left, but the more you take the more you will lose the distinction between what is, with what is not".

"I shan't be taking any more".

Mister Cuddles gave a lop side grin with his lop sided maw and said nothing to that proclamation and five hours later Bar was once again in Polk Alley in Yaonis Fretum.

Rat asked, "How much this time chango"?

"Just enough to take the edge off, don't call me chango either, you koofed up dope-fiend! I don't want to be a snufz-head, give me a sort of cutting down dose"? Bar asked.

"A cutting down dose"? Rat grinned with teeth eaten away by the effects of the fearful narcotic, "So four bags then señor"?

"I said a cutting down dose, I've got withdrawal cramps and sweats and I see things"!

"We all see things señor, I see you".

"No, I see **things**".

"Well good for you muchacho, what about two bags then, you can take it steadily"?

"Two bags, that's the same as before right, one dose"?

Rat Wiley was momentarily shaken from his casual attitude, "You did two bags in one go"!?

"Was that too much, is that where I went wrong"?

"That was too much muchacho, you're probably hooked and caught good on a whamo like that".

"So how do I wean myself off it"?

"Not really the right question to ask a wholesaler like me is it chango".

"Damn you, give me four bags then and I'll work it out for myself"

"Yes señor, a pleasure to do business with such a discerning gentleman customer, that will be three shillin if you please"?

"Three! I'm buying twice as much as before and you're charging me one hundred and fifty percent"!

"Actually I'm charging you one hundred percent junge, one hundred percent of three is three, you don't seem to have a total understanding of how percentages work. Look at it this way, last time you got, what we business men call an 'introductory discount', as a new customer. You only get that once though I'm sorry to say, so if you want four bags, then you give me three shillin".

Bar's sweaty face seemed to register a wave of conflicting emotions and Rat fingered the blaster in his jerkin tentatively. Then the cramps hit him again and he hurriedly handed over the new inflated price,

"Pleasure to do business with you Général, see you next Tuesday"! Rat watched the poor snufz-head limp away.

Bar made it back to his flitter before he had to open the first bag and this time he had no time to make a smoke, he took a pinch and sniffed violently. Then he did the other nostril. A tremendous feeling of euphoria came over him, what had he been worried about?

The stress was gone, the pain, he felt himself cooling down. He turned to the beautiful red-head that was seated beside him, in the front passenger seat,

"You look great Somica, how long's it been and how did you get here"? Bar wanted to know.

"I guess it's been about ten years Takom, I though you'd ping and you did for a short while and then they dried up and I guessed you'd moved on".

"I can't get over how young you look, you haven't changed a bit", Bar drank in the girl's simple beauty. She wore no make up of any sort, but her hair glistened with health and vitality and her freckles were very attractive.

"When did you get to Mars"?

"A few days ago and the first thing I wanted to do was meet the Dep C.E.O. of Martian Future Projects Inc".

"You've been following my progress in business"?!

"I never lost interest in you, Takom. Now then where are we going, back to your place, I could shave you, bathe you, massage you and then ball your brains out, how does that sound"?

Bar gunned the engine, "Like heaven babe, let's go".

He drove up the 'A' road at far greater than the speed limit, but was fortunate that no combmen were patrolling it that morning. As he pulled up to a sudden halt, he turned to tell her that this was his place and the seat was empty.

The silly young woman must have fallen out of the flitter he realised and went up to his apartment. He showered, shaved and dressed in his business attire. If he continued to be beardless, he might consider permanent depilation but for now he preferred to have the option. He realised then that he was ravenously hungry and made himself three thick sandwiches which he bolted down with a glass of dodo-juice. Then looking at his wrist chrono he realised he was particularly late and dashed back to the flitter.

The offices of Martian Future Projects Inc were understandably quiet and sombre as he strode toward his own, after all, they had lost their beloved C.E.O. He was still fresh in his grave and his deputy had been acting strangely ever since. The instant he reached the door Flenkins was standing there, Flenkins had the most ridiculous purple moustache and as he spoke to Bar it wriggled on his upper lip and moved around his face before settling back into place, in it's original location,

".........what do you think Sir"?

Bar tried to concentrate, as he opened the door, he requested carefully, "Run it past me again"?

Flenkins looked momentarily confused, before gulping and doing as bidden,

"I think while you're acting up to full C.E.O. until the board meet and undoubtedly finalise it Sir, that I would make a good right hand man to have around the place, I have the service, the expertise and I won't let you down, what do you think"?

Bar was not listening again, he was watching the purple moustache do a writhing jig with Flenkins eyebrows and then they all settled back into place. A sudden grip of cramp hit him in the midriff and he began to sweat,

'Already!' He thought. Then, *'Still I only took a sniff this time, I've plenty left, just get rid of this imbecile and I can dose up again".*

"I'll give the matter some thought and get back to you", he replied, hoping his tone sounded sincere enough.

Flenkins did not move though, instead he grew angry, "It's that bitch Breem isn't it? She's only been here three years and already she's upper management and we all know why don't we Takom"?

Bar was watching the green steam issuing from Flenkins ears, he'd seen him angry before, but never noticed the phenomenon, it was especially amusing and he burst out laughing,

"In business Flenkins there's always room at the top for two qualities; one is charisma, which I have in spades, the other is a cracking pair of pert tits, which is the quality we all admire in Breem. Now you Flenkins, you're a faithful hound, I'll give you that, but you're a dog is all, so go and pack up your stuff, you're fired"!

Flenkins paled, "You're sacking me! Hades teeth, what for, I've not done anything wrong"!

"I don't like your moustache and I don't like your steam, so you're history matey, goodbye and do not rely on me for a reference. Now get out and have Breem sent in here pronto".

"Roast in the fires of Tartarus itself you blackguard, get your employees to deliver your messages and you won't hear the last of this, I'll ping the board, I'll…".

"You'll get out"! Bar roared in fury, "Or I'll throw you out bodily"!

Flenkins scampered to the door, in real dread and was gone. Bar then burst into laughter. Being on snufz had it's compensations it seemed. He sent a message to his secretary to have Breem come in then and just as he had finished snorting and taking the edge off, there was a delicate tapping at his door.

"Come in", he cried and the graceful honey-blonde slid in and asked sweetly, "You wanted to see me, Mister Bar"?

"Yes, sit down please", he waved to a seat opposite his desk. She glided to the chair and took her place on it, her skirt sliding up in the process revealing the smoothest of taut contoured thigh. She saw him looking at her legs and did nothing to conceal them, in fact she was enjoying the scrutiny, only too aware of the effect she had on men.

"I've been watching you Breem", he began, suddenly able to think very clearly indeed, "And I've decided you are the woman to take Martian Future Projects Inc to another level of excellence".

Breem smiled, expecting the post of Dep C.E.O. to be offered to her, Bar went on,

"So I want to offer you the post of C.E.O. with certain contractual obligations of course and with the resultant approval of the board, which I'm certain they will sanction at the earliest opportunity".

Breem smiled, her dazzling white smile and leaned forward slightly to reply, so that her blouse fell open exactly as she expected and revealed a very impressive cleavage indeed.

"Thank you Mister Bar I won't let you down, but you mean Dep C.E.O. of course, you forgot to say deputy, I assume I'll be working directly *under* you"?

"No I meant C.E.O. I will remain the deputy, I've decided I don't want the extra responsibility, in fact I'm planning a lengthy leave of absence very soon and you may even have to replace me, if you so desire to do".

Breem lost her composure at this revelation,

"C.E.O. of the whole company"?

Bar nodded happily, "The whole ball of wax, Breem, yours to lead".

Breem was suddenly speechless, then remembering something she suddenly asked,

"You mentioned some contractual obligations, Mister Bar"?

"No biggy", he grinned. "In fact once I leave the firm, you'll be free of it anyway".

"So what is it then"?

"I just want a bit of gratitude that's all".

"And you have it Sir, I am very grateful for the opportunity and you can be certain I'll work my socks off for the firm and ……..".

"I'm sure you will, Breem". Bar cut in, "But I meant gratitude to me"!

"Certainly Sir, I am grateful, what do you need".

"Well you could start by getting under this desk and taking it out and showing it a good time", he chuckled.

"I beg your pardon"? Breem was horrified. "I got to my present post by hard work and long hours, Mister Bar and if you think you'll get me to gratify your lascivious needs in order to gain promotion then you've got another thing coming"!

Cloughlin will certainly blow me for the post, but you have by far the better body. In fact I bet Cloughlin will……..".

She flew to the door and tore it open,

"This is sexual harassment and '*The Board*' will hear of it as soon as I get back to my pad and……..".

"You're fired Breem, go and ping the board and I'll ping them to say you're making the whole thing up because I got rid of you for shoddy work. Go and get your things together and get out of the building in an hour, or I'll have security throw you out".

"Now let's slow down here", Breem suddenly hesitated at the door and closed it behind her once again, so that no one else could hear their conversation, "I've worked very hard for Martian Future Projects Inc, Mister Bar as you well know and to fire me because I won't sleep with you is morally outrageous and wrong, we both know that, so let's come to some sort of mutually equitable agreement; please"?

"Oh, alright", Bar felt light headed and capricious, "How does this sound, you stay in your current post and I promote Cloughlin instead"?

"But Cloughlin doesn't have the experience nor knowledge to take the reins, Mister Bar".

"But she does have certain experience and knowledge that I'm interested in right now", Bar grinned maliciously.

"So you're giving her a top senior post because she'll have sex with you? While I get nothing at all"?

"You get to keep your job"!

"You're disgusting Takom Bar. Immoral. Depraved. Why are you behaving this way"?

"You just answered your own question", Bar giggled, "Go away and think about it".

"To hell with that you blackguard, if you think I'm going to let that useless mare Cloughlin get the best job over me".

With a look of angry distaste she began to unbutton her blouse.

SEVEN

THE FOUR BAGS had lasted almost a week before Takom Bar had to visit the Rat again. He bought four more for three point five shillin and cursed the pusher to Hades for his greed, vowing this time to wean himself off the habit forming and addictive narcotic. It was time to visit the grieving widow, who now seemed, to his mind, to be the cause of his current problem.

It seemed a lifetime ago since he had swam in the frigid waters of lake Passionata, made love to her on the cold beach and shared her body warmth beneath the blanket, letting the beginning of the scheme cook in his mind.

Bar - I think it's long enough now, I need to see you and begin to make plans for our future together.

Treet - Please do not ping me again?

Bar - What on koofing Mars do you mean?

Treet - Do I have to keep typing the same message, I do not want to see nor hear from you again. Do not email me either.

Bar - Why?

Treet - You know why

Bar - I did it for you, why are you trying to cut me off?

Treet - Some of what you did; I did not agree to and am disgusted by it, so please leave me ALONE.

Bar - I have to see you, let us talk this out face to face, please?

Treet - *[connection timed out]*
Bar - I will come and see you, unless you reply.
Treet - Tonight eighteen hundred:- at the house.
Bar - I'll be there babe, I love you..
Tree - *[disconnected]*.

The flitter pulled up to a sighing halt and Bar left it once more around the corner. He doubted the combmen would be watching it though. They had turned up no fresh evidence it seemed, nor had they found the stolen jewellery. They would not find the jewellery either, for it was at the bottom of the lake.

He took a good sniff of snufz into each nostril and a tremendous sense of pleasant calm came over him. He could handle this habit, it was not that bad and a great deal of the time he actually felt better than he ever had in his life.

The good times definitely outweighed the bad, as long as his supply was maintained there would be no difficulties. As Lorn was now incredibly rich, he could afford all the snufz he ever wanted.

He left the flitter, walked carefully around the huge lawn and keyed himself into the house.

Lorn was draped on the lounge sofa and her face was purple and yellow one eye bloodshot. She wore a silk nightgown, the garment almost transparent, her body easily discernible beneath the shear fabric.

"I know you're angry with me", he said to her, when she did not move, "But think about it babe, the police are utterly convinced of your innocence, and you did say I could rape you in the future. Sorry about the sock to the eye but it made the whole thing look so much more horrible. The sympathy was all for you, the poor helpless and raped victim. You do see that don't you"?

She nodded slowly, "I do, Tak and that all would have been alright, well not alright, but forgiveable. It's the sodomy that I have so much trouble with, how could you do something so; so, humiliating? Tell me you took no enjoyment from it"?

"Of course I didn't, but you know as well as I do it's what rapists usually do, it had to look convincing".

"I'm afraid I do not know the activities of rapists as well as you Tak, not at all", she returned carefully.

"Well, what's done is done and I have a snufz addiction to thank for the incident too. I did that for you Lorn, I did the grisly thing you wanted from me. Do you mind if I get myself a drink"?

"Don't move, I have something to say and then the whole thing will be over", she commanded.

"Alright, Lorn, say what you have to say"? He stayed over at the door, as instructed.

"It's this Tak. Gilliam is now out of my hair and I'm fabulously rich, I can have any man I want and by your own admission, in addition to being a murderer, you're also a snufz-head. So, I ask myself, do I need you any more and you know what the answer is dear Tak"?

"What's the answer sweetie"? He asked her, totally misjudging the situation.

"It's this", she told him and pulling out a nub nosed blaster from beneath her, she took half his chest away with a single bloody shot!

"Inspector"! Orkwell dashed into Hyde's office, "The Treet house, there's been another break-in and shooting this time"!

Hyde rushed to pick up his jacket and minutes later they were rushing through traffic to get to the property in question.

"Axel on his way"? Hyde asked, at the wheel as Orkwell was frantically using his pad. The rotund constable nodded,

"Alerted and travelling, just like us".

When the flitter ground to a sighing halt outside the Treet residence, the first thing Hyde did was examine the keypad of the lock, once again it was not broken.

"Whoever's in there knows one another", he said to Orkwell and then proceeded him through the doorway. They found Missus Treet sipping Mars-vodka, seated opposite a bloody ruin of flesh on her carpet. It was the corpse of course.

Hyde asked, "Did you shoot this man, Missus Treet"?

The woman nodded mutely.

"Why? How did he get in the house"?

"He worked for poor dear Gilliam, so he knew the combination, came here often to discuss business out of hours with him".

And tonight"? the inspector wished to know, "What was he doing before you killed him".

"He admitted to being the burglar and the rapist and told me he'd come back for some more, some more........".

She broke down at that point and Orwell went over to her and put a comforting arm around her. She then collapsed into the podgy constable's arms.

Orwell said to Hyde quietly,

"Now we know who the killer was and how he got into the house, Inspector".

Hyde looked thoughtful, it seemed just a bit too convenient to him. He suspected Missus Treet had just gotten away with murder.

EIGHT

'*I*VE DONE IT'! she thought with triumph, '*Gotten rid of an unwanted husband and also an inconvenient lover, now all I have is mine and I have no need to share until I meet someone I truly wish to share with*'

She went over to the window, avoiding the damp area where the industrial cleaner had brought the carpet up like new. She was short a few ornaments, some jewellery, but on the plus side of the balance sheet she had all that was left. For quite a while she remained in the same fixed location, looking out into the middle distance before she realised there was a figure standing beneath one of the huge lights that turned Mars into twilight, when it faced away from the sun.

The figure was not tall, it was sort of hunched and the light seemed to bounce off the top of an obviously hairless head. Then terror suddenly gripped her guts with fingers of ice and steel. It was Gilliam!

'*No'!* the scream sounded in her head, even if she did not give voice to it. '*It cannot be, am I losing my mind, it must just be someone who looks very like him and my imagination is doing the rest*'.

She looked back, forced herself to focus on the figure the best she could in the dimness and the distance, looked until her eyes were sore and the more she did so, the more he looked like Gilliam.

Terrified she opaqued the window and went to bed, but as expected, sleep eluded her. She tossed and turned for a couple of hours and then went back to the window, the figure was gone. Had it ever been there, or was it a product of her conscience? Did she have one? Was she even remotely sorry for Gilliam's death? She thought not, but deep in her id perhaps her subconscious mind had produced the figure?

This time she slept, but fitfully and was up at a ridiculously early hour. She needed a plan and she began to form one. The funeral had been a terrible bore, pretending to be the grief stricken widow. She went to the window, and the figure was there again! There was no one to tell. He was just standing hunched in the same position, her husband!

"What was there to be afraid of? A spirit from beyond, a ghost? There were no such things and she was determined not to be going mad. She got on her pad, looked for a retreat, somewhere costly and luxurious, she could afford anything she wanted. She *would* afford whatever she wanted

She chose the spa at Aromatum Pr. A resort close to the equator.Packed hastily, filling just a single case, which she tossed into the boot and then roared down the A44 at a brisk cruising speed. The road was, as usual, covered in dust though and half way to her destination she pulled into a roadside café, for a snack and something to drink.

The place was called Sabaea Opciones, a Spanish owned café in the heart of Terra Sabaea. As she strolled across the courtyard, doing her best to get as little dust in her hair as possible, she saw him again and deliberately drew closer. She needed to see his face, it was Gilliam!

How could it be, Tak had killed him? Or had he?

She had never seen the body, never even been down to identify it in the Constabulary Morgue, someone from the firm had done that. Had there been a huge conspiracy? Was he alive?!

She called to him, but he turned then and went around some outlying buildings and when she hurried to pursue him one of her heels nearly broke her ankle and she knew chase was impossible. Shaking with frustration and morbid mental conjecture, she went into the bar of the café and ordered a double Lichen-vod. Gulping it down. She looked at her hands and saw they were visibly shaking. What was the matter with her, was she losing her grip on reality.

"Are you alright Miss", the Spanish bartender asked her then, "You look very pale, like you've seen a ghost"?

"Don't be ridiculous"! she snapped back at him, "There aren't any ghosts, get me another drink, make it a double again".

For some reason she could not fathom she glanced toward the far end of the long oval bar and there was Gilliam!

"What is it Miss"? The bartender was still solicitous, despite her ealier rudeness. He placed another drink on her napkin.

"That man over there, tell him to go away. He's dead I tell you, get him out of here"!

"Miss, should I call an ambulance, are you ill"?

"He keeps following me, get rid of him and I'll be fine".

"Following you, who is, I'll throw him out for certain, or we can call the constables".

"Combmen! No, it's alright I'll deal with it myself, he's gone now, please leave me to myself for a moment will you? Thank you".

When she looked again Gilliam had sneaked away to make her look ridiculous, just like the old blackguard. She downed the second double, bought a few snacks and rushed back to her flitter. Once she was back on the road, her fractured nerves began to settle a bit. Once she got to the spa at Aromatum Pr she could get some blue Lubies from the apothecary and get a good night's rest.

Lorn thought about the bar, what a mess and the constabulary mentioned, she'd have to be more careful in the future. Whether anyone believed her or not, she could not tell them. She knew the penalty for murder in Ausonia and it was death by lethal injection. The pertinent component of that little scenario that she did not fancy being; *'death'*. She had not come this far. To mess everything up now with hysteria would be folly, so she decided she would not.

Gilliam had been carrying neither a harp nor a pitch fork and he was not dealing with an imbecile! Let him carry on watching her and see where it would get him. Determined to be alright, she finally pulled into the spa and booked herself all the treatments and one of the best rooms in the entire place.

She was just unpacking her case when there was a ping at her door. She glanced at the inspection plate, expecting someone from room service. It was Gilliam!

"No"! she screamed "Go away, leave me alone, I'm calling spa security".

She strode to the room connector and stabbed the button,

"Help me", she cried to the voice who answered, "There's a man outside my door and he's going to hurt me I know it"!

The security was there in just over a minute and used the over-ride swipe on the combination lock of her room,

"What is it Miss", a muscle bound youth of around twenty two or so, asked her, "Did he run off once you pinged for us"?

"Yes, but he's been following me all day, all the way from Ausonia".

"Then it's a job for the Constabulary", he decided, "I'll….".

"No"! she halted him, "Just take down this description for me and make sure I'm not disturbed again please".

"Of course, but….".

"Just do as I ask please and no more. I don't want the combmen involved at this time".

The security operative took down Gilliam's description and left frowning. If she was not careful the combmen would get involved whether she liked it or not. Lorn had to face him if he turned up again, find out what he wanted, or it would be that grim needle for her.

For the next few days she treat herself to all the beauty therapy and treatments the spa had to offer and the description she had given security kept him away. It allowed her to begin to relax, it was almost as if she had imagined it all. She did not even need the lubie's, she was once again in a good place, her head in the right frame.

She watched the Mars Athletics Championships on the Tri-vid in the bar and saw Dirk Straddlemore take the zinc medal in the fifteen hundred metres, for the English Empire. England had won more zinc [fourth] and tin [fifth] medals than any other country and were doing very well, but the Poles (now rich due to their off Earth heavy industries) and the Chinese (rich due to off Earth manufacturing) continued to vie for the table's summit.

At ease and relaxed she waited until the fifth evening to book out and decide to drive back to the house. There she would immediately put it on the market and get rid of it. Then she thought she would try a rocket trip to Venus and then the holiday resorts on the Moon.

As her flitter pulled out and began to take the slip road to junction 23 however, she saw an all black Tefal Sentry 233 catch her own and settle behind her. The windscreen was tinted so she could not see who was at the wheel. Not to worry, it was obviously someone else also leaving the spa. She drove on until she had met the junction and was on the 'A', but the Tefal was still just three flitter lengths behind her.

Then the tinting was suddenly turned down as the road's lights came on full and Lorn Treet saw who was in the flitter following hers. It was her husband Gilliam!

"Alright you *inconvenience*"! She shouted, even though he could not hear her, "Let's see how fast you are prepared to follow me, ass-hole"!

Her foot stabbed at the accelerator and the Morphy-Richards began to gather momentum. The two flitters were doing one hundred and twelve kilometres and the Tefal was still behind her, but she had the slightly more powerful engine in the two fifty and she pressed her foot still further.

One hundred and twenty eight and the Tefal was still there, Gilliam's jaw firmly set. She stabbed violently on the accelerator and the Morphy-Richards was doing one hundred and sixty four kilometres an hour when she lost control and the flitter crumpled against the steel side barriers and the ruptured boiler exploded in a boom of hyper-heated steam and torn metal.

The local uniforms arrived within seconds, sirens blaring, but there was nothing they could do. The human body is not built to withstand that sort of impact, the remains that were removed by the ambulance three quarters of an hour later were not recognisable as Missus Lorn Treet.

NINE

"SOMEONE TO SEE you Inspector", the intercom pinged as Hyde was just enjoying an afternoon pipe of med-bacco. He carried on drawing the calming smoke into his lungs as he asked,

"Have them come in then, please"?

He had half been expecting the figure that pushed through the door a couple of seconds later.

"Gilliam, have a seat, can I temp you with a pipe full of Golden-lich".

"Yes indeed you can Inspector, thank you".

Hyde handed over the pouch and Gilliam filled his own pipe that had resided in a pocket and then thumbed a match from the desk, sucking it into life.

For a few moments there was silence in the office as the two of them enjoyed the flavour of the sweet smelling smoke. Gilliam looked at the wall behind Hyde's head and saw all the two-d images pinned to a very old fashioned cork board. One of them was of Lorn Treet. Beside it his own and beside that Takom Bar.

"You still use two dee's", he noted around the stem of his pipe, "Why Nigle"?

"It let's me see the entire scope of any investigation without having to swipe the screen, I move them around and the rearrangement sometimes helps my thought processes, just an eccentricity".

Gilliam nodded as though he understood, perhaps he did.

"Three to take down now, I guess"? Hyde finally put out for comment, Gilliam nodded.

"The remains were identified by your colleague Axel, as being those of Missus Treet, I guess that closes your case, Inspector".

Hyde nodded, "Do you still think Bar got his just deserts and was killed as an intruder? Or do you now subscribe to my theory that she was the one who had you murdered and then took care of Bar, once he had outlived his usefulness"?

Gilliam grimaced, "Her reaction to my various appearances would indicate most strongly that you were right Nigle'. Lorn was her husband's murderer, even if she used Bar to achieve it".

"What will you do now Gilliam"?

Gilliam's jaw was suddenly set in determined fashion,

"Take over as C.E.O. of the companies, run them as he ran them before. The house and the share holdings are now legally mine according to the precise wording of Gilliam's will. Who is there to oppose me"?

"No one", Hyde agreed, "No one for a very long time, if you outlive all your competitors. It was a very clever clause in Gilliam's will to have you activated in the event of his untimely death, a very clever ruse indeed".

"And I am programmed with all his memories and experience", the android told the inspector, "It's just a shame that the clause did not actually save his life".

"True", Hyde conceded, "But it preserves his legacy to the business world of Mars, the name of Gilliam Treet will be spoken for many, many years to come"!

SICKLE'S COMPASS

Let me not to the marriage of true minds
Admit impediments. Love is not love
Which alters when it alteration finds,
Or bends with the remover to remove.
O no, it is an ever-fix-ed mark
That looks on tempests and is never shaken;
It is the star to every wand'ring bark,
Whose worth's unknown, although his height be taken.
Love's not Time's fool, though rosy lips and cheeks
Within his bending sickle's compass come;
Love alters not with his brief hours and weeks,
But bears it out even to the edge of doom.
If this be error and upon me proved,
I never writ, nor no man ever loved.   William Shakespeare

ONE

THE CIVIL SERVICE was going to be a grand affair and for Miora Herbgadden something unique in her life too. Not so for the prospective groom, Larris Silverwick.

"Are you very happy, Larris, I am"? The blushing bride-to-be wished to know

"Yes darling I am", he told her and he meant it.

"Of course for you, you've been through this all before", she noted almost sadly, "I hope I can make you happy my sweet".

"You can and don't worry everything will be fine, now I have a meeting with Boot, it won't take long, can the arrangements do without me for a short while"?

"Of course", she told him, "I'll call you if we need your approval on anything.

Silverwick left his young fiancée and strode through Silverwick estate, there he was scheduled to meet with one of the solicitor's of Stubbsinge, Shadrack and Boot. It was Glees Boot who was seated in one of the high winged leather chairs that were one of the features of the study.

The oak panelled walls and old world paintings spoke of a time well before the time that men now lived in, but some clung to such memories of the past and Silverwick was one such collector. Boot had even helped himself to a sherry, which was presumptuous of him, but Silverwick deigned not to comment on the breech of etiquette.

"Ah, Silverwick, good afternoon, this sherry is damned fine, how are you"?

"Wishing to hear good news from you Boot and look at your shoes, you've trailed half of Mars in here"?

"Oh, so I have that's a bit thick, sorry. Anyway the good news is that as the sun sets over Mars this evening you will be a single man, Silverwick and free to marry Miss Herbgadden".

"You have the appropriate docx for me to e-sign".

"On my pad, everything is in order. Your former wife Belona will then be declared legally dead".

"I don't see why that gives you cause to smirk, Boot", Silverwick had never liked he who was, in his opinion, the worst partner in the firm.

"I was smiling at your good fortune, Silverwick, this estate, the company holdings, you'll be a very rich man thanks to your former wife's vast interests".

"In that case I'm glad you're happy for me, the docx are complete in every detail I hope"?

Boot chuckled and asked, "Does your former secretary know all the facts connected to this rather sordid little arrangement".

"The most sordid detail in this is your involvement, Boot. In future I will be dealing with one of your partners, for I find your insolence rather tiring".

"Oh, I doubt I'll need to be involved in the future. The strange disappearance of your wife, Silverwick and the subfusc details surrounding it, will keep me quite comfortable".

"What are you implying you seedy little grasper"?

"I'm talking about my continued instalments to secure my silence".

"You'll get the fee for your services and that'll be ballie well all, now get your dirty feet of that Italian Mahogany Long table and tell me what it comes too. Then I can settle it and have done with you"?

Boot passed the pad to Silverwick, who glanced at the numbers, "Three hundred, have you gone out of your mean, grasping little mind"?

"Let's just cut right to the heart of the matter shall we", Boot asked then, "I've found Missus Silverwick! She's not dead as presumed".

"That's a very obtuse lie".

"Then let me ask you if you recognise these earrings".

Silverwick held out a hand despite himself and the solicitor dropped a pair of pearl earrings into it. He scrutinised the back of the ninety nine percent argent and saw the tiniest of inscriptions in the white metal. Going over to his desk he pulled out an eyeglass that he kept for counting perforations in his timbrological collection and it was confirmed, they were Belona's!

"Where did you get these and where is she"?

"I can assure you there is no need for alarm, Silverwick. Simply meet the current fee and then I will set up a bank draft for the fortnightly deduction from your account and you'll never see her again. So, do you sign, or do I produce the first Missus Silverwick"?

He climbed ungraciously to his feet, Silverwick, gritting his teeth e-signed the papers and then Boot's exorbitant bill!

TWO

"YOU DON'T MIND if I remove every scrap of her from this estate do you, Larris", Herbgadden asked him a few days later. "After all I agreed to share it with you, despite it's history".

"Take every bit of it to the attic, or get rid of it altogether, I prefer never to think I was married before", Silverwick agreed. "To find another stately place like this is southern Mars though would be nigh impossible and the study and the den have always been mine and I don't want to lose them".

"That's a good compromise then", she agreed and then added, "You know what Larris? Since that creepy solicitor of yours had that meeting with you, I sense your mind has been elsewhere, did he say something that distracted you"?

"Legality always distracts me, Miora sweetheart, don't let it worry you everything is as it should be".

The door of the lounge opened then and in walked Belona Silverwick!

Larris dropped the glass from his hand in shock and it smashed on the polished wooden flooring. Miora turned around and her hand went up to her mouth. Of course she had seen tri-vid's of Belona, so she recognised her at once. The apparent apparition said rather tacitly,

"Hello, Larris". From behind her another figure entered the room, a distinguished looking man in his late fifties with a handsome shock of thick white hair.

"I think perhaps it best if this next conversation were with just the two of us Miora", Larris said woodenly, "Please leave us to talk privately".

Miora promptly burst into tears of frustration and bewilderment and ran from the room.

"She's very pretty and very young", Belona said and her voice was filled with tiredness and sadness.

"I never thought to see you again, Belona, it been seven years for goodness sake. You just disappeared on me and now you show up like this and who's the gentleman with you"?

"I'm doctor Vandi, Sir.

Silverwick had heard of the distinguished psychiatrist, he went to shake his hand, "Doctor of the Vandi Institute down in Galle, in the French sector. Can I offer you a drink, Doctor? You too Belona, I know I need one! Please have a seat, both of you, while I get us some refreshments".

"Your wife cannot have alcohol, Mister Silverwick; the medication you understand"?

"Well no I don't, Sir", Silverwick admitted as he poured himself a sherry, "But I trust an explanation is on the near horizon, so to speak".

"I'll take a small sherry also if I may", the doctor agreed as he helped the first Missus Silverwick to seat herself comfortably. "Do you have in your employ a solicitor by the name of Boot, Mister Silverwick"?

"Unfortunately yes", Silverwick agreed, "He's not a very good choice. Has he been menacing you, or your staff, or your patients"?

"He came to see your wife, who has been in our care for the past seven years, Sir", Vandi explained, "Asking her for some sort of memento that would prove he had indeed spoken to her. We, of course presumed that you had employed him, to locate her. That you had finally reasoned in some way that she was still alive. Have you found the hidden trust funds in her name? Seen the regular withdrawals from them"?

Silverwick ignored the questions for a moment. He had one of his own.

"Belona why'd you go and how did you end up in a sanatorium"?

"I only remembered once I'd given the man the earrings", the first Missus Silverwick confessed.

Vandi explained further, "Your wife came to me with amnesia and was not in her right mind, Mister Silverwick. The only instruction she gave, when I first decided to take her on as a patient, was to keep her location a secret. The thought of a possible suitor or husband filled her with terror, so reluctantly I agreed".

"Why Belona"? Silverwick knelt before his wife, "We were happy, there was no need to fear me, I don't understand".

"To seek sanity in one who is insane is enter a maze that few can unravel", the doctor answered for her.

'I see'! Silverwick thought, *'While ever the bills were paid, there was no need to delve too deeply eh, Vandi'?*

Suddenly Belona threw him onto a different track asking simply, "Do you love her, Larris"?

"Belona, you disappeared and I thought you dead, what was I supposed to do? I couldn't put my life on indefinite hold, in the vain hope that you would one day surface"?

"She's very pretty. I love you very much though and I need you now I've remembered".

"Need me"?!

"Your wife is not completely cured, Mister Silverwick", Vandi told him, "I can only let here stay here under your supervision, you will have some documents to sign. You must agree to be her guardian, she could easily relapse at the slightest of triggers".

"I thought your memory was returned", Silverwick said to his wife, refusing to look at the doctor. "Are you better, or not"?

"All I know is that I love you very much and need you and can only stay if you say you will look after me".

"Very well then", Silverwick agreed. Though he sounded quite suddenly as though he might have a hidden agenda.

"I will take care of you Belona, I'll take care of you don't you worry".

All I need now is a plan, a way to push my dear wife over the precipice she clings to, into the inky deeps of insanity. I know who I can rely on to help me. We can achieve it together, then all I thought I had will be mine for certain and she'll never come back"!

"Well thank you Doctor, for bringing her back to me", he said to Vandi.

"Show me the relevant docx and I'll e-sign them and let you get on your way".

The doctor did his best to look pleased, but it was evident to Silverwick that he was not really happy to be losing his regular and reliable source of income. Once the butler had shown him out, Silverwick took Belona's hand and asked

"Darling what is the exact nature of your former illness, what did that charlatan Vandi actually claim was wrong with you"?

"The doctor was most kind to me, Larris, you mustn't speak of him that way and I'd really prefer not to dwell on whom I used to be"?

"If I'm to look after you in the best way I can though, surely I should know what signs to be on the alert for. In case you suffer some sort of relapse".

"I feel fine since the earrings brought everything back to me", his wife explained carefully, "I no longer hear any voices nor suffer any delusions".

"Did these delusions ever result in violence? I know this is painful for you, but you must realise I have to guard my own safety too".

Belona looked shamefully, "It seems I struck Dorl once, but I have no memory of it and he said it was accidental".

"Dorl"?

"Doctor Vandi, that's his first name".

"I think you should go and get some sleep now Belona, I'll have the maid make sure you have everything at your disposal. Forget the hour, you look exhausted, will you do as I recommend"?

"Of course Larris", she agreed meekly and after he had called and instructed the maid, he had the task of meeting his fiancée once more.

"What is she doing still in this house"? Miora wailed, "Why've you let her stay? Do you plan to remain married to her and break off our engagement"?

Silverwick took the younger, more lovely woman in his arms and promised, "I love *you* Miora. Belona is now nothing more than a fond memory from my past. If I divorce her though, then all this, all that we have become accustomed to and are happy with, will be snatched from us. It's *me* who's run the financial affairs for the last seven years. *Me* who's built it up to even greater value, while she has vegetated in a lunatic asylum. Should we give it up because her doctor now sees a chance at even more commission"?

"What's the alternative"? Miora was suddenly thoughtful in a calculating way that Silverwick liked the sound of.

"The alternative's to send her back and in a way that means she will never return".

"It sounds sort of unfeeling, maybe even cruel".

"We will act as humanely as possible, but we will keep what we have had for the legal term, seven years".

The following morning he asked his wife, "Belona, do you remember anything of the early hours".

"What do you mean".

"I found you in my room, at zero three fifteen with one of cook's kitchen knives in your hands"!

If it was possible, Belona went even paler and her hands went to her mouth in comical denial of the grim proclamation.

"You let me take if off you without any protest and I took you back to bed, but you see now why we cannot share the same bed for the present".

He did not add that his intended had slipped into his room during cover of darkness and spent most of the night with him in his wife's stead. Had eagerly preformed some of the *duties* required of a spouse from time to time.

"I don't remember any of this", Belona admitted, fear all over her features.

"Don't worry I've asked Miora, who's had nursing experience, to take an active role in your care, to help get you back to full health".

"I don't want *her* help. In fact I don't want her in this house".

"She's accepted your return and the arrangements we made are over, finished. While I need someone I can trust explicitly to take care of you, while I look after the business interests. I can't stay away from the offices for much longer Belona".

"'Trust', what do you think is going to happen, I wasn't in a correctional facility, I was ill".

"And vestiges of that illness remain and Miora is the best person to look after you while I'm not here. Get to know her darling, I'm sure the two of you will get along, otherwise I may have to ping Vandi and let him know you're still having *difficulties*".

"Are you still sleeping with her, Larris"?

"Of course not! Now that you're back she and I are nothing but good platonic friends. She has dealt with you return in an adult and responsible way, I need you to accept her position as your nurse and companion in the same spirit, will you do that for me"?

"I'll do my best then, as long as you and her aren't…..".

"We are not".

THREE

"I NEED TO get out of the house", Belona decided, "Strange how this place no longer feels like mine, but more, Larris' alone".

"He had it maintained and built the new south wing, I suppose some of the interior is different too", Miora noted carefully. "We could always go for a drive in the flitter, get out of here for a couple of hours"?

"Really", Belona's features lit up with excitement, "You mean it"?

Miora nodded, "You're legally in my care at the minute so why not, the change of surroundings will do you good.

"I'll get my parka".

They took the Hotpoint Glide 241 and coasted down the B23 for an hour before stopping on Hebes Chasma plateau overlooking the valley beneath. The wind was quite ferocious and the ever present red dust caught everywhere, but they climbed out of the flitter and gazed at the valley bellow. A rust covered area beneath a pink sky with the odd hint of blue from the lichen furs and the tiny bright yellow point of Sol, twice as distant as any Earther would be accustomed to.

They could breath without the tiny personal oxygen tanks that remained unused in the flitter's boot. With special nose filters, the sand was not a problem and though oxygen was still at a premium, by breathing more rapidly, it was possible to stay outside on Mars for an hour, with ease.

"Life is slowly beginning to come back to this world", Belona noted, "I hadn't realised the gradual changes".

"Sort of echoing your situation", Miora observed neutrally, "Care and nurturing can bring vitality to anything given time. Come on, let's go and eat, I know a great little café on the junction of 22 and 23"?

They took the flitter back to the place that Miora had recommended and while they waited for their orders to arrive Belona finally asked what they had both been waiting for.

"What do you hope will happen to you once I'm fully restored to health Miora"?

"I hope at the very least for some sort of position in one of your companies, Belona and then who knows? I'm young, I'm told I am not unattractive, one day someone will come along, who hasn't got a wife hidden away somewhere".

"Well I can promise you the former at least, if you are capable, tell me what idea you have for any of Silverwick holdings"?

The younger woman began to outline a sales promotion she had in mind for Silverbeauty, one of the cosmetic giants that the older had set up herself a decade previously.

"You've some great insights and some good notions", Belona told her, when they were eating and the verbal presentation was over, "I'll give you a chance to realise them Miora, I know it's not the sort of compensation you were hoping for, but after all, Larris is legally my husband"

"Of course", the former secretary smiled, "I understand Belona. Larris has made his choice and I have to agree with it, there's no alternative.

As she lay with him that night she asked, "She trusts me completely, what's your next move, Larris, I'm growing impatient I want to be Missus Silverwick.

"Tomorrow, we move again, alright"?

Sure enough the following evening Miora was keying some information into her laptop when Belona entered the room.

"You look exhausted Belona", the secretary/nurse declared at a quick signal from Silverwick, "Of course you would be after *last night*"!

"I? What…. I don't….." Belona was confused and unsure of herself.

"She doesn't remember, Miora", Silverwick replied. "It was the screaming, a nightmare we think. Then the walking and general wandering around the estate, but we have a solution. Miora will sleep in your room tonight and keep an eye on you Belona. Now please don't argue, I can see that look in your eye? Once Miora has finished on the lap top she'll get you a draft to help you calm down and see you in bed safely".

"But I don't feel tired", Belona objected.

"Once you're warm and tucked up you'll sleep", Miora agreed. "You go up Missus Silverwick and I'll be there just as soon as I've finished this typing".

"Very well", Belona agreed. Once she was gone Silverwick instructed,

"Give her two lubie's and not the red ones, two blue"!

"Two blue lubie's", Miora gasped. "She'll be out of her tiny tree"!

"That's right, a maniac, out of her mind", Silverwick said with grisly satisfaction. Several hours later they woke Belona abruptly, telling her she had tried to strangle Miora. Understandably she burst into tears, she also believed everything they had told her.

"It was wrong of Vandi to let me come here, I'm obviously not well enough yet to leave the institute, I think it best if I go back, Larris".

"Nonsense Miora croaked as rehearsed, "It's just a set back, you didn't know what you were doing, we'll look after you here, Belona".

"But I could have killed you"! the older woman wailed.

"Just try and get some rest and we'll think of something tomorrow", Silverwick crooned, "Lay down and get some sleep Belona".

The two of them left as soon as she closed her eyes,

"I'm not sure I can keep this up, Larris", Miora said dully then, "It's too cruel, there must be a different solution".

"Patience", he cooed, "We're close". He took her in his arms,

"Do you want to return to your job as a secretary and lose all this, out of sentiment for someone I no longer love? Or do you want to be with me"?

"You know the answer to that", she sighed and they were kissing when his pad pinged.

It was from Boot! Silverwick grinned as he read the e-mail;

> Boot - Checked my balance this morning and your draft
> has not gone in, you'd better explain, Silverwick.

So he had no notion of current developments, good, Silverwick replied;

> Silverwick - Come to the house, all will be explained.
> Boot - Thirty minutes.
> Silverwick - I'll be waiting.

"This is absolutely perfect", he said to Miora and showed her the pad.

"What are you going to do, Larris"?

"Don't you see how truly excellent this is? I get rid of the both of them in one master stroke. She'll have the blaster in her fist when the combmen come in answer to my ping. He with his chest blown open, her supine on the floor holding the murder weapon.

Miora shuddered, "But who will really pull the trigger, Larris"?

"When you want a job doing well, you have to do it yourself", he said. This is the culmination of what the two of us desire. No Boot, no Belona. In her present drugged state she'll believe anything we tell her and she'll confess to the law. Once Vandi declares her legally insane, I become the executor of the estate".

"But how can you marry me if that's the outcome".

"You'll be my wife to all intents and purposes, maybe not in the eyes of the law, but in my heart".

"You mean I'll be your mistress eternally", Miora observed woodenly.

"You know how much I love you, we don't need a contract to prove how much", he took her in his arms, "And you'll be the mistress of this house and the estate in the other sense of the term".

Once more the girl bent to his incredible will and all he had to do then was wait. Wait for the equally villainous solicitor to arrive.

The airlock pinged and Silverwick glanced at the inspection screen even though he knew who was outside. He hit the unlock button and the door swung open. A gust of frigid, dust filled, air blew in from the outside and Boot entered wearing a parka and a filter mask.

"Good evening, Boot", Silverwick smiled, as the other pulled the mask from his face, he nodded in return.

"Come into the lounge and have a drink", Silverwick offered with a gracious wave of his hand.

"I see you're feeling sociable this evening, but unfortunately I have some other claims on my time, so if you explain the omitted draft and rectify it now on my pad, I'll take my leave of you".

Silverwick continued to walk to the study however and Boot reluctantly followed, even though the last thing he wanted at that moment was to be in the mansion.

"Silverwick, what game are you playing here, just sort out the draft and I'm off"?

Silverwick was pouring himself a sherry however and hardly seemed to be hearing anything Boot said. Suddenly from the tray of glasses, he picked up a snub nosed energy weapon of some sort. It was black, metallic and the compression button was in blood red.

"I picked this up in the dingier streets of Shalbatana Vallis the other week Boot, do you know what it is"?

"Frenge"! the solicitor cursed, "What ever it is put it down Silverwick! Listen, forget the draft, in fact forget them all, just let me get out of here with what I already have. You'll never see me again I swear to the Jewish baby what so ever his name was".

"It's one of those new laser pistols", Silverwick smiled. "It seems that they cauterise anything soft they pass through, sealing it from leaking. So convenient if you happen to care what the seared item is going to fall on".

"Silverwick, please......"

"I've set it to a metre and a half, with this dinky dial here and fifty percent discharge should do the trick. Actually I'm really interested to see the effect, of course you won't be in a position to share the findings with me".

"Silverwick! NOO"!

The beam issued silently and Boot's head seemed to freeze for the slightest of time. Then it toppled from his neck and bounced onto the polished floor with a sort of soft thud. Silverwick watched in fascination as the body jerked spasmodically for a couple of seconds, before falling to lay close by the head.

"Miora", Silverwick said, "Take this and put it in Belona's hand while I ping the local Constabulary". At the door his fiancée, white as a sheet walked over to him stiff limbed, like a zombie. To comply with his nefarious instruction.

FOUR

"**D**ETECTIVE INSPECTOR HYDE", the portly combmen introduced himself, "And this is my Detective Constable; Orkwell".

"Come in gentlemen and on into the lounge where the corpse is".

A third figure was behind the duo, tall, rather flabby and totally bald, he struggled to get past the other two, to be in the room first,

"I'm forensic", he told the owner of the mansion, "Axel, Stel Axel".

"Well there you are gentlemen! You'll find the weapon used, in the hand of my poor demented wife, she's up in her room, I doubt she'll remember anything, she has episodes of amnesia".

Belona appeared behind the three combmen,

"Who's this, Larris"? she asked, "Did you call the constabulary yourself? I'm so glad you've decided to come clean"!

Silverwick's jaw dropped at the apparent change in his wife. She seemed serenely calm in and in full control of herself.

"What are you doing here"? Silverwick demanded, "How are you still awake, with what…….".

"With the amount of drugs I was supposed to give her", another woman was in the lounge doorway, an attractive younger woman.

"You'll find the weapon in my room, Inspector, just as this murderer said you would".

Belona's words had an icy calmness to them. "It's exactly where my depraved husband put it after he had murdered poor Mister Boot".

Hyde looked to Silverwick, who had suddenly lost all of his self composure,

"No"! He gasped, "She did it, get this Axel fellow to check, her prints will be on the weapon which admittedly will have my own as it belongs to me".

"I've not touched the gun, Inspector", Belona reported calmly. "I hate firearms and begged Larris not to buy it. I couldn't have guessed he intended to use it so quickly after the purchase".

Hyde looked at the other woman, who silently nodded her head,

"Then *she'll* have left some prints", Silverwick blurted desperately, "When I gave it her to…..".

"My assistant has not touched the gun, Inspector", Belona stated calmly and with certainty. For she had supplied Miora with the single cellular gloves that had since been burned in a wing grate of the estate.

"Feel free to scan all three of us, only my murdering husband will have energy residue on his hands and sleeve".

"You frenging bitches"! Silverwick suddenly understood how perfectly duped he had been, "I tonked you both and the pair of you have betrayed me".

"I'm afraid you'll find him rather delusional Inspector. The evidence though, the evidence will prove irrefutable" Belona told Hyde.

The Inspector said to his constable, "Tie wrap Mister Silverwick, Orwell, you go and get the gun Stel".

Then he turned to Belona, "The forensic team will have the remains removed at once, Missus Silverwick, then we'll get out of your way. You'll have to give witness at the trial of course. Capital punishment trials can be rather upsetting, but my department will see to it that the whole process is as little taxing to you, as possible".

"Thank you inspector, my assistant and I will retire to another room while your men do their valuable work".

While Silverwick was screaming abuse and being lead away by Orkwell, who looked like he would suffer no resistance, the two women went to another wing of the opulent house of Silverwick.

The instant the door closed behind them, Belona took Miora in her arms and the two kissed passionately,

"I told you it would work", said the now totally sane Missus Silverwick.

"Vandi really did give you another lease on life didn't he", her homosexual lover gasped, "And your performance was totally convincing, you fooled both Larris and Glees Boot completely".

"They were easy", Belona returned, "You had the harder task sleeping with that slime-ball of a husband of mine, but now we're together and for always".

"Convenient of Boot to supply us with a means of getting rid of him", Miora grinned. "And so clever of you to cancel the draft and force him here".

"I knew how Larris would react, he was always greedy and grasping", Belona nodded. "Let's forget all about them though and plan our future. We can run the estate and companies together, but before we do I plan a holiday for us. Let's get away, now that the plague is over and the place is being recolonised, how do you fancy a fortnight in a luxury hotel on Venus"?

Lightning Source UK Ltd.
Milton Keynes UK
UKOW04f0604301117
313609UK00001B/48/P